RIFTS AND REFRAINS

USA TODAY BESTSELLING AUTHOR

TIYE

WITH KEISHA MENNEFEE

HONEY BLOSSOM PRESS

To our fathers,
Ronnie Perine and Robert Mennefee, Sr.,
whose wisdom and guidance inspire us every day.

This book is a tribute to both of your legacies.

ONE

Amara

Why did it always seem to rain during a burial? Not the downpour of a storm—rather the constant drizzle that keeps you squinting and unsure if you should pull out an umbrella or brave the temporary discomfort. Or maybe rain at a funeral was the standard setup in what I'd seen in the movies, since I'd never actually attended one until my grandfather's.

"Here, baby." A kind, Black, wrinkle-free woman whose gnarled hands were the only clue to her advanced age gave me another foil-covered dish to add to the others that covered the small kitchen table. "Your granddaddy loved my sweet potato casserole."

"Thank you, he would've appreciated this," I replied politely, hoping she didn't try to strike up a conversation with me like almost everyone who'd dropped off a dish. Hard to talk about a man I barely knew with people who knew him well—or at least knew him. His friends were curious about the granddaughter they'd heard about and hadn't seen. The only family pictures in the house were of my grandparents holding my father as an infant and me, at six years old, with missing teeth, smiling wide at the camera, and then another of me in my cap and gown from high school. The photos were centered on the small wooden shelf above his ancient TV, which still had a protruding back in his tiny living room filled with guests. His worn leather recliner had been pushed to the side for the repast, though you could see the outline on the floor where it had been normally positioned. Strange to be the center of attention of a man I'd only seen twice.

"That man loved you so. He talked about you all the time." The mourner patted my hand. "Did he leave you anything? Rumor has it he has money stashed somewhere in this house."

"No, ma'am. I don't think he stashed any money either." I glanced around the crowded home, hoping for a respite from this curious woman and this dreary home that I *had* inherited. My mother stood near the door, greeting people and receiving condolences. She seemed at ease, and conversed with the guests about my grandfather. My father, the quieter of the two, held down the back of the living room with a slight smile that didn't reach his eyes. He had remained stoic during the funeral. Or maybe it'd been easier for him to regulate his emotions because he wasn't attached to the very man whose seed had created him.

I envied that my parents had known the man who may have understood me more than anyone else in the world. Music and wanderlust had infused his spirit like mine. My memory of him was so faint I might as well have not known him. There were no photos of him and me, so I couldn't even conjure a scenario in which we were together. The last time I saw my grandmother alive, she'd caressed my cheek and said that God had blessed her again with the husband she'd loved through me. Too young to understand the meaning, I could feel the potency of her love for my grandfather, even as a little girl. As far as my father was concerned, my granddaddy didn't exist.

Marcus Johnson, Jr., my staunch father, who believed in education, routine, and wearing ties to work, stopped speaking to my non-traditional, free-spirited musician grandfather the day of my grandmother's funeral. My gossiping Aunt Vera on my mother's side once told me that my grandfather showed up drunk and a bumbling mess, apologizing to my grandmother and hugging her casket. My father had been appalled, and they almost came to blows as he attempted to physically remove my grandfather from the funeral. After that, we weren't allowed to mention Marcus Johnson, Sr. ever again.

The woman with the gnarled hands leaned closer and whispered, "I'm telling you, before you and your parents leave, you might want to check the house in case the vultures descend. They can't wait until you leave to tear up this house."

I nodded. "Probably a good idea. I'll tell my parents. If you'll excuse me, I need to run to the bathroom." I left before I screamed, searching for a spot to hide in plain sight. I wasn't comfortable being upstairs alone in any of the rooms, since we'd been staying at a nearby hotel. Being inauthentic required a rechargeable social battery, and I needed to be plugged in again.

I moved slowly through the small crowd to the stairwell, careful not to make any eye contact. I started up the stairs to take a breather in the bathroom. On the way up, I realized that the way the stairwell curved at the top protected me from people seeing me, though I could see guests coming in and out.

From my perch on the stairs, I could sit back and freely observe the strange mix of people who'd arrived to pay their respects to my grandfather. For a man my father seemed to despise, my grandfather had a lot of friends or people who appeared to care about him. Some had money, based on their personal grooming, tailored clothes, and shiny shoes. Some barely had a thing, if faded pants, well-worn dresses, unkempt facial hair, and old wigs meant that in Memphis. In Atlanta, the land of the fab and still more fab, one could never tell anyone's financial status if clothing were the only indicator.

The small, dilapidated two-story house my father had inhabited as a boy appeared lonely. Even as a child, I always thought the front of a house resembled a face. The windows were the eyes, and the door the mouth. I remember being a child staring out the back window of my mother's car, judging the level of happiness of the family who lived in those homes based on the faces of the houses. I'd been right over the years, based on conversations with my friends and family. Houses did reflect the emotions of the people living within. And this house that my grandfather lived in alone, long after his wife and son left, had been depressed with possibly suicidal tendencies.

The front door opened again as yet another guest entered the repast, and I caught a glimpse of my grandfather's freshly packed mound across the street. Why would anyone choose to live across from a cemetery? Seemed a morbid place to raise a family. Then again, maybe my grandfather wanted a constant reminder when he first purchased the property that we all had an expiration date and to not take life for granted. Maybe that was my imagination talking and not his reality. More than likely, this location was probably all my grandfather could afford.

Before the door closed, a man pushed it open almost impatiently. He didn't fit in, even in this room of misfits. This guest was a tall man, probably around my age, wearing shades and an expensive dark suit tailored to fit his muscular frame. His skin, the color of chocolate, swirled with caramel. He removed his fedora when he walked inside. He didn't seem like a man who wore hats often. His haircut was too fresh to be frequently covered. Probably only wore the fedora to protect against the annoying light rain. At the burial, I'd noticed him standing apart from the small crowd while I played my guitar and sang a rendition of Bill Withers's "Ain't No Sunshine" at my mother's request. I assumed he'd already left the burial, as I hadn't seen him since the repast began over two hours ago.

He scanned the room before catching my curious gaze and removing his shades. His eyes were the color of a shiny new penny, or maybe it was the peeping sun's reflected light. When he strode my way, I gulped and wanted to retreat upstairs. The stranger had been the only one to notice me from my position on the stairs. Even my parents mingled through the living, dining, and kitchen, speaking to people as if I no longer existed. The stranger stopped three steps below me, placing us almost at eye level. Grateful for my long dress, I pulled it over my knees and greeted the stranger with a smile.

"Um…if you're here to pay respects to my grandfather, we're asking guests to sign the book on the table over there." I pointed to the end table next to the door, though his focus remained on me.

The stranger nodded slightly. "I've paid my respects while he was alive, unlike some people here. I didn't realize Stoney Johnson had a granddaughter who could sing."

"Is that what you called him?" I'd only known my grandfather as Marcus Johnson, Sr. In the obituary my father created, he had been listed by his government name. We didn't make a program for the funeral at the request of my grandfather, who knew he was dying of prostate cancer and had left specific instructions about his funeral and burial to my father.

"You don't know that?" The guest raised one thick brow. "We all called him that. I wondered why the obituary didn't mention the name most of us knew him by, or any of his accomplishments."

"It's what my grandfather wanted," I answered, though I wondered the same thing. Although I didn't know much, I knew that Granddad had been a struggling musician who had seen a small level of fame.

"Really? Or is it what you and your family, who never visited him, wanted?" He twisted his lips.

Acid burned my stomach as I rose, stepped down, brought myself closer to him, and snapped, "Listen—not that I owe whoever you are an explanation—we are only following his wishes. This day is hard enough without having you question me or my family. If you'll excuse me. I'm sure you know your way out."

"Jake." He blocked my path, his stern face softening with the slight curve of his lips surrounded by a mustache and goatee. "Jake Barnes, and I was a fan of your grandfather. Stoney was a friend of my father, and I considered him an uncle." Jake pressed his hat across his heart. "My apologies and condolences. You're right. Today must be hard. Sometimes, I forget that a thing called manners exists."

I touched his forearm at the genuineness of his apology. "It's okay. Today feels surreal. Needed a moment away from everyone. We thank you for coming out and celebrating his life. If you'll excuse me…Mr. Barnes."

"Jake." Still blocking my path, he reached inside his jacket and passed me his pale blue business card. "What do you do?"

"Why?" I held the card with embossed lettering without reading it. Jake was an attractive man who could also charm, yet I didn't sense his interest was personal.

"Humor me, since you won't look at my card." His broad, dimpled grin, so disarming, elevated his looks to handsome.

"I'm a music teacher at a middle school in Atlanta."

His questioning eyes assessed me. "A teacher in a city these days is damn impressive."

I scoffed, "Yet you say that like you're not impressed at all."

Jake smiled. "I will never knock the profession, because we need teachers. Just think that it's a shame someone like yourself only teaches."

I bristled again. "What does that mean? I love what I do."

He held his hand up and took a step down. "I told you. I forget about my manners. Let me compliment you in another way. I was about to leave until you strummed that first note. Haunting and beautiful. And the best was yet to come." Jake tapped the banister, watching me. "You ever thought about singing professionally?"

"Doesn't every kid dream?" I shrugged nonchalantly like my pulse hadn't jumped at his question.

"With a voice like yours, it might not be a dream. Atlanta wouldn't know what to do with that mezzo-soprano." His cell buzzed, and he pulled his phone from his jacket pocket to check it. He backed down another step. "If you're ever in Nashville, look me up."

"I have no reason to travel to Nashville. Why would I look you up?" I still held his card and moved closer to him subconsciously before I caught myself.

"Mari?" Mama stood at the bottom of the stairs as a couple of guests passed her. "Is everything okay?"

Jake turned around and placed his hat by his side. "Everything is divine. Just telling *Mari* that her voice is mesmerizing and embodies the soul of our people with every note."

"Thank you. I have never heard my singing described quite like that," I replied, admittedly pleased by his flowery compliment. I joined him on the stairwell. He was taller than I first thought, and I had to bend my neck slightly to meet his gaze.

He replied softly, "The melody and the timbre when you sing are like the pain and the triumphs of a people who want to be heard. Just like when Stoney used to sing."

Mama beamed. "She gets her talent from me, too."

I bit the inside of my cheek to suppress the giggle. A mathematical genius with the gift of gab and making people feel warm and cozy, Mama didn't have a creative bone in her body. Jake must have caught the amused look on my face, and his mouth twitched. Something about the small shared secret engendered trust. I glanced at his card, and my heart skipped a beat. "You work for Evelyn Hart?" Evelyn Hart was the biggest country star. Period. She'd had number-one songs in each decade since she first began singing in the seventies.

"I'm a part of her management team and always looking for talent." He grinned. "I'll be here for a couple of days. Hope you use my number, Ms. Amara Johnson."

Before I could ask how he knew my name when we didn't have a program, my mother proudly corrected him. "Ms. Amara Johnson, soon to be Mrs. Phillip Graham."

His brown eyes sparkled as he tilted his hat toward me. "Congratulations. Mr. Phillip Graham is a lucky man."

"Thank you." Warmth flushed my face at my mother's blatant attempt to block any further conversation between me and Jake.

Jake smiled at Mama and me again and strode out the door, taking his energy with him. Belatedly, I realized his presence had lifted my dour mood. Energized me. He'd been the charge I needed to get through the rest of this strange day.

I folded my arms. "Mama, why did you tell a perfect stranger I was engaged?"

She placed one hand on her hip. "I know when a man is interested in a woman, and I can tell he's a smooth one."

"He manages Evelyn Hart. His interest was business. You heard what he said about my singing." I beamed despite myself.

Mama pushed back a tendril of her relaxed hair behind her ear. "He had you hemmed in and wouldn't have let you leave until you agreed to call him."

"I'm thirty years old, and you still treat me like I don't have the good sense you gave me. Even if he was flirting, I know how to handle men like him."

Her lips twisted. "Hmm…I saw how you looked at him. Didn't realize you were grinning all in his face. You're about to get married, Mari."

"If I looked at him in any kind of way, it is because he works with Evelyn Hart, Mama, and he said he knew Granddad," I insisted.

"My girls." My father placed a possessive hand on my mother's back. "Can you lower your voice? This is a small house, and we don't need anyone else in our business. That man isn't even here, and we still have guests." He then addressed me. "Why don't you go upstairs and call Phillip? You're probably missing him."

I frowned but held my tongue and did his bidding. My father ruled our household, and whatever he said was the final word. Although I'd lived on my own since I graduated college, whenever we were all together, I reverted to that little girl eager to please him. I stomped back up the stairs and chose the last of the three doors on the second floor for privacy. The guest room, formerly known as my father's bedroom.

The twin bed was neatly made, and my mother had dusted and cleaned the blinds and the lone wooden chest of drawers yesterday. I rested on the bed, staring at the peeling ceiling, and lifted the card. Jake Barnes. A man associated with one of the greatest to ever do it loved my voice.

I reached into the pocket of the sweater I wore over my dress and fingered the card before I called Phillip. When he answered, I replied, "You really should be here with me."

He sighed. "Is it that bad?"

"The parents are pretending that we were one big, happy family. This fakeness is slowly killing me."

"What else are they supposed to do?"

"Not this. Feels too disingenuous."

"Those people don't know your father hasn't spoken to your grandfather in years."

Jake Barnes, who didn't even live in Memphis, knew we hadn't been involved with my grandfather. "This is a tight-knit community. Trust me, they know."

"Maybe. Your parents are still doing the best they can. I can't imagine my father dying, and I had no clue that he was even sick until the last moment." We both had close relationships with our parents. In fact, our mothers, who were sorority sisters, had orchestrated our meeting in the first place. We'd dated for two years and had been engaged for three months but had yet to set a date, much to our mothers' dismay.

"How's the contract going?" I crossed my ankles, needing to keep the conversation going so I wouldn't feel compelled to return downstairs.

"Slow." Phillip worked as a project manager for American Express, and his days were long and nights short.

"Hopefully you can wrap up before I come home."

He chuckled sarcastically. "You'll be home in a couple of days. Doubtful."

I turned over on my side. "Why don't we get a hotel downtown like we're tourists when I return? Order room service and have lots of back-breaking sex."

"You must miss me," he crooned. "Baby, you know I can't be distracted right now."

"Bring your laptop. We can work and play," I suggested, hating that I sounded whiny even to myself.

"You're the multitasker. Not me. We can get a hotel once I finish the project, or maybe go somewhere for the weekend."

"We were supposed to take a trip to Puerto Rico when we first got engaged. It's been three months."

Phillip drew a long, irritated sigh. "I really have to get back to work. We have our whole lives together, can take many trips, and stay in hundreds of hotels. Call me tonight once you get ready for bed, okay?"

I mumbled, "Okay."

"Love you."

Frustrated that he'd blown me off once again, I didn't say it back to him as I ended the call. I pushed to sit up and looked out the sole window at the hundreds of plots and headstones of those who'd gone before me in the graveyard across the street. This was what my father had woken up to every single morning. Death. The final resting place. No more time to spend with loved ones. No more time to make things right with family. No more time to pursue your dreams. No. More. Time.

I moved to the window and stared at my grandfather's burial site. "Did you lose everything because you risked it all for your dreams? Or did you have a taste of success that left you unfulfilled? What happened to you? What made a man who loved his wife and son dearly abandon them as if they never existed? Why did you leave me this house in desperate need of therapy? And why did you request I sing at your funeral when I had no idea you knew I could sing?"

I didn't know how long I stood at that window, waiting for answers that would never come.

TWO

Amara

As I stared out the window, words jumbled around in my head. Words that demanded to be released. I turned around, scanning the room for my leather bag. When I didn't see it, I went to my grandfather's room, a few feet away on the other side of the bathroom. His room was only a little bigger than my father's old one. It was large enough for a mirrored dresser and the queen-sized bed where I found my leather bag next to my mother's purse and my father's gray flat cap.

I perched on the edge of the bed and scrounged through my bag containing an extra outfit to pull out a black gel pen and my red journal, where I jotted down notes for songs, random thoughts, and poetry. I'd been writing since I could remember. Some of what I wrote went into simple music for my students to learn, while everything else was for me. Words I would recite to myself. Songs I would write for my ears only. Poems I created when my emotions were too overwhelming to process, and I needed an outlet. At home, in my closet, I had countless notebooks filled with the Amara that no one knew, and I'd never shared with another soul.

I opened my journal to a fresh page, and thoughts tumbled out of me:

> *Rain whispers on a Memphis day,*
> *Through silent echoes of a past astray,*
> *Here I walk, tracing roots entwined,*

In a house of memories that bind.

"Hmm." I paused at the last sentence and stared at the words on the page. Something about that last line spoke to me. I scanned the sparsely furnished room with bare walls and noticed the half-opened closet door filled with his clothes hanging neatly. My grandfather had kept an organized and tidy home, and maybe because he didn't have a lot of possessions, maintaining his house had been easy.

I held my journal to my chest and entered the small closet. I closed my eyes and inhaled the faint scent of mothballs and masculine cologne that reminded me he was real. I fingered one of his suit jackets and imagined how handsome he must have looked when he was dressed up. In the few pictures I'd seen of him, he'd been an attractive man, especially in his youth—tall, lean frame, caramel skin, light brown eyes, and curly hair. Hair my father and I had inherited. I looked down at four pairs of worn and used shoes lined up against the wall. After finally giving up on music, he'd been a bus driver and had probably alternated wearing these shoes for work. The shelf at the top of his closet contained a Memphis Grizzlies baseball cap and a black fedora like the one that Jake Barnes had worn.

Jake had been an interesting man who knew my grandfather in ways I was sure my father never knew. Hell, Jake knew that everyone called Marcus Johnson, Sr. "Stoney." What other sides had he seen? Did he know the type of liquor my granddad preferred or what made him laugh?

I reached into my pocket again and looked at his card. Did Jake really mean it when he said he liked my voice and that I had potential? Crazy how no one had complimented me on my singing since I'd sung in front of my sixth-grade class, and a man who just happened to work for Evelyn Hart heard me at my estranged grandfather's funeral. The possibilities of a music career fluttered in my stomach.

I quickly quelled the excitement and placed the card back in my pocket. No one would take a music teacher seriously anyway.

I sighed away the tingling of regret whenever I thought of my musicality. That I could've done more with my gifts. I could sing in most ranges, was adept at guitar and piano, and knew enough of most instruments to teach to others. Yet I had done nothing to cultivate my talent because a music career wasn't viable or acceptable in my household.

Becoming a music teacher had been my compromise with my parents. This compromise brought some joy to my life because, as a teacher, I could surround myself with instruments and had an excuse to play my guitar and the piano. Standing in his closet, I saw the evidence of my grandfather's broken dreams, and pride still seeped through that at least he had taken a risk on himself and his passion.

I touched the sleeve of his work uniform shirt and chuckled. "My fingers glide over whispers old." I then pushed the shirts to one side, revealing a guitar case against the wall hidden by the clothes. I smiled triumphantly. "In every corner, tales untold."

When I pulled out the black guitar case and placed it on the bed, anticipation filled me. I unclicked the case, and an old, still-beautiful maroon and black Yamaha acoustic guitar nestled inside. I picked it up gingerly, sat back on the bed, and admired it. One of the gold-plated tuning pegs on the head of the instrument was broken. Something that could easily be fixed. I hugged his guitar, anxious to play it, and ran my fingers over the strings. It needed tuning, but it was still viable, and now it was all mine.

As I positioned the guitar on my body, I looked back in the case to see if he had a pick and instead found a brown journal. I eyed my own notebook and then retrieved the leather-bound notebook. I flipped through it, and my heart impossibly swelled with every page. His musings, his thoughts and lyrics, smiled back at me in damn near perfect penmanship. I couldn't believe that my grandfather kept a journal like I did. We were more kindred spirits than I realized. Glancing over a few of his words sparked my creativity, and I reached back on the bed for my notebook to add to what I'd just written.

My voice, a bridge from past to now,
Through history's chords, I take my vow.

I continued to turn the yellowing pages in disbelief that I found my grandfather in his scent, his guitar, his words, and, most importantly, in me. Renewed energy coursed through my blood as I whispered,

*"A quest not just to uncover my tree,
But a search for self, in melody."*

At the end of the journal were two folded papers, probably letters, and an old, tattered photo of my grandfather as a young man with his arm slung over a woman's shoulder. The top of the picture had been torn across part of his shoulder and her head. I couldn't clearly distinguish who she was because she wore a sweater and slacks, though I had enough to determine that the woman wasn't my grandmother. Who was she? Why did he hold on to this photo? I sank back on the bed and stared at the ceiling.

"Oh, what a tangled web you must have woven in your life, Stoney Johnson." I took a deep breath, the low rumble of mourners who didn't know my grandfather all that well still present in the background. "And you left it up to me to unravel it all."

THREE

Jake

Alcohol had become my best friend lately. She was the only one who got me. Comforted me on a lonely night. Understood my need to relax and chill when my thoughts of the past and the unknown unsettled me. The only one I could trust to be honest with me when I lied to myself and others, I mused while I emptied my second Old Fashioned of the night as I jotted down notes on my phone sitting at the hotel bar. Instead of lounging out here, I could be in my room, reviewing the contract for the drummer my father had hired. Being holed up in a hotel room drinking seemed clichéd and like I was this desperate and lonely alcoholic instead of a man on the come-up. Besides, I loved the buzz and the people around me while I hung out in the Corner Bar of the Peabody. Never knew who would walk through the doors of the historic Memphis hotel.

"Another one?" the pretty barmaid asked before biting the corner of her lips from behind the cherrywood bar.

"Why not?" I smiled, contemplating whether I should ask her to my room, until I remembered that I had sworn off random women and flings. I would be thirty-four on my next birthday, and if I wanted more for my life, I had to be the man I wanted to be and not just pretend. "On second thought, maybe a sweet tea."

"Come on, you've only had two drinks, and the night is young." She leaned over the bar, giving me an ample view of her perky breasts.

I dragged my lusty gaze from her chest to her face. "Naw, I'm good. Been a long day. Probably crash in a little while."

"For the long day." She slid an empty glass before me, dropped a square ice cube, and poured the bourbon, brown sugar syrup, and Angostura bitters. Garnished my glass with an orange peel and cherry. "On the house."

"If I didn't know any better, I would think you were trying to get me drunk." I picked up the glass and raised it in her direction. "Last one, and thank you."

The pretty woman's voice lowered. "We'll see if it's the last one." Her smile faded, and she stood up.

Flowers layered with honey wafted under my nose, and I turned my head to the right as Amara Johnson slid onto the stool next to me. My breath hitched at her unexpected appearance, and I could only say a soft "Hey."

She raised her brows and asked the barmaid, "Can I have an Old Fashioned, too? I can tell you mixed him a good one."

The barmaid stole a glance my way before answering, "Coming right up." She moved away from the counter to prepare Amara's drink near the sink, giving us privacy.

I half faced her, pleased with her company already. "Somehow, I didn't take you for a hard-drinking woman."

Amara's forehead wrinkled prettily. "An Old Fashioned is hard drinking?"

I chuckled. "Forgot you're from Atlanta. What are you doing here?"

"Looking for you." Her ruby-red lips curved into a bright smile, and her natural allure tempted me to flirt. I had to remind myself to remain focused, since she could be a potential client, and she had a man. *No random women or flings.*

"You took a big chance I would be here. I did leave you my card. Could have just called."

"I figured even if you weren't here, I planned to have the drink I so desperately need, catch the ducks that march through the lobby, and call you later. My instincts were correct that you would stay at the Peabody and be at this nice bar on a Friday afternoon."

The barmaid placed Amara's glass before her and busied herself with another customer.

I raised my glass. "Want to get to know each other better, or are you ready to hear my spiel on why I would be the best person to represent you?"

"Actually, neither." She peered at me impishly over the rim of her glass as she sipped.

At Stoney's home, she'd been a beautiful, delicate wallflower. Here, away from that depressing house and her family, Amara blossomed before my eyes. She quietly demanded attention. I'd loved her voice and wondered how best to use it when I'd given her my card. Initially, I thought her raspy, soulful tone would suit background vocals or a track or two on a movie soundtrack. The woman sitting beside me, with her honey-brown skin and gold-flecked brown eyes that danced, could legit be a star. She'd swapped her long black dress for a simple pink peasant blouse and jeans with black peep-toe heels. Her raven, shoulder-length, wavy hair had been brushed into a fun, bouncy ponytail. Cute and sexy at the same time. Disarming, warm, and welcoming. An intoxicating combination.

I leaned on my elbow, watching her. "Okay. I'm not getting the vibe you're interested in afternoon delight…so?"

She laughed. "How old are you? No one says that anymore."

"Oh, but you're old enough to know what it means. Don't make fun of me." I swallowed more of my drink, enjoying our light banter.

"I'm not. I'm looking out for you. Can't have you telling women that tired old line to get their attention."

"I'm good in that department. No worries." I scanned the intimate, dark bar. "Care to get a table? Maybe share an appetizer if you're not still stuffed from the repast."

"That was a lot of food I didn't touch," she commented. "We convinced most of the guests to take food home with them. I don't know why people think food will somehow make it all better." She lifted her glass. "When this right here makes it all better."

"I couldn't agree more. But you probably want to slow down on that drink if you didn't eat." I signaled to the barmaid. "Can we just move to that table?" I pointed to a small, empty table in the corner of the dark restaurant.

"Yes. I'll send a waitress over there."

I quickly read her tag and smiled. "Thanks, Lila. If you change your mind about the complimentary drink, just add it to my bill."

A look of disappointment crossed Lila's features. "It's yours."

"Okay." I guided Amara through the restaurant with a light hand on her lower back, aware of her intoxicating scent.

Once we were settled at the table on opposite sides, I became keenly aware of Amara as our knees grazed. She dropped her gaze from mine before the waiter appeared. She smiled politely at the young man. "I don't need a menu. Just bring whatever popular appetizer can feed us, two glasses of water, and a saucer of lemons."

The waiter smiled back. "You got it. I'll surprise you."

I protested, "You're a bossy little thing. Maybe I have a gluten allergy, or I'm a vegan."

"Then order something else, although nothing about you looks like you eat that clean," she commented, matter-of-fact.

"Wow." I touched my chest. "Should I be offended?"

"Not at all. Well, unless you do eat clean." She tilted her head. "Do you?"

"Hell no. I need my pork ribs and mac and cheese." I chuckled and patted my flat stomach.

"Then we should be good." She took another sip before staring into her glass. Her mood suddenly dipped back into that melancholy space it'd been when I met her earlier, sitting on the stairs. Then I realized she'd probably escaped here because she didn't know anyone else and didn't want to be in that house of unfulfilled dreams any longer.

"I know we just met…" My voice trailed off when she looked up at me. Her eyes no longer danced. "If you need me to be quiet or a listening ear, I'm here."

She straightened her shoulders and lifted her chin. "I want you to tell me about my grandfather. You were the only honest one of all the people who came in and out of the house today. The only one to remotely question why he didn't want his accomplishments to be noticed, or why his family, who hadn't been in his life for years, are now calling the shots." She blew out a breath. "I'm not like my family, who want to brush away any memories of him. I can tell my dad just wants to move on, and my mother will do whatever he wants even if she feels differently. My grandfather is the last one of his mother's children, and my father is an only child. I have a few second cousins who couldn't care less about an old, grumpy man who had been estranged from everyone else for years. I'm the only one who can carry on his legacy. Except I have no idea what he's done. I tried to google him. Turns out, Siri doesn't have all the answers."

I wryly replied, "Think Siri is Apple. You want Bixby or Alexa."

She giggled and sniffed back tears. "Sorry. I shouldn't be saying all this to you. I didn't know anywhere else to go."

I inhaled and exhaled, wondering where to start discussing a man who'd also been an enigma to me. "I met your grandfather when I was nineteen, and we'd kind of kept in touch since then. The best way I can tell you about him is to show you." I checked my watch. "Let's get the food to go and come with me. I have a car."

Amara's eyes lowered. "We can't just stay here and talk?"

Impatiently, I waved my hand. "Call your fiancé or your mama and tell them you're going to the Rock 'n' Soul Museum." I pulled out my cell to text an old friend who managed the place. "You can catch an Uber and meet me there if you're more comfortable."

She shook her head. "No, I trust you. I'll ride with you."

I quirked a brow. "You sure? Because I saw that look in your eyes, like *this man might cut me up in a million pieces and scatter my remains to the wind.*"

"Dark much?" she teased. "I'll text my mother where I'm going."

"And not your man?" I questioned before I could stop myself, noticing her now-ringless left hand. *Focus, Jake.*

"Well, if my instincts are wrong and you do mean me harm, he's too far away to help anyway. And Mama can describe you from head to toe," she informed me.

"Point," I said, and rubbed my hands together. "All right, if I help you get to know Stoney, then I need you to agree to come to my family studio in Nashville and sing for me."

Amara frowned as she stumbled over her words. "I…I have to go back to…Atlanta and work."

"Well, getting to know your grandfather isn't a one-day event. We'll hit the museum today, and you'll learn why he's relevant in blues." I leaned back in the chair. "If you want to know anything else, the summer is coming up. Schools will be out. Take a weekend. Bring your fiancé or whoever you want to bring and cut a track with me."

Her eyes widened. "You have a song you want me to sing?"

"Sing one of yours." I pushed my empty glass toward her half-drunken one in the middle. "Bet you write your own stuff."

She blushed and ducked her head. "Mostly poetry. Not sure if it's any good."

I whistled. "Shit, girl. Poems are the verses to any song. You can sing 'Twinkle, Twinkle Little Star' with that voice and make it a hit."

Amara dipped her head as her hands wrapped around her glass. "You only heard me once and already believe in me?"

"Once is all I need with a gift like yours. So, if you want my help with your grandfather's legacy, let me help you have one of your own." I tapped the table with my knuckles. "Think about it."

I settled back in my chair. What did I just suggest? Men and musicians like Stoney kept secrets for a reason. Men like my father. Men like me. And could I ignore the tingling that traveled my spine whenever she looked at me with her beautiful, big eyes?

Amara gulped down more of her drink and extended her hand. "We have a deal."

I couldn't tell if I felt excitement or anticipation. Either way, I felt like I'd just won the prize of my life. I took her hand in mine and ignored the spark when our hands met, which caused her smile to wilt. *Damn.* She didn't want to be attracted to me either. Maybe her reticence and her engagement would remind me that she belonged to someone else. I'd wanted a taken woman before. I wouldn't travel that road again, especially when cultivating Amara's talent was far more important than any chemistry between us. Or at least that's what I told myself until she licked her pouty lips when the aromatic oysters and lobster frites, a lightly fried seafood dish, were presented before us.

Amara Johnson had already invaded my mind with her astounding voice. I would have to fight like hell to keep her from piercing my heart when I knew all that I would do was break hers.

FOUR

Amara

"**H**ow much time do we have to get to the museum?" I asked before popping a piece of the scrumptious lobster that practically melted in my mouth. "Kind of want to eat these while they're hot. If we get it to go, the Styrofoam container may make the crispiness soft. Plus, I want to order another drink. This time, a classic Manhattan."

Jake texted someone. "You always drink like a man?"

"I like what I like. Who says it's a man's drink?"

"Apparently, everyone but you. Go ahead and order. We have a half-hour or so." He nodded in the direction of a piano in the corner. "Do you play?"

"Yeah," I mumbled with food in my mouth. Ordinarily, I wouldn't be so messy around a man, especially an attractive one like Jake. Being engaged made it easier to be carefree, and I wanted to somehow make myself less appealing to him. "I play guitar, piano, and drums. Experimented with the violin. I wanted to play the sax because it's so sexy, but I couldn't seem to figure out the right blowing technique."

"Blowing technique?" He smirked while squeezing lemons over the plate of food without asking if he knew what I liked, which I did like. The waiter placed two glasses of water on the table, and Jake promptly picked one up and gulped like he was thirsty while I ordered my Manhattan.

After the waiter left, I used my oyster-speared fork to point at him. "Poor choice of words in front of mixed company. I meant to say I've always been better with my hands than my mouth." Belatedly, I realized my second double entendre of the evening and groaned.

"You're getting more interesting by the moment." Jake chuckled. "Can't wait to get you into the studio and let you just go for it."

"I've never been in the studio, sooo…let's take it slow." I blew out my breath, exhaling some of the nervousness when thinking about being in an actual studio.

"You'll adapt. Where do you play?" he asked.

"I haven't performed publicly since high school. Now, I play in my classroom to teach my students and at home."

Jake pressed his knees against mine. "Play something for me."

"Now?" I quickly downed the last of my Old Fashioned and stuffed another oyster in my mouth, more out of avoidance than appetite.

"Yeah. The singer isn't here until tonight."

I swallowed my food past the nervous lump in my throat. "We can't just start playing a piano in a bar. It's like trespassing or something."

"Trespassing in a public bar?" He sucked his teeth. "Stop being scared. Guarantee, once you start playing, no one will stop you."

"Um…" Nervously, I scanned the small area. Ten people besides the staff occupying the bar and countless guests walking past in the lobby might hear me. I had only performed in front of nonjudgmental students who had no clue about what was considered good music or the mash-up of mourners who were too curious about Stoney's estranged family to focus on my voice.

"Take a risk." He pushed the Manhattan that had been delivered by the waiter to me before he chomped on another piece of lobster.

"Easy for you to say. You're not the one who'll be publicly humiliated if I'm told to stop." I imbibed a bigger gulp than I intended, allowing the cool liquid to warm my insides and hopefully lessen my inhibitions.

"Even if you're told to stop, who in the hell cares?" he cajoled me with a dimpled smile. "Go on, Mari."

I corrected him, "Amara. Only close friends can call me Mari."

"We're about to be best friends. You, me, and Phillip Graham." He winked.

I giggled. "You remembered his name?"

"I think your mama wanted to be sure I remembered." Jake wiped his mouth with the napkin.

"I'm sorry about that. My parents seem to forget that I'm thirty and have been on my own for years whenever we're all in the same room."

He waved his hand. "I get it. You're a beautiful woman. Any reasonable man would step to you. She didn't know that I'm only interested in your talent."

"That's what I was trying to tell her. You only gave me your card because you liked my voice," I replied. However, it stung my ego for Jake to say he wasn't interested in me, especially because I wasn't wearing my ring.

"So, show me your voice again." He sighed loudly when I hesitated. "Give me your phone."

"Why?"

"Your playlist."

"Which one?" I slowly pulled out my phone and found my Spotify.

"Just give me your phone." He held his hand out, and I reluctantly relinquished it. Jake scrolled up the screen and wryly commented, "Eclectic taste, from *Porgy and Bess* to Lil Wayne. Miley Cyrus. Tina Turner." His brown eyes lit up before he returned my phone. He ambled to the piano, tickled a few keys, and started playing a tune I had trouble catching. Maybe because I'd been caught off guard that he could play music simply by looking at the song, but I couldn't pick up the tune. He remained standing while his hands expertly traveled the piano like he was caressing the curves of a woman. Jake looked over his shoulder at me and beckoned me with his head.

It was now or never. I took a deep breath, joined Jake, and leaned against the side of the piano, facing him as he eased down on the bench. I glanced around the elegant room, but no one seemed to care, as Jake had predicted. He started again and softly demanded, "Sing."

A light switched on in my mind, and the tune he played connected. I closed my eyes and began singing "Do Right Woman, Do Right Man" by Aretha Franklin. All reservations and shyness disappeared from the moment the lyrics glided from my mouth. I became lost in the world of a woman asking her man to treat her the way she deserves. The type of woman who doesn't have a problem stepping out on the relationship or leaving if he can't love her how he expects to be loved by her.

When I finally opened my eyes after finishing the last note, a small crowd had gathered, and they clapped enthusiastically with beaming smiles. Embarrassed that I'd been caught in another realm as I sang, I bowed playfully and gestured toward Jake. "A round of applause for my piano man."

The crowd clapped, and a smiling Jake shook his head slowly from side to side, his eyes gleaming with excitement. "Where have you been all my life?"

I beamed, proud that I had impressed him and an audience who were not my students.

An older woman with blonde hair in a severe bun, wearing the hotel uniform, approached us with pursed lips. "We don't allow anyone to touch the piano unless you're hired help."

Still riding on a high from the pleased audience, I no longer cared about management complaints. I moved to stand behind Jake and tapped his broad shoulders lightly. "Our apologies. We're here on vacation and couldn't resist in the land of blues and country music."

He placed his hand over mine and smiled at me before addressing the manager, exaggerating his natural Southern twang. "Thank you. Me and the little lady couldn't help ourselves. We'll get out of your way."

The woman stepped closer. "I actually wanted to know if we could hire you. We don't get that type of crowd participation from our regular band."

"Oh wow," I exclaimed, stepping back to allow Jake to stand.

Jake rose with his charming smile, and the manager's cheeks flushed. "We take that as the highest compliment, but we don't live here. If you have a card, I'll take it. Maybe we can stop in on occasion, since we're in Nashville."

Her smile faltered as she gave him a card from her pocket. "Definitely keep us in mind. Just next time, you can't use the piano without permission."

"Got ya." Jake picked up my hand and led me out of the bar. "We really have to go."

The moment we were out of the manager's sight, we hurried out the sliding doors, laughing. "What about the bill?" I asked.

"They'll either figure it out and bill my room or comp us for the free entertainment. I figure they owe us. The bar is full now."

"Seriously, your grandfather used to give me unsolicited advice about women. I guess he figured since I wasn't married, I needed help." Jake used one hand to maneuver the silver sedan into a tight parking spot I would've driven past because I would've deemed it impossible.

"Okay, tell me what type of advice he gave you." I smiled. On the short car ride from the hotel to the museum, Jake's affable manner had made a potentially uncomfortable ride pleasant and relaxing.

He quirked a brow. "You ready for these change-your-life words of wisdom that he offered?"

I slapped my thighs in jest. "Yes. I have patiently awaited your answer for the longest five seconds ever."

Jake turned off the engine. "He told me to never watch *Jeopardy!* with a woman I'm interested in because she'll quickly find out how smart or dumb I am."

I gasped before I covered my mouth.

His forehead wrinkled. "You good?"

I slowly lowered my hands. "Just that *Jeopardy!* is something my father and I used to watch together. We still do when we're together and happen to catch it."

"Maybe your father used to watch it with your grandfather."

"I wouldn't know. My father won't talk about him. It's why I have to do my own research."

Jake pointed to the Memphis Rock 'n' Soul Museum and unlocked the car doors. "Well, here we are."

He jumped out and hurried around to open my door, and we walked inside the closed building on historic Beale Street. The museum celebrated music and the significance of Beale Street to African American History. I'd learned about the greats like Ida B. Wells, who co-owned and edited an antisegregation paper based on Beale Street. The legendary B. B. King, who got his start in Memphis and was known as the Beale Street Blues Boy, and W. C. Handy, who considered himself the father of the blues and performed on Beale Street.

We chatted excitedly about the exhibits and our varied musical influences. He loved Andre 3000's refusal to be pigeonholed into one category and still considered *The Miseducation of Lauryn Hill* the best album besides Kendrick Lamar's *To Pimp a Butterfly*, While I argued that *DAMN.* had more hits and was the better album. I preferred H.E.R.'s versatility and musicality, the brash voice of Tina Turner, and the bluesy sounds of Al Green. He suggested I listen to Reyna Roberts and Mickey Guyton, two African American female country artists. We had free rein in the museum courtesy of Jake's friend, Sweetie Jay, who had enough Southern hospitality and personality for Memphis. She greeted us and demanded a pic with Stoney Johnson's granddaughter. She then excused herself and told us she had work to finish in her office.

As Jake and I moved through the museum, discussing music, I mused that this had to be the best non-date I'd ever been on with a man. We clicked, and conversation flowed so easily that we talked over each other. Jake clearly had an ear and an appreciation for music that Phillip and my parents didn't share. I was almost certain he had a woman or two somewhere. He was too handsome, charming, and self-aware to be alone. I traced my ring finger, wondering why I'd neglected to put it back on once I decided to find him. I'd only taken the ring off because I was advised by my father that we were going to a rough neighborhood and the expensive diamond solitaire might attract the wrong attention.

"Since you sang for me, it's only fair that I show you this." He waved his arm with a flourish at a small exhibit discussing the blues wave that occurred in the seventies. Planted between a red electric guitar and a saxophone on the wall was a portrait of Marcus "Stoney" Johnson and a plaque highlighting his contributions to music. I traced the metallic words detailing his legacy as a talented singer and musician who fused Memphis blues and country music. He was also a talented songwriter for local and nationally known musicians. I blinked back tears at the smiling man who shared my hair, eyes, and button nose as he held a guitar in his hand, a painting that seemed familiar to me in the background. I'd never seen this picture of him. I'd only seen a few in which he usually wore a frown or his eyes seemed sad. In this one, his eyes were bright and hopeful. He'd been happy, and something took away that smile and turned him into a grump that eschewed family.

Jake picked up the headphones attached to the glass. He used a nearby antibacterial wipe to clean the ear cushions before gingerly placing them on my head. The twang of my grandfather's pick on the first string resonated with my soul, and I grasped the headphones, needing to stem the flow of tears threatening to spill over. Then I heard the clarity and strength in his gravelly voice that spoke directly to me. He sang of a man searching for the right woman while nursing a broken heart from an unrequited love. The more he sang, the more I wondered if he meant more than his desperate hunt for a woman. Maybe he meant his dreams. I replayed the song without thought, his music soothing a piece of my heart I didn't realize needed a balm.

After replaying the sample two more times, I finally pulled the headphones off and looked around. Jake had disappeared, probably allowing me privacy. I snapped pics of my grandfather's portrait and the plaque detailing his influence on the blues in Memphis with my phone, and with my head held high, a surge of pride and inspiration coursed through my blood. I would go to Nashville and let go, as Jake had suggested. I wanted to see how far my talent would take me while on this journey of getting to know my grandfather—the good, the bad, and the ugly of Stoney Johnson.

FIVE

Amara

After spending more than two hours in the museum, I reluctantly left my grandfather, or that was how I felt. He was alive again as I listened to his music. I experienced a tremendous sense of loss as I walked away from his exhibit, much more than I had at the funeral. Maybe because I saw an authentic glimpse of his voice and his talent and had more regret that I'd never really known him.

On the way to the hotel where my parents and I were staying near downtown, Jake must have sensed my need for quiet, because he didn't say a word beyond asking me where I was staying so he could drop me off.

I stared out the window at the blackness of the night, lost in my own world, trying to again find the balance that I thought I had when I first arrived in Memphis three days ago. I felt off-kilter and so damn unsettled because I couldn't figure out what was bothering me.

When Jake drove up to the sliding doors of the hotel, I didn't want to leave the comfort I'd found in him during the last few hours we'd spent.

He quietly announced, "We're here."

I softly chuckled. "I know."

"Listen, I'm serious about getting you in the studio, and I'll help you find more information about Stoney in any way."

I turned to look at him while still laying my head on the leather headrest. "I might just take you up on that offer after hearing my grandfather's song tonight."

Jake smiled slightly. "You could feel his voice in your soul."

I nodded slowly. "Like my voice."

His smile widened, and the two dots in his cheeks deepened. "Glad you hear what I hear. Now, do you believe me when I say you need to come to Nashville and do something about your talent?"

"I do." I sighed. "Kind of scary to know that something I've buried deep inside might be allowed to come to light."

He hit the steering wheel and grinned. "Yes, Mari. Yes. Come to the light with me. Let me set you free."

Although Jake teased, his innocent words seemed to take a new meaning in the close confines of the car. We locked gazes a tad too long, and I opened my own door this time before I got sucked into his dark, beautiful eyes. "Thank you again, for everything."

When I exited and stood by the car, Jake got out on his side and tapped his roof. "You still have my card?"

"Yes."

"And you plan to use it to see me in Nashville with all expenses on me?" He nodded slowly. "Move your head with me and say yes."

I laughed and spread my arms wide. "Yes."

Jake's smile slowly faded, and his eyes drifted to my lips.

"Um...I better go inside." I kept my eyes trained anywhere but his sensual mouth, though I hadn't taken one step away from him.

"Yep." He came around the car and stood beside me. "I'm just making sure no one kidnaps you in the short walk through those doors. Wouldn't want Phillip Graham coming after me for not protecting you."

Internally, I acknowledged his subtle reminder that I had a fiancé who trusted me and awaited me back in Atlanta. I needed to run far away from this tempting man.

"Bye, Jake." This time, I took a step toward the hotel.

He wore an amused expression. "Later, Mari. If you're ready for your destiny, call me."

"Promise. I'm a woman of my word, since you did keep yours."

"I did, didn't I? So you owe me." His face broke into such an infectious grin that I hugged him and kissed his cheek without thinking. Jake's eyes darkened with desire as he lowered his head slightly, and the urge to kiss him on the lips overwhelmed me.

I backed up from him. This time I waved before I turned around and resisted adding an extra sway to my stride, since I felt his heated gaze on my ass.

A month later, I sat at the piano in my bright classroom at the end of the day. A tune tumbled around in my cluttered mind to match the words inspired by my brief time with Jake.

Your name, a whisper on my tongue,
A secret melody, unsung.
The air between us charged, a dangerous spark,
On a path I tread, marked by the dark.

I hadn't called Jake as I reconsidered his offer to visit Nashville. Once I returned to my life and away from Memphis, the familiar, though not the best fit, had worked for me thus far. Why would I risk everything for a dream I'd never fully realized? Still, I did at least owe Jake a call to tell him I'd wavered on what I wanted to do and thank him again.

"Nice song." Stacie, the sixth-grade math teacher and my work friend, walked into my room with a large smile. "Did you sing that while you were in Memphis?"

"I was at a funeral, remember?" I said with more irritation than I meant as I pushed back from the piano, embarrassed that she'd heard me. I felt uncomfortable playing my own music around people, even friends and family. "What's up?"

She walked closer to me with her phone in her hand. "You. Why didn't I know that you could sing like this? And who was that fine-ass man playing the piano for you? Like, is he single? Because I need his number, unless you're stepping out on Phillip, and if you're doing that with *this* man, I don't blame you." Stacie grinned wickedly as she twirled one of her thin braids.

"What are you talking about?" I asked, though my pulse raced as she held up her phone.

"You just went viral. Almost two million in not quite a week since it dropped."

I picked up her phone. There I was, singing in that hotel piano bar while Jake played the piano and admired me. Like, really admired me. *Shit.*

"Girl, who is he?"

"I met Jake at the funeral. He knew my grandfather, and we just kind of hung out so I could get to know more about him." I scrolled, reading some of the glowing comments about my talent, and that Jake and I should be performing together somewhere. "How did you see this?"

"I'm always on TikTok, and everyone is seeing this video. If you ever check your social media, you'll see I tagged you and commented on your name."

I gasped. "Why would you do that?"

She frowned. "Because people should know who you are, Amara. Why are you tripping?"

I leaned against my desk. "I don't know. Not used to the attention. I'm like the background person."

"Um…not from this video. Baby, you are front stage and killing it." She snapped her fingers. "People will start contacting you, trying to sign you."

I stared at the video, and the chemistry between Jake and me was palpable. Phillip couldn't ever see this. "Jake already did."

"The man playing the piano is in the music industry?"

"Yeah." I looked up at Stacie. "He's an agent and works with Evelyn Hart."

Her eyes widened. "That Black man works with the biggest country singer?"

I nodded.

"How in the world did that happen?"

"No clue. Just know if Jake was lying, he wouldn't choose to say he was representing an aging country star."

She pointed at me. "That part."

"He invited me to Nashville for the weekend to sing for him in the studio. He suggested that I bring Phillip, too."

Stacie squealed. "You really should do it. The summer is here. What's the harm? In the worst-case scenario, he's not the right one to represent you, and you still had a free trip to a fun city."

"True." I nodded, still looking at her cell.

She took back her phone. "You keep staring at the video, so you might as well go and perform whatever song you were just singing." Stacie headed to the door and tossed over her shoulder, "Sounds like you were thinking about *that* man anyway."

I was grateful she kept walking, or she would've seen my blush. I grabbed my phone off my desk, and within seconds, I started watching Jake and I perform beautiful music together. The more I replayed the footage, the more I became clearer on what I wanted to do.

SIX

Jake

The alarm sounded, and I slid deeper under the covers. I stretched my arms and legs and found an empty space. Opening my eyes burned, and my temples pounded from the heavy drinking and strenuous sex with a woman whom I met at a bar last night while listening to a band I was contemplating signing to our agency. I'd hoped that she understood that it was a moment and not make it more.

I slowly swung my feet over the side of the bed and held my head in my palms. I'd had way too many mornings like this, trying to fill an unexplainable void within. This fast life was taking its toll on me, and I sometimes felt powerless to stop it.

The few hours I spent with Amara had stimulated my own musicality and creativity. Her wide-eyed curiosity and enthusiasm about her grandfather evoked warmth instead of numbness. I wanted to be different for her. I didn't want to be the manager that her family probably and rightfully assumed me to be—a charming fast talker with the glorious gift of gab, only interested in the money my clients could bring. I'd been that person with clients I'd signed, and would've been that way with Amara after hearing her poignant singing at the burial until she popped up next to me at a bar and somehow seeped into my hardening heart.

Amara Johnson was beautiful, and had immense talent and a rich backstory that would automatically grab the music world's attention, especially with a voice like hers meant for the grittiness of country music. Truthfully, Amara had crossover appeal, and the range for popular rhythm and blues, jazz, and hip-hop with the right rapper. Despite starting the game late, she could quickly rise to the top under proper guidance. I wanted to be the man who led her to superstardom. The man who made all her dreams come true. Like my father had been to Evelyn. Without him, Evelyn would have been a local star, maybe even a one-hit wonder.

I'd been groomed to follow in the footsteps of the only father who gave a damn about me—my stepfather, who married my mother when I was eleven years old. He'd been several years older than my mother and a white man, which had been an awkward transition for me after being raised in a predominately Black community in Houston. My biological father floated in and out of my life until my mother met William Barnes when he needed her legal services. He fell in love with her and wanted to continue to raise her son as his own. William asked to adopt me when I was fifteen. By then, I'd grown to love him and considered it an honor to change my last name to his when, in the words of Shaquille O'Neal, my *biological didn't bother.*

For years, I'd been content to be in William Barnes's shadow and loved that most people didn't make the connection we were kin because of our appearance. I'd signed various artists to our management team over the years. It was initially an uphill battle because my father wanted to focus solely on country music. I had to show him the error of his thinking, that we could make more money and impact by being the management team that could deal with any record label regardless of genre. Lately, I'd wanted to do more than sign on new talent for my father. Wanted more than hustling, hungry artists willing to sign any contract to have a chance. Wanted an opportunity to sign an artist under me and not William Barnes.

My father had taught me how to get the best deal, even if it may not have been the best deal for our client. His philosophy had been that without us, our artists would remain among the obscure, nameless, talented people. With our magic touch, they would make the money they'd never imagined.

If their career slowed down or ended, our responsibility wasn't to ensure they were financially secure for the rest of their lives.

During the last fifteen years that I'd been in this career, I'd seen artists explode and soar and then others crash and burn. Some of the implosion was the artist's fault. All too often, it was the tide of the business, and certain artists were meant to have only a moment and not a lifetime. Unfortunately, those artists who couldn't believe their spotlight had shifted to the next new shining act spent the rest of their lives chasing the same dead dream instead of finding a new one. Rene had never recovered from her meteoric rise and traumatic fall from grace.

I inhaled and exhaled deeply as the familiar sorrow lumped my throat every time I thought of her.

I checked my phone on the bedside table for the first time that morning and already had twenty-one messages and four missed calls. Still no contact from Amara. It'd been a month since the funeral. A month since she'd surprised me with her voice. A month since she'd asked for my help. A month since she'd agreed to come to Nashville and sing for me. A month since she'd impulsively kissed my cheek and hugged me in gratitude for our museum trip. Her action had been innocent and genuine, yet when she backed away, her gaze briefly drifted to my lips, and my gut tightened. I wanted to pull her back to me and kiss the shit out of her. Amara had lingered as if she wanted me to do more than acknowledge her thanks as I stood outside my car, watching her as she finally waved and walked into the hotel where she and her family were staying. A month ago, she'd told me she was a woman of her word and would contact me to make arrangements for her visit.

As weeks had passed with no word from Amara, I wondered if her life in Atlanta had reclaimed her. Maybe her man had talked her out of traveling to Nashville for something as crazy as cutting a track with a man she just met. Or maybe her mother had reminded her of the life she was building with her future husband, and going to Nashville wasn't a part of that plan. Or maybe Amara realized it was best to stay away from me.

I wanted to call her and reaffirm that our relationship would only be professional. But doing that would only draw attention to the attraction that flared whenever our gazes met or we causally touched each other. When she'd possessively placed her hands on my shoulders at the bar, I wished for a second that I was hers. Playing the piano for her and being with her at the museum felt normal and right. Watching her walk away from me physically ached, and I couldn't recall ever having that experience with another woman. Missing a woman I'd only known for a few hours didn't make sense, and I didn't like that she stayed at the forefront of my mind weeks later.

For that reason, I hadn't called or contacted her. I wanted her decision to come to Nashville to be her own. I would even prefer it if her man accompanied her so that I could focus on her gift and talent, and not how I wanted to hold on to her and never let go.

My cell rang again, and this time I picked up. "Morning."

"Uh oh, I can tell you had a late night. Is she still next to you?" My best friend, Nathan Price, snickered.

"It's daylight. What you think?" I grinned as I rose from the bed and padded across the dark, thick carpet to throw on a robe from my massive walk-in closet.

"I thought you told me you were tired of the same old."

"I am. Habits are hard to break. She came on to me, and I was too drunk to fight her off." I searched through my color-coordinated closet, looking for a shirt and slacks. I had a meeting with Evelyn and my father later today. We were planning her farewell tour, and everything had to be perfect and fit the needs of the queen of country music. "But I know you didn't call to bust my balls. What's up?"

Nathan asked, "Why didn't you tell me you knew Stoney Johnson's granddaughter?"

I paused from pulling a shirt off the hanger. "How do you know I know Stoney Johnson's daughter? How do you even know Stoney Johnson?"

"Duh, do you remember what I do for a living?"

"Funny. I helped you get on at the paper… Why you playing?" I sat on the plush bench in my closet. "Seriously, Stoney isn't B. B. King or Z. Z. Hill and definitely not W. C. Handy, so why do you know about him?"

"Just realized those blues singers like a lot of initials." He chuckled again. "Seriously, you and that fine-ass woman at the Peabody went viral."

"What do you mean? That happened a month ago." I shifted my phone to my other ear to make sure I heard correctly.

"Well, apparently, a guest at the hotel filmed you and dropped it last week, and one of Amara Johnson's coworkers recognized her two days ago. Your name isn't mentioned except as Rene Star's ex. I didn't know you played the piano. Y'all be like Ike and Tina."

"Prefer Jay and Bey," I drily commented. "Where is it?"

"On TikTok... I just sent it to you. It has two million views."

"Two million views once she was identified?"

"I don't know. I just saw the original post dropped a week ago and that her coworker tagged Amara Johnson two days ago."

I clicked on the link, and we looked like an established musical duo. We were attuned to each other. The ebbs and flows of her singing matched the stroke of my keys. She glanced approvingly at me as I played the piano like we'd rehearsed for hours. My eyes were glued to her, never wavering the entire time she sang. Wearing a soft smile, I adored her from the first to the last note.

"Shit," I said aloud before I could stop myself. Amara probably hadn't reached out because I looked like a fucking lovesick puppy. I stared at the video, wondering why that woman affected me so. I'd been with women who were sexier and more beautiful than her and had known talent. Yet here I was, on damn TikTok for the world to see that I was positively smitten with Amara Johnson.

Oblivious to my inner turmoil, Nathan said, "I did some deep diving and heard a couple of her grandfather's songs. Uncanny how she has his cadences. They must have sung together."

"Naw... She barely knew him, and she wants me to help find out more information about him in exchange for her voice in the studio." *Or at least, she* wanted *my help.*

"Why didn't you call me? This is what I live for," he exclaimed. "Never mind. Probably trying to keep her to yourself. I can tell she has a body underneath that blouse."

I shot up from the bench. "It's not like that. She's engaged."

Nathan scoffed. "When has that ever stopped you before? A man is another word for challenge. When you want something, you go after it and fuck the consequences."

My blood boiled at how insensitive he sounded, and I wanted to lash out. Except he didn't know about Rene. No one did, and no one ever would. "She's different, and I'm not rocking like that anymore."

"Says the dude who told me he was done with random hookups."

"All right. Let me go." I didn't hide my irritation this time.

"Hold up. I'm playing. You say she's different, then I believe it. Shit, she got you playing the piano, and I've known you for years and didn't know you played any instrument."

I rubbed my hand over my hair, which needed combing. "I play piano and fiddle. Dabble with the guitar and drums."

"Get the fuck out of here. I had no idea my best friend was a musician. Should I be offended?"

"Moms made me play until I finished high school. Thought it would come of use. In some ways, it has." I loved to play and did it in my spare time. My father always told me I had more career longevity in managing talent than being the talent, and I rarely showed anyone my skills.

"You do know that video blew up because of both of you. She sang that song, and you played the hell out of that piano. I watched it five times already. So when can I meet her? Is she recording in the studio anytime soon?" Nathan often sat in the studio and jammed with my recording artists. He loved raw talent and aspired to start his own magazine dedicated to all genres in the music world.

"I don't know," I admitted glumly. "I haven't heard from Amara since then. Maybe she changed her mind about finding out about her grandfather and coming to the studio."

"Did she say that?"

"I just told you I don't know."

"She ghosted you?" His tone dripped with disbelief.

I stammered, "I mean…no… She just hasn't called me, and I haven't called her."

"Oookay. And it's nothing between you?" Now his tone suggested skepticism to the highest degree.

"No."

"Then, if it's business, why haven't you called her?"

I slapped my thigh. "I wanted the decision to record to be hers."

He grew quiet, and I finally grabbed my slacks and shirt. It was already after nine, and I had a busy day. I hurried out of the closet, cradling my phone as I picked up my Louboutins on my way to the bathroom.

"Hello…you still there?" I asked.

"Just wondering why you're not pushing up on her. She's probably getting hits from all kinds of agents with this video. Do you want someone else to have her on their roster?"

"No. I just don't want to pressure her. She's a music teacher who isn't even aware of her star power. Not every person has aspirations to be a star. She might be that person."

"Or she needs the right person to guide her. Come on, you know that she's gold… Correction, platinum. Stop being scared."

"I'm not scared."

He guffawed. "I see how you were looking at her. Get over yourself and get her here. She's more important than your ego or lust."

"Yeah…yeah… I need to get ready."

"Not getting off the phone until you man up and get that woman to Nashville. You need her for your brand."

I could hang up the phone, but he would continue to harass me until I gave in. He was a topnotch journalist for a reason. I did want Amara Johnson for my brand. "You can meet her when I sign her, and she can decide if she wants you to do her story."

"Now that's the cocky Jake I know. Not this 'give up before you ever really try' vibe you're giving me because you don't want to feel for her."

"I'll let you know when she gets here," I promised, ready and willing to do whatever it took to get her in the studio. "I guarantee she won't want to leave once she's in Nashville." I clicked off without saying goodbye, and before I overthought, I found her number and called.

"Hello," Amara answered as I prepared to leave a voicemail.

"Hey…it's Jake Barnes."

"I know." I could hear the smile in her voice, and my nervousness dissipated. "I've been meaning to call you."

"Then it's a good thing I called you, because you sound like you plan to let me down easy."

She giggled. "No. I wondered if you still wanted me to come down to Nashville. Maybe you had second thoughts, especially after that TikTok video."

"You saw it?" My face flushed. Would she say anything about how I looked at her in the video?

"My coworker, Stacie, showed me a couple of days ago. She was the one who identified me. She was so excited and asked if we were a duo or something. Predicted I would get a record deal. So, when you didn't call, and I received a couple of calls from other agents, I thought you'd changed your mind."

"Why didn't *you* call me? You said you would." I heard the soft accusation in my tone, as if she owed me, and I quickly dialed it back. "Doesn't matter. We're here now, and I need to know when you're coming. I can make all the arrangements. Everything is on me, and you don't have to do anything but show up. Three days tops. We can try a couple of songs and see what you think."

"What if I want to spend the whole summer?" she asked. "I still want to learn everything I can about my grandfather. I found a journal, an old photo of my grandfather, and a woman who wasn't my grandmother. I also found two letters at his house."

"Letters? What kind of letters?"

"Love," Amara replied.

That simple yet complicated word floated in the air between us. "I'm guessing the letters are not between Stoney and your grandmother?"

"They're not." She continued, "I'm not asking you to pay for my entire stay, though if you have any recommendations on where I could stay for a reasonable price, let me know. Since I've been home, I can't shake this feeling that whatever I need to know is back in Tennessee, whether it's Memphis, Nashville, or somewhere in between. I know you're a busy man, and I don't expect you to spend your days helping me find out what happened with my grandfather."

"Not too busy to help you. I promised you. Plus, I admired him, and he was like an uncle to me."

"Still, it might take more time than I thought. His story may be deeper than that of a man with shattered dreams."

"What do you mean?" My curiosity was piqued.

"I can show you better than I can tell you," she slyly remarked.

I chuckled. "All right, guess I'll have to wait until you get here. And when will that magical day be?"

"Next Sunday, June third, and it'll probably just be me. Phillip and my parents aren't happy about my decision, but I have to do this for me."

Unbridled joy spread across my chest at the thought I would see her in a few days. "That works. I can arrange for you to stay on the grounds of Evelyn's compound. It's where the studio is, and she has several cottages for guests. Everything is still on me."

"Evelyn Hart? I get to stay at her home?" Her voice lifted almost to a squeak.

"Yeah. A lot of our artists stay there while we work on their records. Once you sign with me, you have the option to stay longer if you decide."

"Once? And not *if* I sign? I'm getting offers now because of that video. I need to keep options open."

"Yet you already chose a date to be here and plan to spend the summer with me…with my team." I closed my eyes in embarrassment at my slip. Words I would've normally said to another potential client felt more intimate with Amara.

"If I'm being real with you, I'm not sure what I want to happen with my music. I'm not the aspiring singer hoping for a break. Music has been a part of me for as long as I can remember. Whether I ever record a song or not won't change that. I've been in this unexplainable funk, and hearing my grandfather's music has woken something inside me. Maybe it's to discover what happened to my grandfather when he had so much talent, or maybe it's about really learning who I am. All I know is that my soul won't rest until I have answers. If it ends in a musical career with you as my manager, that's what it'll be."

"Fair enough. I have a couple of meetings today, but I'll get my assistant to set up your flight. Call me if you have any burning questions or need my advice."

"Thank you, Jake. Thank you for everything."

"No need to say thanks. I want to help you however I can, especially if it means I get to sign you as a client," I teased.

"So, I guess I'll see you soon." She seemed reluctant to get off the phone, like she did leaving me in Memphis.

"Yeah," I replied, just as reluctant. "Soon."

SEVEN

Amara

I ended the call hating myself for lingering when the conversation was clearly over. Hearing Jake's voice again reminded me of the few hours we spent together and that I had to drag myself away from him. His mouth had twitched with humor as he'd watched me take my time to get out of his car and finally into the hotel. Jake was a part of the entertainment business and probably used to women reacting like I did. He'd been a gentleman and accommodating, respecting my unspoken boundaries, though I'd sensed his attraction to me. Then I started second-guessing whether he'd changed his mind about inviting me to his studio when weeks passed without any contact.

I'd been surprised that his number had popped up on my dashboard as I tapped the steering wheel of my car, gathering my strength to tell Phillip that I planned to be gone most of the summer. I'd been sitting in the parking garage of his condo, trying to figure out the best way to tell him that wouldn't end our relationship. I wasn't sure if Jake's invite to Nashville was still open, so I'd planned to travel between Memphis and Nashville searching for answers after discovering the letters in the guitar case I found at the top of the closet in my grandfather's room. My potential music career had been secondary motivation for my trip, even after the calls from talent agents and managers clamoring for my attention. Hearing Jake's voice again brought the idea of a music career to the forefront. He'd made me feel like the most talented singer in the world, and that I had star power. That I had my own legacy to discover. I wasn't sure if Jake had been gaslighting me until I'd seen the video.

I was glad that Phillip had never been into social media and didn't have any accounts, because I wouldn't have a leg to stand on about being in Nashville for the summer. He would've looked at the video of me and Jake and accused me of an affair. Jake appeared positively enamored as he played the piano and gazed at me longingly. I'd replayed the video countless times, trying to be unaffected by his open admiration. Replayed it until my stomach stopped clenching. I prayed that the object of Jake's attention was my talent and not me. I wasn't looking for love when I already had it, and I wouldn't ruin my relationship because of a little crush. The more time I spent with Jake, the more, I was sure, his flaws would become apparent, or maybe he had a woman, and the focus could clearly be my music and Stoney Johnson. I just had to tell Phillip and get him to understand why I *had* to do this.

The tap on the glass scared me out of my freaking mind. Startled, I looked out the window, and Phillip stood there, holding his leather satchel with a confused smile. "Why are you sitting in the car? You have a key."

He opened my door, took my hand to assist me, and kissed me when I stood before him. He had reddish-bronze skin, pearly-white teeth, thick hair that he wore slightly unruly, and the leanness of a basketball player. I'd been instantly attracted when our mothers set up the date.

I hugged him and smiled warmly. "I was waiting for you. Wanted to walk in with you."

Phillip wryly commented, "That's sweet, I guess."

I pinched his taut stomach. "You're such a grump."

He squeezed me. "A grump you love."

"I do." And I did. No man was perfect, and he'd been good to me. We were comfortable with one another. Rarely argued.

He suddenly grinned. "Let's go get something to eat. We're already outside, and I bet you're hungry."

"Yes, I would love that." I returned his smile. Phillip was rarely spontaneous, preferring to plan our dates, as much as I encouraged him to be open and flexible. Pleasantly surprised at his demonstration of flexibility, I suggested, "There's this new soul food place at College Station I know you would love."

"Don't want to drive that far."

"Thirty minutes? Any place worth going is at least twenty minutes, and I can drive if you're tired."

He gestured with his thumb. "We can go around the corner."

"It's just sandwich and pizza shops, and it's only seven on a Tuesday. There won't be crowds. We could be sitting and eating some oxtails and rice by eight." I started shaking my hips playfully while still in his arms.

Phillip frowned. "Some of us have to work in the morning, and I still have more emails to finish tonight. We can check it out on Saturday."

I refrained from sighing loudly. "Saturday is your fraternity fundraiser, remember?"

He nodded. "Oh. Yeah. Let's eat there Sunday, then."

Well, Phillip left the perfect opening. I might as well dive in. "I'm flying to Nashville then."

He dropped his arms from around me. I became cold despite the warm late spring air. "You still on that?"

"Yes," I replied firmly. "I want to go to Nashville. You're not going to miss me. I'll fly home every other weekend, and you can fly down to see me."

His brow furrowed deeply. "Wait…you're talking like this is more than a week's vacation. How long do you plan to be there?"

"I tried to bring it up before, but you shut me down. I want to spend June and July there. I'll be back at the beginning of August."

"Why do you want to be away for so long?" He crossed his arms, clearly awaiting my answer.

I gulped down my growing nervousness. "You know I want to find out more about my grandfather, and I want to see if I have a real chance at music."

"Can't you try that here in Atlanta? We're engaged, meaning we should at least be in the same city together."

I reasoned, "We don't live together—your choice, not mine, by the way— and you work crazy hours. We spend maybe three nights…four tops out of the week together. Being in Nashville isn't going to hurt us. The summer will flash by in a second."

"Damn right it'll speed by, because you're not going. One week was too long, and now you're discussing a whole summer. Where will you stay? You don't have that kind of money, and I'm sure not going to pay for it."

I folded my arms and leaned against the car. "Why do you have to be an ass about this? I never asked you for any money. I get you're upset, but you're not trying to hear me. I've watched you work like a dog for the last two years, promise me trips that never happened and dates you've canceled, and I didn't give you a hard time because I can tell you thrive with your work. You love what you do. And I don't. Do I love my kids? Of course, but am I living up to my potential? The answer is no."

He bit out, "You're chasing a fucking pipe dream that you never even had."

"Maybe I never had that dream because I was never allowed." I lowered my raised voice and pressed my hand against his chest. "Baby, music is in my blood. It's in my DNA. I am more my grandfather's child than my father's. He had hopes and dreams of being this star. Someone took that away from him, and he died a lonely, bitter man. It's like Langston Hughes described in *Montage of a Dream Deferred*. Either I'm going to wilt and die or explode if I don't see this out. I'm asking for the summer. A summer to find the me I was always supposed to be."

Phillip crossed his arms. "What am I supposed to do while you're gone?"

"Support me. Love me. Marriage is a winding road. If we can't figure out how to grow individually and together, our marriage will fail anyway."

He sighed and dragged his hand down his face. "Listen…just give me until July, and I'll take a week off, and we'll go together."

I patted his chest. "If I truly believed you would take the time, I would. I don't want to wait for the opportunity to come when I have it right now. At least take off Monday and fly down with me on Sunday, so you can see where I'm staying and the people I'll be working with. Then come back in July for the week."

"You have a place to stay? Obviously, you've already planned this. It doesn't matter what I feel anyway."

"The management team just offered me a space on Evelyn Hart's compound right before you walked up. It's a crazy opportunity to be in the presence of greatness." At his continued skeptical expression, I added, "I want you there with me. To experience what I experience. Because I'm going doesn't mean I'm not considering your feelings. I've been sitting in this car for over an hour, trying to figure out what to say to you, because as much as I don't want to lose you, I also can't deny what my soul is telling me to do."

He scoffed, "Yeah, right. Your soul says leave your man behind and go sing and decipher some old love letters?"

"I'm not leaving you behind. I would love to have your full support as my future husband."

He stepped closer. "And as my future wife, you'll respect my feelings and stay."

I rubbed my arms and changed tactics. "You want to go back to school one day, right?"

Phillip didn't answer.

"You even asked me if you had to move temporarily away from me to attend school so that you weren't limited to Atlanta, would it be okay? What did I say?"

His nostrils flared before he sullenly replied, "That you would never interfere with a goal or a dream and that we could work out anything."

"Then why can't you give me the freedom in our relationship to grow?"

"I said what I said." He jammed his hands in his pockets and started walking toward his condo. "If you go to Nashville, then it's over."

I slunk against the car. Anger, hurt, and frustration fought for the first position in my burning heart. We'd never broken up or even hinted at breaking up. Our relationship had been easy and simple. We'd both been nearing thirty when we met. We'd established careers and were ready for the next step. Within three months of dating, I knew the altar was inevitable for us. Our families already knew each other, and our small circle of friends had welcomed our respective partners. Our love should've been enough to withstand long distance for two months.

Except Phillip was a planner, and our plans had aligned until after my trip to Memphis. Now, our plans didn't and may never align again. He apparently couldn't handle it. I still wanted to work through this. We still had a future. Following one path didn't necessarily close off another one.

Why couldn't he see that I needed to do this for me? Or that I was afraid that I would end up like my grandfather. Why couldn't he attempt to support me on my terms and not his?

Those thoughts raced in my head as I remained standing by my car, debating my next move, whether to leave or stay. Pride wouldn't allow me to run after him and confront the selfishness he'd just offered in return for the selflessness I'd always given him. Determination finally gave me the strength to dry my tears and get in my car. The conviction in my spirit hit the ignition and drove me away.

EIGHT

Amara

The morning of my flight, I strummed my guitar in my bed. I'd chosen a late-afternoon departure, hoping that somehow Phillip would change his mind. We'd never been at odds like this. I was supposed to go with him to his fraternity gala, and if he'd called, I would've dressed and been by his side. When he didn't, I rolled up into a ball and cried, fighting with myself about the decision I'd made to possibly lose everything I'd known for the unknown. My parents were also pissed with my decision and weren't speaking to me. We'd been here before, like when I decided to get a tramp stamp and a ring on my belly button for my sixteenth birthday without their permission. And again when I decided to major in music instead of pre-law, as they'd expected. No matter how upset they were with my decisions, we would eventually speak again. My mother would give in first and convince my father that I'd always been a dutiful daughter. Any decisions I made were usually sound, even if they disagreed.

This time felt different. My mother was upset and worried that the wedding she'd been waiting for since I was born wouldn't happen. Phillip had apparently confided in his mother that we weren't speaking because I'd decided that chasing a futile dream was more important than my future with him. His mother called my mother, which only upset Mama, who hated that I was the cause of any discord in my relationship with Phillip. She

49

expressed her hurt and frustration that I would throw away everything I'd been building with him. I should feel lucky that I'd met a handsome and ambitious man who wanted marriage and family.

I'd been irked that she said it like he wasn't fortunate to have *me*, and I'd corrected Mama. To her credit, she immediately backtracked to say that I was beautiful and talented and that it wasn't her intent to ever suggest that any man was better than her daughter. She still ended the call, telling me not to call back until I came to my senses.

My father didn't even attempt to convince me to change my mind. I'd called him the next day after Phillip threw down the gauntlet on our relationship. When I told him that I would spend my summer in Tennessee to learn more about my grandfather and wanted to explore my music, he remained silent for a long time before saying, "Music will break your heart like it did my father." He hung up before I could respond.

I didn't bother to tell my small set of friends, whom I knew wouldn't understand because they never acknowledged my music. They took my ability to sing and play instruments for granted, and it was a good way to keep my job as a teacher. So, for the past few days, I'd packed up a large suitcase, a carry-on, a backpack containing my grandfather's letters, the tattered photo of an unidentifiable woman, and an old journal containing some lyrics. Once settled in Nashville, I would spread his belongings around me and search for clues. Between having the safe space to explore my music and being in a place where people seemed genuinely interested in Stoney Johnson, I felt confident that this journey wouldn't be in vain. And maybe after my two months in Nashville, I would have satisfactory answers for Phillip and my parents, and we could move past this hurtful silence.

Unable to sleep, I'd been writing poems and trying my hand at lyrics most of the night in my guest room, which also served as my music room. I figured I would rest when I laid my head down tonight in Nashville. Jake had texted me and told me that one of his people would receive me at the airport and drive me to the compound. We would meet and discuss expectations of the next two months tomorrow. I'd been grateful he texted me and didn't call me back with the plans. I also appreciated he wouldn't be the one to pick me up. If he did, it would seem more personal than professional. I still loved Phillip and ached that he hadn't contacted me.

I checked my watch. I had a couple of hours before heading to the airport.

A key rattled in the door and my heart lifted. Only Phillip had a key. I quickly put down my guitar and hurried to the front. When I entered my living room, he had just closed the door. The usually well-groomed Phillip needed a shave.

He looked at me, his eyes tired. "I figured you might still be here."

I rushed to him and pulled his head down to kiss him hungrily. In between kisses, I murmured that I missed and loved him. He grabbed me up and walked me backward to my bedroom. We removed each other's clothes frantically. By the time we made it to my bed, we were both naked and expressed our troubled emotions through our bodies.

Afterward, I snuggled underneath him, wanting to be close to him because I would miss him. He'd been my world for the last two years. Phillip would soon be asleep. His breathing had slowed down, and his arms around me had relaxed. I rubbed the soft hair on his forearm. "Once I know my schedule, I'll plan a trip back home."

His body grew rigid. "I thought you changed your mind."

"No, my flight is later today. In fact, I need to get up in a second." I looked over my shoulder at him. "You came over to prove I wouldn't leave without your permission?"

Phillip's head jerked slightly. "Consent? I wouldn't say that. Thought you wouldn't want to do anything that I was against."

"I don't, which is why this has been the hardest week. We've never gone a day without talking. I don't want to lose you. I'd hoped you were here to tell me you support me." I slid from his arms and turned to face him.

His forehead furrowed deeply. "I can't support something that will only take you away from me."

I grabbed his scruffy face with both hands. "Can't you give it a chance before you write us off? Maybe this will bring us closer. I need a man who'll let me be me even if we don't always agree, because you trust that being me won't hurt us as a couple." When he narrowed his eyes, I pulled his face close to mine. "Give me three weeks. And if I can't somehow show you what I'm doing makes sense…if I can't give you a reason beyond what I'm giving you now to stay in Nashville the rest of the summer, I'll return home." I sat up and reached for my phone, which had gotten tangled in the sheets during our hot sex. "I can book a flight to be home in three weeks, and I'll come straight to you. Please…" I allowed the sheet to slip down, displaying my breasts.

His gaze darkened, and he took the phone out of my hand and pushed me on my back for round two. "Three weeks."

"Of course," I promised as his mouth found my erect nipple. I had three weeks to make an impact because I had no intention of returning home with my tail between my legs, admitting defeat.

Later that evening, I stepped off the plane and entered the Nashville airport. When I heard a live guitar in the near distance, my spirits lifted. I strolled past pictures of old and famous country stars like Minnie Pearl, Hank Williams, and Patsy Cline while I searched for baggage claim. Memorabilia of Dolly Parton and guitars inside glass cases dominated the décor. The airport was alive with music, lights, food, and people. I walked around excited that I may eventually be a part of this tapestry of music. Gleefully, I grabbed my large suitcase and hooked my and my grandfather's guitar cases on my back, anticipating the beginning of my journey. Even the air felt different as I strolled through the doors, looking for my ride.

"Mari." A familiar voice called my name, and I breathed to quell the flutters in my stomach. Jake stood outside some badass sports car with butterfly doors a short distance from me. Why did he seem even more handsome than the last time I saw him? It had to be the expensive car and the envious looks of women who walked past that made him seem so appealing. I loved the man I'd left behind, and Jake was a manager and an agent who would probably do and say anything to get me to sign a deal with him. I had to remember that as he hurried to me with a wide, dimpled smile to grab my bags from me. He didn't attempt a hug as he took my guitars off my back and placed them on my rolling suitcase. "How was your flight?"

"Great. I've never flown first class. Thank you."

"With your talent, that's about to be your norm." He started walking toward his car. "I was able to get out of a meeting earlier than I thought. Figured you could use a familiar face in a new city. We can grab dinner, and then I'll take you to the compound. You hungry?"

I should have told him I was exhausted after many sleepless nights. I should have told him I would rather wait until I settled in my new space, ordered food, or picked up something on the way to the compound. With his infectious, expectant smile and my energy having lifted exponentially at the sight of him, my response became a simple yes.

His grin widened like his opening doors, and I slid into the passenger seat, waiting for him as he loaded my bag and guitars into the trunk. I picked up my cell and texted Phillip, letting him know I'd made it to Nashville. He replied,

Good. See you soon. Call me when you get ready for bed. 6:32 p.m.

Will do. I love you. 6:32 p.m.

Miss you already. Will always love you. 6:33 p.m.

I pressed the phone to my chest. I couldn't get lost in this new world that Jake could offer me. Just the walk through the airport had invigorated me in ways I'd never experienced.

When Jake slid into the driver's seat, his magnetic presence looming large in the small car, he glanced down at my chest and how I held my phone. "Phillip Graham?"

I met his inquisitive gaze. "Yep. We love each other and can't let this time apart break us."

Jake looked away before his lips curved slightly, and I noticed the crinkles around his eyes, evoking warmth and trust. He would continue to respect my boundaries as he'd done a month ago. "I want whatever you want for your career and your time here. Regardless of Phillip or your family's beliefs, you have a long and fruitful musical career if that's what you choose."

I sighed, "I hope so."

"Maybe you can tell me what you found at your granddaddy's house over dinner? Rumor has it he left cash in the wall." Jake chuckled as he started the car with a swipe of his hand in front of his console.

"Did that old lady with the young face at the repast tell you that, too?" I laughed. "Not going to lie, when I found the letters, part of me kept expecting to find a hidden door or something."

"What are you going to do with his house? Give it a few years, and it'd be worth a lot. Gentrification is encroaching on Memphis." He drove smoothly out of the airport onto the highway.

"Plan to keep it for now. At some point, I want to go back and pack up my grandfather's stuff this summer. My father had an alarm system and Ring camera installed to protect it as much as possible, at my request."

"Tell me when you want to go, and we'll go," Jake reassured me.

I shifted slightly in my seat. "You're a busy man, and I won't hold it against you if you can't come with me."

He gave me a side glance. "You're a woman of your word just as I am a man of mine. You're my priority while you're here."

"Is that why you're here instead of one of your peeps?"

Jake's lips twitched. "Guess I can be honest. I wanted to pick you up because I didn't want to wait another moment to know what was in those letters. I'd been visiting Stoney since I was nineteen out of a favor for my father and pictured him as some sort of monk. He didn't seem to care about any woman outside your grandmother, whom he mentioned with stars in his eyes whenever I visited."

"Mr. Barnes, I didn't think you were into gossip and drama," I teased, loving that he'd been intrigued by the letters when I only received a lukewarm reaction from Phillip and my parents.

"What gave you that impression? I listen to Breakfast Club faithfully and follow all the gossip blogs, determining if what they say follows what I know or experienced." He chuckled as he weaved in and out of the slow-moving airport traffic. "I could probably start my own blog with all the shit I know from working in this crazy industry that can chew you up and spit you out and not give two fucks."

"That's what I'm afraid of, honestly. I'm a small fish that could easily get sucked in by the sharks."

He glanced at me and held his right hand up. "Give me your hand."

I did, and he clasped it.

"I got you. I won't let anyone hurt you. *I'm* that big, bad shark that will protect you from everything else in the ocean. You may not trust my words yet. You will sooner or later," he promised while squeezing my hand.

We held hands a little longer than necessary, and a tingle in my lower belly urged me to let go first. I stared out of the passenger window. I was here now, and I had to release any reservations to see this journey to the end. The bright city lights of Nashville loomed in the distance. It'd never occurred to me that this journey I had to take might be a never-ending one. Then another thought occurred: the man beside me might be better equipped for this journey than the man I left behind.

I pulled my knees to my chest, and tears gathered. Phillip hadn't been controlling or selfish. As a man who focused more on the future than the present, he'd clearly sensed that as much as I kept trying to make this a summer of exploration, it was more than that. He rightfully feared losing me.

I felt Jake's concerned gaze, and I shifted away from him. I had to build a wall to protect my heart from him when it still belonged to Phillip. I owed my fiancé that much.

NINE

Jake

Amara changed up on me abruptly, which probably had something to do with her man. Maybe she'd recalled his text, and it reminded her that he trusted her or something. Or our entwined hands triggered a retreat response. All I knew was that I felt her withdraw like a blossomed flower that suddenly had to close to keep out a pest. I wouldn't be a threat to her relationship, and at some point tonight, I would address the proverbial elephant in the room. I could admit to myself that I was more than attracted, and seeing her at the airport in leggings, a fitted T-shirt, and a jean jacket did wonders for my already rampant libido.

Yet she was more than a woman I could coax into bed. She was my potential Evelyn Hart. I refused to fuck this up by allowing my dick to take control. I'd learned my lesson with Rene and wouldn't repeat it with Amara.

"Hey, if you'd rather rest up and have dinner tomorrow, it's cool. I can take you straight to Hartland," I offered after we'd driven silently for a few miles.

"Hartland? I love that name. Simple yet profound, right?"

I nodded. "I think so. One of the reasons Evelyn changed her last name. 'Hart' can be used in so many ways."

"What's her real name?"

"No idea. She changed her name so long ago that we would have to dig up her birth certificate to find out. The world only knows her as Evelyn Hart, which she prefers."

"Hmmm…what would my name be?" She playfully tapped her index finger against her temple, and I could see her guard slipping again.

"Mari Johnson," I replied.

She lifted one arched brow. "Told you, only friends and family call me that."

"Yes, and you have that personality that welcomes people into your home, and that's how we'll present you. If people believe you could be their next best friend, your fan base will grow like *that*. Oprah grew so fast because she seemed more real and accessible than other talk show hosts. Taylor Swift sings and dances to everyone else's songs at events. Amara is a beautiful name that means 'grace,' but it also means 'bitter.'" I gave her a knowing glance. "Unless you're adept at hiding who you are, I'm guessing your parents went for the Nigerian rather than the Italian meaning. And you know we must keep the Johnson, even after you're married."

She turned her head and looked at me. "Sorry I got quiet on you earlier. Just a lot of thoughts about everything. We can have dinner because I really don't feel like waiting to order food once we get to Hartland. I'm starved."

"No worries. I can be a listening ear anytime. I'm excited about your being here and ready to get started. I can be demanding and pushy. If I'm taking you too fast, just say 'kindergarten,' and I'll slow down."

"Are you always this nice?" Amara wrinkled her button nose.

"What was your first impression of me at Stoney's house?"

Amara promptly replied, "You didn't fit in with everyone else. That you were arrogant and kind of pushy. Judgmental. At the same time, charming."

I quirked a brow. "And I'm all those things. I'm human, just like you. Do my best to keep my fuck-ups at a minimum. Might say something mean or uncalled for. Or be the sweetest man you've ever encountered. Don't try to pigeonhole me as any one type, because you'll never get me."

"Okay, first impression of me." An impish smile graced her face, making her that much more beautiful.

"Depressed…no…melancholic, a wallflower, guarded, outspoken, feisty, unbelievably talented woman who had no clue of her potential or power."

"I am also all of those things." She touched my hand, which rested between us on the console. I ignored the jolt in my pulse as she asked, "Where are we going?"

"Going to a spot on Broadway, the most popular street in Nashville. Want to give you a little taste. We'll probably hit that street a lot for inspo while you're here. Are you sure you're not too tired?"

She smiled. "I'll rest once I go home to Atlanta at the end of the summer. Is this place we're going to have dessert?"

"I can do better than any restaurant. Evelyn is out of town, but her staff are still there." He spoke into the air. "Call Hartland."

A pleasant-sounding female voice answered, "Did you pick up our guest already?"

"Yeah. We're going to head there. Think you can scrounge up some banana pudding or a peach cobbler?" I glanced at Amara for approval. She nodded happily.

"You know I can. How long?"

"We're headed to Broadway for dinner first. You have time."

"Sounds good. Bring her to the house first and let Craig get her bags to the cottage." The woman paused. "Am I on speaker?"

"Yes." I smiled.

"Sugar, welcome. Can't wait to meet you. Jake's been talking about you nonstop. We are a family at Hartland, and Jake and his father are the best. Evelyn is a piece of work, and I'm not talking about her behind her back. She knows I'll tell her to her face how I feel, which is why she loves me."

"Appreciate that, ma'am," Amara said.

"Ma'am seems so formal. Call me Jess."

Amara firmly replied, "Mean no disrespect, but I was raised to call people older than me ma'am. So it might take me a little while to conform."

"I like you already."

I chimed in. "Told you she was special. See ya soon." I hung up. "I have to make a couple of calls to check on clients. Is that okay?"

Amara nodded, placed buds in her ear, and closed her eyes. She slunk down in her seat, and her chest slowly rose and fell. She already felt safe with me, and I would keep it that way. I would prove my father wrong, and I needed to prove to myself that I could manage a career on my own without fucking it up.

I hadn't told my father or Evelyn about Amara because I wanted them to be wowed by her talent and not just take my word. I also wanted Amara to be my muse, not my father's or Evelyn's. After hearing and seeing her in action, they would fight to work with her. My father would insist on being her lead manager. Evelyn would suggest that Amara perform background vocals for her records in the studio and on stage while she was on tour.

No. Amara Johnson was all mine, and we would rise to the top together.

TEN

Amara

His deep chuckle caressed my ears as I slowly opened my eyes. "How long was I asleep?"

"Ten minutes." He placed his finger over his mouth briefly. "You need to go on tour. The money isn't in record sales unless you're Beyoncé or another top-tier performance. With the merchandising and shows, we'll recoup the money spent on the studio time and marketing. Don't worry, I have some thoughts for your tour that will make you a lot of money. All right, get on my schedule, because I need to go grab something to eat."

A male voice asked, "Where you headed?"

"Twelve Thirty."

"I love that place. Is tonight for songwriters?"

"I have to check the schedule."

While Jake finished his conversation, I lowered my window, allowing some of the atmospheric, crowded streets and the bars and restaurants into the car. The buzz of the nightlife in Nashville re-energized me. I rested my chin on the door, observing the mix of people wearing cowboy hats, boots, and smiles. I'd stayed home for college, attending Spelman, since I earned a full ride. Although I lived on campus, I'd been studious and rarely partied hard. Being here, away from anyone who knew me, I could reinvent myself.

Jake and I valeted in a garage within walking distance of the restaurant next to the National Museum of African American Music. The restaurant had three levels. Each one had its own unique style and décor. We walked in while a country band rocked the floor. The vibe was casual and fun. I bopped my head to the music, and Jake smiled. "You like?"

"I do."

We listened for a few more minutes before he grasped my hand and pulled me behind him. My hand fit perfectly in his, and the way he led me felt right. Jake nodded at others as we walked up the stairs to the next level. With the darker lightning and red décor here, I felt underdressed in my leggings and sandals, especially because Jake wore slacks and a polo shirt. Once we stepped deeper into the second level, a man playing the guitar sang to a small audience sitting at small tables and chairs. Each table had a candle, giving the room a soft glow. My attire no longer mattered as we listened to the man sing beautifully about comparing falling in love to the beauty of cherry blossoms in bloom. I whispered to Jake, "Who is he?"

"I don't know. Between here and Music Row, some bars host songwriting series for new singers hoping for a break. You sit and write lyrics, and then you perform the song. If you're a good writer and singer, odds are someone will sign you, or, at the very least, you'll secure a gig to perform at the many bars and restaurants in this area."

I stepped closer, fascinated by the concept. Impressed that these hopeful performers could be that vulnerable and courageous to play original songs. "Is this something you want me to do?"

Jake shook his head. "I discovered you. You skipped ahead of this. If you want to do this on your own, feel free. I can tell you all the places that host songwriters." He nodded in the direction of the rooftop bar. "Come on, let's get something to eat."

I followed him as he greeted a few patrons warmly, and he introduced me by my first name only and as a friend. He charmed his way to the entrance of the rooftop bar. A pretty hostess wearing a tight black shirt and pants opened the glass doors. She hugged him and flirted as he asked if JT was in town. She batted her fake lashes and kept her hand firmly around his bicep, ignoring my hand, which he still held. The hostess replied that JT wasn't in town and she would tell him that Jake had asked about him.

Nashville might have been new to me. Thirsty, aggressive women weren't. Annoyed rather than jealous, I squeezed Jake's hand, and he received the message. He informed the young woman, "Send the finest whiskey. We're going to the corner table."

An oasis of green foliage, hip music, pretty cocktails, good eats, and a cool breeze against the illuminating backdrop of Broadway awaited us. People milled around at the bar, in cushy loungers, or at tables and chairs. Jake led me to a table in the corner of the roof, easily the best one in the restaurant and bar if you enjoyed sitting outside.

As we settled across from each other, I mused that we appeared to be on a date. The setting and ambiance of an intimate dinner for two under the stars screamed romance. Was this Jake's intention, or if this was where he brought all potential clients? "It's nice here. What's the name of this spot?"

"Twelve Thirty Club. This is Justin Timberlake's restaurant. He has live music and songwriting events here all the time."

My eyes widened. "You mean you know Justin Timberlake?"

He shrugged. "Yeah. When he released his country-inspired album, he cut some songs at my studio."

"Oh wow. You think you can get his autograph for me?"

"Stick with me. He's going to want to do a duet with you." A waiter promptly approached our table with menus. Jake flashed his dimples at me. "You have to try the whiskey here. Tennessee is also known for its whiskey because we have so many distilleries."

"I saw that on one of the billboards in the airport." I rubbed my hands together. "I can't wait."

"We need to order you some food too." He addressed the server. "Let me get the Asian shrimp, the wings, sweet potato fries, and a Caesar salad."

I teased, "And what am I eating?"

Jake raised a brow. "Habit. Used to making decisions for others. Do you need to look at the menu?"

"No. Everything sounds good, and that Caesar salad better be for both of us."

"We're sharing everything." Jake pointed to a large, churchlike structure slightly behind and on the side of the restaurant. "That's the famous Ryman Auditorium behind you. It's designated as a Rock and Roll Hall of Fame Landmark and used to be the Grand Ole Opry for years."

"Do singers still perform there?"

"It's still fully operational. Shows happen all the time. It's even open to comedians and all genres of music, although it's most famous for country music. We can tour it one day."

He crossed his arms on the table. "Tell me what you want to happen while you're here."

I glanced around the rooftop. "It's crazy that just this morning, I had no idea I would end up here. First, listening to an amazing singer and then vibing on the roof of this restaurant overlooking the city with you and all these beautiful people…feeling like I deserve to be here for once." I exhaled my self-doubts and insecurities and lifted my chin as I answered Jake's question. "I want to feel like I belong. I've been on the outside all my life, hoping to get an invite inside. When I sang at the Peabody for the first time, I belonged. Seeing my grandfather in the museum and hearing his song, I belonged. That last piece of the identity puzzle I could never get to fit finally did. I want to see how far I can go. Even if it's not very far, I can at least say I tried."

He nodded slowly. "With me, you'll go far."

I debated whether to tell Jake about the three-week time frame I'd agreed upon without his input. Then I changed my mind. Tonight was about relaxing and getting to know each other more. "You seem so sure of my success. How do I know you're not full of shit?"

Jake chuckled. "I'm almost certain there are people in this world who believe I'm full of shit. The best way I can tell you is that you're here now on an all-expenses-paid trip, and we've yet to discuss or sign any contract for me to be your manager. I've never conducted business like we're doing right now because I believe in you, and I want you to trust me."

"Why me?" I asked. "You've probably seen such great talent."

"Exactly why I know. Have you checked the video from the Peabody? It's eleven million views and counting. Already have a couple of labels asking about you."

"I bet most of those views are women checking you out," I teased.

He leaned closer. "Stop deflecting from your talent."

"You need to as well. I searched for you online and didn't see any photo or video of you playing an instrument. Women love a handsome and talented man. How often do you play publicly?"

"I don't."

"Why?" I asked, genuinely curious.

"This isn't about me," he replied as our drinks were placed before us.

"How am I supposed to trust a man I don't know?" I sipped the whiskey, which had to be the smoothest liquor I'd ever had. "This is damn good."

"Tennessee whiskey."

"And I thought it was just a song." I tasted some more.

"I don't play because it's not what I do." Jake tapped the table a couple of times. "Okay, if you want to get to know me, treat me like a date. Ask whatever you need to make you want another date with me."

"Is that why you brought me to this restaurant meant for a romantic time? Wine and dine me to convince me to sign? Because I have to tell you, both times I've gone out with you have been great. And if I were still single, I would be so gushy over you with one eye open."

He chuckled again. "Why one eye open?"

I pushed through the butterflies that had swelled every so often since he picked me up from the airport, staring into his dark, alluring amber eyes. "You're too good to be true. So, either you're only giving me surface level, which is expected on a first date, or you're hiding who you really are from me."

Jake shrugged. "Technically, this would be our second date, and maybe what you see will be what you get. Not hiding who I really am. I'm a thirty-three-year-old man who is lucky or blessed to be a product of a hardworking attorney mother and a stepfather who earns millions managing talent. I inherited their work ethic and determination, earning my own money. I love making deserving, talented people's dreams come true. I'm demanding and bossy. Used to getting my way and can be selfish. But also crazy loyal to a fault and a man of my word, right or wrong. I drink too much, and I probably, excuse my language, fuck too much. Not the best in the relationship department, though I believe in friendships, lasting love, marriage, and family. You have no reason in the world to trust me except your gut. You came looking for me in Memphis because of your gut and possibly have given up everything because of your gut. I don't take any of that or you lightly. I will be good to you and promise to be honest with you." A waiter with our meal approached the table. "Shall we eat?"

Admittedly pleased with his response and intrigued by the man before me even more, I raised my glass slightly. "Yes."

ELEVEN

Amara

"Hey, we're here," Jake's voice announced from a distant fog as he gently shook my shoulder. I opened my eyes to the grandest home I'd ever seen. Correction: grandest mansion I'd ever seen. The well-lit face of the house with a nose and a smile made of stone and glass beckoned strangers and family from near and far. Green bushes peppered with fuchsia-colored flowers lined the circular driveway and the pathway up the five stairs to the expansive glass double doors.

The flat land surrounding Hartland, interrupted by five small guest houses on one side, a corral and a stable on the other, could be seen for miles because of the diamond-shaped tall lamps and the in-ground lights that dotted the expansive lawn and sparkled in the darkness. Jake opened the car's butterfly doors, and I stepped out in awe. I hugged myself. This would be my home away from home, and I'd never felt luckier. Jake grabbed my bags and guitar case and strode to the house, and I followed.

"Is it okay if I take pics? I know the NDA doesn't allow me to post or say anything about Evelyn Hart. I can't remember if it said anything about pics," I said. Jake had sent over an NDA for me to sign two days ago and told me he wouldn't send a contract until we could discuss it in person.

"You can take pics to mark your time here but can't post until you sign the contract with me. And if you decide not to go with me for some reason, you can't ever post any pics involving Hartland."

"Got it." I turned around with the mansion in the background and held up my phone. "My first night."

I inadvertently caught Jake in the background, walking away with my guitar cases on his back. It was a natural shot, and he looked good in the picture. So I kept the pic and took another when he moved from the shot. I would never post that pic of him in the background. If we did part ways, I would have something to commemorate the first day of my journey that wouldn't have happened without Jake.

After the selfie, I walked up the stairs to the obscenely wide and long porch that stretched the width of the mansion. Several beautiful, handcrafted rocking chairs were scattered across the polished wooden floor. I was inspired by being outside next to these soothing chairs, where I could see the stars sprinkling the darkened blue sky. Fireflies in the nearby woods sparkled like tiny diamonds. The sounds of crickets and frogs communicating flitted through the warm night.

"You can sit out here anytime you want. You have free rein of the bottom floor and the basement where the studio is located. The second floor is off-limits," Jake said. "There'll be times we'll go into the city so you can catch the vibe of Nashville and use my own studio."

"I can't imagine you live on the grounds."

His eyes crinkled. "Why can't you imagine that?" he asked as he held one of the large doors open for me.

"You don't want people in your personal business." I smiled as I walked past him. "This home feels like family, and family loves to get all in your shit."

"Ooh. Ms. Johnson curses."

"Don't sound so surprised. I get frustrated or pissed, and you'll have to cover your ears," I boasted.

"Jake? I thought I heard you drive up," the voice from the phone earlier called out, and an older, curvy woman with long gray locs, wearing a t-shirt, jeans, and an apron, walked into the main room from somewhere in the back of the house. Jake promptly put my belongings down and playfully lifted her in a bear hug. "Put me down, boy. Embarrassing me before I get a chance to meet her."

Jake placed her on her feet. "I had to mess with you. It's been a minute since I've been here."

"Five months, to be exact."

"Come on, Auntie, you know I stay busy, and my artists don't like driving way out here to work." He kissed her cheek. "Missed you too."

I warmed seeing this side of Jake. Made him seem more personable.

"Jess, this is Amara Johnson, our next big star," Jake proudly introduced me.

"Hi, so nice to meet you," I replied, stepping closer to shake her hand. Instead, she pulled me into a big hug.

"I hug. Hope you don't mind," Jess said when she backed up.

"Not at all. Love hugs, and when I hug all day when I'm with my children at school."

She smiled wide. "Come on this way. She can stay in the Royal room tonight, and Craig can take her things to the cottage tomorrow. He's in the stable with the horses."

Jake nodded. "Good idea."

Jess saucily tilted her head. "All my ideas are good."

"I can't, and I won't argue." He grinned boyishly, showing off his deep dimples.

"I won't either, because I heard you make the best desserts," I added.

"Good. You better enjoy this peach cobbler before Jake has you eating rabbit food," Jess said as we headed toward what I assumed was the kitchen or dining area. "He can be a health nut."

I looked back at Jake, who'd moved toward another hall, and he gave me a sheepish grin. *Damn.* I forgot that my appearance might have to change and that I would have to watch my diet. I'd always had a round face and curves. We definitely had a lot to talk about, because I had no intention of being a stick to fit anyone's definition of beauty.

The three of us chatted and laughed about Jake's wild younger years in the nook of the large kitchen designed to cook for an army of people. At one point, Jake and his mother had lived here with his father, William. He'd been rebellious, sneaking off with one of his parents' cars while they were asleep to drive back to the city and hang out with friends. He'd been doing it for a while until one night, he had too much to drink and believed his mother's car had been stolen. In a panic, he called William because he couldn't call the police and report it. He begged his father to lie and pretend that the car was stolen off Hartland's property. William agreed to calm his panicky son, but when his father came to pick him up, his mother was in the supposedly stolen car. Jake had forgotten he'd taken his father's car, and the sixteen-year-old started crying real tears because his father drove a Maybach.

Jake chuckled. "I cried like a baby all the way back to Hartland, a blubbering fool to my mother, who hadn't said one word to me the entire time. I didn't know what waited for me at home for stealing a Maybach when I had my own car, a sensible Honda Accord. When we pulled up into the garage, my father's car was parked there. Confused as hell, I'm wondering, what car did I drive there? Then I swore off drinking because, apparently, it made me forgetful. My parents let me believe I was losing my mind for a good solid month while I was forbidden to drive except to school and back."

"So, what really happened?" I pushed my empty plate away from me, wishing the three of us hadn't devoured the heavenly cobbler with the flakiest of crusts and the sweetest and juiciest peaches I'd ever had.

He shook his head ruefully. "I had forgotten where I parked my father's car. He had a tracker, and once he realized that I'd taken his car and not my mother's, he tracked it to a bar a few blocks over from where I believed I'd parked. They wanted to teach me a lesson and didn't speak to me for that entire month I was on punishment. They relayed everything through Auntie Jess or the other staff. Their silent treatment and disappointment worked better than if they'd yelled, which I expected."

"Yes. Silence works better than yelling. I couldn't stand it when my mother didn't speak to me. She's a chatterbox. On the other hand, my father is a quiet man who only speaks when necessary." I yawned as I giggled. "Oh…excuse me. Guess I'm more tired than I thought."

Jess immediately picked up our plates. "Go ahead. I'll see you in the morning. Are you spending the night, Jake?"

"Not sure yet. I have early meetings." He rose and placed his empty glass of almond milk in the sink.

"Can I help?" I stood with my glass in my hand.

"It's my job, and I love it. Yours is to make beautiful music. Can't wait to hear you in person. Saw that video of yours." Jess twisted her lips at Jake. "You make a good team."

I knew what that look meant. Had seen it when my mother and Phillip's mother wanted to match us as a couple. Jake ignored it and tugged on my short-sleeved shirt, beckoning me to follow him.

I hugged Jess. "Thank you for the compliment and the best peach cobbler I've ever had. Goodnight, Jess."

She waved us off. "Night."

As we left the kitchen, Jake asked, "How often do you play your guitar?"

"All the time. I don't have a set time."

"You need to get on a schedule. A time for the guitar, the piano, and the drums, and I want you to get better with the violin or, in country music language, the fiddle. I can teach you some things, but bringing in a coach would probably be better." He walked slightly ahead of me, and his tone had lost some of his friendliness. "Tomorrow, we'll go into the studio, and I want to hear you play to see if you need more coaching with the instruments you say you play well."

"I do play well. I might not be in a band or sing professionally, but I've always been a musician," I said.

He looked down at me. "As a teacher, you should know that any skill can be enhanced."

I nodded and resisted folding my arms at what I perceived as a slight against my talent. "Where are we going?"

"The porch." He brought me back outside. "Choose a chair. I'll be right back."

I settled in a chair that provided the best view of the starry midnight-blue sky. Jake returned with a shiny acoustic guitar that wasn't mine and gave it to me. "Play whatever inspires you."

"I prefer my guitar."

"I know." He gave me a pick. "Play."

"What if I don't play on demand?"

"You will now." His tone left no room for argument, and he moved to lean against a pillar on the front porch with his arms folded. "Working with me won't always be easy. I'll push you and challenge you. You might even curse me and hate me. As long as you're real with me, we're good."

"And what about you being real with me?" I placed the unfamiliar guitar across my lap and strummed the strings without the pick, listening for the tuning. Of *course* it would be tuned already.

"You say that like you have something else on your mind." The cords in his forearms bulged like he expected the worst.

"I do. I'm exhausted and haven't had much sleep this past week. No one wants me to be here, especially Phillip. I promised him I'd come home if I couldn't show him why I needed to be here in three weeks."

Jake scowled and retorted, "If he can't see that already, he won't in three weeks."

"He's never really seen me play or sing. I want to impress him when I go home for a visit," I meekly explained.

"How can he not? You just told me you play all the time." His scowl deepened.

"We don't live together, and I play in my classroom or when I'm home alone."

Jake's forehead scrunched. "Listen, if you're not really going to give this a chance, then I don't need to waste my time."

"I wouldn't be here if I didn't want to give it a chance." I lifted my chin, determined not to let the irritation in his voice silence me like my parents had done most of my life.

He countered, "Are you? Because it seems to me you have one foot in both doors, and I need all of your feet in this door while you're here."

"What if I can't do that? I have to keep my feet on solid ground even if it's in two places."

He blew out his breath and tilted his head back against the pillar. "I saw how you looked at this house…this porch. Play how this night makes you feel." Jake closed his eyes.

I scanned the diamond-lit sky and felt the heat that hadn't lessened just because we could no longer see the sun. A large pool of blackness gleamed from the moonlight in the distance—probably a river or a lake. I held the pick between my thumb and index finger, hitting a few strings before catching a rhythm in the air. "Summertime" from *Porgy and Bess* flowed from my lips. The lyrics about an easy and protected life were similar to the life my parents had provided for me. One day, she would fly free and on her own. She was no longer protected by her parents. Again, like me.

I looked at Jake as I finished the last note. His eyes were still closed, and when he opened them, they were glassy.

"If he doesn't know this side of you, then how can he ever say he knows you?" he asked quietly. "Why do you hide who you really are from him?"

I protested hotly, "I don't hide who I am from him."

Jake shook his head. "This is the third time I've heard you sing, and I'm moved to tears each time. If you can't see this is who you are, you might as well catch a flight back to Atlanta and return to your nice little life. We don't need to wait three weeks."

"Stop telling me to go back home. You told me we can go at my pace, and the minute I tell you my timeline, you dismiss it," I retorted.

He shot back, "If the timeline was yours, I would respect it. But it's some bullshit time to please your man who'll never accept that you're meant to be more than a teacher."

Breathing through my building anger, I calmly reminded him, "You asked me for a weekend. I offered a summer. Three weeks is a compromise."

Jake narrowed his eyes. "And if he wants you back home after that, then what happens here?"

I shrugged. "Whatever song or songs we create are yours to do whatever with."

He pushed off the pillar and kneeled in front of me. "Don't ever give your songs away to anyone, not even me. Your grandfather didn't know his worth, and I refuse to let you follow his path. He gave away songs that he'd written. From what I understand, he gave them away for little to nothing to whoever asked because he didn't believe they were worth much. My father gave him money out of empathy. If you turn your back on your music… on who you are, you will end up like him. Maybe the dressing will look different. You might have a husband, a couple of kids, and a dog, and live in that nice suburb." Jake pointed at my heart. "In here, you'll always have a void, wondering what if. A void that will never be filled until you know and accept that your path is meant to be extraordinary."

"I don't want to lose Phillip," I admitted, wiping my falling tears.

Jake's jaw clenched. "And if you lose yourself holding on to him, it would be a fucking shame."

"It's not just that. I have to keep my feet in both places. When I asked you to be real with me, I also meant that we have to ignore this." I gestured between me and him.

"Agreed." He continued to kneel in front of me, and his gaze dropped to my lips before meeting my eyes again. "You're afraid of our attraction, and I'm not. I'm fully aware that though you might fight it, you would give in to me if I put pressure on you. Do I want you? More than I've ever wanted a woman. But I would be no different than Phillip if I allowed my own selfish needs to get in the way of who you're meant to be. We didn't meet to have a few nights of fun that would forever ruin our ability to work together. Stoney brought us together to fight for his legacy and to begin yours. I saw how you looked at the museum listening to his music. Stoney is your kindred soul. You found his letters, his music, and you found me. To walk away from your destiny because you're afraid to lose a man who doesn't even know you in the first place is disrespectful to your grandfather's legacy."

My heart pounded at his rawness, at the desire that he didn't hide as he made his plea. I could get so lost in Jake and forget the love I already had. It would be so easy. Here, away from everything I already adored, in this beautiful, romantic home. "I did find his letters. Letters of love between him and a woman who wasn't my grandmother. My grandfather died brokenhearted because he lost my grandmother and father chasing after his dream and fell for a woman who seemed to understand him more than my grandmother. But we both know that affair didn't end in a happily-ever-after. Kind of like you and me if we give in to temptation because you already get me. Maybe I'd rather have a void than end up brokenhearted and alone. I don't want that future either."

Jake's eyes softened. "We don't know his whole story."

"We don't. We only know the beginning and his end." I sighed. "Can we really work closely together and not act on our attraction?"

He smirked. "Am I that irresistible?"

"Well…the fact that you've been kneeling a long time does work in your favor," I flirted.

The playful light darkened to desire in his eyes, and he stood and turned away from me. "As long as you don't say shit like that to me, we'll be fine."

I realized I'd gone too far in my teasing and wanted to lighten the mood. "Got you thinking about sex, huh?" I took the pick. "This song will really get you going. A violin would be better, but I think you can still figure it out."

Jake ran his hand down his face over his goatee. "Really, Mari?"

"Yeah, we're friends again." I smiled and started playing a few strings. "Guess what I'm playing, Jake?"

He jammed his hands in his pocket and started grooving in place, and a smile erased the frown. "Not the 'Thong Song'?"

"Yep. You remember the lyrics?"

"Do I?" He arched a brow. "I couldn't wait to get to the beach when I was a little boy to see them thongs." Jake started singing and rapping as I played.

Jess came out on the porch, laughing at Jake's performance, especially when he grabbed her hand and twirled her around. "Can I make song requests?" she asked.

I bragged, "I can pretty much play by ear, and if I can't, Jake got it."

The rest of the night went by harmoniously as I took their requests and played for them. Jake took the guitar from me and showed me he was also a musician during several songs. It'd been the best time that I could ever remember. My cheeks hurt from grinning so hard, and I could honestly say that when I finally laid my head down to rest, my soul smiled.

TWELVE

Jake

My eyes popped open before the alarm. Excitement that I would get Amara in the studio today jolted me awake better than a cup of espresso. Before returning to Hartland, I had a few meetings and phone calls. I'd driven the forty-eight-minute ride home, though it was after two in the morning. Spending the night with the kinetic sensual energy between me and Amara was a bad idea. So I'd told Jess to show her to her room, and I got my ass in my car and drove home.

I jumped in the shower, allowing the water to soothe me. Last night had been hard. We'd been vulnerable and truthful with one another. A perfect prelude to making love all night. Seeing her visible pain and hurt at the thought of losing another man stabbed my ego. I had to remind myself that she and I had just met, and she'd been with him for some time. That Amara Johnson wasn't meant for me. All I needed to remember was what happened the last time I'd mixed my personal life and business, and my longing crept back into my heart. Amara's man would fully accept and support her musical ambitions in the best possible world. Then she wouldn't have regrets. Still, I couldn't help but wonder why she'd kept a large part of herself from him. Last night, Amara had glowed with the peace that only came from true happiness. Why wouldn't she allow her future husband to see that side of her? The true beauty within.

Soon after my shower, I headed to my first meeting with one of our older talents who had an upcoming tour. My phone rang as I exited the road, driving up Broadway to Garth Brooks's Friends in Low Places Bar, where Conrad was practicing for an intimate show tonight.

"Hey, Dad. On my way to catch Conrad's rehearsal, and then Daybreak to negotiate their contract with Warner Music."

He commented, "That shouldn't take long."

I agreed. "More of a formality. Warner still wants Daybreak, and the band isn't asking for much more."

"Wish all of our roster was that simple." He lightly chuckled. "Heard that the new singer you neglected to tell me about impressed Jess last night. When do I get to hear her?"

I didn't know how I forgot that Jess couldn't hold water. Of course she'd told my father. Probably Evelyn, too. "We're going to be in the studio all week. If you have time, stop by Saturday before you head to New York and check her out." My parents were traveling to New York to speak with the reps at Madison Square Garden for Evelyn's first stop on her upcoming tour. My mother had been a corporate attorney and become an entertainment lawyer once she met my stepfather. She often helped negotiate and draw up contracts for him.

"Probably won't have time. Evelyn will be back at Hartland. She can sit in, and we can get her thoughts." He cleared his throat—a sign that he needed to ask me something that made him uncomfortable. "I haven't seen her contract. Why the secrecy?"

I gripped the steering wheel tighter. "I want to try my hand again."

"I thought that might be it. I don't know, Jake. If she's as good as Jess says she is, she probably has longevity. You're better at finding talent, and I'm better at managing their careers."

"What do you mean you don't know? I was younger and got caught up. I've made you money for years, finding and acquiring talent. I've even helped you manage most of them. I want this one for myself."

My father retorted, "Then why haven't you nailed a contract before we host her? You have her at Hartland and singing in the studio I built."

"Is that your way of saying not to use your studio? It's our studio any other time, and Hartland is open to anyone we want to work with. Well, she's the one I want to work with personally." I tried to check my rising anger, though I was sure my father knew I would get upset. It was why he was hesitant to ask me any questions about Amara.

He quietly said, "I don't want to argue with you. But I don't operate without a contract in place. It's business, and I can tell you're already going down that path you did with—"

"Will you ever let me move past Rene?"

"She could've ruined us. All that I built could've gone in a second because you couldn't do your job," my father shouted.

I cursed silently. My father rarely raised his voice, so I lowered mine. "And because she loved me, she didn't ruin us. Mistakes were made, and we've moved on." I tamped down the guilt that I'd spoken an untruth about Rene. She hadn't fully recovered, preferring to spend most of her days isolated and barely making music. I had the best mental health professionals working with her, though I'd only seen some improvement when she fired them all. "If you prefer, I can arrange for Amara to live in the city and use my studio."

He said quickly, "She can stay where she is. Wouldn't want her to think Evelyn doesn't want her there."

"We definitely wouldn't want her to think that," I said sarcastically. "We have to protect Evelyn Hart's brand at all costs, right?"

"Don't do that, son. I wouldn't have my career if it wasn't for her. You wouldn't have the life you have without her either."

Tired of hearing how Evelyn saved my father's career again, I snapped, "Really? My mother was a six-approaching-seven-figure attorney when you met her. I received athletic and academic scholarships and graduated with honors in business from Tulane University. We both would've done all right without you."

He grew quiet before finally saying, "I'll see you on Saturday."

I hung up, hating whenever I had conflict with my father. We only butted heads in business. I needed to prove him wrong, which required a guarantee from Amara that this wasn't an experiment. I called her, and she answered on the second ring. "I hope I didn't wake you."

"No. Been up for a while. Hard to sleep in a strange place, even in a heavenly bed like this." She paused. "I can tell you're driving. Already hitting the streets before nine like a banker."

"Yeah. Be there later, by two. Jess can show you your cottage, and you can make it your own while staying there so you'll be more comfortable." I tapped the steering wheel. "Listen, we didn't finish our conversation. I need to know you're here for more than three weeks. We can produce a couple of demos, but that can't be all for our work together. What I do takes time, and three weeks won't cut it. We need to decide how we want to present you to the world. You honestly fit any genre, but we want the right one for you. I already talked to my friend, who's a journalist, and he's dying to help with Stoney. And you still want to take a trip to Memphis with everything else we need to do for your music. I made serious plans for us once you told me you would be here for the summer."

She replied earnestly, "I want to be here as long as needed. I also want to honor my word to my fiancé. I'm willing to work hard with little sleep. I have three weeks to prove to him that I can be this star you seem to think I can be."

I shook my head vehemently like she could see me. "Nope. *You* have to envision it. Not just me."

"Then make sure I see it too, and I guarantee I won't have any more drama with Phillip. Ultimately, he just wants to make certain I'm not going anywhere, and as long as he can be open to whatever this career brings me, I won't." At my silence, she continued, "Jake, look at this as a challenge. If there's anyone who can make me a star in three weeks, it's you."

I bumped my head on my leather seat twice, her belief re-inspiring me. "I know what you're doing, and unfortunately for me, it's working. If we do this and your man still doesn't approve, all I ask is that you be honest with yourself about whether this is the career you want or not and that you don't make a decision out of fear of losing him."

She squealed. "I promise."

"That means we have much to do, and I want to see those letters tonight." I added, "And you'll have smoothies for breakfast now for more energy. I hope you enjoyed that dinner and peach cobbler last night."

"I'm all for being healthy, but I refuse to be a stick, Jake. I love my natural curves."

"I'm looking out for you. If Auntie bakes like she did last night for you three times a day, you'll be twice your size in a month. Your bod is already hot, speaking professionally, and I want you to keep it that way for stamina." I grinned, sensing her blushing smile on the other end. "We need a stylist who can show you the best way to wear your clothes, makeup, and hair."

"I won't argue there. Years of being a music teacher and my overall wardrobe sucks." She giggled self-deprecatingly.

"Today will be your easiest day because we're about to do a boot camp for the next three weeks, and I'm arranging a performance at a club in the city. Then Mr. Graham and whoever you invite can see you in your element."

"Woah. You mean a real performance with an audience and not just in front of a few people?"

"Yes. I'm making you a star like you asked. You're showcasing cover songs and at least one original song." I parallel-parked in front of the bar. "We're giving the world a piece of new recording artist Mari Johnson."

"I don't even know my genre or my style. Like, who am I?" Her voice rose.

I reminded her quietly, "You are always Amara Clara Johnson, and I'll see you later. Bye."

"Bye." She ended the call sounding surer than she had a few seconds ago.

I wanted to call and cancel the rest of my meetings and go straight to Hartland. Amara's challenge to have her ready in three weeks really inspired my creativity and flow. My thoughts were flying nonstop as I jogged into the bar to watch one of our long-term artists, Mel Conrad, a traditional country singer from Austin, Texas.

THIRTEEN

Amara

As soon as I hung up with Jake, the shrill ring of my cell sounded again.

"I thought you were supposed to call me once you settled in your place?" Phillip barked.

"Morning," I politely replied, though I cursed silently. I'd forgotten to call him. Barely made it to the shower before I collapsed in bed. "I crashed. I hadn't been sleeping well with you and the parents upset about my decision. Then, with the travel, I fell asleep. Sorry."

"It's already starting. You're moving differently."

"That's the whole point of this, Phillip. What's the sense if I do everything the same way I've always done? I apologize for not calling you, but my schedule isn't that of a school teacher anymore. We'll probably be up all hours of the night until we capture the right song." I propped myself up on the fluffy pillows. "Can we start over? Let's say good morning and that I already miss you."

He grudgingly replied, "Miss you too."

I questioned, "You sure? Because you seem mighty irritated with me, though you have gone out of town for work and forgotten to call me before. I don't recall ever being upset with you."

"Hate when you bring up something I've done to make a point."

"It seems to be the only way you hear me." I pulled the sheets higher. "Come on, baby. Be cool, okay?"

"Okay." This time, when he answered, he dropped his irritation. "What did you do last night?"

"I got to see Justin Timberlake's restaurant, and then I had the most fattening and delicious peach cobbler from the chef here. Then I practiced my guitar and did covers of songs. It was a good night. Told my potential manager that you and I agreed to see what happens in three weeks. He's getting me ready to perform and wants me to sing several songs at some bar in Nashville. I want you to fly here and be there for me. Then you can see why this is important."

"I get why it's important to you. I'm just trying to understand how this new lifestyle will fit with mine…the life we were building."

"Be patient with the process. Maybe we can figure out how to navigate my new life together. I'll get the exact date, but be prepared to come here around that time." I curled into a fetal position. "We can make the trip romantic."

"And are you prepared to return with me if I don't think you should pursue this career?"

Jake's cautioning words reverberated within me. Three weeks was an arbitrary date for a man who may never accept that I was meant to perform. The acid in my stomach burned as I stated, "I need you to have an open mind about this. I'm sorry I never showed you how much music means to me. Give me a chance."

"The fact that you're there against my wishes and we're still together *is* my giving you a chance," he replied sternly.

"Are you remotely interested in seeing me perform?" I curled tighter, waiting for his answer.

"Of course. Just wanted to make sure you remember the compromise we made."

"Hence the show, so you can truly see me. I got it, Phillip." I paused, trying to say what I needed to say without angering him or hurting him unintentionally. "Seriously, don't come if you can't just be here for me without an ulterior motive to get me back to Atlanta."

"You mean home?"

"I meant Atlanta. Home is you," I said as I pushed myself to get up and swung my legs over the side of my bed.

He whistled. "All right…tell me when, and I'll be there."

I breathed a sigh of release, and the pain in my stomach eased. "Just plan to take the following Monday off so we have time to see the city together."

"I can't make promises. This is our busy season."

"Every day is your busy season. We agreed to three weeks. If you want me to uphold my end, you do your part. I'm pushing the management team to help me perform for you."

He sighed. "Mondays are difficult. I can take off Friday and leave that Sunday."

I twirled around. "Thank you. Can't wait until you see me. I'm getting a new look."

"You know I don't care about that."

"I know, but my appearance becomes a part of my brand, and we're supposed to find my right look."

"You're beautiful as you are. I need to get back on the job. As long as you're happy." His voice still held doubt. I was determined to prove we would be fine.

Once I ended the call with Phillip, I danced around the massive bedroom in my bra and panties in anticipation of finally getting into a studio. Searching through my suitcase, I chose a yellow t-shirt that showed a glimpse of my stomach over slightly tan baggy cargo pants. I pulled my wavy hair in a ponytail on top of my head. I stared into the full-length ornate mirror attached to the wall nearest the window. *What would Jake change about me?*

Probably my hair. Make it straight and longer. Might even change the color. Would he make me sexier or more folksy? Definitely sexier. He was a man's man. He had way too much alpha in his blood to not want to make me more feminine in his eyes. Thankfully, I was comfortable in my skin and not attached to any particular style. Now, granted, I couldn't and didn't want to be SZA or Megan Thee Stallion sexy, but I could show some skin. I looked in the mirror again at the diamond that sparkled in the center of my belly, and then my round ass. I could pull off most outfits.

I marched out of my room, searching for Jess. She was in the kitchen, tidying up, and a delicious-looking, frothy smoothie with a straw rested on the counter. She looked up from the sink when I walked in. "How did you sleep?"

"Mixed because of the strangeness of a new bed, which I know will fade. I need the thread count. Sleeping between those sheets was simply divine, and I'll need to buy some for my own bed at home. Well…if I can afford it." I grinned.

Jess pushed the smoothie toward me. "If you're here with us, you're about to be able to afford whatever you want and more. This is your breakfast from here on out. It's filling and gives you energy. Jake didn't tell me if you had any allergies."

"I don't have any." I received the smoothie. It didn't help that one of the television monitors in the corner was set to a food channel. Images of Trisha Yearwood soon flashed on the screen as her cooking show was coming up next. "So, I never get to have any of your delicious food again?"

Jess laughed. "I'll make sure you get a couple of my meals a week. I also drop off food while you're in the studio. I rarely cook healthy food for hungry people. The band and background singers will be here tomorrow. Today, it's just you and Jake."

I inhaled deeply and exhaled slowly. "Just me and Jake makes me more nervous than performing in front of others. Before, he's been cool and laidback and supportive. Now, he's preparing me for the stage. I'm not so sure how he'll be. Is he intense?"

She nodded and dried off the sink with a yellow dishtowel. "You *want* him to be intense. That means he believes in you." She said, stepping back. "Did you know a Black woman helped write that song?"

Jess pointed to the screen and turned the volume up just enough for me to hear the show's theme music.

"That one? No, I didn't know."

"Alice Randall. Look her up when you get a chance. She's one of the first Black women to write a number one country hit. Donna Summer was the first."

"*The* Donna Summer?"

"The one and only. What you showed us last night proves that with Jake's special touch you're going to be someone worth knowing about, too. Jake is good at spotting talent and normally leaves the cultivating to his father. But he wants to work directly with you, and after last night, I understand why. Together, the two of you are pure magic. A lot of talent has passed through these doors, and your light shines more than any of them," she paused. "Let me stop before I say too much. Jake hates it when I compare his acts. He believes in anyone he signs. Drink up, and if you need anything from me, let me know."

"I do. Is there, like, a Victoria's Secret or a lingerie shop around here?" I quickly held my hand up, and my diamond sparkled. "I'm not trying to seduce Jake. I'm engaged. Just trying to figure out my look, and I had an idea."

She laughed. "I noticed that pretty ring. You might have to remind Jake a time or two that you have a man. Better yet, bring him here so Jake is clear."

I shrugged as I took my first sip. "Jake and I talked about it already. Boundaries are in place."

"Like I said, bring your man here to reinforce those boundaries." She opened a drawer and retrieved some keys. "There's a nice outside mall, Crossing Landing, about twenty minutes from here. Take the silver BMW in the garage."

I gulped. "The silver BMW? I can get an Uber."

"Nonsense. Jake already arranged for you to have the car while you're here."

"Do you have something that's less expensive for me to drive?"

Jess hugged me quickly before placing the keys in my hand and closing my fingers around them firmly. "Yep, a woman with my sensibilities. It's fine. We trust you'll take care of the car. Even if an accident happens, we're insured and more concerned with your safety than replacing the car. Now, go and be back by two. Jake hates tardiness. I'll move your things to your cottage while you're in the studio. He or I will show you around your living quarters. Until Evelyn returns, it'll be just you, Craig, and me. Craig works the ranch and lives in the main house. If you get scared or nervous, I'm a yell away."

"Thank you for making my trip here already special."

She grinned. "You're welcome. Now get out of here. Time's ticking."

After gulping down my smoothie, I hurried back to my room. I grabbed my leather Coach cross bag, which contained one of my grandfather's letters. I'd been carrying this letter around to feel closer to him. I needed his spirit to guide me while in Nashville.

In the silent hum of twilight's pause,
Your gaze meets mine, a silent applause.
The world retreats, leaving just you and me,
In this crowded room, where no one can see.

I strummed on my grandfather's guitar as Jake pulled up fourteen minutes after two. He stepped out of the car, wearing a tailored suit and shades. He exuded wealth and prosperity as he approached where I sat on the porch strumming. I couldn't see his eyes, though I sensed his gaze had traveled my body, and the slight curve of his lips indicated his approval.

"You're late," I said, pointing out the obvious.

"I am. Won't happen again." His forehead wrinkled slightly and then relaxed. "I liked what you were just playing. One of yours?"

"Yes. Started working on it last week."

"Lyrics?"

"Spoken word."

"Then we have lyrics." Jake held the front door open for me to pass beside him. He smelled good. No, the cologne blended with his natural scent well. "You look good," he complimented me, though he kept his tone neutral.

I twirled as soon as I walked deeper into the foyer. "Working on my appearance. I know I still need a stylist, but I wanted to get into a different mindset for the studio."

"Thinking you want to be sexier?" he asked.

"Thinking that's what you want."

He shook his head. "I want whatever makes you feel confident and comfortable. You on the porch last night was sexy."

"You don't like it?" I gestured to my lace bra under a denim jacket and fitted jeans.

Jake smiled. "I just complimented you. If this is another part of you, then I'm down. And we can get the stylist to give you a variation of this for your showcase. I got you a gig on Broadway in the city. They'll give us thirty minutes. Figure you can cover three or four songs and present two original songs."

"We have enough time to record two new songs?"

"You already have lyrics and know how to compose your own music. I say we're good, at least for a raw copy." Jake moved ahead of me while he led me to the studio in the mansion's basement. "Today, I want to define your genre more. Your voice is too strong for popular R&B. I want the industry to be clear on categorizing you." He looked at me as we walked alongside each other. "How do you feel about country music?"

"Me and country music?" Several country songs popped into my mind. Songs that made me feel. "Won't I seem disingenuous to choose a genre not typically deemed for us?"

"First, all music is for us. We both grew up in the South, and country music is in our blood as much as jazz, blues, rap, and soul. We've been conditioned to believe that we're not country music. We have some amazing Black country music singers right here in Nashville, and I want to expose you to them, too."

I mulled over what he said. "Why country?"

"Why not? You can be molded for any genre." He used his hands as he explained. "Besides, you have the gravitas and honesty for the grittiness of country. You create spoken word like a natural storyteller. Country is about our everyday struggles. The working class. The blue-collar worker who needs this music to take their troubles away. Your voice reaches deep down and grabs your soul. The origins of country music are rooted in African American folk music and a little blues anyway, which Stoney knew." We started down a flight of stairs. "What instrument do you associate with country besides guitar?"

"The banjo," I immediately answered.

"The banjo was originally an instrument of our enslaved ancestors. With your voice and musicality, we can bust this genre open. It's time people respect that country music is a part of our history…a part of us, too." He gave me a side glance. "Your grandfather dabbled in country at one point in his career."

"Really? Thought he was strictly blues."

"I found a rough copy of his country song today, and I'll play it for you later."

We hit the bottom of the stairs, and two large studios faced me—one a royal purple, and the other a glittery solid gold. The purple one contained a black and gold drum set. The gold held a large keyboard. Large monitors and computer workstations were in both control rooms. Mics and equipment I'd never seen before or could identify loomed in the backgrounds.

My stomach fluttered, and I clasped my hands together in front of me. "Confession. Do you remember that I've never been in a studio?"

"Not even as a field trip with your students?" he asked incredulously. "I thought you meant you'd never been in a studio to record. Still hard to believe no one suggested you perform professionally. You must never sing in public."

"Not even in a church choir or since high school. My father resented my grandfather and anything related to music. Blamed music for breaking up the family. My father barely played any records in our home and never praised me for my natural inclination or gifts," I said nonchalantly, as if my father's disinterest in my music didn't affect me.

Jake regarded me for a long second before he spoke quietly. "I know what it's like to not truly be seen, too."

I brushed off his sentiments. "It's cool. I know it wasn't personal."

Jake touched my arm. "You don't have to deflect or suppress your feelings here. Channel whatever emotion that's bottled up inside when you create or perform."

"In some ways, I am my father's child. Holding in my emotions is almost second nature. Might be difficult to truly release how I feel." Ruefully, I shook my head. "I told you I'm in kindergarten, and you have to get me to college in three weeks. Or at least a senior in high school."

"I can get you a master's in three weeks," he bragged as he swept his arms wide. "All right, which studio do you want to use? The purple room or the gold room?"

"Purple. My favorite color."

"Duly noted." Jake touched the doorknob of my choice. "This is your studio to use at will as long as you are here with us. The other studio may be used by other artists."

"Wait. So I don't have to share?"

He flashed his dimples. "Well, only Evelyn if she's in the mood to make music. You're going to be my star. I plan to start my own agency, separate from my father. I make you a star, and then people will be clamoring to work with me."

"Thanks for adding more pressure." I slid past him into the comfy room with plush purple crushed velvet chairs to lounge on. I surveyed the studio where dreams were formed and inhaled slowly and deeply. This was the same studio that had generated hits by Evelyn Hart and other top-selling artists. "This is freaking surreal. Two months ago, I couldn't have ever imagined this."

Jake tossed his jacket in one of the chairs, then unbuttoned and rolled up his sleeves before plopping down on the sofa near me. "Tell me about the letters."

"Now?" I touched my pocket protectively.

His gaze followed my hand. "You have one of them with you?"

"Ever since I found the journal in his guitar case, I've carried his letter around." I pulled it out of my pocket and carefully unfolded it. "There were probably more than two. Maybe he destroyed them, or maybe they're somewhere else in the house."

"Did you read them?" He pushed his sleeves higher.

"Just this one. The other was from the woman, and it somehow felt like a betrayal to my grandmother to read hers, so I stopped. It already feels invasive to read his personal thoughts and feelings, like I'm reading his diary. I also have a photo of them embracing, but it's so worn and tattered that I can't make out her face. I didn't want to explore any more until I came here." I closed my jacket and chose the leather swivel seat. "Why do you want to talk about the letters now?"

"Your grandfather is the reason you're here. The studio will be full tomorrow. I have two background singers. One of them plays the steel guitar and the bass. Then we have a percussionist. My journalist friend might pop by, too. Right now, it's only you and me. I want to start producing your sound using whatever you feel when you hear this letter." He reached his hand out. "Can I read it to you?"

When I passed him the letter, he grabbed my wrist and tugged me beside him. The sudden action surprised me, and a thrill coursed down my spine. He immediately slid over, giving me space, and held the letter up to read. Slightly dazed at his unexpected nearness, I glanced at him, and he seemed unaffected as he squinted to read—until I noticed the slight tremor in the paper from his hand. I settled back on the sofa, satisfied that I could make a man like Jake nervous.

FOURTEEN

Jake

I had impulsively grabbed her to me because I didn't want her in that chair. Not yet. She was the recording star. The person in the booth wasn't the person in the control room. I'm a stickler for a process, and I didn't want her in the producer's chair.

My bullish behavior excited her. I noticed it in the widening of her eyes and how her breathing sped up. I wanted to forget what I'd inadvertently done, and the thought of kissing her clouded my mind. I picked up the letter to escape my rebellious thoughts of using this tempting moment to my advantage. I hated that she noticed the tremble in my hand. Hated that she appeared smug because she recognized my nervousness. A nervousness I only held because I had to refrain from doing what felt natural and right. To hold her. To touch her. To kiss her.

"Are you going to read it?" she asked with amusement lacing her words.

Clearing my throat, I then improvised, "Yeah. Yeah. Just thinking that Stoney had excellent penmanship." Luckily, he truly had some of the neatest and most legible handwriting I'd ever seen.

"Right? It's just so perfect. His handwriting could've been used on greeting cards," she said, beaming. She was already proud of her grandfather… Ready to believe in him whether her father would ever do so again or not.

Her chatter gave me time to rein in my errant thoughts and focus on our purpose in meeting each other. "Sit back, close your eyes, and I want you to express your emotion. Let go, Amara, however you want to let go, as I read Stoney's letter."

She crossed her ankles, slumped on the sofa, and closed her eyes. Her chest rose and fell slowly. Satisfied that she'd followed my instructions, I began.

April 11, 1974

Dearest Heart,

I miss you. It's only been two days, and I can't stop thinking about you. I wish we were still in Nashville together, making beautiful music. I've never felt so attuned with another soul. It's amazing that we're so connected that you can finish my sentences. You understand my thoughts. My heart. My music. You understand me. You. Get. Me.

Yet I recognize that being with you is a pipe dream, a fantasy that will never come to light. A love that, as perfect as it is, isn't meant to be. My mind is spinning with so many questions that may go unanswered. How is our love possible? Why would God allow me to fall for you when I already am tethered to another? Why would he tease an unattainable paradise with you? Why would he bring me so close to my destiny to take it away? Why would he have us meet seven years too late? Why would my dreams of music be entwined with meeting you?

I still question my sanity that I never visited Nashville until you invited me. How can I sincerely call myself a bluesman and a true musician if I've never traveled the three hours between Memphis and Music City to hear the glorious diversity of all sounds? You opened my eyes to so much in such a short time.

Being in Nashville, where music flourishes and is firmly planted with roots clinging to the earth, fueled me in ways I'd never experienced before. I became alive, vibrant, and intuitively creative. Lyrics and notes poured out of me like a newly burst oil well down in Texas. Creating songs that derived deep in my soul will soar me to the next level. The level where the world sees me and not just Beale Street. The level I've worked and sacrificed my whole life to reach.

And I owe it all to you. Maybe I shouldn't have kissed you in gratitude for the gift you'd given me. Aiming for your cheek, I touched your lips and tried to apologize. Then I became powerless to stop when you welcomed me into you.

You asked if I love you, and I didn't answer you, disappointing you. Hurting you. Too afraid to express words that I couldn't take back. Too afraid to admit my true emotions, because if I did, my fall into you would be fathomless and impossible. I didn't tell you my heart, knowing the cost of loving you is too high. A price I can't afford when you know I also love my wife dearly and promised her forever without ever knowing someone like you existed in this celestial world for me. A commitment I can't ignore despite how I yearn to be with you.

You probably don't want to hear or know this and wish I only loved you. But you asked for my honesty, and to answer your question, can my beating heart sustain space for two great loves at the same time? Can I truly love you when I still profess to loving my wife? Once upon a time, I would've thought that impossible. I loved her that much. Since I met you, my answer is yes.

Until we meet again,
Stoney

I slowly re-folded the yellowed paper, understanding why Amara had hesitated to read any other letter. We were privy to his most private thoughts. Thoughts he'd only wanted one person to read. Intimate thoughts that he'd never wanted his wife to ever know, let alone the granddaughter he'd never really had a chance to know. The tangible excitement and happiness expressed in this letter, emotions I'd believed he was incapable of experiencing in the years I visited him, only saddened me. He'd initially appeared dour and moody when I stopped in and chatted with him before I gave him an unopened envelope of money. Over time, I realized that my visits had been a ray of sunshine in the middle of his rainstorm, and that it had inevitably returned when I left him. He'd clearly loved the woman he wrote as much as he loved the woman he'd married. An understandable dilemma, especially because the other woman understood his passion. Understood his very reason for being more than his wife. *How do you leave your heart for your soul?*

Amara hadn't opened her eyes, though tears streamed down her cheeks. I squeezed her thigh and rose to pick up her grandfather's guitar and place it on her lap. I turned the leather chair around to face the booth. My back to her, I sat quietly, waiting for her to begin.

A few minutes later, she began to play without using her pick, apparently preferring rawness to a richer sound. She hummed with every brush of her fingers on the strings, alternating between minor and major chords, evoking sadness and relishing happiness. She made me feel every heartfelt word in his letter. Amara's translation of her grandfather's wistfulness and hope thrummed through each note. Through her music, Stoney became that young man again. The young man who believed he was on the cusp of greatness. The young man who realized the complexities of love when he'd always thought it to be simple.

I listened to her and watched her create for hours. I never uttered another word, allowing her the space to just be. My instinct had been right to seek her out after she performed at Stoney's funeral. Amara "Mari" Johnson would be a star.

FIFTEEN

Amara

I swear my head had just hit the pillow in my bed in the cozy cottage when I heard knocking on my door. Startled, I shot up. "What?"

The knocking continued, and whoever had the audacity to bang on my door so early in the morning would be cursed for eternity. Especially if that person was Jake Barnes. I threw off the covers and, unable to find my robe, wrapped the comforter from the bed around the panties I'd kept on once I stripped and hopped in between the sheets, too tired to do anything else after we finished in the studio late into the night. I swung open the door to an amused Jake in joggers and a tank displaying his sinewy biceps and triceps.

"I hate morning people," I grumbled. "Why do you look wide awake?"

"It's after seven. Time to run." He jogged in place.

"Are you fucking kidding me?"

"Potty mouth so early in the morning." He grinned wider. "You must be getting pissed."

"I just went to sleep."

"You went to sleep five hours ago. That's enough time to get going. We have a lot to do in a short time. Your timeline, not mine… I mean Phillip Graham's timeline." His lips twitched. "Last night was just the start. We have to build your stamina, since you play instruments and sing. You exert

94

a lot of energy when you do both, and we can't have you winded after two songs." His eyes roamed over my comforter-covered body quickly, though I caught a flicker of interest. "Throw on workout gear, and let's get it."

I groaned. "Don't really own gear because I rarely work out."

"You have muscle definition in your arms and abs. You do something…" He answered himself. "You play instruments and sing. Do you have shorts, a T-shirt, and tennis shoes?"

"Yeah," I reluctantly answered.

"Then meet me outside in five minutes." I closed the door before he finished his last word. He shouted, "Five minutes, Mari, or I'm throwing you in the shower, comforter and all."

"My name is Amara," I yelled, and kicked out at the air like a spoiled child.

Six minutes later, I joined him in shorts that barely covered my ass and a long t-shirt I knotted so it wouldn't fall past the length of my shorts. "I'm here."

"Stretch." He bent over and easily touched the ground, extending his arms. Jake obviously worked out. "Are you just going to stare, or are you going to warm up?"

"As my future manager, all this bossiness got to stop. I hate being told what to do." I slowly rolled my hips and lifted one foot to touch my butt. No way could I bend over in front of him, flashing my cheeks.

"Aren't most teachers bossy?" He quirked a brow. "Just dishing out what you give all the time. And as your manager, anything I tell you to do is for your own good."

I rolled my eyes as he started at a light jog ahead of me. I had to run faster to keep up with his long legs. "Slow down. I told you I don't exercise regularly."

"Sorry. Used to jogging on my own." He slowed his pace to match mine.

"I can only run so much before I pass out. FYI." I kept up with him. My lungs and legs had cooperated thus far.

"You won't pass out. While you're here, you jog every morning. Even if I don't spend the night here, you still exercise."

"I guess you didn't go home last night. I thought you left after you got that phone call. Wouldn't want you to get in trouble," I said, curious about the person on the other end of the call, whom he immediately muted once he saw the name.

"You are my priority." He smirked. "And stop trying to get in my business. Trying to figure out who would call me late at night."

"It's only fair." I started to pant a little. "You know…I'm…engaged. Are you seeing someone? Just a conversation between friends."

"We're not friends."

"Then stop calling me Mari," I quipped, unfazed by his words.

"Fine, Amara." He laughed when I popped him in the side. "Save that energy for singing."

"Okay, Mr. Barnes, is this how you'll be? Two can play that game marvelously if our communication and flow will always be one-sided." My breaths were getting shorter and shorter.

He relented. "I'm always seeing someone. Not into relationships."

I snorted. "Of course you're not. I bet women throw themselves at you. Why have just one?"

Jake shot a glance my way and continued to jog. "I'm not the player you think. Just too busy for the time a woman needs to feel secure in me and in us."

"I've always heard you make…time for what you want. Maybe you haven't found…the woman you want." I panted more. Felt a slight twitching in my lungs.

"Or maybe I have, and I can't have her." Jake's dark amber eyes danced when our gazes connected. His lips curled into a slight smile, and my inner core clenched tightly. "Do you have any more questions about my love life?"

"No, I think I'm good." I looked away first. "You're right, I don't need to know about your personal life."

"No, you don't." He turned around to jog backward. "Do you know 'Jolene'?"

"Dolly Parton or Miley Cyrus?"

"Guess you do know the song." Jake's dimples flashed. "Sing Mari Johnson's version."

"I love that. My version." I raised my hands in victory as I continued to jog. I'd only sung a couple of bars of the famous song of a woman begging the other woman to leave her man alone when my voice cracked. I stopped running. My voice never cracked. Like, ever.

Jake still jogged backward. "Come on. This is what I'm talking about. You must learn how to control your diaphragm and your lungs while performing. That voice cracking can and will happen again if you don't practice singing and exercising. Now sing again."

I nodded and started slowly jogging as I sang the next set of bars. Still shaky, but better.

"Good. We'll jog with singing and then without. Even if you can't run anymore, do a fast walk. Thirty minutes, okay?"

Instead of answering, I sang the chorus again. This time, I forced my breath past the burning sensation in my lungs. I almost sounded like myself. I inhaled and exhaled, controlling my breathing and panting as I sang again.

When we finally stopped near the corral where three magnificent brown horses roamed, I collapsed flat on the ground. Jake followed suit. We both stared up at the bright sky. "Can you give me my grandfather's music? I want to play it while I prepare for the day. Might give me more ideas."

"Yeah. I'll send you a link. You should play it in the studio, where he was meant to be heard. Clear, crisp, beautiful. I have a couple of phone calls, so feel free to go to the studio and listen after you clean up and have breakfast. Everyone is supposed to be here at noon."

"Are you going to be there?"

"Yeah." His voice lowered. "Better to be around others. I think we need some distance between us before things get confusing and muddled."

"Even when I run in the mornings?" I teased, agreeing with him.

"Now, I might have to show up for that." His deep, throaty chuckle traveled through me, and I ignored the tingling of desire. "I'll have to spend the night here at least two or three times a week to make sure you're doing it."

"Aw, shit," I lamented, although the thought that he would be sleeping nearby on some nights comforted me. "I'm in trouble."

"Hmm…mmm… Better use some of that profanity in one of your songs. Might have to pen a song called 'Smutty Mouth.'"

"I love it. It can go after the song I'll name in your honor, 'Seeing Someone Man.'" I sang the title in the tune of Nina Simone's "Sinnerman."

He laughed again and pointed at me. "That's going straight to number one."

"I know, right? Got to add the lyrics to my notebook." In the studio the day before, I'd spat out poetry after listening to my grandfather's bittersweet love for a woman who wasn't my grandmother. Some old ones. Wrote two new ones. Tinkered with the drums, keyboard, and electric guitar, letting my waves of emotions guide my choices. Jake had been so quiet and contemplative that there were times I'd forgotten he was in the room. My flow had erased his presence. Jake no longer existed in plain sight. "So, you got all you needed from me to produce a song before we meet with the others?"

He turned his head to look at me. "I have enough for an album."

I blinked rapidly and sat up. "Enough for an album in one day? I thought what I did yesterday released years of frustration, anger, joy, and hurt. I was all over the place. Writing poems, singing riffs, and trying different chords. Nothing and everything made sense. But you're telling me I could have an album of songs from what I did?"

Jake remained on the ground, looking up at me. "We need to do more work on each of them. But yeah, we have enough. You have at least twelve songs, most potential hits, rattling around in that fascinating mind of yours, and we're just getting started."

His words drifted over me. What I'd done last night, I'd done most of my life. Maybe not quite like yesterday. Yet I'd composed poems and music ever since I was a child. Never thought it would amount to anything anyone else would listen to or enjoy. They were my musings. Amara's musings.

"How can I have so much inside of me, and no one cared to see that? Not my parents, teachers, or even me. Oh, God. I can't blame Phillip for not accepting my gifts when *I* didn't even accept them. One night in the studio? One night? I wasted so many years hiding from myself…from my talent. Never thinking I was good enough for more." I covered my mouth with my hands, and tears pricked my eyes. I started rocking, almost angrily. "Damn, I'm so tired of crying about every little thing. Lately, I can't breathe without the threat of a tsunami of tears. I swear I'm not this mushy person."

"So, what if you are and were never allowed the space to be that?" he reasoned calmly. "Nothing wrong with tears. Shit, I told you that you make me cry every time you open your mouth. My eyes should be swollen shut after last night. You move me, Mari. Just like you're going to move the world."

Shaking my head, I mused, "I don't think I'll ever meet another man like you."

He placed his hands behind his head, stared at the sky again, and smiled. "Nope, you won't. And don't you ever forget me when you rise to the top and I'm just the guy who helped you get started."

"Impossible to ever forget you. You're stuck with me now." I held out my fist to his, and he bumped mine. "I want to start looking at the contract."

"I'll send one over to you later this week to review and negotiate your terms, but I don't want you to sign until after the showcase." Jake continued to look at the sky. "I want you to be sure before you commit. Want you to accept that your peeps may never change their minds if Phillip or your parents don't approve after the showcase. If you can accept and not regret choosing this life, then sign. For what it's worth, I hope that Phillip Graham sees you on that stage and asks you to marry him all over again. Then you can have everything you want."

"Thank you." I studied the profile of his face. The long lashes, the full lips, and the slight hook in his nose only made his face more interesting. "It's worth the world for you to say that to me."

He nodded slightly, and we lay on the lush grass a little longer as I savored this last moment of togetherness. "I want to hear 'A Born Legacy' again."

Like he did, I propped my hands under my head. I started reciting a poem that I had begun in my grandfather's bedroom about finishing your family's incomplete dream while charting your own course.

> *"Rain whispers on a Memphis day,*
> *Through silent echoes of a past astray,*
> *Here I walk, tracing roots entwined,*

In a house of memories that bind.
My fingers glide over whispers old,
In every corner, tales untold,
My voice, a bridge from past to now,
Through history's chords, I take my vow.
Not a legacy left, but one I found,
In the blues, where my roots are sound,
I sing the bloodlines of my heart,
Where my journey ends, and did start.
A quest not just to uncover my tree,
But a search for self, in melody,
Each note I play calls me back,
To the roots that fill what once was black.
This journey, my song of return,
To the fire within, that will always burn,
My legacy, reborn through what I play,
In old echoes, I find my way."

"And that is your first song." Jake smiled with pride and contentment.

SIXTEEN

Jake

"Take it from the top." I adjusted the synthesizers. We'd been rehearsing for five hours straight. I'd called my favorite drummer, Domino, to sit in the booth and play for Amara. A slim, tall man with wild locs who usually ate Jess out of house and home, which she loved. He now counted out for Amara, who stood in the booth with headphones on, a mic before her, and a mic aimed at her guitar.

Sophie, our background singer, served triple roles. She could play the steel guitar and bass. Sophie was also our social media manager and had successfully grown Barnes Management from half a million to almost nine million on Instagram. She was two years younger than Amara and a ball of energy and optimism, and the two had immediately clicked like old friends reunited. They swapped fav songs and made plans to hang out during breaks. I smiled, watching them sing together. Even their voices blended well.

Sophie moved in and around the studio, snapping pictures. Although she'd taken plenty of photos of Amara while she created and rehearsed, she wouldn't post any until the showcase. We wanted to keep what we'd been working on under wraps.

Then there was Tavion, the thirty-something with a voice that could send chills down anyone's spine. He and Sophie were the types of singers who preferred the background. Neither was comfortable with being the star.

I'd placed Amara in the same role when I initially heard her sing at the funeral when I'd believed she was a wallflower. Had she not eased beside me at the Peabody with just the right amount of intrigue, the world would've missed out on Amara Johnson.

"Ready?" I asked.

Amara started picking at her guitar and added a capo to her strings to change the key. She locked eyes with me. I nodded, and she continued playing. Domino easily chimed in, and we began recording her first song.

While everyone lounged in the studio, I sent the file to my laptop and went into the gold studio to hear Amara's song. I wanted to produce most, if not all, of her album, which also would be a first. I dabbled in writing and producing. I'd helped my other talent or producers when they grew stuck, but never on a whole song. I'd only planned to do a demo with her and determine the best producer later. After observing her in action last night and how she created her words and sounds fascinated me, and I wanted to produce her songs. I could watch her all night long. She mumbled, wrote notes, and then tried it on the guitar before turning to the keyboard. Her eyes were closed most of the time, and she seemed to be in another dimension as lyrics sprang from her lips. Sometimes clear. Sometimes incoherent, though I could fill in the blanks. I doubted anyone could condense her beautiful chaos into a complete song like I could.

Placing the headphones on my ears, I lay back on the sofa, allowing the music to flow over me. If there was an unexpected rift, I had to smooth it out. My heart swelled as I listened to the song we'd devised from her poetry and her quest to discover her grandfather's legacy. I had an ear for music, which my father had used to his advantage, having me pick out hits for most of our artists. This song was worthy of a Grammy. A Grammy that I would win as a co-writer and producer on the song. A dream that I'd never had or ever thought possible. Being a manager brought money and perks but rarely fame or recognition. Working with Amara had opened me up to the possibilities of a new life. To think beyond my immediate vision.

I listened to the song twice before changing tracks to Stoney's country song. Genetics ruled how they sang a song's cadence in the nurture and nature battle. Fucking unbelievable, actually, that similarities existed in two very different songs with decades spanning between them. One of the lines toward the end of his "A Man's Luck" seemed familiar. Maybe it was the lyrics or the rhythm, but I'd heard it before.

The door opened before I could replay it, and Amara smiled at me. "Jess brought us dinner."

Pushing off my headphones, I couldn't hold my grin as I sternly said, "She better have bought you a salad."

"She brought a huge salad for us all, along with brisket, baked beans, and jalapeno cornbread. And if you think I'm not going to eat that, then you're not a real Southerner." She stamped her foot at my silence. "Come on, Jake. I had nothing for lunch and sucked down that smoothie after jogging. I'm hungry."

I crossed my ankles, settled back against the sofa, and closed my eyes.

"I'm only supposed to eat the salad?"

Placing the headphones back on my ears, I asked, "What do *you* think you should eat, since you want to wear a bra on stage?"

"I'm not succumbing to the pressures of looking like every-damn-body," she replied crossly.

"Then why are you mad at me?"

"Because you're not telling me it's okay to eat the brisket."

"If I tell you it's okay, will you let me get back to my music?"

"If you say yes."

"If I say no?"

She moved to stand over me. "Then I'm going to harass you until you relent."

"Why?"

"Because I want you as a man to accept women have bumps, bruises, and curves, and our bodies are not meant to be perfect. And I can choose to wear a bra on stage whether I have a flat or round stomach." Amara had a glint in her eyes that suggested I needed to tread lightly.

"And here I thought you could be the submissive woman I've always wanted…needing my permission." I covered my head instinctively, expecting a punch or a hit. When it didn't come, I cautiously lowered my arms, and she pinched my nose hard and hurried back to the door.

"When will you men learn that a woman is happy to submit to a man who deserves her respect and love?" Amara flounced out of the studio and tossed over her shoulder, "I'm eating that brisket along with my salad."

I shook my head, wondering if she captivated me because of her talent or personality, or maybe it was both. Or maybe because I knew I couldn't have her. Forbidden fruit always tempted more.

I readjusted the headphones and closed my eyes, ready to disappear into Stoney Johnson and not his granddaughter.

"Seems I wasn't invited to the party." A deep, rich voice with the strongest Tennessee twang interrupted my musings.

Startled, I sat up. "Ms. Evelyn? Dad said you wouldn't be back until the weekend."

"I heard that something magical was happening at Hartland." The petite and shapely woman, with her trademark auburn-red hair, smiled warmly. She belied Mother Nature, appearing at least twenty years younger than her age. She continued to be as lithe as a much younger woman because of years of the best care, yoga, and Pilates that her wealth afforded.

"Auntie told you?" I asked, though I knew the answer. Jess was Evelyn's best friend and house manager. She probably couldn't wait to call Evelyn and tell her about the ingenue that graced Hartland. I rose to my feet when she entered fully into the studio with outstretched arms. I hugged her to me. "Good to see you."

She pulled back. "Darling, you need to stop by more. We're family, Jake."

"My mother says the same thing," I automatically responded, and the light dimmed in Evelyn's eyes. Guilt flamed my face, though I didn't apologize. Evelyn demanded and fully expected people to comply with her wants and needs. Some of it was her personality that leaned toward the dramatic, and the rest was how the world treated her. Evelyn Hart could have whoever and whatever she wanted or desired. She wanted my family to live at Hartland. Ultimately, my mother had decided otherwise.

"Then maybe you should visit her more, too. You're still her baby, no matter how old you are." Evelyn weakly smiled and took a step back.

"I will." I nodded toward the other studio. "I'm here for most of the summer working with my new singer, Amara."

She looked toward the other studio where Amara and the others were eating, oblivious to Evelyn's sudden appearance. "William says you haven't signed her yet, and she's staying here?"

I clenched and unclenched my jaw. "Ms. Evelyn, was I wrong to assume that this was always my home and I had free use of the studios? As I told my father, I can pack up and bring Amara to the city."

Her green eyes flared. "Jake, you still sound like that spoiled boy who took his parents' cars without their permission and snuck girls here. That threat might have worked with your father, but not me. Hartland is open to all musicians and singers. This is always your home, even if your mother disagrees. But if someone lives on my property, I need to know beforehand and see if she's worth her salt."

Properly chastised, I humbled myself. "I brought her here because this is where the magic happens. I wanted her to be inspired. This house and these grounds have had years of melodies and hits from you and other amazing, talented artists. I want you to hear her and get your honest opinion, because you know more than anyone the challenges of breaking into the good ol' boys' club."

She placed one manicured hand across her chest. "You want her to sing country? Jake, you know she won't get much traction. The more things change, the more they stay the same."

"Yet that didn't stop you from demanding a place at the table."

Evelyn countered, "Do I need to point out the obvious? I have fought for a seat at the table because I'm still relatable to the powers that control this industry. At least start her with rhythm and blues, get a pop crossover hit or two, and gradually add a country song later."

"Why go through all that when she could be the one who breaks down that last arbitrary wall that country music is only for white folks? DeFord Bailey, Charley Pride, and Darius Rucker can't be the only Black people country music accepts. What about the women? You can be instrumental in joining the old and new school of country… One legend who broke down barriers, leading the way for a future legend."

She tilted her head. "You just thought of that at this very moment, or you would've presented her to me openly and not on the sly."

I pushed the headphones around my neck. "Maybe I just thought about your role in Amara's career. I wanted to keep it separate at first, but the more I think about it, the more we both know it makes sense. The truth is that all of this happened suddenly. We're working on her first showcase in three weeks. I met her about five weeks ago, and I wanted to coach her a little bit, since she'd never sung professionally before I brought her to you. She's an unassuming music teacher from Atlanta, and I didn't want you to intimidate her."

"Now, you know I wouldn't intentionally do that." She crossed her arms and arched a perfectly tattooed brow. "I'm not that type of diva."

I uncrossed her arms and spun her around playfully. "Just who you are is intimidating. *The* Evelyn Hart, who's broken all kinds of records, your judge and jury on your potential career? I don't know what else could be more intimidating, especially for someone like Amara."

"Such a charmer. I'm the least of her concerns if this is the world she wants." She patted my cheek. "If this Amara plans to be a country singer and wants any endorsement from me, she must pass the test of impressing me first."

"Can't argue with that." I held the door open for Evelyn to pass through. The room was eerily silent when I opened the door to the other studio. Only Amara stood with clasped hands, stars in her eyes, and a slightly bowed head. Domino, Tavion, and Sophie were quietly around the coffee table of food, apparently waiting to see what would happen now that the queen had returned to her palace.

Amara stepped forward slowly, her wavy hair pulled back in a severe ponytail, emphasizing her natural beauty. "I'm such a fan, and your home is amazing. I can't thank you enough for your hospitality."

Evelyn studied Amara up and down, from her heels and jeggings to her t-shirt tied at her waist, hinting at her belly. She pursed her lips when she glanced at me. "Well, I can see at least one reason you want to work with her solely."

Tavion and Domino snickered while I warned her, "Evelyn, don't start. I don't mix business and my personal life."

"Anymore, you mean?" Evelyn blew a raspberry and waved my protest away. "Too many years I watched my tongue trying to be the lady as defined by men. Now I say whatever I damn well please and dare you to argue." She pulled down her denim jacket firmly. "I call it like I see it, Jake. You're fascinated with that face and body. Don't forget I've known you since you were that mannish teenager. So, is she going to sing?"

"Yes, she is," Amara answered softly yet firmly, and headed to the booth.

Evelyn swiveled her head in surprise. "Sing now. Not in the booth but out here without the help of that room."

"Um…" Amara looked at me. Her eyes widened, and she softly gasped. I tilted my head. She straightened her shoulders, walked into the studio, and grabbed her guitar. Then she returned to where Evelyn had moved to the producer's chair, expression revealing no emotion.

I almost felt sorry for Amara. *Almost.* She had to get past any doubt about her talent. She had to pass this test, or I would cancel the showcase and slow everything down. Or switch to the more familiar R&B lane—a lane that still wouldn't fully embrace all that Amara could be.

Amara started strumming her guitar with her fingers, and I smirked at her boldness when she started singing "Jolene." The world knew that Evelyn and Dolly were frenemies. Evelyn gave nothing away. She didn't flinch or nod while Amara performed. Her soulful voice and the acoustic guitar reverberated through the studio until the last note. Amara bowed her head fully in deference to Evelyn.

Evelyn's green eyes lowered to almost slits before she nodded slowly. "You showed some spunk playing my enemy's song in my own house. Either you had no clue that that's the worst song to perform before me or didn't care about that."

I drawled, "She didn't care."

Her red-stained lips curved into a wide smile. "My type of woman." She rose from her throne like the queen she was and closed the small space between them. "The only thing I suggest is using a pick when playing this song. I like the rawness of using your fingers when you play, but the lyrics are raw enough."

Evelyn held her hand out, and Amara quickly took off her guitar, which Evelyn pulled over her head. Amara passed her a pick. Evelyn strummed "Jolene"'s first few notes with her pick and then used her fingers. "You hear the difference?"

Amara smiled. "Yes."

"You never want instruments to drown out one another. The listening ear should be able to detect the distinctive sounds of the guitar, the fiddle, the keyboard, or whatever instrument you're using." Evelyn touched Amara's chin. "Your mouth is also an instrument. Never let your music overpower that beautiful, clear voice of yours. Remember that if you ever take anything away from being here at Hartland."

"Yes, ma'am."

Evelyn strummed the guitar longer. "This is a good guitar. Well taken care of." She asked Amara, "Mind if I stay awhile and see what y'all cooking, especially since I see Jess made brisket?"

Everyone scrambled, making room for one of the greatest singers to ever do it. Sophie rushed to make her a plate. "Do you want everything?"

"Just the brisket and a little bit of that cornbread. Pile the meat high, since Jess won't let me eat too much brisket anymore. I'll eat in a second." Evelyn tapped my arm. "All right, my Jake, she's not just a pretty face. After she does her showcase, we can talk more about my endorsement." She moved inside the studio and settled on the stool before the mic, picking at the guitar. Serenity graced her face. This was Evelyn's happy place.

Amara's hands were clasped in front of her heart. She probably didn't realize she'd been standing like that since she gave Evelyn her guitar. I squeezed her shoulder. "You passed the first, most crucial test. Think you ready for middle school?"

She finally let out her pent-up breath. "Did I really just play in front of Evelyn Hart?"

The normally reserved Domino said, "No, you just impressed the queen."

Amara positively glowed as she held her fist for me to bump. I wanted to grab her in a bear hug and lift her off her feet. Instead, I jammed one hand in my pocket and bumped her fist before I did what my heart urged me to do. "You better go in there with her and get some more life lessons. She doesn't ever work with new talent."

She looked in the studio where Evelyn had started playing one of her hits, her voice just as strong and vibrant as when she'd started in this business fifty years ago. "Maybe she wants to be alone."

Not a second after Amara had voiced her hesitation, Evelyn looked up from the guitar. She beckoned Amara to come inside the booth.

"You better learn quickly that you take heed when I tell you something," I commented, passing her an electric guitar.

She rolled her eyes to the sky and entered the studio.

Satisfied that Evelyn was halfway on board to becoming a major supporter of Amara, I smiled as I sat back in the producer's chair. "Sophie, I hope you getting shots of this."

"You know I'm on it." Sophie moved to stand beside me. "Started taking them the minute she passed through those doors, boss."

We bumped fists, too, as we all gleefully observed Evelyn Hart in her element, teaching the new school about the facets of playing an instrument and singing.

SEVENTEEN

Amara

"**S**he jammed with us, baby. Made me feel special that she wanted to give me pointers about my voice and used my guitar the entire time. Absolutely insane how much talent and knowledge about music Ms. Evelyn has. I forgot that she could play the hell out of a guitar and keyboards." Tucked in one of the comfy chairs in the sitting area of my cottage, I relayed the events of the day with Phillip.

"You sound excited. I don't think I've ever heard you sound like this," he said with amusement.

"I haven't… Besides the day you asked me to marry you," I quickly added.

Phillip chuckled. "My ego can take that you were more excited by Evelyn Hart than my grand proposal." He'd proposed while we were at dinner right before our second anniversary. His ask had been simple, sweet, and old-fashioned. He'd gained permission from my father for my hand in marriage and bent on one knee in a small, intimate restaurant. I'd been pleased.

"Sorry." I snuggled deeper under the quilt I threw over me while I listened to my recordings through the wireless speakers throughout the cottage. Jake advised me to listen with a critical ear and decide if I wanted to revise anything. He also encouraged me to play my grandfather's music for more inspiration. He said that before he left to meet with Evelyn about her tour. We'd wrapped up earlier than I thought we would, freeing me up to relax and process my day.

"I told you my ego could take it, and I've taken off that Friday as you asked."

"Yeah?" I said. "Then you can meet everyone. I'm hoping Ms. Evelyn pops in on my showcase."

"I really can't wait to meet that potential manager of yours," he commented sarcastically. Or maybe it was all in my mind.

"Jake?"

"Oh, that's his name. You've told me everyone's name but his."

"I guess because he's the boss around here, and everyone else is more like me. All performers." Had I purposely not said Jake's name around Phillip? I racked my brain, trying to figure out whether I had. Maybe subconsciously, I didn't want to draw attention to a man I was attracted to. As much as I wanted to be truthful with Phillip about Jake, I knew that would be yet another reason for him to demand I come home. Besides, I rationalized we planned to be married forever, and to be tempted by others was highly possible. I was pretty certain that Phillip often attracted women with his good looks and ambition.

"You see yourself as a performer now?" Thankfully, Phillip had moved on from Jake.

"What else should I call myself?"

"I don't know. Just have trouble picturing you as this entertainer on stage. You're my Mari, the music teacher the students love who lives down the street from her middle school." His voice held wistfulness.

I tucked the quilt tighter around me. "I get all this is a lot. It's not your fault I never felt comfortable singing and displaying my musicality to you. I'm always writing and practicing music when we're not together. Even at work, I compose songs for my students to play. It's in my DNA and blood, and it's not fair for me to be angry at you for feeling uncomfortable about my decision to be here."

"Thank you, because I was starting to believe you didn't care about my feelings at all. It's like all of this came out of left field. Why are you just telling me now if performing means so much to you?"

"My father never welcomed my talent, and I stuffed the biggest part of who I am into a package more appealing to him. I was so used to being that way with him that I behaved like that with everyone. I don't want to hide who I am from anyone anymore, especially my future husband and father of my children."

"It is a lot, but I don't want you to keep anything that important to you from me moving forward." He paused. "Why does your father hate your grandfather so much? Your father is like this cool, laidback person, and it's hard to imagine that he has hatred for anyone. Was your grandfather abusive or something?"

"I don't believe so. I can only hypothesize about their relationship, because my father always refuses to mention him. Seeing my father's childhood home was definitely depressing. However, I can't say it was always a sad home simply because a graveyard was across the street. Back then, Black folks weren't allowed to buy homes in any neighborhood." I curled into the fetal position under the quilt. "What I do know is that my grandmother took my father and left my grandfather when Dad was eight years old. They moved to Atlanta, where one of her sisters lived, to help raise my father. From the bits and pieces of conversation I heard over the years, my grandfather had been unwilling to give up music to make their marriage work. My grandparents struggled to put food on the table, and she wanted him to get a regular job. He didn't want a job that would take away his freedom to travel on a whim or to write when he was requested by record companies and singers. Now that I found some of his letters, I know he had an affair. Maybe my grandmother found out about it, and that's the real reason she left him."

"Maybe that's why your father is still angry and never wanted anything to do with music. He knew about the affair, too, and assumed it was also someone in the music business."

I replied glumly, "Yeah. That seems plausible for his refusal to forgive my grandfather. It didn't help that, apparently, my grandfather showed up at my grandmother's funeral drunk, and he and my dad almost physically fought."

"You found anything else in the letters?"

"I only read one in depth and wanted to wait until I arrived here to look into it. My manager—*Jake*—has a journalist friend who wants to help me dig for more information. Stoney Johnson went from potential star to nothing, and I want to know why."

"Isn't losing his wife and son, whom he loved, enough to make a man give up? I know losing you would be hard for me, and if we had children, I wouldn't know how to handle it."

I smiled. "I forget sometimes you can be the sweetest man. It is enough. Except my gut tells me it's more and may have something to do with whoever the other woman is."

"Sherlock Holmes, good luck in your search, and I hope that whatever you're looking for will bring you back to me."

As much as I wanted to reassure him that our life would remain the same once I left Nashville, I couldn't. I'd already changed after two days. "I want to pursue this. I know it's scary to you, but this isn't something that will go away."

"I know," he answered rather testily. "Let's get off the phone before we ruin a good conversation."

I needed to say more, yet I knew more wouldn't resolve anything, so I bade him goodnight. I drew the quilt around me tighter and pressed play on my phone. Soon, my grandfather's deep, smoky voice permeated the room, and his voice lulled me into relaxation. As my eyes drooped, a knock on my door awakened me. Thankfully, I still wore my clothes from earlier today.

Jake waited outside with his hands in the pockets of his khakis. "I was hoping I didn't wake you."

"Naw, just listening to Stoney." I stepped outside and shut the door. "Don't want to let mosquitoes in."

"Yeah, those bastards are annoying. Craig keeps the citronella sprayed around the main home, which should help."

"It does." I looked around him and stood on tiptoes to glance over his head. "I keep hearing about this Craig and have yet to see him. Is he like this mystical creature that lurks in the background, handling everything and vanishing when people appear?"

He laughed. "Quite an imagination. No, Craig prefers horses to people, and that's where we can find him. He lives in the main house with Evelyn and Auntie and watches over them. I'll make a point to introduce you so you don't stumble upon him and scream."

"Yeah, think it's best so my imagination can stop running wild."

Jake shook his head. "No, no. Keep that imagination going. You have such beautiful songs in that head of yours. Stoney had a way with lyrics, too."

"Right?" I smiled. "I'm keeping that country song on repeat."

"I can hear. Going to listen more on my drive home." He gestured behind him to where his car was parked on the circular driveway in front of the main house.

"How far away do you live?"

"About forty if there's no traffic."

"Why don't you just sleep out here?" At his pause, I hurriedly added, "None of my business, right?"

"It's not like that. Just prefer to be in my own bed. I was considering asking if Sophie and Tavion wanted to stay out here, since we have five cottages on the property. Keep you company."

I hugged myself to keep the night chill away. "I would like that. I love the people you're surrounding me with already. I enjoyed today, and I'm starting to feel like a real performer."

He shuffled from foot to foot. "Was proud of you today. Not trying to sound condescending or thinking that you need me to say that to you. I just wanted to hug you when you had the nerve to sing 'Jolene' to her. Not often does anyone catch the queen off guard, and you did. That's the part of you I like the most. You have the surprise attack personality. You're all meek and humble, then strike like a cobra if you're remotely put on defense."

His description of me was spot-on and, coincidentally, how I would describe my father. "I don't try to be that way. Being ignored or feeling like I'm being judged is a trigger. And I could see how Evelyn can be triggering to someone like me."

"She means well."

"I know. Still, her large personality can't help but consume a room, and I refuse to be swallowed."

Jake smiled hard, his dimples on deep display. "Keep that energy when you perform in front of a crowd. We'll start working on the actual show tomorrow. Today was about learning the band. I thought about hiring a keyboardist, but I want to keep it simple now. A drummer, you, and the background singers, since Sophie can play the guitar and bass."

"Are you waiting to bring in a producer once I sign with you?" I noticed that he had been arranging the songs.

"Why? You don't like your song?" he replied with a nonchalance that he didn't quite sell.

"I love it. I only asked about a producer because I'm sure you didn't plan to spend this much time on me. You have other artists who need you, too."

"I know more than you about my obligations," he drawled. "Maybe you're inspiring me as well."

I folded my arms. "Really? In what way?"

He rested his hand on the doorjamb, partially caging me in. The neck of his polo shirt was slightly open, revealing a hint of a tattoo on his chest. "I never thought I would be a producer. I've finished one of your songs and am eager to get to the next one. I want to produce your first album. Probably not all the songs. We might need to change it up a little."

I squealed and clapped my hands. "I love what you already did. Makes sense to me for you to continue. We can be like Janet, Terry Lewis, and Jimmy Jam, or Aaliyah with Timbaland."

He leaned closer. "Or Mari and Jake Barnes. You're an original. Never forget that."

"Don't think you'll let me." I straightened the collar of his polo shirt, needing to touch him in some way. "That was bothering me."

Jake's brown eyes danced. "And you let me go all day looking crazy?"

We grew silent. It was the quiet that messed with me. I couldn't ignore the longing I saw in his eyes or how my body hummed at his nearness. "Umm… I need to get back to listening to music so I can get an early start, and you need to get on the road."

Jake lifted his hand off the door. "Need you to do what we did this morning. I won't be here to wake you up. I'm trusting you."

His cell buzzed in his pocket, and he silenced it through the material. Only a woman would call him this late. I ignored the twinge of jealousy that knocked on my heart, especially after Evelyn's doubtful words that Jake's interest in me was purely business. Seeing an embarrassed Jake try to explain himself to her was flattering.

"Studio by nine. Nathan dropping by tomorrow. After the studio, we can all do some sleuthing. I'll be Easy Rawlins, and Nathan will be Mouse."

"You like Walter Mosley, too." Amused, I leaned against the door as he backed away. "If you're Easy and Nathan is crazy-ass Mouse…who will I be?"

"The Devil in a Blue Dress, duh." He chuckled before he disappeared into the darkness.

"I guess so, since I did approach you to help me." I snorted before closing the door, hoping my mystery ended better than that story did.

EIGHTEEN

Jake

With erotic thoughts of the beautiful woman I'd just left, I smiled as I strolled to my car. I almost didn't notice Evelyn, who rocked on her porch as I walked past her. "I figured you went to check on her. Surprised you didn't stay the night."

I turned toward her and placed one foot on the first step of the stairs. "Told you I don't mix business and pleasure…anymore," I amended. Evelyn knew my past and would call me on it as she had earlier.

"Good advice that we rarely follow when there's attraction. Even that ring on her finger won't matter when the heart wants what it wants." She gestured for me to sit next to her.

"It's late, and I have to get back here in the morning."

"You could stay. You still have clothes from the last time in your old room." She patted the chair.

I sighed loudly and plopped down next to her. "I thought you said all you needed to say in the meeting."

"That was about work. This is personal."

"I'm listening."

"Amara may not be as young as the others who start out in this business, but she's naïve and defers to you. She has eyes for you despite that ring on her finger. We both know that you have a way with women. If you hurt her, things could get ugly, and we don't need another Rene."

I gritted my teeth. "She was years ago, and I'm not that man anymore."

"Maybe not, but women don't change. As sweet as that woman that you've brought here is, she has a bite. And like any animal, she will defend herself regardless of who's impacted if she's hurt or feels you betrayed her."

"She isn't Rene, and I'm keeping my distance. I respect her engagement and hope she and her future husband make it because that's what she wants." I shifted in my chair to face Evelyn. "Amara already means more to me than sex, and I won't jeopardize what we're building. I will start my own team, and Amara will be my first talent. It's way past time that I'm my own man. I'll always appreciate what my father has taught me, but we differ in our approach."

"If you're so insistent on branching away from William, why didn't you establish yourself by having her in the city at your studio? Why start her career here? You certainly didn't think about my endorsing her until a few hours ago, and you can't convince me otherwise. Isn't the best way to prove to your father that you don't need him anymore is to show him that? Being here tells me that you're not ready to be on your own as much as you would like to believe."

I bristled at her words. "Because that woman a few feet away is meant for greatness, and I want her to believe that as much as I do. Hartland has a long legacy that my studio doesn't have yet. This place isn't just for my father. This place is for all musicians—your words and not mine. Besides, I brought her home so you could meet her, because you're my family, too. And I'm not bullshitting you either," I finished firmly. Evelyn had been a surrogate grandmother to me. Never forgot my birthday. She was genuinely happy for my successes and encouraged me through my failures. Coddled me when my parents were strict with me and offered me sound advice whether I wanted it or not.

"One thing you've never bullshitted about was your love of family." Evelyn started rocking again with a smile. "You are my family, and Amara has great potential. You're right about Hartland being the place for her. She can stay as long as she needs. Then maybe I'll see you more, too."

I teased, "Ah…always an ulterior motive to get me to come back here."

"Seems everyone always leaves me and doesn't want to return," she said quietly. My gentle teasing had triggered her loneliness. "Even my own daughter hates coming here."

"Ellie is busy traveling the world." I consoled her, though I knew she spoke the truth.

"With my money," she retorted. "No time for me until she needs money."

At fifty-five, Ellie behaved like a petulant teenager, demanding money from her guilt-ridden mother when her latest business venture went bankrupt or a relationship ended. In short, Ellie Hart was a damn mess who continued to break her mother's heart. My excuses for her disrespectful behavior were futile. Despite millions of adoring fans, Evelyn needed to feel like someone cared about her as a woman, which was why Hartland had been a home or respite for so many people over the years.

I placed my hand on top of her hand, gripping the rocking chair's arm. "I'll do better and visit you more, okay? Just don't tell my mother, or she'll be jealous."

She tittered, and I bent over to kiss her cheek before heading down the stairs. Once I reached the bottom, Evelyn ordered me, "Handle Rene before I do. She's threatening me again."

Fuck. "Told you—you always have an ulterior motive." I turned around and headed to my car. "Consider it handled."

Perturbed that Rene continued to harass Evelyn, I sped away from Hartland. Whenever I thought I could have peace, I was reminded I couldn't. All because I'd allowed my dick to make decisions for me when I knew better than to deal with a woman like Rene.

I waited to calm down, which didn't happen until I'd been on the highway for twenty minutes, before I called her. "Rene?"

She accused me, "You must be dealing with other women. Why haven't you called me? I've been trying to get in touch with you."

"Been busy. I'm calling you now. What do you want?" I tapered the irritation from her whiny, shrill tone. It was a wonder that she'd made millions as a rapper and songstress with such an annoying speaking voice.

"Need to see you," she said. "It's been weeks since you stopped by."

"Seven weeks, to be exact, and we're not together anymore."

"You're never going to forgive me for leaving you?" Rene lamented. "I made a huge mistake and want one more chance."

"Rene, we're not good together. I've been over that part of us." I sighed. "I don't want to rehash that chapter anymore. Turn the page, please, and stop threatening Evelyn with whatever you think you have over her head."

"It's a fact. She's done people dirty."

"Has she ever done anything to you except welcome you on her land and in her home?" I asked her. Rene had been the last woman I invited to Hartland to start her career—eight years ago.

"And? Doesn't mean that she hasn't done someone else wrong." She paused. "You never ask me what she's done. Maybe you already know."

"I don't want to know *if* she's done anything. Everything is fair game in this fucked-up industry, and she came up during an era when women weren't respected. I can imagine she did whatever she had to do. Loyalty is the only value remaining in this business to which I can cling. Apparently, it means nothing to you. Evelyn helped you get started. I don't know why I expect you to be different from what you've shown me." She'd fucked around with other men while we were together. I wasn't an angel either during that wild time, so we'd argued often. "You're only trying to lash out at her to get a rise out of me, and my attention. I need you to stop it."

"I know you still care, or you wouldn't check on me. Why can't we try again? I've been sober for a year."

"You confuse love with caring about you. I will always care and want the best for you," I said softly. Despite infidelity on both sides, I blamed myself for how we ended. How her career ended, and her suicide attempt. Guilt kept me bound to her. "Are you taking your meds? Seen your psychologist lately? You start up with Evelyn every time your manic phase hits."

She growled. "Please stop talking to me like that. Like I'm someone to be pitied."

I snapped, "All right, have you started writing music, taken a drive, or tried to fucking *live* again? Anything besides threatening Evelyn and bothering the shit out of me?"

Rene disconnected the call, and I closed my eyes briefly before focusing on the road again. She wasn't the only one who needed therapy, and I needed to see what information she had on Evelyn. I would get Nathan on it while he helped Amara with Stoney.

My old college roommate, Nathan Price, worked people like a snake charmer. He could get the most guarded or dangerous person to open up and willingly confess. Nathan had worked overseas in combat zones and in the mean streets of Chicago and New York to gather information to quench his never-ending thirst for knowledge, and to write an award-winning series of articles about the origins of killers. After his last stint overseas, when a bomb landed a few feet away from him and he was almost killed, he'd called and told me he wanted a safer job. A job that still held his interest but wouldn't endanger him. Nathan had a fondness for all genres of music and had been fascinated with my life and the varied people I met. Since his move to Nashville a couple of years ago, he'd been a freelance writer for *Rolling Stone* and other music magazines and a journalist for the local paper, highlighting old and new talent.

Two days after my conversation with Evelyn and Rene, Nathan dropped by the studio at my request. He was just as enthralled with Amara as I had been at the Peabody.

"Man, I see why you wanted her back here. She's the real thing."

I beamed. "She is. I reviewed the contract with her yesterday and think she'll sign it, since I'm offering an advance."

"I didn't know you did that." He lifted both of his brows.

"My dad usually doesn't. I want to be different with some of my new artists who need financial support while waiting for a record deal or a gig. There's no way Amara could afford to stay here and pay for expenses back in Atlanta. I had to give her a reason to sign with me."

"Shit, I would sign." He grinned.

We dapped while we watched her in the booth as she expertly played the acoustic and electric guitar and then tickled the ivories. She had the bravado of Tina, Aretha Franklin's soul, H.E.R.'s musicality, and the earthy sexiness of SZA. Something about how she gripped the mic, with her pouty lips almost touching, could tighten my pants if I wasn't careful to change my thoughts.

Nathan applauded like he was at a concert when she finished singing Adele's "Rolling in the Deep." We were trying on different songs, trying to determine which three she would perform while I worked on her original tracks.

Pressing the mic, I announced, "Let's take a break.'

Domino, Tavion, and Sophie piled out of the booth, followed by Amara. She walked out smiling with an outstretched hand. "You must be Mouse."

Nathan looked at me curiously as he took her hand. "What?"

"I'm Easy, and you're Mouse," I said wryly.

"I'm the unstable sidekick who will kill on a whim instead of the actual detective?" he asked incredulously.

"Yeah. I mean, of the two of us, who's more levelheaded and less likely to be on the run?" I leaned back in my chair, waiting for him to deny that, for years, he'd welcomed danger.

He still held Amara's hand as he answered with a self-deprecating grin, "I guess I am your Mouse. Mind if we step to the other studio and chat a little bit? I can't wait to hear what you have on Stoney. He was a fascinating man from what I've discovered already."

"Need to extend break time, Jake," she told more than asked me, and I nodded.

Nathan held the door open. His interested gaze rested briefly on her curvy ass once she passed him, and I averted my gaze before I resented my best friend. I really didn't blame him. She looked damn good wearing a top that bared her sunburst tramp stamp and the diamond-pierced belly button that teased me every time the studio light reflected off it. She'd French-braided her hair, giving her a youthful and vibrant appearance.

"Better watch yourself. Staring a little too hard," Tavion commented from behind me.

"Just making sure I don't have to step in. Nathan can come across strongly when he's trying to gather information."

He sucked his teeth. "Dude, I saw that video of you, too. And in person, I feel the chemistry between you."

I swiveled to look at him. "Drop it. She has a man."

Tavion raised both of his brows. "Noted that you didn't deny the vibe between you."

Domino and Sophie wore big, knowing smiles. They'd been with me for years, working in the studio and being an impromptu band when I needed them to back up an artist. We were like a family, teasing and caring about each other.

I threw two middle fingers at them.

Tavion scoffed. "Save that, Jake. That's what you want to do to Mari."

"Ha… Ha… Ha." I turned back around in my chair while they laughed. "Everyone has jokes. I'm just fascinated with her talent. That's it."

"Sure. Tell that to yourself if it helps you sleep better," Domino called out.

Jerking my head, I crossed my hand over my heart, feigning hurt. "Not you, too. I thought I could rely on at least one of you to have my back."

Sophie approached me from the side and draped her arms over my neck. "I got your back, boss. You want me to give her a note from you with the checkboxes asking her if she likes you too."

I playfully pushed her arms off me while the two men cracked up. "All y'all fired."

My threat only made them laugh harder, so I shook my head and placed my headphones back on to tune them out. No sense in denying my feelings for Amara. I accepted my fate. I couldn't hide that I was falling for her from the people closest to me, but she and I would never be.

NINETEEN

Amara

The night before the showcase, we were all frustrated with each other because everything that could go wrong had. Domino had sprained his wrist helping his girlfriend move, and though he valiantly tried to push through the pain, it became apparent he wouldn't be able to run through five songs. A pissed Jake sent him home after Domino bungled the beats.

We had to adjust without drums while Jake impatiently made calls to find another drummer who could pick up at least the three cover songs by tomorrow. We hadn't decided on any songs outside "A Born Legacy," though we practiced three other originals. We'd moved into the city near Jake's studio because he had more space there to practice a full band. I would alternate between the electric and acoustic guitar and the keyboard for the showcase. I hadn't practiced on the keyboard with the band and didn't have time outside the studio, which became more evident the more we rehearsed. To make matters worse, the studio's air compressor broke, and Jake refused to move. So we'd sweated bullets most of the day until the air conditioner was repaired a short time ago. We were cranky, hot, and miserable, and Jake didn't mince words. He yelled and cursed every time one of us messed up, and no one responded likewise to the boss. We just did whatever he demanded.

"Shit," I mumbled when I tickled the wrong key while singing "River Deep – Mountain High" by Tina Turner. It would be my finale, displaying the strength and range of my voice. "Sorry…sorry. Let's start over. Not having the drums is messing up my count."

Jake bellowed, "This is the fifth time. We haven't even rehearsed your songs because we're stuck on this one."

"For three weeks, we rehearsed with drums, and not having them is throwing me off," I explained, careful to keep calm despite his unreasonable irritation.

He scoffed, "Drum or no drum, you didn't fucking follow the practice schedule I gave you. If you did, you wouldn't be messing up once again."

"You know I've been up to the wee hours of the morning in the studio and waking up early to jog, and then I'm back in the studio for the rest of the day. When did I have time to follow your damn practice schedule, too?" I shot back. In my peripheral vision, Sophie and Tavion grew still. This was the first time anyone had challenged Jake.

He hit his fist in his palm. "Three weeks was your idea. Not mine."

"It was your idea to have a concert when I know nothing about singing professionally." I wiped the sweat off my brow.

He crossed his arms. "Stop using that excuse. Stop fucking hiding behind that bullshit excuse." Jake glared at me. "Again." He jumped on the drums and grabbed the sticks. "I'm counting off."

Determined not to miss another key, I started playing again and opened my mouth to sing. I needed to ignore his mood and prove I could do this. My voice would make him forget my bad keyboard playing. "River Deep" was one of my favorite songs, and I'd been happy that Jake agreed it would be perfect for my first show.

But as I made it to the chorus, he waved the drumstick curtly, stopping me. "No. No…no. Do you want this or not? Because the way you're singing isn't worth shit."

I bit the inside of my cheek to stem the jab to my heart at his insult. "I'm doing the best I can."

"Bullshit," he roared. "You're stuck in your head. Too worried about what others are going to say or think. Too worried that people won't like who you really are." With the contempt with which he spoke, I knew he referred to

Phillip. "Tomorrow, I'm presenting you to Nashville, and you're performing like the music teacher you are and not the star you say you want to be."

I balled my hand into fists. "Your energy is not helping me."

His scowl grew deeper. "You think I give a fuck? You have to perform your ass off, no matter the energy. People are ready to dismiss you anyway for daring to sing country. Perform like it's your last show, even when you fucking miss a note or a lyric or have a judging audience. You make people respond to you. You make them feel that nothing matters but your voice. No one knows you, and you can't wait until the vibe is right to prove you got it. Make them want to embrace you from the minute you walk on that damn stage." He dragged his hand down over his unkempt beard. "Again."

I slapped my thighs. "Why? So you can curse me again? We've been at it for hours, and nothing I do is right."

"Maybe we need a break," Tavion suggested. "It has been a long day. Give the studio time to cool off." He fanned himself with the bottom of his Bob Marley t-shirt.

"Again," Jake repeated as if Tavion and I hadn't spoken.

I rolled my eyes so hard I hurt them as he started the count. I grabbed the mic with one hand, closed my eyes so I couldn't see his scowl, and started playing with the other hand.

"Nope. Not good enough."

A disapproving Jake, a ball of anger and disappointment, sat behind the drums, intimidating me. I finally threw my hands up. "I can't work like this."

Jake growled, "You can and you will."

I took off my headset and placed it on the mic. "I'm out."

He moved from behind the drum set and strode to me. "You walk out that door, don't come back."

I turned and marched out the door to the street, refusing to shed a tear. My pride kept me from crying, which I badly wanted to do. I wasn't cut out for this. I checked my watch. Too late to catch a flight. It was a four-hour drive back to Atlanta. I could rent a car and get the hell out of Dodge. No way could I expect to stay at Hartland if I wasn't going to work with Jake. I could go to Memphis, back to my grandfather's place, and focus on the letters and his journal. Even if I couldn't make it in the industry, I couldn't go back to the studio or home until I figured out what had happened to Stoney's music. Nathan had been working hard after the three of us read the letters and the journal one night after practice, and I expected answers soon.

The hotel Jake had reserved for me over the weekend was within walking distance of the studio. Once I reached my room, I collapsed on the edge of the bed. As much as I hated to admit it, Jake was right. I couldn't seem to relax and let everything flow. I was partly worried about how Phillip would receive me. The larger part of me feared I would let my grandfather down. I wanted to finish the dream he'd started and be a force in the music industry. The way I'd been performing all day wouldn't cut it. It just hurt to feel Jake's disappointment in me when he had supported me.

I shut my eyes tight, willing myself to push away the irrational thoughts evoked by my emotions. I was in my feelings, and Jake's nerves were on edge. A lot rode on my shoulders, and I'd succumbed to the pressure. If I left the minute we hit a snag, I wasn't the woman I thought I was. I had gumption, and damn it, that asshole Jake wouldn't push me away from my destiny. Even if I had to find another manager to help me get there.

I pulled my cell out of my jacket pocket, checking the time. Phillip should be arriving within a couple of hours and would be staying here with me. Well, at least he'd be happy that my time in Nashville might be cut short. I sighed. Maybe seeing him would comfort me and remind me that my life in Atlanta had been good. Maybe I could find a manager back home. A manager with whom no attraction existed. My phone buzzed.

Call me. 6:05 p.m.

"We'd already talked a few hours ago. What else could happen now?" I muttered aloud as I called Phillip. "What's wrong?"

"Everything is right. I helped secure the deal with the Koch company," he announced excitedly. Phillip had worked diligently over the last few months to make this happen. "The bonus for this deal is crazy. We can look at the house in Buckhead you wanted."

Dread filled the space where excitement should have rested. He could've given me that news in person. "Congratulations, baby. We can celebrate late tonight when you get here." I cleared my throat, already fearing his response. "Shouldn't you be on a flight here?"

"That's why I called. I can't leave. We have meetings tomorrow to wrap up everything. I can come next weekend, or maybe you can fly back here on Sunday morning."

I slowly sat up. "What? Tomorrow is my showcase. I did this for you."

"No, you did this for you. I didn't ask you to do a show. I was coming to support you and spend the weekend with you."

"So once again, your work is more important than me," I accused him hotly.

"Just like yours is to you."

"Don't do that. For two years, I didn't say a word when you canceled at the last minute on me for work. This time, I'm shouting from the rooftop that you need to choose me." I hit my chest.

Phillip practically hissed. "I've been working on this deal for months and didn't expect it to close today. But I can't dictate when shit happens. It's out of my control. What am I supposed to tell the execs at Koch? Huh? I have to fly to Nashville to see my fiancée perform?"

I doggedly replied, "Yes. That's exactly what you fucking say. We compromised on three weeks."

He blew out his breath. "Okay, fine. You have my support to stay the summer, all right? I won't complain or say another word about your being in Nashville. I'll fly down next weekend, and you can sing for me and only me."

I fumed silently. How could he do this to me again? I'd tried to accommodate him yet again, but he had yet to do that for me. Jake and I were beefing now because I'd challenged him to get me ready in three weeks, and he'd failed. Jake hated failing and had warned me not to allow Phillip to dictate my career. And now Phillip was suddenly agreeable with my staying the summer?

"Think how much fun we can have when I come later," he said. "Just you and me in Nashville with my bonus. I can get us a penthouse suite with a piano at the most expensive hotel, and then you can give me a private show. This deal sets me up for a promotion and a large salary increase. We need this. Please, Mari. Give me grace again. You won't regret it."

Someone knocked on the door, and my pulse raced. *Jake. Not now.*

Quelling my nerves and refusing to rush to the door, I stood up when the second knock followed. "I'm serious, Phillip. You have to put me first. We're getting married."

"Yes, we are, and I want you to be happy. Have fun tomorrow. Get someone to record and send me the video. Call me as soon as you finish killing it. I know you'll be amazing."

Phillip's belief in me seemed genuine, so I relented. "Okay. But you better be here next week."

"I will. Look, I need to run to meet the Koch executives for dinner. Love you."

"Love you," I responded out of habit and with little emotion before we clicked off the call.

Now, to deal with Jake. I steeled my shoulders and pushed down the door handle. I immediately relaxed at the sight of Sophie and Tavion, both wearing cowboy hats, big smiles on their faces like they were mischievous kids.

Sophie spoke first. "We're going out now."

"Not up for it." I leaned on the door. "Appreciate you trying to help."

Tavion grabbed my hand. "We're going before you make the second biggest mistake of your life."

"What was the first?" I dragged my feet as he pulled me out of the room.

"Walking out on Jake. But then he cursed us all out and told us to get out of his face. So we need to blow off steam before I lose it on him."

I slowed my pace. "Guys, I'm sorry. I know you've been busting your asses. I just couldn't take any more."

Sophie shrugged. "He's still going to pay us, and we got a break. Come on, Mari. Time to party. We'll deal with Jake later."

"Might as well. Phillip's not coming," I announced, surprisingly feeling more relief than disappointment. In the past three weeks, I'd spent all my time with the crew, as we were calling ourselves, and I had no idea how or if Phillip would fit in with my new friends.

"Oh no. Is everything okay?" Sophie asked with a worried frown. She'd moved into the cottage next to me, and we'd become fast friends, staying up late, creating songs together, and sharing our past loves and current hopes. She was single after a horrible breakup, yet she remained hopeful of a forever love.

"He just secured this big deal and can't get away." I shrugged.

She stepped in front of me and narrowed her eyes, studying my face. "Are you okay? I know how important it was for him to be here. Why we're even doing this in the first place so soon."

"I'm good." At her raised brows, I squeezed her arms. "I really am. Let's go paint the town red, and I'll let Jake cool off before I call him."

We stepped into the elevator, and Tavion grinned wickedly. "I know someone who'll be thrilled to know your man's not coming."

Sophie punched him in his chest. "Shut up."

"Hey!" He chuckled. "It's no secret that Jake got a thing for you. He's really mad because he thinks you're fucking up because of your man."

Sophie hit him again while I blushed. I'd caught Jake staring when he thought no one had paid attention, and he never dropped his gaze whenever I caught him. I had no doubt that our attraction hadn't waned. We just chose to ignore it for the greater good.

"Why do you keep hitting me? We're supposed to be able to tell each other shit, right?"

I allowed my head to flop against the back of the elevator. "Jake isn't mad because he's jealous. He thinks it's stupid that I'm considering Phillip's feelings about my music, and after what just happened, I can't say he's wrong."

Tavion nodded. "Because he's not. You're badass, and no one should take that from you."

"Phillip's not taking it from me. It's just…" I struggled to find the words.

"What she's trying to say is she has to figure out how to keep her man and sing. It's what we women have had to worry about since the beginning of time. Men don't have to figure out how to have it all, while we have to do a juggling act, especially if we decide to have children." Sophie threw her arm around my neck. "I got ya, sis."

I grinned. "Thank you." I pointed at Tavion. "Because these negroes don't get it."

Tavion held his hands up. "Maybe I don't, but I do know the stinger of jealousy is what's up Jake's ass."

"Ooh, that visual is a bit much." Sophie giggled. "But if we're being honest, then yeah. He might be a little jealous."

"Is he really that into me?" I asked. "His phone is always ringing late. I know he has women he's running off to when we're done in the studio, and he's probably messed around with some of his artists before, as Evelyn said."

Sophie replied, "We've been with Jake for years, and he's different with you. If you weren't engaged, guarantee he would be all up in that." She playfully tapped my ass.

Tavion clapped his hands. "So glad you're engaged, because we probably wouldn't get any work done if you weren't. Hell, girl, every other song he looks like he wants to drag you off somewhere."

"All right, stop it. He's more into my music than me," I offered, trying not to think of the times Jake had looked at me with pure, unadulterated desire.

"Yet I don't hear you saying that you wouldn't give him some if you weren't engaged." Tavion nudged my shoulder.

Giggling, I pushed him off me. "I swear you're messier than any woman I know."

He tilted his head, and a sardonic smile crossed his face. "What? You didn't know that men are messier than women? We just hide it better."

"Facts," Sophie said. She and I dapped.

The doors opened. "Where are we going?" I asked.

They both shouted, "Karaoke."

I said skeptically, "Really? We need a break from singing, so we go to a place to sing?"

Sophie nodded vigorously as we exited the elevator. "Yes, really. You need to sit in these bars and feel the energy. You might know music, but you don't know the heartbeat of Nashville. You need to feel it through your soul. Have you even been out here since you arrived?"

"No. Jake was supposed to bring me back downtown, but we jumped right into my music, preparing for tomorrow."

She snapped her fingers. "That's why something's missing. Nashville is missing."

"I can receive that. All right, I'm game." I had nothing to lose, and if I stayed in the hotel, all I would do was wallow in my room until I ignored my pride and called Jake.

As we walked past the studio, Jake and I locked eyes. He stood by his car on his phone, smiling. "Meet me at my place, and I'll order dinner."

My heart ached at the grin on his face as he called his latest woman to tell her his night had ended earlier than he'd anticipated. Jake looked away first and slid into his car like we didn't exist. We were like strangers.

Once we were out of his earshot, I asked, "Did Jake say anything about tomorrow?"

Tavion answered soberly, "No."

Sophie replied, "Yes."

They exchanged nervous looks.

"He just pretended he didn't know us." My heart dropped to my stomach. "He said we're not doing the show, didn't he?"

Sophie shrugged. "Well, Jake told you what would happen. He's not the man you walk out on." She ticked off on her hand: "He's stubborn, has a big ego, and has the power to end your career before it starts. Sometimes, you have to take what he dishes out to get what you want."

My temple thudded painfully. I'd walked away in anger and frustration and thought I could return to his good side once my emotions settled. Being ignored by him and knowing he'd canceled the show hurt. Like, really hurt. Still, I defended myself quietly. "He doesn't get to talk to me in any way he wants."

"It's his way. When he loves what you're doing, he tells you. When he doesn't, he also tells you," Tavion reminded me.

"His way wasn't helping."

Sophie chimed in. "No disrespect, because you know I think you are the bomb-dot-com. Jake's put his rep on the line for you. It's unheard of that he hasn't nailed you down for a contract, and he's produced three of your songs for free. He's spent time and money on you, paying for the venue tomorrow, neglecting his roster to coach you through this, and today you were off. It never got better. You're performing like you're too stuck in your head. Your first show is tomorrow, and you're letting your nerves take over. He doesn't want you to choke in front of all those people. Some want you to fail because they don't want Jake to succeed. Or plain don't believe a Black woman should sing country. We all know Jake's heart is in the right place, no matter his mouth."

I turned slightly to let a guy hurry past me on the crowded sidewalk. "I know he's worried. So am I. Jake was borderline abusive. He can't talk like that to me, and I can't allow him to think he can because he's my unofficial manager." Broadway's bright lights and music became our backdrop as the three of us walked and talked. Colorful, loud bars and busy restaurants blasting country music, old and new, tickled our ears as we discussed what had occurred earlier.

"Then pull him to the side or speak to him after rehearsal. Don't just leave like you did," Tavion added. "This show is important to us, too."

I shifted to the middle of them and wrapped my arms around their necks. "I apologize for my part and for not thinking how my actions might impact you. Come on, you must admit he was a real bastard."

"Maybe, or maybe he knows you can do better," reasoned Sophie.

They were loyal to Jake and would ride for him. I was the newcomer who needed to humble herself. I squeezed my new friends to me. "I'll talk to him—beg him, if I must, to give me another chance to perform tomorrow night."

"Or you can just bat those naturally long lashes at him and press your palm on his chest when you do it, and he'll give you whatever you ask." Sophie winked.

I protested, "Hey, you're supposed to be on my side."

"I am. But I need to work, too." She strolled into one the brightest and loudest venues, AJ's Good Time Bar. "This is the one. We're about to get so lit."

We squeezed toward the bar and ordered drinks. The staff remained all smiles despite the place being packed. The line to sing karaoke was long. People were all cheers and supportive as participants of varying levels of talent walked onto the small stage. The vibe here was crazy, and I smiled for the first time that day, allowing positive energy to pass through me. Most of the people who walked on the stage could sing. Impressed, I clapped and hooted loudly with everyone. The beats and twang of the different country songs appealed to me more since I'd been working with Jake, and I knew more songs than I'd initially thought I would. By my third whiskey sour, I tapped Tavion and shouted over the music, "When are we going on stage?"

He quirked a brow and yelled back, "You'll be after the next guy."

My stomach lurched. "What? I was kidding."

"We're not. I signed you up an hour ago." Sophie rested her arm on Tavion's shoulder.

I lowered my eyes. "You two were in cahoots?"

Tavion put his hand behind his ear like he couldn't hear me. "Huh?"

"This is a huge and loud crowd." My apprehension grew as I scanned the room of a sea of white faces with a sprinkling of color.

"The crowd will be worse tomorrow because they know they're about to see a show. Tonight they're drunk and don't give a shit if you fuck up. Time to get on that stage, Mari Johnson." Sophie grinned.

"All right, y'all better have chosen me a good song." I gulped down my drink and slammed it on the bar, grateful for the liquid courage coursing through my veins.

My personal fan group jumped up and down, egging me on. I tied the ends of my t-shirt behind me to show off the diamond in my belly button. I snatched Tavion's white Stetson and placed it on my head while standing at the small stage's edge. Two women celebrating twenty years of friendship wrapped up their rendition of "Friends in Low Places" by Garth Brooks before my name was called.

I took a deep breath and walked on the stage. "I'm Mari Johnson. My friends told me I should come up here and show out. I still don't have a clue what I'm singing. I'm fresh out of Atlanta and loving Nashville, especially this bar." I picked up the mic instead of keeping it on the stand, as everyone else had done, and adjusted my hat.

The audience whistled and roared when the first notes of "Since U Been Gone" by Kelly Clarkson blasted. My inner teenager, who loved this song, smiled at the heavens. I spread my arms wide before bringing the mic back to my mouth to announce, "One of my favorites, especially because I might just be a little pissed with the man who put this on my finger. Got me doubting if he's worth it." I waved my left finger, and my diamond blinged under the spotlight. This time, the women in the crowd howled in solidarity.

From the very first note, I had the audience hooked. I pranced around the small stage and hit every freaking note perfectly. My anger, frustration, and disappointment at the two men in my life bled through each lyric as I sang the hell out of the ultimate song about feeling suffocated. By the end, everyone in the crowded bar sang along, and when I extended the last note, the applause was deafening.

When I lifted the hat and bowed playfully, I rose up to a clapping and catcalling Jake in the audience. His lips curved as two men scrambled to help me from the stage. Our gazes never wavered as I sauntered to him and poked his chest. "Is that good enough for you, sir?"

His dimples flashed before he turned away from me and shouted at Sophie and Tavion, "Studio, now. We have a show tomorrow. Our star is finally ready."

I impulsively hugged him from the back. He looked over his shoulder at me and lowered himself slightly. "Hop on."

"Seriously?"

A few patrons heard him and helped me climb on his back while I squealed. I settled against his strong back, wrapped my arms around his neck, and whispered, "You better not drop me."

He hefted me higher. "You just make sure you hold on."

Bursting with joy and pride from the performance I'd just killed, I gave him a big kiss on his cheek, and the four of us left the bar ready for whatever tomorrow night would bring.

TWENTY

Jake

I cursed myself even louder once I'd cleared the studio with my temper. I'd been known to rant and rave when situations weren't going my way, but never like the way I'd just behaved. I could blame it on my growing nervousness due to the fact that it was the first show I'd produced in totality, from the song choices to the order in which Amara would perform. I'd even planned to play the guitar and keyboard myself to add another layer of richness to her sound.

I could also blame my irritation on Amara's rather lackluster rehearsal. And if I did, I would be lying if I attributed my foul mood to anything but jealousy. I prided myself on not lying to myself, even though I may not have always been truthful with others. I'd been a wreck because Phillip would be in Amara's bed later tonight.

Jealousy and envy reigned supreme over my rationality and supportiveness. I'd overheard Amara talking to him on the phone when she arrived at the studio. I'd run to my office to review a contract for one of my other artists, but the mic from the studio was never turned off. Amara's voice had been sexier and deeper as she expressed her excitement about seeing him that night, about the fun weekend she'd planned for them. He'd only laughed in amusement and didn't sound at all like a man who couldn't wait to see her and get his hands on her the way I would've. I'd spent such a short time with her and already had been spoiled with her daily presence.

I silenced the mic when they neared the end of their conversation. I didn't need to hear them express their love for one another. Recognizing that she had a man and knowing she had one were two different things. I'd joked and teased her about Phillip as if he were an imaginary person, but he was real. A man who'd won her heart and future. A man she was determined to keep and who she worried wouldn't accept her journey into the music world.

Granted, Amara couldn't seem to capture the fire she'd consistently caught in rehearsals the past three weeks. My irate mood didn't help matters. I'd become her guide, her teacher, her mentor…and she looked for my praise and encouragement, which I refused to give out of pettiness. Her confidence and performance suffered because of my criticisms, and I only rode her harder. I hated that she saw me and respected me in a managerial role, but she didn't see me the way she saw Phillip. She might have been attracted to me and had a crush that she didn't hide very well, but she loved the man who would be with her in a suite I'd paid for.

I needed to get out of there and figure out what would happen tomorrow. I could cancel the event or postpone indefinitely until Amara cooled off and we discussed what she wanted to do. She'd left without looking back and hadn't texted or called. She might be done with this "experiment," especially with her man in her ear, telling her to come back home with him and continue the life they were beginning. Twenty-one days of arduous practice and little sleep compared to life around her loved ones and regular routines? That might appeal to her more. A man who didn't talk to her as ugly as I had would definitely be more appealing.

I poured some bourbon from the minibar in my office and gulped it down before pouring another one. I walked to my window, overlooking the flashing lights of the city. If I didn't get a handle on my emotions, I would lose her. I needed to be truthful with her and apologize for being jealous. I also needed to be honest and tell her that she couldn't let anyone rattle her or take her off her game. She needed to rise above her emotions if she wanted to have longevity, because she would have haters and doubters.

I gulped down my second glass and turned away from the window.

As I left the building, Naomi, a pretty songwriter I'd dated a couple of years ago, called. I answered with flirtation in my voice, determined to escape inside of her tonight. "I hope this unexpected call means you want to see me."

She giggled. "I just touched down in town to meet up with one of my singers. Hoping you were up for a little fun."

"Always." I smiled. Perfect timing. Naomi already knew what was up and didn't have any expectations beyond good food and great sex. I opened my car door and noticed my crew walking past with large smiles. Amara and I locked eyes, and her smile faded. I'd hurt her more than I realized. Unable to face her, I returned to Naomi. "Meet me at my place, and I'll order dinner."

I didn't hear Naomi's response as I slid into my car and watched them pass on their way to have a good time and forget about me. I inhaled deeply and pulled out into the busy street on my way to do what I did best—lose myself in women and alcohol.

As I circled the block, trying to shake the encroaching depression, Mama called. I hesitated to answer. She didn't always approve of my choices. My decision to follow her husband into the music business was one of them. I only answered because I'd promised Evelyn that I would do better in staying connected to family.

"Hey, Ma."

"What's wrong?" she asked. My mother had uncanny intuition and always knew when something wasn't right with me, though I didn't always admit my feelings to her.

"Nothing. How are you?"

"I'll tell you when you stop by for dinner soon. Not taking no for an answer."

"Why do I feel like it's an ambush or some sort of intervention?"

"It's not. Just miss my only baby."

I thumped my head against the seat. "Miss you too."

"So, you'll add me to your calendar?"

"My life is crazy busy right now, but I do want to see you. Are you coming with Dad to see my showcase tomorrow night?"

"Did you invite me?"

I refrained from saying something smart, which would've gotten me backhanded when I was a boy. "Mama, would you like to come tomorrow night and see my new artist?"

She chuckled. "Was already planning to go with William. Just wanted *you* to invite me."

"All right, you made your point." I drove through the streets slowly, not yet ready to go to the loneliness of my condo. "Ma, how did you get over *him*?"

"Oh…you haven't mentioned Jakobi in years. Why do you ask?"

"I remember how much you loved him and how hard it was to get over him."

"It was tough, especially because you're so much like the good part of him. Time and recognition that the relationship wouldn't work is my only answer." She added quietly, "I thought I hid how hard it'd been letting go of him from you."

"No. I just pretended that I didn't hear your arguments or your tears. Made me hate him because he hurt you." Memories of growing up in a household with a father who came in and out of our lives on a whim still tightened my chest.

"Hate is such a strong word."

"You're right. Hate implies energy, and I rarely think of him anymore." The last time I saw my father was at my college graduation, and he didn't stay long. He was too uncomfortable to witness my mother happy with another man. Once Mama met William and truly moved on, my father stopped pretending he gave a damn about us. About me.

"Did Jakobi call you or something?"

I scoffed, "I wouldn't answer the phone if he did. Just wondering how you get over someone you love when you know being together is impossible."

"I knew something was wrong. I could hear it in your voice. You haven't asked for my advice since you were a boy. Never wanted to listen to anything anyone had to say."

"Thanks for reminding me why I don't," I retorted. "You and William can't seem to let go of who I was in the past. How can I grow if you won't give me the room?"

She sighed. "Hey, I don't want to argue."

"I don't either."

Her voice softened. "Then let's talk. You asked me a question, and I want to answer."

"I'm listening."

"Why is loving this person impossible? Why can't you be together?"

"It's complicated…and I'm not just brushing you off." I turned the corner and realized I'd absent-mindedly been driving in circles. I couldn't leave the area until I made things right with Amara. "Maybe love is too strong a word. She's someone I care deeply about, and I know that, ultimately, it wouldn't work. I just want to stop thinking about her so much."

"I don't know…"

"Don't know what?" I asked.

"If you can't stop thinking about her, maybe it's a sign that things are different with her. After all, that's how I felt when I met William." She chuckled. "Before you write the possibility of this woman off, make sure it's not you getting in the way of love."

I tightened my grip on the steering wheel as I scoured the tourists and locals enjoying the nightlife of Nashville, hoping to catch a glimpse of Amara. "For once, it's not me getting in the way."

Mama exclaimed, "Oh, really? Well, I hope this conversation means you're finally ready to settle down with the *right* woman?"

I wryly commented, "I'm ready for something different, that's for sure. Just trying to find my way."

"Jake, if this call is any indication, you're finding it. And I'm here for it."

"All right, Ma. You made me feel better. Let me go before you throw more slang my way." I chuckled. "Love you, and see you tomorrow night at the showcase."

"I wouldn't miss it for the world, and I love you too." She sounded pleased with our brief conversation, which made me smile. I would do better by the woman who'd always been there for me, and we would have dinner soon.

I pulled into a no-parking zone as soon as I ended the call before texting Tavion.

Where are you? 8:23 p.m.

A few seconds later, he responded.

AJ's Bar. We just signed Amara up for karaoke, and she has no clue. Better get here, and don't start no more shit. She found out her man's not coming tomorrow. 8:24 p.m.

My heart soared like helium-filled balloons released into the sky. Phillip wouldn't be here to share her special night. AJ's wasn't too far from me. I just had to quickly find parking and cancel my plans with Naomi.

As I walked into the bar, I spotted Tavion and Sophie cheering. Then I was entranced as Amara exceeded my expectations regarding her command of a diverse audience. She exuded confidence and sexuality as she entertained the crowd. She'd channeled her palpable anger and frustration into every lyric. I knew some of her emotions were directed toward me. I willingly accepted that if it propelled her to perform like this. She had to be the darling of the night as she finished to a deafening applause. Amara's victorious smile widened when she saw me, and she added an extra sway to her hips as she approached me through the crowd that spread like she was Moses and they were the Red Sea.

At that moment, I knew she wanted to kiss me as much as I wanted to kiss her. Before we did something she would regret, I turned away and called for Sophie and Tavion. She grasped my back, apparently needing my touch. Instead of pulling her in front of me to hold her like I yearned, I hefted her onto my back. I would be strong for her. I would be her friend and mentor or whatever role she wanted me to be. Whether she knew it or not, she'd become my inspiration to be a better man.

As she held on to me while we headed back to the studio, she pressed her face against mine. "I shouldn't have walked out on you like that."

"And I shouldn't have spoken to you like I did." Tavion and Sophie were slightly ahead and couldn't hear our conversation. "I was jealous because I knew he would be here with you this weekend, and I have no right to be."

She squeezed my neck. "I get jealous every time you look at your phone, and I damn sure don't have a right to be. So let's scrap today and work harder at not being jealous, because we have a long future together. I need my future manager and producer to be focused and fair."

"I need my singer confident, sexy, and commanding like you were tonight."

"You thought I was sexy?" Amara giggled in my ear.

"You know you were tying your shirt so everyone can see your belly ring and that sexy-ass tat on your lower back."

"I asked you if *you* thought I was sexy, not what I know." Amara slipped a little bit, and I hefted her higher.

"Glad you drink smoothies and jog now. You're getting heavy." She nipped my ear playfully, and I cursed before I could stop myself. An inebriated Amara was way too tempting. "Behave, or I'll make you regret it."

"Hmm…I imagine that you like rough sex."

I looked ahead. Tavion and Sophie were still out of earshot, and we would be back at the studio in a few minutes. "Depends on the woman."

"How would you be with me?"

"Amara, you have a man, and I'm trying to respect that fact."

"A man who doesn't put me first," she lamented. "Makes me wonder if something is wrong with me. Why doesn't he miss me?"

Her self-doubt incensed me. We passed the doorway of a closed flower shop, and I ducked inside the space. I shifted her around so that she straddled me, pressing her against the glass door. Before I allowed reason to intervene, I cupped her neck and captured her lips in a deep, soulful kiss. Amara was only momentarily caught off guard, then she wrapped her arms and legs tightly around my waist and kissed me back. My tongue joined hers, and we moaned loudly in each other's mouths. I could get drunk just from the taste of her. Amara moved her hips sensually against my hardness. If she wore a dress, I would've easily slipped her panties to the side, entered her raw, and dealt with the consequences later.

"Umm…do we need to scrap going to the studio? Looks like you need a room," Tavion announced from behind me. I broke the kiss and rested my head against Amara's heaving chest while she laughed.

"Busted," Sophie called out from farther down the street.

I chuckled, not remotely embarrassed we'd been caught in a passionate embrace. "Give us a second, and we're going to the studio."

"You sure? Because Sophie and I have no problem partying more while y'all talk or do whatever this is."

Without turning around, I repeated, "We're going to the studio. If you want your jobs, leave now."

"One day, I might just quit on you," Tavion threatened as he walked away.

"Boy, you're not going anywhere." Sophie chuckled as their chatter grew softer.

A contrite Amara placed her feet back on the ground while remaining in my embrace. "What did I just do?"

"It's what I did. I kissed you in a way that made you respond. I didn't like that you were doubting yourself because of him and had to do something. If you were mine…" I shook my head at the trust in her eyes and stepped back. "Momentary lapse in judgment. Won't happen again, because you're not mine."

She grabbed my hand before I walked away. "I feel like my grandfather must have felt, wondering why I met you two years too late."

"Well, we didn't meet then. We met now, and apparently, you can't drink around me."

"I'm not drunk, Jake."

I sighed. "Why can't you let me believe that you wouldn't kiss me back if you were sober? That you only have a temporary crush on me?"

"You prefer that I lie?" she asked in disbelief.

"Yes," I said emphatically, and her head jerked back. "What do you want me to do, Amara? Everything we're doing right now is so that you can keep your man. You can't keep looking at me with your big, pretty, brown, soulful eyes and expect me not to react."

She frowned. "Call me Mari. You're getting mad again. Why?"

"Because this isn't easy for me. I thought I could handle how I feel about you. I hate that I'm so attracted to you. That I wake up with a smile because I get a chance to see you. To hear your voice. That I'm only nervous around you because I want to grab you and never let go. That I'm so fucking jealous of a man I never met. A man who doesn't know what he has." I touched her heart through her shirt. My palm briefly curved to the fullness of her breast. "Tell me, Mari, before you met me, did you think he was the one? Did you have any doubts? Has he been good to you? The kind of man who doesn't drink to excess and doesn't have a rep with women? The type of man you trust with your whole heart? The kind of man who doesn't have daddy issues and comes from a strong family who believes in marriage and family?"

"Yes. He's all of those things," Amara confirmed. "But he's not you."

"Exactly. And I'm all those things he's not." I clenched and unclenched my jaw, trying to find the right words to explain why we couldn't allow the purpose of our work to be clouded by our undeniable chemistry and passion. "If we don't stop, then you're repeating your grandfather's mistakes. You chose Phillip for a reason, like Stoney chose your grandmother. I won't let you fuck up a good relationship because of this temporary passion between us. I will always be your friend, your manager, and your producer for however long you want me to be. I refuse to let you be more to me." My chest was heaving up and down by the time I finished. "You and I will move past this. You were amazing on stage, and you'll be amazing tomorrow. Don't tell Phillip about this because he probably won't forgive you. And please make that man recognize what he has, okay?"

Amara hugged herself, tears brimming in her eyes. "Okay. We'll move past this."

"Okay? I don't know… You don't seem okay. I'll tell Jess to make you some of her hot chicken if you say we're good." I smiled, trying to lift her mood.

She grudgingly smiled back. "Hot chicken with lots of fresh-cut fries."

I started walking again, hoping she would follow. "Why do you keep insisting on eating bad and then want to show off your belly?"

She punched me hard in the arm. "You better run, or I swear I'll hurt you."

Picking up my speed, I teased, "I don't really have to run that fast. You're still slower than me."

Amara yelled, "I swear I'm going to get you when you least expect it. You better not take any naps around me."

Looking over my shoulder as she sprinted toward me, eyes still bright yet determined to get me, I asked, "You do know I'm teasing, and I think you're sexy and beautiful just as you are?"

She grinned. "Stop trying to talk yourself out of this beatdown. Sleep with one eye open."

A short time later, she strapped on a guitar back in the studio. "'Wreck Me' is the second song."

I checked the set list. "You don't have a song titled that."

"I'm about to create it right now. About an infuriating man who causes destruction to a woman's heart. Trust me, it will be a hit.

> *"Wreck me, in the shadows we find,*
> *A love so fierce, it's one of a kind.*
> *In your kiss, I find my defeat,*
> *In your arms, my heart skips a beat."*

She sang the words with the perfect melody and arched a brow, daring me to argue.

Sophie clapped. "Already love it."

Tavion and I exchanged glances, and I conceded, "Guess we have a long night ahead of us as we add a brand-new song to the show."

Amara nodded with a glint in her eyes that I couldn't read. "Whatever it takes for my success, right?"

I stared at her from my producer's chair. "Right."

She added a slide to her index finger, and I sat back and let her genius take over.

TWENTY-ONE

Amara

The day of my showcase sped by in a blur. With only a few hours of sleep, I had two steaming cups of black coffee to get me going. The hairstylist and makeup artist arrived at noon to make miracles of me and Sophie. The stylist crinkled my hair and added blonde and purple pieces to make it fuller and funkier. I planned to wear a lavender cowboy hat, so Jake wanted my hair to hang long beneath it. Lashes were added, and my makeup had been airbrushed on my face to last through hours of sweat. Sophie wanted her hair to be extra long, so the stylist braided it in cornrows and installed a raven-black hair that complemented her cocoa-brown skin.

Jake sent a car to pick Sophie and me up from the hotel and transport us to the bar, where we would change clothes thirty minutes before the show. He didn't want me to be seen until I walked on the stage. I hadn't directly communicated with him. He'd been relaying messages through Sophie. I wasn't sure if he was avoiding me or not.

I hadn't had time to think about that mindfuck of a kiss he'd planted on me, or that he'd then told me I should forget about it and just be with Phillip. Granted, my flirting, touching, and questioning how he would be as a lover had him hot for me. Still, I didn't expect him to turn off the heat like a switch when we were caught. I wanted to challenge his feelings for me more, but I relented at the pleading look in his eyes. Whether it was because he respected my engagement or didn't want to mix business and pleasure, Jake didn't want more with me. I needed to see Phillip and remember why I loved him. I had been content until I met Jake. Maybe a dose of my old reality was what I needed to reorient myself to the man I belonged to and not the man I wanted.

Someone knocked on the door to the room I'd been given to change in and prepare for the show—a room big enough for a large vanity and a small sofa and coffee table. Jake had Jess deliver her smoothies and fruit for me to nibble on, although I hadn't had an appetite all day. For the first time since arriving in Nashville, I wondered if I'd made the right decision to pursue this career. No one from home was here to support me. I'd known everyone who was here for me for such a short time. This was the first time I'd done something so significant without the support of family and friends.

The knocking continued. I had about fifteen minutes before showtime. It might be last-minute instructions. When I opened the door, my mother stood on the other side. Ugly tears sprang from my eyes and fell down my face.

Mama, whose tears mirrored mine, hurried past me to my vanity and pulled a tissue from a box. "Stop, Mari, before you mess up your makeup."

I laughed. "Mama, this makeup isn't going anywhere. I just need to hug you." I grabbed her tight to me, and we hugged. "I was just feeling sorry for myself because I didn't have anyone here for me."

Her brown eyes softened. "You didn't tell me. I would've been here earlier if I'd known you had a show."

"I didn't tell you because you weren't speaking to me." Overwhelmed with emotions, I hiccupped. Phillip must have told her and asked her to come, since he couldn't attend. God, how I wished I could see him and thank him personally. We were off tomorrow. Maybe I'd fly home and return on Tuesday. Surprise him.

She pulled me into a hug again, rubbing my back. "Shh… Calm down. You only hiccup when you get too upset. Everything happened so fast. One minute, we're making plans for your wedding. Next, you tell me you want to stay in Nashville for the summer to explore music and learn more about your grandfather. I just needed a moment to process."

"And is Daddy here?" I already knew the answer. They would've been together if he was.

"Your father will need more time."

"It's okay. I know how Daddy can be. Just glad you're here. I'm sorry, Mama. I should've tried harder to get you to understand why I needed to come here. I don't want to do this without you."

"I'm here now. You're not doing this without me." She pulled back slightly. "You look so beautiful. Like the star you've always been to me." I twirled so that the light reflected off my sparkly purple bra underneath my lavender jean jacket. I shoved my hands into my black jeans and tapped my purple cowboy boots on the floor.

I inhaled and exhaled. "Thank you. I needed to hear that." I walked toward the door. "I need to tell Jake to find you a good seat to see my show. It's packed and has standing room only, so it might be hard."

"Stop worrying. Jake knows I'm here. He has a seat for me in the roped-off area on the side of the stage with his other special invited guests."

My thoughts swirled. "How long have you been here?"

"I flew in about two hours ago. It was such short notice that I didn't have time to breathe. Jake called me this morning and asked if I could be here for you. He arranged for me to fly and had a car to pick me up. First class all the way." She peered at me, and I was sure varying emotions must have crossed my face. "Is there something I should know about you and him? He seems to really care about you."

I smiled weakly. "He knows I was disappointed by Phillip not being able to be here. Guess he wanted someone in my corner."

"Phillip was supposed to be here?" my mother asked sternly. "Then why isn't he?"

"He signed a big contract yesterday and needed to finish up this weekend."

She frowned. "Oh no. He'd better get his act together if he wants to marry my daughter. This was an important day for you. Work can't always come first."

I laughed at her indignation. "Right?" I kissed her cheek as Jake knocked on the partially opened door.

"Showtime. We have to get your mother seated."

My stomach clenched at the sight of him. He had a fresh haircut, his beard and mustache were trimmed, and he wore a tailored maroon suit that hugged the dips in his arms just right. His eyes swept my body quickly, and a flicker of interest curved his lips before he grinned.

"Mari Johnson, are you ready?"

"Now that Mama is here, I am." I hugged my mother once more as she hurried out of the room to follow him. "Jake?"

He poked his head back in. "Yeah?"

"Thank you. What you did… Bringing my mother here… Words can't express."

He nodded. "I wanted my mother to be here tonight. Thought you might want yours, too."

"See ya on the stage. Did you ever find a drummer?"

"No worries. You got this," Jake shouted as he headed back out on the floor to take my mother to her seat.

I stared at my reflection and whispered, "Hope you're looking down on me, Granddad."

With bated breath, I walked down the short hall toward the stage with my guitar. When the host announced me, I waved to the audience with a smile. I acknowledged Tavion and Sophie, who were already in place to sing background. Sophie had her own guitar strapped on and ready to go. My smile grew wider when Jake waved his silver stick from where he sat behind the silver and purple drum set he'd had designed with my name on the kick drum.

Mama sat on my right, beaming proudly with clasped hands as I greeted the intimate, standing-room-only bar, "How's everyone doing tonight?"

The mostly white audience yelled different words of good vibes.

"Thank you for being here. I know some of you saw me performing at the Peabody on the viral video, and others have never seen me before. Tonight is special in so many ways. My mother is here cheering me on. This is the first time I have performed professionally. I get to honor my grandfather, a local blues musician born and raised in Memphis." Some of the audience clapped.

"I dedicate this performance to my grandfather, Stoney Johnson, a bluesman who loved country music too. I hope I make him proud."

More loud applause and the spotlight kept me from seeing the people clearly in the audience past the front. I could feel my nerves attacking me, and I held my pick in my hand for a moment too long, steeling myself to start with Chris Stapleton's rendition of "Tennessee Whiskey." Suddenly, I felt an arm around my waist and a chaste kiss on my cheek. Jake whispered, "This is your legacy. No one can take this from you."

His touch and reassurance instantly relaxed me. "My own cheerleader, everybody. My producer and friend, Jake Barnes."

The audience oohed and aahed as Jake waved at the audience on his way back to the drums. Remembering his words about relating to the crowd, I informed the audience, "I've always been a whiskey drinker, but damn it, since I've been here, I have to say, there's nothing like a Tennessee whiskey."

I strummed the first chord, and the crowd went wild. By the time I started singing, I owned the audience.

TWENTY-TWO

Jake

The night was pure magic. Amara held the audience's attention during the entire thirty-minute set. Even when she performed her original songs, she had some people singing along by the end. Based on the crowd reaction, although it was still a work in progress, I would discuss releasing "Wreck Me" first with Amara. It had a crossover country-pop feel and would likely shoot to the top.

I played the drums until she sat at the piano to wrap up her set with "River Deep – Mountain High." I grabbed my fiddle, which I'd placed near the drums. Tavion knew enough of the drums to replace me as I moved near the keyboard with my fiddle, smiling at my muse. Amara sounded as strong and raspy yet clear as Tina. Sophie jammed with the tambourine, and her vocals were perfect for the energy of this song, too.

Amara played the keyboard just as furiously as she sang. She was meant to be on the stage and to entertain. She had the crowd clapping and yelling their approval as she finished the set with a flourish. She blew kisses at us and then went to the center of the stage and bowed. I gave her the acoustic guitar, and she played "Jolene" as Evelyn had instructed. She walked off the stage onto the floor for an encore to resounding applause. Amara shifted the guitar behind her back and bowed again.

When she looked for me this time, I grabbed her in a bear hug, lifting her off her feet. "You did it."

Her eyes were bright. "*We* did it."

I put her down and gave her space as fans approached her while she moved toward her mother. My usually reserved and regal mother, who had a seat next to Mrs. Johnson, rushed forward to hug me. "I didn't even know you still played any instruments. Oh my God, that was amazing. I don't know what else to say about what I just saw. She has it, Jake, and those original songs produced by you… Wow. Wow." She hugged me again and kissed my cheek. "So proud of you."

Chuckling, I said, "Thanks for being here." I looked past her. "Where's Dad?"

Her forehead wrinkled, and she looked over her shoulder. "I thought he was behind me. We were both stunned by you tonight. He probably saw someone he knew. We drove separately, so we haven't been keeping up with each other." She grabbed my hand. "Introduce me to your new star."

"All right." I scanned the small crowd of one hundred or so people looking for Amara and spotted my father on the phone, holding one ear to block out the noise. He seemed upset, and my instincts went into overdrive. "Um…did Dad enjoy it too?"

"Of course—he kept staring like he couldn't believe it. Just ask him yourself. He's going to want to sign her yesterday." She suddenly bounced up and down. "There she is. Come on."

I looked back over my shoulder at my father, and when we locked eyes, he averted his gaze. *What the hell?* Did he suspect that I planned to sign Amara myself and not under his company? I returned my attention to Mama as she pulled me to where Amara and her mother stood in the roped-off section.

Amara's face brightened when I approached, and my stomach flipped. I cursed internally, reminding myself that I hadn't known her long enough and to give it more time. My body would eventually stop reacting when she smiled. "Mari Johnson, this is my mother, Tanisha Barnes."

Mama immediately hugged her and pulled back to praise her. "Phenomenal. I can't believe you'd never performed before."

Amara gushed, "Thank you. Your son got me stage ready. We worked together for the past three weeks for this show. I might have the talent, but he boosted my confidence by believing in me."

Mama raised a knowing brow. "I see. Well, I can't wait to enjoy more shows." She turned to Amara's mom. "You must be a proud mother. She looks just like you."

Mrs. Johnson wrapped her arm around her daughter's waist. "I couldn't be prouder, and I would've missed this moment if Jake hadn't gotten me here. You have a thoughtful and talented son. You should be proud, too."

Mama positively beamed as she leaned her head on my shoulder. "Prouder than I ever thought I would be."

"Stop before you make me cry," I said half teasingly. My cup was full after Amara's successful showcase, and if anyone else said anything remotely sentimental, I would lose it. "Listen, if you'll excuse me, I must circulate."

Everyone nodded and continued to engage in small talk. I headed toward my father. I needed to know what had made him look like he'd seen a ghost. As I squeezed through the crowd, some of my artists patted me on my back in congrats. Two asked to meet with me. I was sure they would also demand that I produce songs for them or insist that I channel the energy from Amara's show into their sets. I'd started something that would keep me even busier than I had been. And I couldn't wait.

He'd disappeared when I finally made it near the second-floor entrance where I'd last seen him. A woman wearing a black suit with only a button protecting her naked chest from being exposed wore her fedora pulled down to partially hide her face. She peeked up at me as I neared.

Rene. *The fuck?*

I hurried to her and kissed her cheek politely. "Hey, I didn't expect to see you. Glad you're out of the house. Didn't even know you knew about tonight."

She didn't smile. "I guess you really have moved on. She's talented in more ways than one, I'm sure. See why you like her."

"She's just my talent." Referring to Amara as if she didn't mean anything more didn't sound right to me.

"Just like I was to you?" Her mouth formed a stern line, making her appear older than thirty-four.

"Did you drive yourself?" I asked, changing the subject. Jealousy usually only added fuel to Rene's fiery temper.

She rolled her neck. "Why? Trying to get rid of me? Don't want your new ingenue to know about your old one?"

"No. I know you don't like driving at night. I can get a car to take you home."

Rene hissed. "I want you to take me home."

I hugged her to whisper, "Tonight is Amara's special night. I'm not dealing with your irrational jealousy. Please believe I'm not trying to hurt you. Let me get you a ride home. I can bring your car to you later."

"Then let me come home with you like we used to after one of your people had a good show." She rubbed my bicep. "You always were sexier on nights like this."

Rene could be relentless, and she wasn't going to leave. She was too concerned with who I'd be taking home with me. I'd planned on being alone, though Naomi had texted me several times, trying to convince me to stop by her hotel, which was not far from the bar. After the kiss I'd shared with Amara last night, no other woman appealed. Besides, I was exhausted and looked forward to a day of rest. A woman in my bed meant strenuous sex and a late morning.

"I'll text you the code to my car. Just go and wait for me. I'll be done in a little while, and I'll take you home, okay?" I pulled out my cell and sent her a text.

She grinned like the Cheshire Cat and kissed me before I could protest. As she sauntered down the stairs, I breathed a sigh of relief. I didn't need her starting shit with Amara.

"I thought you and Rene were over." Nathan approached me as I scoured the bar, hoping Amara hadn't seen that kiss.

"We are." I finally noticed Amara talking and smiling with a small group. Her back was to me, and I sighed in relief.

"Then why is she here?"

"I didn't invite her and had no idea she'd even heard of this showcase." I moved closer to Nathan. "This is Amara's night, and I didn't want any drama. So I texted her the code to my car so she could get in and wait for me to take her home. It's the only way I could get her to leave."

"Why do you keep letting her control your life?" Nathan asked with a scowl.

"Done fucking talking about her." I glanced around the still-crowded room. "Did you find anything on Rene?"

Nathan snorted. "Besides the fact that she was trouble before you signed her…no. I can't figure out what she knows about Evelyn, either. Maybe she's bluffing."

We both looked toward Amara as she took selfies and greeted people. I crossed my arms. "For Evelyn's sake, I hope so. In her own warped mind, Rene is a woman scorned."

"I'll keep looking into Rene. She may be the least of your problems." Nathan squeezed my shoulder. "Check this out. Your father came up to me and asked what I'd been working on lately. In all the years I've known him, he's never asked me that. Never seemed to care about my projects."

"How did he seem?"

"Bringing it up to you now because he asked how I knew Amara. He approached her to congratulate her while she and I were talking. He just seemed distracted, like something troubled him, and not like himself." He patted my chest. "By the way, bro, that was one of the best performances I've ever seen, and it was just her first show." He whistled. "You found yourself a real one."

"Yes, she really is," I replied, and as if she'd heard me, Amara caught my gaze from across the room and smiled. I nodded before I returned my attention to Nathan. "So, my father seemed distracted?"

"Trying to hide that he was worried about something. He headed downstairs right after we spoke."

"Did you tell him what you were working on?"

"Fuck no. My instinct told me to keep my mouth shut."

"Good. Something tonight triggered him. Maybe Rene isn't bluffing. I'm taking her home. I have a nice, long drive to see if I can get some answers."

Nathan grinned. "Aw shit, are we really like Easy and Mouse right now?"

"I don't know. My gut tells me something isn't right. My father lives for these types of events, yet he doesn't talk to me about Amara before he dips, and he introduces himself to her without me? That's not my father. Why don't you stop by my place on Monday? I'll make sure Amara is there. We need to put our heads together, especially if I get some information from Rene tonight."

"Bet."

"What are you two talking about?" Amara slid her arm around my waist, and I hugged her to me. To the naked eye, it was a friendly hug. We both knew differently.

Nathan replied, "We just got invited to Jake's place to discuss your grandfather more on Monday."

"Is he providing food and drinks? I want steak, potatoes, and whiskey," she said to Nathan as if I wasn't standing beside her.

"Love a woman who isn't afraid to eat—and stop hogging her, Jake." Nathan held his arms out to her, and she laughingly went into them. He flicked his tongue at me.

"All right…all right. That's long enough." I pulled them apart when he held on too long.

"Jake, I'm ready to go." Rene had come back up the stairs. She looked at Nathan and waved. "I thought that was you. It's been a while."

"It has." Nathan's lackluster response didn't invite any more conversation, and Rene didn't offer it.

"How much longer?" She ignored Amara, who stood silently next to me. Tension bounced off her in waves.

"Give me a few. Just go to the car."

"Not going to introduce me?" She sauntered toward us, staring at Amara. "I'm Rene Starr. You might have heard of me."

"Amara." Neither woman attempted to shake hands.

Rene squeezed my arm possessively. "Don't leave me waiting, baby." She strolled back down the stairs.

Nathan kissed Amara's cheek. "Good show again, and see you on Monday." He dapped me off and threw me an *I'm glad I'm not you* look.

Nervously, I started, "Listen, maybe we can celebrate with the crew tomorrow night, or after we meet at my house on Monday."

She lifted her chin and waved a hand dismissively. "You've done a lot already. Sending for my mother is all the celebration I need. We're going to grab a late dinner and then go back to the hotel. If you don't mind, I wanted to show her Hartland tomorrow."

"Sure…sure. Um… I…" I stumbled over my words. "Rene… She's someone…"

Amara held her hand up. "You don't have to explain who she is. You already told me you didn't want to be more than friends. I'm good. Tonight was amazing. Go have fun, and I'll see you on Monday. And if I decide to go home with Mama tomorrow, we can talk by phone or Zoom about what's next."

Hearing her say that she would call or Zoom me struck me like a dagger through the heart. "When will you come back?"

"Maybe Tuesday or Wednesday. I'll text you tomorrow and let you know my plans." She hugged me quickly and disappeared back into the heart of the bar.

I wanted to run after her. *And say what?*

I caught the eye of my mother, who now stood near the stairs, preparing to leave. Her lips curved in a slight smile as she commented, "It's been a night."

"It has, and I'm about to head out. Do you need me to walk you to your car?"

"Your father arranged for me to have a driver. The car is right outside." She hugged me tightly. "Call me, and then you can tell me whether it's Rene or Amara you need to get over. My money is on Amara. I saw that rock on her finger and how you look at her."

I surveyed the surrounding area and warned her, "Talk about it later, Mama."

She raised her brows. "It better not be about Rene. That woman has always been bad news. Can't believe you still messing around with her."

"I'm not. Goodnight, Mama." I hugged her firmly before I heard a lecture again about women like Rene, whom she'd never liked.

"Night, my Jake. Still proud of you." Surprisingly, she started down the stairs without further talk. I knew she had more questions and comments.

I turned back once again and saw Tavion and Sophie laughing while Amara hugged herself, watching them, a phony smile on her face. Seeing Rene with me had fucked up her mood. This was supposed to be a night where she experienced all joy and no pain. Although I knew it was best that we remained friends, it didn't mean it would be easy to not comfort her. I shoved my hands in my pants and headed down the stairs to greet a few more people on the first floor, and then to my car to deal with a woman who'd never deserved my heart.

TWENTY-THREE

Amara

I sensed his concerned gaze on me before he headed down the stairs. If Phillip had been here, the roles would've been reversed, and Jake would've had to watch me leave with him. Maybe he'd invited Rene Starr because he thought Phillip would be in attendance.

Tavion nudged my shoulder and passed me a cocktail. "Welcome to the nasty part of the music world. And I do mean nasty. A world where relationship lines are blurred. Infidelity is the norm, and faithfulness is rare. You keep wearing your heart on your sleeve, Mari, and you're repeatedly asking for heartbreak. Remember that man you have back home, because people like Jake and monogamy don't mix." He nodded toward a woman wearing a sparkly cowboy hat standing near the entrance to the rooftop on this floor. "Teresa Cromwell, a popular country singer and one of Jake's old women, or maybe I should say they slept together. Rene Starr was the only woman he's claimed since I've known him. And one of the many men Rene cheated with while she was with Jake is Teresa's new man, or maybe he's her old man. Who knows?"

"Seriously?" I asked, looking at the handsome man who smiled at Teresa's face. These were the same people who took selfies with me and clapped loudly during my performance.

"Girl, in Nashville, partners switch beds like they switch their linen. Several of Jake's women were here tonight. They were either with their men or knew their place, so they kept their distance." He used his thumb to wipe my imaginary tears. "So, cheer up, and don't let Jake Barnes and his women fuck up your extraordinary night."

I assessed my new friend, who had only concern in his dark eyes. "So Jake has been playing me, pretending to be into me to keep me hooked, making it easier to manipulate me? Be honest. I swear he won't ever hear it from me."

Tavion pulled me toward the dressing room before he replied, "We all love Jake, and he's a damn good manager and just proved he's a hell of a producer. He knows you're hooked on him. Is he using it to his advantage? Probably. Is he playing you? Doubtful. If he's keeping a wall up between you, let him. He knows himself, and you have real potential. You're not built for the dirt that men like him and the women he usually deals with do. Loving him might just bury you."

"I've been looking for you." Mama's voice carried from behind Tavion.

He smiled and hugged me tightly. "You can trust him as your manager and friend. Keep that in mind, and you'll have a bright future with Jake's skills and connections."

"Thank you."

Tavion let me go and waved at my mother on his way back to the floor.

"Everything okay?" Worry lines etched her forehead.

"Yeah, Mama. Just feeling overwhelmed in this moment, you know?"

She nodded and rubbed my back. "Let's go back to your hotel room and talk more. My stuff was already placed in your room courtesy of Jake. He really does think of everything."

Trying to shake my negative mood, I inhaled and exhaled deeply. "He really does."

Mama helped me carry my travel bag and the accessories from my performance back to my hotel room. We'd decided to be low-key, order room service, and veg out in front of the TV. Otherwise I would've ended my great night lonely and feeling sorry for myself with everyone going home with someone. Tavion had introduced me to his boyfriend, who was hanging out tonight. Sophie left to spend time with her family, who'd driven in from Gatlinburg. Jake had Rene. I hadn't realized he'd been instrumental in her career until tonight. I'd done a quick social media search on her during the limo ride back to the hotel.

"You can go out with your new friends if you want. I'm fine in bed watching TV, and we can talk later," Mama offered as we stepped off the elevator and trudged toward my room.

"I might be into performing, but I'm still not a party girl. Besides, I want to lie next to my mommy." I leaned my head on her shoulder before I opened my door. "So glad you're here."

"Me too. I recorded most of it and sent some of the videos to the family. They are so excited."

I moved straight to the king bed and flopped on it. "I'm exhausted."

Mama started putting my things away. She believed in neatness and orderliness. Unfortunately, that good trait hadn't been passed down to me.

"Mama, it's late. We can pack my stuff tomorrow. What do you want to eat? My appetite hasn't come back yet."

She placed her hands on her ample hips. "You were hungry until after you went looking for Jake to see if he wanted to grab dinner with us. You've been quiet ever since. What did he do?"

I threw my arm over my face. "Nothing, Mama. He's just my friend."

She scoffed, "An attractive, wealthy man who seems smitten with you."

"He's respectful of my relationship."

"Are *you*?" She sat down on the side of the bed. "You like him."

"How do you know?" I peeked at her from underneath my arm.

"Your face lights up whenever he speaks to you. Now, you know I didn't like him at first. I thought he was a little too pushy. But after the effort he made to have me here for you once he knew Phillip wouldn't be, I know he's a good man and cares about my daughter."

I moved my arm to my side. "He has been good to me, but we know we should maintain a working relationship if he's going to be my manager. I think we both hope that whatever attraction we have will pass. He knows I want to marry Phillip and wants that for me."

Mama fell back on the bed with me. "Which just makes you want him more, right?"

I groaned. "Yes. It didn't help that Phillip blew me off this weekend, and I did this showcase to prove to him that I was meant to be a performer. He wasn't even here to see my big moment and hasn't yet sent a text or called asking how tonight went."

She replied with certainty, "He'll call."

"I'll fly back with you, and he and I can spend time together. Maybe I'm so caught up with everything here because it's been such fun. It's like the best party every night. I need to go back and remind myself of the life I already have."

"You will not fly back with me and go see that man. He needs to come here. I love Phillip, but he was wrong. You need to see if he's willing to compromise, and that means he needs to come here and see you like I did. He's not going to get how special you are on that stage. I'm still pinching myself that the fierce, uber-talented woman who performed tonight belonged to me." She looked at me. "I'm sorry that I almost stopped you from this. This is your legacy. You are your grandfather's child. You're a beautiful musician and talent, and deserve to be recognized as such. I've never been prouder… and to think I almost missed this because I'd been too stubborn to see who you really were." She sniffed. "You need to stay here the rest of the summer like you planned, and if Phillip can't make an effort to come see you here, then he's not the one for you."

"Mama!" I exclaimed. "I can't believe you're saying that to me. All you've been talking about is my wedding."

"I know, and I still want the two of you to marry. But he was supposed to be here with you on your big night. Celebrating and toasting your success. Singers marry people outside of the music industry all the time. If you're meant to be, you'll work out." She pursed her lips before she warned, "In the meantime, stay away from Jake."

"I don't think that'll be a problem. He has someone, too. I met her tonight, and if he likes someone like her, I know he and I aren't right for one another." I pressed my forehead to my mother's. "But I will take your advice about Phillip. I need to see if he's willing to truly be there for me."

"Sometimes we have to force their hands to do right. I had to do that with your father, who wasn't ready for commitment after we'd been together for a year. I made sure he knew I was dating someone else, and he proposed a month later. And we've been happy ever since. If I hadn't done that, your last name would've been Rodrigues, not Johnson. You know I love me some Hispanic men." We both laughed. She watched baseball with Dad so she could drool over the players without my father knowing.

"Speaking of Daddy," I said, "will he ever come around?"

"With me backing you, he will eventually. I've told him for years to forgive his father, but he refused."

"Did you know my grandfather?"

"Talked to him a few times on the phone, especially when he would call your grandmother and chat with her. Your grandmother's face would light up just like yours does for Jake. Something about musicians is irresistible."

I propped my pillow under my head. "They really are."

"I believe if your grandmother lived longer, your grandparents would've remarried. I liked him and wanted your father to reconcile so your grandfather could get to know you, too. But you know your dad."

"Why didn't you put your foot down with Dad about me getting to know my grandfather?"

"Because he was your father's father and not mine. I had to respect his feelings about Stoney. I wasn't there when their family fell apart. Maybe it'd gotten ugly between his parents, and your father didn't want anything to do with him because he was loyal to your grandmother. As much as Daddy and I talk about everything, his father is still a touchy subject. Even more since he died. He's shut down now that you want to chase this dream that your father believes destroyed his family."

"Did you know that Granddad cheated on Grandma with another woman? The letters I found are love letters between him and the other woman."

Mama sighed. "No. I didn't know, though I suspected. Not too many women divorced their husbands during that time, so if she left and took your father away, it was for more reasons than her hating that he was a musician."

"I don't think she hated it. I believe she didn't understand his longing and desire to play when she wanted him to work a regular job to pay the bills. When he refused, she blamed their problems on his music. And if she knew about the affair, then she definitely blamed music. Her feelings toward her husband's music may have trickled down to Daddy. And I grew up with a father who never valued my natural, God-given talent. Daddy wouldn't even let us play music in the house and never celebrated my talent. For most of my life, the real me was never allowed to shine."

"That part." Mama nodded sadly. "Watching you tonight had to be my proudest moment in a lifetime of proud mama moments. I have so loved being your mother and won't allow your father to continue ignoring who you really are." She shifted on her side to face me. "You will have your parents' support if this is what you truly want."

"I do. Jake gave me the contract and asked me not to sign it until after tonight to be sure this is what I want."

"Do you like the terms he's presenting?"

"I do. I trust Jake, and this isn't because I have feelings for him. I trust that he'll protect me in this industry."

And I did trust him with my career. My heart was another matter.

"Well, as a precaution, get a lawyer to review it and then sign it. Maybe only sign for a couple of years, so if you need to shift to someone else, you can." She tapped my nose. "Just have to get over those feelings for Jake, because something tells me you have a bright future as Mari Johnson, and Phillip better get a damn clue."

Relief and joy that I could continue this journey with support from the woman who'd loved me first spread through my being. "I love you so much, Mama."

"Never as much as I love you."

TWENTY-FOUR

Jake

Nine years ago, I'd observed the allure and potential star power of Rene Kitchens. Scouting for new talent, I frequented bars and clubs throughout the country. At twenty-four, I'd already earned a few million for Barnes Management with the roster of young country artists I'd procured. A young Black man in the trenches searching for country singers was an anomaly and intrigued most of the people I encountered. I didn't think it mattered that I searched for talent in that genre. I'd only followed after my father. Being born in Houston and living in Nashville, I found cowboy hats, rodeos, trail rides, and country music to be as near to my heart as rap and soul music. The lyrics, the music, and the grittiness that described the fluctuations of everyday life appealed. I had an ear, and the artists I signed prospered.

Rene wasn't supposed to be a talent with our agency. She was a rapper who could also truly sing like Lauryn Hill. I'd stumbled upon her while I was visiting my maternal family in Houston. Two cousins invited me to hang out in the third ward, where Black people partied. We entered one small bar and restaurant, and Rene had just stepped on the stage. With the flow and sex appeal of Nicki and a voice like Jazmine Sullivan, she would go far.

That night we kicked it, we fucked, and the next day, against my father's wishes, I offered her a contract with Barnes Management and Rene Kitchens became Rene Starr. She was bad news from the start. A rebel in her family and life, she hated any rules and did whatever she wanted. She had a bipolar diagnosis that I'd mistaken for rebellious freedom and boldness. Caught up in the dollar signs and in the very sexual Rene, I never considered who she was as a person. Never considered that her instability wasn't just a result of growing up impoverished and that money wouldn't cure all ills.

For five years, we had a tumultuous and toxic relationship. We worked hard and partied harder. We had public arguments about each other's infidelities and hot make-up sex. I continued bringing talent to the company as I managed Rene. As her star rose, her drinking and drug use increased exponentially. I ignored it because she'd become the top talent under Barnes. She started missing shows or, worse, arriving inebriated and high, and I had to physically restrain her from going out on stage. Our fights were the worst when her behavior resulted in costly lawsuits. My father had long washed his hands of her and wanted to drop her from our roster.

My ego wouldn't allow me to admit that she needed help outside of me. My ego wouldn't allow me to admit that I'd failed, that I'd made a bad decision signing and getting involved with Rene. That I'd become addicted to her chaos. So I argued with my father to keep her because she still made millions, and her behavior hadn't yet tarnished her in the eyes of her fans. Shortly before her third album's release, she got caught in bed with the husband of Cherry Hill, a pop singer whose rabid fan base far outnumbered Rene's.

Rene was vilified, and that third album that was supposed to send her into the stratosphere tanked. I'd reached my limit with her because of her addiction to drugs, sex, and drama. I broke up with her, and my father was finally able to drop her without further protest from me. She believed she'd lost everything, and in most ways, she had. Three months after the release of her album, she called me repeatedly, and I ignored every call. I wasn't falling back into the vicious cycle we'd had for years. Her highs and lows had impacted me. Her push and pull on loving me hard and then hating me had driven me to other women and substance use. Trying to be there and love her through her insanity impacted my own mind. I started popping pills, drinking more, and having more alcohol binges because I felt truly powerless to help her, because I did love Rene—or the woman I wanted to believe existed under the complicated layers of abuse, trauma, neglect, poverty, and neurochemical imbalance that she'd experienced most of her life.

With all those thoughts, memories, and emotions twirling in my head, I ignored her calls. Then she posted a short note on IG telling the world that she was tired of the endless pain and hurting other people and that no one would ever have to be hurt by her again. I'd be forever glad I saw her post as soon as it went live. My heart pounded as I sped to her home and used my code to get inside. She was in the sparkly dress from her first album cover on her stomach, unconscious, with an empty bottle of liquor and pills littering the bed. I'd already called 911 on my way, and they arrived shortly after. I rode with her in the ambulance, holding her hand, promising myself that I would finally get her the help she'd needed all along.

Now, she rode next to me, and as much as I hated that she still expected me to drop everything for her, I understood. I'd been the only person in her life who'd stuck by her. Her dysfunctional and abusive family hadn't, and with her trust issues, she hadn't made friends.

Rene jabbed my arm. "I watched you tonight with her. On and off the stage. You love her, don't you?"

"I care about her." I hoped she didn't continue this conversation, because I would be honest even if it hurt her. "I've only known her for a little while."

"She's the reason you've been distant and distracted. You don't check up on me like you used to."

"No, she isn't. I've been pulling away on my own. You can't be so dependent on me. You're getting stronger every day, and it's way past time to let people besides me in." I glanced at her. "You're still beautiful, smart, talented, and young. It's been four years since everything went down. Don't you think it's time to stop hiding?"

She quietly admitted, "I'm scared. So scared that the minute I step back into that world, I'll lose my mind again."

"You don't have to go back into music. You still have money. You can invest, go to school, start a business, figure out your other passions."

"My passion is music." She hit the glove compartment with her fist. "How many times do I have to tell you that? I am nothing without my music."

"And how many times do I have to tell you that you are more than your voice?"

"You don't get it, Jake, and you never did." She crossed her arms and pouted.

I glanced out of my side and rear mirror before darting through traffic to pull to the shoulder of the highway.

She yelled, "Are you trying to kill me?"

I turned in my seat and exploded, "No, you're still trying to kill yourself, and you can't see that. How dare you tell me that I don't fucking get it? This is so fucking stupid. I understand you more than you understand yourself. I see you better than you see yourself. You have gifts and talents that can be used in fields other than entertainment. We keep having the same damn argument. This business is too cutthroat for you, and it triggers your mental health and your addictions. It's a reminder of the abusive home you left back in Houston. I firmly believe that if it's not for you, it's not for you. If you can't handle the music business, then it's not for you. Period. Countless therapies and medicines, and nothing has changed because you *want* to be stuck. You want to be stuck and blame everyone else around you for your failures." I jabbed my finger at her. "You want to stay stuck because you believe this is the only way to keep me. Why won't you believe I'll always be there for you even if you soar again? I'm not just here because you failed. I'm here because I want to see you rise."

Her eyes and cheeks glimmered with tears. "And if I rise, will we be together again?"

I chuckled sardonically. "When you rise again, you'll attract so many men that I won't matter. You still want me because I've been there when everyone else abandoned you. Love is much more than loyalty. We trigger each other. We just do. Nothing good will happen with us."

"You really believe that," she stated rather than asked.

"I do. You need to move forward and release the past. Release me." I reached across the short distance between us to squeeze her hand. "If you've ever trusted me, trust what I'm saying now. The world hasn't always been fair to you. Yet it has given you more than most people will ever have. You can focus on the negatives of your life, or the greatness. You can spend the next five years lonely and bitter or vibrant and alive. The choice has always been yours. Regardless, I've done all I can for you, and no matter your threats, I won't allow you to make me feel guilty anymore."

Rene stared at our joined hands before averting her attention out the passenger window as I slowly pulled back onto the highway. We drove in silence for a few miles before she quietly said, "When I stayed at Hartland, I overheard Evelyn on the phone arguing with someone about songs. I couldn't hear everything she said, but it sounded like maybe she didn't give credit to the actual songwriter or that she was being accused of stealing them. I could hear in her voice that she was angry and scared. And we both know Evelyn Hart isn't scared easily. She got off the phone and saw me standing nearby. She threatened to ruin me years ago, though I told her it wasn't my business to tell. I guess she got the last laugh, because I ruined myself."

Evelyn had become one of the most famous performers ever for her singing and songwriting. And if there was a possibility that she'd stolen songs, then she could lose everything. I gritted my teeth and gripped the steering wheel. "Why are you telling me this?"

"Now you know the secret I have over Evelyn's head, I can't use it again. Trying to show you I'm ready to get back to the living." She squeezed my hand tighter. "You know I don't like admitting shit, but since I'm trying to be the better person… Mari is the next big thing. Watching you and her perform awakened something inside me that's been dead for a long time. You inspired me."

"That might be the best thing I've heard all night," I commented with a silent prayer that Rene would continue to fight against her demons and win. I also prayed that whatever Evelyn had done in the past wouldn't haunt her as she embarked on her last tour and headed toward her induction into the Country Music Hall of Fame later this year.

On my drive home, lingering thoughts about Evelyn nagged. If she'd stolen songs, that would change how people saw her. It would change how *I* saw her. Evelyn had always been this superwoman to me, able to leap buildings in a single bound. Able to accomplish the impossible. Able to far exceed anyone's expectations. But if she'd stolen songs, on whose backs did she rise to fame, and at what cost to those writers?

Who was on the other end of that call that day? Who had accused her? Was it the writer or someone who'd found out like Rene had? More importantly, was her manager, my father, involved?

TWENTY-FIVE

Jake

The following morning, I woke to a pounding withdrawal headache on my sofa. I didn't know how much I'd drunk last night. I held my hands in my head. I had to stop this self-destructive behavior when my thoughts troubled me. At least I didn't have a woman in my bed.

I chuckled to myself. Maybe Amara had cured me of my *mannish* ways.

Amara. Amara. Was she already on her way to Atlanta to be with her man and possibly forget about me and her music career? She hadn't mentioned signing the contract again.

I wouldn't pressure her to sign, and I would relinquish any rights to her songs if that was what she wanted. Even if Amara decided against working with me or being in this industry, she'd opened a new path for me, and I would follow it. She had awakened the creator in me and inspired me to pursue a dream I'd once had as a youth to produce music. I was more than a talent scout and manager. I also had musical gifts I hadn't cultivated because my father, like Amara's, hadn't approved. Considering my talk with Rene last night, I also needed to release the past. No more excuses. If I expected Rene to move forward and lay her demons to rest, I had to expect nothing less from myself.

I pushed up from the sofa and had to stand still for a minute to regain my bearings once the room stopped spinning. I stalked to my bar at the back of the room and placed all the bottles of expensive liquor in a couple of boxes I had behind the counter. I would give Nathan or my mother the boxes, since she frequently hosted events. I had to get it together. These last weeks with Amara and the crew had been the most fun I'd ever had. We weren't drinking, using drugs, partying, or sexing. We were having fun because we were blessed to do what we truly loved. We were having fun because the studio had become our safe space to be our most creative and best selves. After a night in the studio, I woke up energized and refreshed, not in pain and grumpy. It was way past time for Rene to rejoin the living, and it was way past time for me, too.

With a clearer head, I took a swim in the pool in my backyard before I showered. I then drove to my office and prepared to review my roster of talent to schedule meetings, then Evelyn called.

"Jake, how are you, darling?"

"I'm good. You must have heard about the show for you to call me this early on a Sunday." I leaned back in my chair.

"I did. Congratulations on discovering another hot new talent. Heard you had an amazing show last night. Would've loved to see you play the fiddle. I thought you stopped back in high school."

"I still dabble. I played the drums, too. Would've loved to have seen you last night," I commented, though I suspected I knew why she didn't come to Amara's show.

"I would've gone to support her, but I didn't want to draw attention away from Mari's night. Those days of upstaging my competition are long gone." She chuckled. "Darling, need you to come to Hartland."

"I'll stop by tomorrow. I need to check on Amara anyway."

"No, today. Be here within an hour." She hung up before I could say anything else.

I called my father. "Miss Evelyn just told me to be at Hartland. What's going on?"

"We'll tell you once you're here."

"You're already there?" The weight of dread replaced the lightness of optimism I'd felt since I decided to give away my alcohol.

"Yes. We need to talk to you. See you soon." He clicked off.

Drumming my fingers against the desk, I racked my brain, trying to determine the cause for the urgency of the meeting. The last time I'd been summoned like this, it was after the story of Rene's affair broke. Did Rene wake up on the wrong side of the bed this morning and decide to threaten Evelyn again? Or, more than likely, Mama had told Dad, or my father saw me with Rene, and they had concerns.

I pulled up next to my father's pristine white Aston Martin as Amara and her mother arrived in my BMW. Had she been called to the meeting too? I stepped out of my car, hurried to open her mother's door, and assisted her out of the vehicle. "Morning…well, afternoon," I corrected myself. It'd just turned noon.

"Thank you, and good afternoon," Mrs. Johnson said once I released her hand. "I didn't know we would see you today."

Amara came around the car with her hair in a bun. "I thought you were going to be resting."

She looked summery in her off-the-shoulder floral dress and sandals. Pretty. Perfect dress for a brunch date. Under other circumstances, in which she was a single woman and not a potential client, that was where we would be headed. Would've loved to spend a sunny day like this with her. Just talking, flirting, and vibing. I tried not to think about the taste of her lips and her skin as she smiled at me.

"Thought so too. Evelyn wants a meeting. Did she call you?" I kept my tone neutral. I didn't want to alarm her in any way.

"No. I'm not important yet." She smiled. "Wanted to show Mama Hartland while she's here, remember?"

"Oh yeah. Go ahead. Feel free to explore. I don't know how long this meeting will take, but hopefully, I'll see you before you leave. What time is your flight?"

"Mama has a late one, and I'm not going anywhere. I'll just work on music before I come to your house tomorrow." She glanced at her mother and quickly amended, "To see you and Nathan to talk about my grandfather."

I tried to bite my lip to hide the grin at the fact that Amara wasn't going home. "Sounds like a plan."

Mrs. Johnson shook her head. "Next time, try harder not to smile." She beckoned me in for a hug. "In case I don't see you again. Thank you again for everything."

I hugged her warmly. Whether Mrs. Johnson liked me or not, I liked her and her natural charm. "Anything for Mari."

She stepped back. "Amara, give me a second with Jake. Walk to your cottage. I'll catch up."

"*Mama,*" Amara said.

"Go," Mrs. Johnson commanded, and we both watched Amara reluctantly walk away.

"Whatever you have to say, I've already said it to myself," I started.

"Okay. Since you have all the answers, what do I have to say?"

"You want me to stay away from your daughter because she already has a man, which I plan to do. You want me to care for and watch over her because you believe you can trust me. Well, you trust me with one eye open," I teased.

She pursed her lips, though her eyes twinkled. "What else?"

I frowned. "I don't know. I thought I covered everything."

"Make sure you keep me posted. I know my daughter. She says she's glad I'm on board with her new career, but she's a lot like her daddy. She'll keep things close to her vest and not tell me. I don't want to miss out on anything, because if you hadn't called me, I would've missed my baby's special night. You think you can do that?"

"With pleasure." I pretended to zip my mouth. "And I won't tell her what we discussed."

"Me either, and it will kill her to know what we're talking about." Mrs. Johnson laughed, and I could see Amara in her pretty face. "I better let you go to your meeting. Hope I get to meet Evelyn Hart while I'm here."

"I'll do my best to make that happen," I promised, hoping I could make good on my word. I had no idea what awaited me on the other side of those glass double doors.

I marched inside and headed for her office. We always held meetings there. It was Evelyn's way of separating her personal life from business. I didn't bother to knock, and entered the large yet cozy room decorated in shades of pink and red. My father sat in one of the red Victorian chairs before Evelyn's cherrywood desk. I chose the seat next to him. "Why am I here on a Sunday?"

From behind her desk, Evelyn peered at the small security monitor on her desk. "Is that Amara's mother outside?"

"Yeah, she wanted to see where her daughter is staying. She also wanted to meet you before she left."

Evelyn clasped her trembling hands on her desk. "I don't know if that's a good idea, because Amara can't stay here."

"What?" I scooted to the edge of my seat. "Why can't she stay?"

Evelyn focused on her hands as she carefully stated, "She's your artist. Not William's. She should be in the city with you."

"We just sat right out there on the porch, and I told you why she's here, and you welcomed her. Sang with her in the studio and everything." I then turned on my father, who'd been uncharacteristically quiet. "You've wanted her out of here since I told you my intention. Last night, she was amazing, and you still haven't complimented her or said one word to me about her. Is this your way of getting back at me, since I want my own company?"

"No. We don't want a repeat of Rene. We allowed Rene to stay here because it's what you wanted. You wanted to be solely responsible for her career, so I allowed it, and when things went sour, I spent millions trying to pay off her lawsuits and canceled shows."

"Millions I brought to Barnes. You keep forgetting my eyes and ears for talent brought you millions. I lost big, too."

"You broke up with her. Years later, she's still harassing Evelyn to get back at you."

"Harassing or scaring you?" I retorted, and studied Evelyn's expression. She was uncharacteristically nervous and refused to meet my gaze, so I pushed forward. "Rene overheard you arguing with someone about songs that you didn't write. I won't ask if it's true because I don't want to know."

My father replied, "No one has stolen songs. Rene overheard things wrong and has been dangling that over Evelyn's head."

Evelyn narrowed her eyes at me. "Why don't you want to ask me if it's true?"

I hunched forward and clasped my hands together on the desk. "I'm not blind to the fact that to get ahead when you're dealing with an old boys club, sometimes you have to do things that aren't always right just to get a seat at the table. So if you did something, I would rather not know."

"I didn't do what she says I did," Evelyn insisted. "I need you to know that. I'm not scared because I didn't do anything wrong."

"Then why worry and kick Mari out?" I asked.

"We're in a cancel culture, and if there's a hint of scandal, people are ready to judge and persecute. I have too much at stake to tarnish my image in any way," Evelyn explained.

"I handled Rene. She's not going to call you anymore, and she was never going to reveal anything. Where she's from, they don't snitch anyway." I moved my chair closer to her desk. "Why don't you want Amara here? You spent time with her in the studio. You know she's nothing like Rene. She's a middle school teacher from Atlanta with good parents and a fiancé waiting for her back home. She's a good woman who wants to follow her grandfather's legacy. A musician like yourself. He's a man she had never had a chance to know, and this is her way of feeling close to him. A man I grew fond of over the years because Dad gave me money twice a year to give him. A man who still died alone, lonely, and broke."

Evelyn's eyes widened, and she looked at my father as she placed her trembling hands under the desk.

My father cleared his throat. "It's not about her. It's about you. Obviously, you're personally involved with Amara, and I can't take that risk again. If you want to continue to work with her, do it. Just not here."

"I'm not that man anymore."

My father scoffed. "Two months ago, Tavion called me to come get you at your studio because you were too drunk to drive, and he was afraid you would insist. I can only imagine how often you drink and God knows what else when no one's around."

I closed my eyes wearily. "She loves it here. She's crazy about Jess and Craig. She was geeked because Evelyn Hart took the time to use her guitar and taught her lessons." I opened my eyes and implored Evelyn, "If I tell Amara she can't stay because of my mistakes, it'll crush her."

"You don't have to tell her why. Just say you want her closer to you. That the commute is too far for you." My father crossed his legs and planted his hands on the arms of his chair.

"I don't ever want to lie to her. I'm trying to be different, and if I lie, then I'm the same person you're afraid will fuck up again." I shook my head. "If you don't trust me anymore, consider this my last day."

"I knew you would threaten to leave because you didn't get your way," my father blustered.

"If that's what you think of me, even after all these years of working side by side, that I'm a fucking spoiled brat, then I should've left a long time ago. I made one mistake, and yes, it was a major one. I've spent the last four years making up for it, and I'm done fucking proving myself." I rose from my chair. "Ms. Evelyn, if you'll excuse me for my language."

"She can stay for the rest of the week," Evelyn said quickly. "She's a beautiful, talented woman with a bright future, and I don't want to hurt her. Stay with her, show her Hartland so she can carry it with her, and *then* move her to the city closer to you. Then you won't have to lie. You've wanted to be on your own and know how to do it. I support your decision."

"I don't want you to quit," my father protested. "I…just…wanted you to be aware…"

I shook my head firmly. "I haven't been happy for a long time, and I refuse to stay stuck. Starting my own company is the best way to move on. This may not be what we wanted, but it's what we need. We can figure out the best way to handle business matters next week with cooler heads, okay?" I didn't want to argue with my father anymore because I did love and respect him.

He slowly nodded. His blue eyes brimmed with sadness.

"In the meantime, Ms. Evelyn, I would appreciate it if you would be so kind as to meet Amara's mother."

She nodded and rose from her throne. I held my arm to her, and she grasped it. Then we went to meet and greet Mrs. Johnson.

TWENTY-SIX

Amara

I hadn't considered myself a morning person until Hartland. Something about the crisp air, even in the summer, invigorated me. Each morning was a fresh start. I could erase what I did the day before and begin anew. Now that I'd been jogging every morning until this past weekend, I'd realized I also enjoyed being one with nature. Feeling the burn in my chest and my shins and calves reminded me that I was still alive.

Jake would be proud once I told him I'd woken early to jog this morning. I still planned to drink smoothies for breakfast while I was here. If I could find someplace in Atlanta that offered smoothies as refreshing and good as Ms. Jess's, or if I could re-create her recipe, that would be my breakfast moving forward.

Atlanta. My home. I'd been in Nashville for less than a month, and it felt like I could live there. Although Jake's father had sent over my contract again via email and increased my advance to triple one year of my teacher's salary, whether or not I would return to teach in the fall still depended on so many factors. What was the estimated pay for my first album if we went with a traditional record company or decided to go indie? What would be required regarding costs and travel to promote my record?

Jake and I had so much to discuss. How would my career look if I wanted to remain in Atlanta to teach, because I did love my students, and work with him in Nashville? Then I had to make decisions with Phillip without disrupting my life with him. When I spoke with him again last night, he'd reaffirmed his commitment to me and made plans to visit me next weekend.

Mama left last night with promises to visit again before the summer ended. She wanted to see more of Nashville. I missed her already and couldn't wait for her to visit a second time. I also couldn't wait to catch the vibe in the city. Maybe after the meeting tonight, I would see if I could convince Nathan and Jake to accompany me to visit downtown, or I would explore on my own. Either way, I was excited to discover Music City. With the showcase behind me, I could breathe and focus on creating and enhancing the music I'd already made. I could travel to Memphis, breathe my grandfather's morning air, and bring his songs to life.

Although his letters told of a forbidden love, the journal relayed his work. The lyrics and how he envisioned songs. Spending hours developing my ideas, poems, and thoughts into songs drew me closer to my grandfather. I held the journal closer to my heart than the letters.

Once I finished running, I wanted to take a shot at playing the music he'd created. He was primarily a horn and piano man. From what I could decipher, he only played the guitar when he dabbled in country music. I often played the country song we'd found while I prepared for the day in the morning and before I crashed. This week would be about my grandfather.

I smiled and increased my speed, feeling grateful for so many things. Most of all, for being alive and well.

After re-checking my GPS, I made sure that this was the correct address. The grand townhome right outside downtown was simply gorgeous. Three stories of glass with a touch of red brick would be the simplest way to describe it.

I couldn't decipher the face of this home. Maybe neutral and unsure. The mood would shift from happy to sad, depending on how the sun fell.

I pulled into the driveway as the sun dipped, making way for the rising moon. Why would Jake settle down? His looks alone made him a catch. Add his car and this home to the package, and he could have his pick of women who would put up with his ways. He didn't usually carry the airs of a man of wealth. This luxurious house spoke differently.

I pressed the doorbell and waited patiently. I called Jake, but there was still no response. When he didn't answer the door after I rang again, I stepped back, trying to see if there was a way to go around and knock on the back door. I peered through the window, and I could see that on his TV screen was a basketball game. He was here.

"Sorry about that. I lost track of time." He stood at the door wiping off his bare chest with a towel, wearing only jogging shorts. "I needed a swim. Didn't expect you for another half-hour."

I averted my gaze from the gold rope chain that draped over the tattoos on his muscular chest. "I can come back. Thought would take me longer to get here."

"Why?" He opened the door wider. "Feel free to walk around while I take a quick shower. Dip your feet in the pool or whatever. There are some snacks in the kitchen. I don't have any alcohol, but I can order something if you want." He followed me as I slowly walked through his artfully decorated foyer and living area. "Nathan will probably be late, as always."

"Okay."

He started up the stairway and looked back at me. "You good?"

"Yeah. Go ahead." I needed him to leave before I started drooling. The man was fine as fuck. Much finer than I'd imagined. His clothes didn't do justice to his body. I had to clear my mind of his virility. So I pulled out my cell and focused on a picture of me and Phillip. When my thoughts drifted back to Jake, I started jumping jacks as I walked around his home until I worried that he would see me through some hidden camera looking positively foolish.

I couldn't come back to his home after today. I would always suggest that we meet at Hartland or the studio. Here, all alone with him, felt too personal. He even seemed different, completely relaxed and comfortable. Walking around his home while he showered felt intimate. Almost more intimate than the kiss we'd shared. That damn kiss.

Okay. Focus on my music. Believe that a home like this is in my future if I keep my eyes on the prize and not the man who could help me get the prize.

I walked past the living area, which opened to the turquoise-blue pool that beckoned me to join it. I ignored the allure of dipping my feet in the water to remain focused on the point of my being here. This wasn't a leisure visit.

I stopped in my tracks when I strolled into the next room. "What the hell?" The room contained every instrument imaginable. Some were attached to the wall. Others were placed on stands. Two grand pianos graced the corners of the glass wall, giving a view of his backyard's corner. I was like a kid in a toy store, wanting to try every single instrument, and I touched the strings of a golden harp.

"Mari?" he called from somewhere near.

I shouted, "I'm in your music room and may never leave."

Jake soon appeared at the door, wearing a Henley shirt and joggers. He chuckled when he saw me with a flute in one hand while I sat at the piano. "Not sure where to start?"

"Not at all. You collect instruments?"

"Yeah, but I also wanted to teach myself how to play them all."

I turned my legs back across the bench and stood. "That's my dream too."

"You're probably closer to that dream than I am, since you've been teaching music for years."

"Maybe. This is amazing. I could live in this room."

"You can always stop by anytime while you're in town. Thinking I need to move you closer to me anyway. Once you sign the contract, you will be the first talent on my new management team. Regarding the contract, it would be with me and not Barnes. I might not have made that clear."

I put the flute back on the black velvet cloth on a small table and moved to the French horn perched on a stand. "I'm going to be your very first client? I thought I would be signing with you, but under Barnes."

"You'll be under my management. No team yet. I have the revised contract upstairs, and you can sign it tonight or get a lawyer to review it before you sign. Regardless, I need it signed before the end of the week." He slowly walked around the room, circling me like the shark I'd envisioned him to be. He trailed his hand across the sax and the trumpet on their respective stands while he regarded me without a hint of warmth. Something bothered Jake.

"Do you think I'll change my mind?" I was trying to understand why his playful mood had shifted to this indescribable one once he brought up the contract.

He shrugged. "Until you sign, it's always a possibility. The other night was amazing, but you still may have reservations about signing with me. Other people better suited for you may have approached you."

I moved in his direction, and he stopped walking. "You say that like you already know."

His eyes slowly rose to meet mine. "Were you approached by Evelyn or my father?"

"Evelyn never mentioned anything business. She met my mother and showed us around Hartland. That was it." I shrugged, and then my chest deflated. "Damn. Your father sent an email. I thought it came from you until this very moment. I haven't signed anything." I took another step closer. "I'm not trying to start trouble between you and your family."

"You're not." His eyes flashed fire. "I'm going to find you a place near my studio, so I don't have to commute. Are you ready to leave Hartland?"

I wasn't, yet I sensed that it was time. "Kind of feels like home already. But I'm open to staying somewhere else."

The edges of his lips curved as he picked up a trumpet and blew a few notes of Louis Armstrong's "What a Wonderful World" before he spoke again. "All right. Let's spend a couple more days at Hartland so you can enjoy the whole property. Evelyn and Jess will probably invite you to dinner. We can ride horses, swim, and chill. I'll stay out there, too. We can invite Sophie and Tavion if that makes you more comfortable."

"I want to focus on my grandfather this week, so I'd rather wait to make plans after speaking with Nathan. In case I need to go to Memphis."

"We," he corrected me as he placed the trumpet back on its stand. "If we need to go, then we'll go."

Jake said it with finality, and even if I wanted to go alone, he probably wouldn't allow it. I didn't know what was happening between him and his father and why his dad had sent me a contract behind Jake's back. All I knew for certain was that the man in front of me had faith in me and, so far, had kept his word.

He picked up a shiny brass trombone and pushed the slide until it grazed my breast.

Ignoring the spark of desire he'd just ignited, I grabbed the end of the slide. "If the only thing you changed on the original contract you sent me is your name, then I'm ready to sign."

Jake tugged the slide until I was in his embrace and wrapped his arms around me. "Thank you for trusting me."

I tapped his chest, backed up, and held my hand out. "From now on, we shake hands. All of this is way too tempting when we both have someone. You knew what you were doing opening the door with no shirt, tatted chest all glistening."

His head fell back in laughter before he shook my hand. "Done. I'll get the contract while you open the door for Nathan. He texted a short while ago. He's five minutes away. He's probably parking now."

I found my way back to the front door and opened it as Nathan parked a dusty 4Runner. I walked toward him as I teased, "Finally, someone drives a regular car like me."

Nathan chuckled as he climbed out of his SUV. "I hear you. Being around Jake makes you feel like you need to do more with your life. Have you questioning every choice you made that he ended up living like this and you didn't."

"Right? We're all around the same age, and I thought I was good with my Maxima and nice two-bedroom apartment. Then I meet Jake, who walks around like money is a given."

Nathan hugged me when we neared each other. "He can't help it. He's always had money. Even before his mother married his stepfather, she did pretty well for a single mother."

"How was he when you first met him?" We started toward the townhouse.

Nathan chuckled. "We were in New Orleans for college. What do you think?"

I nudged his shoulder. "That bad?"

"Worse."

"Maybe I don't want to know."

He raised one brow. "You don't."

We approached the front door, and I asked, "Did you find anything?"

"I've been digging around trying to see exactly who your grandfather wrote for. From what I can tell, he's received credit for some of the songs. Probably not all. In the only letter that the mystery woman wrote, it was like she felt horrible that Stoney's hard work and dedication hadn't resulted in a reward. He didn't have any vices, from my research. Lived like a monk once he was divorced. If he had other women, it wasn't serious. He wasn't a gambler, nor a drug user, or an alcoholic, and yet he lived like he didn't spend his money wisely."

"What about the songs in the journal? Are those published?"

Nathan shook his head as we crossed the threshold into Jake's home. "Is there anything else I need to know that you've thought of?"

"There's a song of my grandfather's that reminds me of another song, but I can't quite figure it out."

Jake jogged down the stairs holding a black iPad. "Must be the part of the song I keep replaying." He went to Nathan, and they dapped and hugged. "Y'all hungry?"

"Yep," I answered for Nathan.

Jake headed to his kitchen. "I'll cook while we talk."

"We can just order," I offered.

"You said you want steak, right?"

"Yes."

"Then I'll make you steak. Mine are better than most restaurants."

I whispered to Nathan, "He cooks too?"

Nathan twisted his lips and nodded.

Whew… Whoever landed Jake would be one lucky woman.

TWENTY-SEVEN

Jake

We replayed Stoney's song for the fifth time, trying to catch the rhythm. "I hate that this song is familiar, but what it reminds me of keeps escaping," I said. We were in the kitchen finishing eating around my island.

Amara pushed her almost-empty plate away. "That had to be the best steak I've ever had. Like, seriously. I want to take some back with me to the cottage."

"I have plenty. I'll wrap you some to go," I offered.

Nathan chimed in, "Add me. I need lunch for tomorrow."

As I stood, Amara hopped up. "Let me wrap the plates. That's the least I can do after that delicious meal."

I sat back down. "The foil or Saran Wrap is in the drawer under the island."

Nathan held a magnifying glass over the letters and opened the journal. "Is the song playing one of the songs in this book?"

"No, I don't think so," she said. "Jake has a better ear for lyrics. Let him see the journal. I could be wrong."

Nathan passed me the magnifying glass.

"I can see." I shook my head.

"Dude, I'm not blind. The paper is old, and sometimes ink or pencil fades. We may pick up on something that can't be seen with the naked eye. Take the glass."

I snatched the magnifier and used the glass to study each page.

Amara asked, "You visited my grandfather for years. Why, again?"

"My father met Stoney years ago at some blues festival in Memphis, and they would see each other from time to time. He connected my father with a few artists that he signed. Stoney refused to be paid or sign any contract because he considered my father a friend. For years, he didn't take any money. When my father discovered Stoney was struggling, he asked me to start visiting him. I would get advice about music and pay him for the advice, so Stoney wouldn't feel like a charity case. I looked forward to our visits and enjoyed talking to him. He had a dry sense of humor, and man, did he know music. You could ask him about any genre, and he had an answer."

I looked at Amara, who stood across from me, preparing to-go plates. Her expression was open and curious despite the regret in her eyes.

"If he'd come to your showcase, he would've sat in the front row with the biggest gap-toothed smile, proud of you. I used to be so angry at you and your family. Used to judge you and wonder why you couldn't see how great he was. Those pictures of you and your father in his house were centered on his wall because you were his center. He rarely talked about you and your father, probably because it pained him. But every day he woke up and sat in his chair, he needed to see your face. So whatever Nathan finds or whenever you want to go to Memphis, I want to be there because I want him to win, whatever that means."

"Through you, I feel like I know the good of him and not just the bad." Her lips curved slightly as we stared at one another.

Nathan sniffed. "Look, I didn't come here to cry. Just answer my questions. I'm in reporter mode. We can reminisce later."

I chuckled at my old friend. "All right. All right."

"Jake, can you ask your father if he remembers exactly the artists he referred to Stoney, unless you know their names already?"

"No. That was before I started working for William."

"Did your father ever call him or visit? Or had you become the only connect?"

"Sounds like I'm a dealer or some shit. I don't know if they contacted each other at all. Stoney would always ask about my father but never hinted or suggested that it'd been long since they spoke." I wryly added, "Guess I'll add that to the list of things I need to ask."

Amara shot me a worried glance, and I shrugged.

"What did you and he talk about? Did he ever mention anyone he wrote for?" Nathan asked.

I continued to scour the journal for anything. "He didn't really say who but talked about performing with the greats like B. B. and Bobby Blue Bland. He met Elvis a couple of times."

"Wow. What if he wrote songs for Elvis?" Amara said as she cleaned the dishes as if she lived here. Normally, I would've stopped her and told her I would do it or get my cleaning service to come in. But she moved easily around my kitchen like it was ours, and I didn't want to break the fantasy.

Nathan replied, "Back then, songs were stolen from us, so anything is possible." He unfolded one of the letters. "Can you read it to me? Sometimes hearing content helps me decipher it better."

I observed Amara carefully as she slowly took the letter from Nathan and stared at it as it trembled in her hand.

"I can read it." The protective side of me interfered with my gut, which said she needed to do this herself.

She closed her free hand and said with resolve, "I got it. I need to face whatever we're going to find out about my grandfather. He had time to get rid of his letters if he wanted to. Maybe he wanted someone to find them and do what we're doing right now. Stoney wanted the truth to be known even if it made him appear uncaring about his wife and son."

I eased back in my chair as she began to read,

"Dear Heart,

I have amazing news. I played two of the songs you wrote, and my label loved them. They want them to go on my album. Can you believe they are finally talking about a deal after all this time? If it wasn't for you, I wouldn't have this opportunity. I can't thank you enough. I wish you would travel more to see me. I know you worry about your family, and I worry about mine. But can't you see we are meant to be? We can rip this music world into pieces with your songwriting skills and my voice. We can be this team in work and in love. Oh, God, I pray you will hear me.

It's been two months since I've seen you, and I keep hoping my feelings will fade. My love only grows, and with this confirmation from the universe that they want to use your songs, you have to consider that this is our sign. This is our time. Don't we deserve to be happy? Haven't we worked hard and sacrificed enough? A love like ours can survive and withstand anything.

Yesterday, I drove past the Ryman and thought maybe, just maybe, it was within my reach because of you…because of us. You are making my dreams come true in music, and if we are together, then my dreams will come true in love. No man has ever made me feel like you, and no man ever will.

Love you always.
Your Lovely Heart"

Years of knowing the history of country music triggered a thought, and I snapped my fingers. "What if his secret love was Linda Martell? She would've been a little older. She was the first Black woman to perform at the Grand Ole Opry, which was still at the Ryman around that time, if I'm not mistaken."

Nathan pointed at me. "Grand Ole Opry House was there until 1974, which tracks if she thought it was within her reach. She already had children and may or may not have been divorced then. Two Black people trying to break into a genre that, until this point, except for Charley Pride killing the country and pop charts, was damn near impossible."

Amara frowned. "I never heard of Linda Martell."

"Most people outside Nashville have never heard of her," I replied. "Sorry I haven't told you about her. Figured we could do a deep dive into the history of Black folks in country music while you were here. Planned to do that first until we started focusing on your showcase."

Amara pulled out her phone and quickly found images of Linda on Wikipedia. She held a guitar in her hand with a black cowboy hat cocked on her head. If the page was correct, she was still a pretty woman and currently lived in South Carolina. Amara looked at me. "I need to hear her songs."

"We can play them later tonight. Think she'll be a big inspiration, especially if she knew your grandfather." I started rubbing my hands together, feeling victorious that we were slowly solving the puzzle of Stoney Johnson. "Do we have enough information to ask if she knew Stoney?"

Nathan leaned back. "I don't know if we want to approach her about a forbidden love, especially if she didn't give him credit for her songs. I can do a deep dive into her works and see if his name pops up. Do we want to accuse a legend of possibly stealing a song when she's already been through a lot in the business? And if they were a couple, maybe he would have given her permission, and when they ended things, he might have changed his mind. Breakups can be brutal."

I whistled. "Crazy brutal, especially if Stoney ended things, and it looks like he may have, since this reads as if she was trying to convince him to be with her."

"Still, I don't want to accuse her of anything. I can only imagine the racism…"

"And sexism," Amara added.

"…and sexism she experienced. It was the 1970s in the South, right after the Civil Rights Movement. Crazy remarkable that Linda or Charley or any singer or musician who wasn't white and male would dare to sing country." Nathan looked at Amara, who now had an iPad on the island. "Which brings up my next point—what do you want to do with the information I find? Before, you told me you just wanted to know more about Stoney. Knowing that this story is entwined in country music, the path you're on now, there's so much you can do with this information."

"What do you think?" Amara asked me.

"Think you should let Nathan write you and Stoney's journey in music because it will be an ever-winding road. Time has only moved the needle a little bit on country music executives' acceptance of us in this industry. I can pull some strings but will have an uphill battle without Evelyn or my father's backing—a battle I'm more than willing and able to win, because your talent is undeniable. With the facts of Stoney's life and his continued legacy through you, we could potentially have a *New York Times* Bestseller and a top country album if we release simultaneously. An album we can finish if you're done signing," I said, looking pointedly at the iPad she'd just closed.

Amara picked up the tablet and passed it to me. "It's signed. I want Nathan to take a pic of us, as a witness to my being the first artist to sign with Jake's new talent agency."

Nathan grinned as she gave him her cell. "Man, that's awesome. It's about time."

Elated that I finally had her legal permission to move forward, I wanted to grab her up in the biggest hug and kiss her. Instead, we respectfully stood beside each other while I held up the screen. "I was just waiting for someone like you who inspired me enough to take the plunge."

Amara blushed. "Take the pic, Nathan."

"Yeah, Nathan, take the pic. She hates getting mushy." I looped my arm around her shoulders and drew her closer.

As soon as he snapped, her phone rang with a video call. Nathan frowned. "It's your man."

She looked sheepishly at me and slipped from under my arm. "I need to answer it."

My pulse quickened, though I pretended otherwise. "Take it. We need to get used to each other anyway."

Amara nodded and clicked on. She smiled. "Hey."

"Hey. Checking on you. You usually call before now." His diction hinted he was an educated man—much like mine did, depending on the situation.

"I was going to call you on my way back to the cottage. I'm meeting with Jake, my manager, and Nathan, the journalist, tracking down information on my grandfather." She turned the camera around to Nathan first. "Nathan, this is Phillip, my fiancé."

He nodded with a smile. "Hey. Congrats on your engagement. She's cool people."

"Thanks, and she is."

I tensed when she turned the phone to me. Phillip was clean-shaven and thicker than I'd thought he would be. He appeared to be a solid guy still wearing a shirt and tie from a day at the office. "This is Jake. I'll be working with him the most, since I officially just signed a contract."

Since the phone faced me, I saw the frown he quickly hid to greet me politely. "I heard she did her thing the other night."

"She did. Hate you missed it. Told her that had you seen it, you would've proposed to her all over again," I improvised.

With cold eyes, Phillip lightly chuckled and boasted, "I can't wait for the private show when I see her this weekend."

Amara snatched the phone back. "*Phillip.*" She started walking away and muted the phone to tell us, "I won't take long."

Once she left the room, Nathan looked at me with raised brows. "He is going to be trouble."

"Her trouble; not mine." I slunk back in my chair.

"Okay… Let's see how long her trouble stays separate from you."

"Are you saying I shouldn't have signed her?"

He shook his head vehemently. "Definitely not saying that. She's a gold mine. I just think you have to back off because she's engaged. That man ain't stupid. He just marked his territory. You can't keep openly swooning over her while you swear to everyone else she's just your client. For God's sake, you're making plans to travel out of town with her."

"It's for her grandfather, and I figured you would come too."

"Bullshit. You only half know I'm here when that woman is around. You have to treat her like you do everyone else. It's the only way it's going to work." Nathan looked over his shoulder before he whispered, "She's halfway in love with you and this lifestyle. What do you think is going to happen if you continue to treat her as special instead of as your client?"

I leaned toward him. "I swear to you, I'm trying to keep my distance. But it's not natural to fight what feels right."

"Then fight for her. She's not married yet. But this passive-aggressive game you're playing is draining, and you'll end up hating each other. It's all or nothing, my friend. Pick a side and stick to it."

"I wish my feelings were the only thing I was fighting." I ran my hand down my face in frustration. "I just found out my father tried to poach her from me."

"What? What's happening between you and your father?"

"I have no fucking clue. He's an astute businessman and will do whatever it takes to seal the deal. I just never expected that he would go behind my back. He emailed her a contract last night. It's why I decided to finally start my own. He said he didn't trust me to work with Mari alone because he could tell we were involved and didn't want another Rene."

"Rene had issues long before she got with you. Amara is as stable as they come. She's a middle school teacher from Atlanta. You don't get more stable than that. Those women are nothing alike, and you're different now."

I thumped the table with my fist. "Why can't my father see that? He's afraid that if Amara somehow gets pissed with me, she'll ruin Barnes Management or do like Rene and threaten Evelyn with a conversation she overheard a few years back. It sounded like Evelyn may have stolen songs or not been given credit that was due to a writer. Even had Evelyn agreeing that Amara shouldn't stay at Hartland if I'm going to be the only one working with her."

Nathan hit the back of his hand with his other hand. "You do know how to use a cell, right? Why am I just finding out you knew what Rene held over Evelyn's head?"

I looked past his shoulders for Amara. "Shh… Your voice carries. I'm telling you now."

Nathan sat back on the cushioned leather barstool. "Too many bits of information at once. Yet taken together, they mean something."

Through the pause in our conversation, I could hear Amara's raised voice. We both grew quiet. I tried to make out the words. Nathan was closer to her.

I asked, "What are they arguing about?"

He waved his arms like a wild man to shut me up, then narrowed his eyes and listened to her faint voice for a minute. "Uh oh. He's mad about the contract. Guess she signed it without his permission, and he's pissed. She's not backing down, either." His eyes were lit with mirth. "I need to hang out with you more often. You have a regular soap opera happening."

I whispered, "You think they'll break up?"

"Wouldn't *that* make your life easier."

"Only if she wants it. Otherwise, I'm dealing with a depressed and heartbroken singer."

"That might work in country." Nathan snickered.

"True." We bumped fists right as Amara walked back in with a flushed face.

I stood. "You okay?"

"Think I need to head back to the cottage." She looked at Nathan. "Sorry if I wasted your time tonight. Can I call you and finish going over everything or something?"

"You didn't waste my time at all. I forgot that Jake actually talked to the man over the years. So I'm about to quiz him until we have more answers."

I picked up her wrapped plate to bring back to the cottage. "Let me walk you to your car. I'll be back in a second, Nathan."

"Bye, Amara. Okay, Jake. I'll be waiting." Nathan tilted his head and quirked a brow at me.

I opened her door when we got to the car. "I can tell you're upset. Are you all right?"

"I will be. Growing pains of a relationship." She sighed more in annoyance than worry or hurt.

"Say less. I'll call you in the morning about plans for the week. Just get back safe. I'll tell Craig to look for you and text me when you get inside."

"I will." She looked up at me and then glanced at my lips. The hot kiss we'd shared permeated my mind.

"Get in the car, Mari," I growled.

"Yep," Amara agreed, and hopped in. I watched her until I couldn't see her taillights.

I turned around to head back inside, and Nathan's words hit. *Too many bits of information at once. Yet taken together, they mean something.*

I faltered in my steps as the pieces suddenly formed into the truth. A truth that placed me between a rock and a hard place. A truth that could destroy the people I loved.

TWENTY-EIGHT

Amara

Jake watched me until I turned off his street, and I wondered for the umpteenth time since I'd met him why he'd come into my life like he was meant to be there. Four months after I agreed to marry another man. A man who I'd loved and still loved. Phillip and I were simple and flowed. Now, we stayed at odds. Maybe Jake appealed more because he'd been the easy that Phillip and I once were. Or he just appealed. Period.

Phillip demanded that I leave Jake's home and call him when I did. He probably wanted to yell more at me for not telling him I planned to sign with Jake. He didn't understand why I had to sign it before he arrived in town for the weekend. I reminded him that I'd sent him the first contract the day I received it and asked him to review it and give me his opinion. I'd asked him about it more than once, and he kept telling me he would look into it eventually.

My phone rang again, and I hit the button in the car. "I'm not there anymore, before you say another word."

"I think you should fly home tomorrow, and I'll fly back with you to Nashville this weekend if you still want me to."

"Of course I still want you to come here. Why do all that traveling when you plan to be here in a few days?"

"You need to remember what you're leaving behind. You have a life here with me. It's not just the music. It's the whole scene. You don't hang out with men. Never had a male friend, and you don't go out in public wearing a bra showing the public what's mine. I don't fucking like how close you and your manager are. Everything you're doing right now is destroying us. Come home, and let's talk."

"Maybe if you'd come to my show like you promised, you wouldn't feel so threatened by this whole scene. I have made friends with people here. Those two men are helping me with Stoney. We aren't just wilding out." I stopped at a red light on Broadway and sank back into my seat. "I need you to see the life that I'm creating. I am having fun and want you to be here with me. I can arrange to be based out of Atlanta and maybe travel to Nashville once a month or every other month. Maybe more or maybe less. This can work. Mama wasn't a believer until she saw me perform."

"Baby, I've seen your video from Saturday night. You can sing, and you can play the hell out of your guitar. That still doesn't mean you should devote your life to it now."

I yelled in frustration, "I can't keep going in circles with you! You dismiss what I want to do like it's a damn hobby. I keep trying to compromise, and you haven't compromised beyond giving me permission to stay the whole summer. You only agreed to that because you stood me up for a show I did for you."

A horn blared behind me, startling me. *Shit.* I hadn't realized the light had changed. I couldn't fight with him and drive on unfamiliar roads, so I searched for a place to park while I argued with Phillip.

"I left Jake's house as you demanded because I respect your wishes. I even apologized to you because I shouldn't be at another man's home and won't do that again. Any further meetings will be at the studio or at an office." He didn't respond as I focused long enough to park in front of a bar. "Hello? Are you still there?"

"Yeah," he grunted. "Come home, Amara."

I inhaled deeply then slowly exhaled. "I'm not coming to Atlanta until after you visit here. It's your turn to show me that I'm a priority. Come here like you promised, and then we can talk. This arguing on the phone isn't helping."

He hung up, and I stared at my console in disbelief. I picked up my cell and called his number, but before I pressed the phone symbol, reason reared its calm head. Phillip may not answer, which would only anger me more, and if he did answer, it would only involve more arguing. So I exited the car and blew off steam by walking.

Peace settled over me as I wandered down Music Row. The melodic sounds and the busy chatter engendered a feeling of warmth and belonging. My anger drifted into the surprisingly cool night air. Maybe there was a small efficiency or loft within walking distance from here that could be my place for the remainder of my time in Nashville. I wish I had my guitar or notebook as words and thoughts crowded my mind, hoping for their own space. This street of bars, restaurants, and clubs inspired me to create.

A woman's deep, soulful voice caught my attention, and I strolled into the open door of a relatively calm bar. People sat at tables and enjoyed food and drinks, and Sophie was on the stage. She stood front and center, gripping the mic with her eyes closed, singing a song I'd recently heard, "Raised Right," by a Black country artist, Reyna Roberts. She wore her long blonde wig in two braids, jeans, and a fitted T-shirt. Sophie looked and sounded amazing. When she finished, I clapped and howled louder than anyone.

She noticed me and smiled. "Hey, y'all. Before my time is up, I have to bring my girl on the stage with me. She just performed for the first time ever at Casa Rosa Saturday night." She beckoned me forward as the patrons clapped. "Normally, she has her guitar strapped to her back, so it's weird to see her without it. She does a mean version of 'Jolene.' Y'all want to hear it? Mari Johnson!"

The crowd cheered as I stepped on the small stage. "Another round of applause for Sophie." I waited until the patrons quieted. "As Sophie just said, I always have a guitar or a piano when I sing. Feel kind of bare."

A tall cowboy appeared out of nowhere with an acoustic guitar. "You can use mine."

"And they say chivalry and the Southern charm is gone." The crowd howled and clapped as I thanked him. I pulled the strap over my head and pulled Sophie next to me. "We're going to sing this song together."

And together, we rocked the small bar.

With raised drinks, Sophie and I toasted her performance and my signing on with Jake. She took a sip of her whiskey before she asked, "Are you excited? Jake has so much in store for you."

"I am excited. I want to see what we can do together. The showcase was just a start," I said, and we clinked glasses again. "You were good up there. Why haven't you signed on with Jake?" I picked up a chip and dipped it in the bowl of salsa that our waitress had just delivered.

Sophie raised an arched brow. "Because I don't want to be this star who travels the world. I'm content living here near my family, singing background, and having nights like this. Jake pays me well, so I can focus on singing and songwriting. I've made decent money on a couple of songs I already sold. I'm an old-fashioned girl who wants a ring and a bunch of babies. Husbands want their wives at home."

"With the right man, you can perform and still have a marriage and a family. There are plenty of married women who are singers," I argued.

"But how many are really happy?" Sophie studied her glass. "I watch the women in this industry, and it's hard to keep a relationship going. Most end in divorce or don't even make it to the altar. Look at Evelyn. She's been married and divorced two or three times. Then you have to take bullshit to be seen, especially for us Black folks. Is it even worth losing your man over it?"

The liquor burned a trail down my throat, and I chased the discomfort down with another gulp of whiskey.

Sophie touched the space between us on the table. "I didn't mean you and Phillip. You're right, plenty of marriages also survive."

"Might as well mean us," I glumly said before taking another swig of alcohol. "That's where we're headed. How was I supposed to know when I accepted his proposal four months ago that my life would change so drastically? He doesn't want me to pursue my music. We got into an argument because I signed the contract. He should be happy for me, and instead he's pissed. Could I return home to my teaching job and marry him? Yes."

"You wouldn't be happy," concluded Sophie.

"I thought I would be happy with Phillip until I met Jake, who opened me up to this new world. Maybe I still can be happy with Phillip. What is happiness, really?" I looked at Sophie. "My grandfather pursued his music because he believed he had no choice if he wanted to be happy, and in the end, he didn't seem too happy."

"If music makes you happy then you at least have to try. I've been through shit with my last boyfriend, but I refuse to be bitter about relationships or life. To be happy is a choice that I'll gladly pick every single fucking day." She punctuated her words with another sip of her whiskey.

I propped my elbow on the table and rested my chin in my palm. "My parents are happy. Or at least that's what I think happiness looks like. They're the best of friends and genuinely like each other. They also enjoy their chosen professions. And from what you just said, you would be content with your husband and babies and occasionally doing music. I used to be sure. Marriage. Family. Teaching. I don't know anymore. Maybe happiness is on a constantly moving scale, and that's all we can expect."

"You can release a couple of songs and do a few shows. Be more of a local artist," Sophie suggested while crunching on her chips.

"I don't want to place a ceiling on how far my music may take me. Being with Phillip requires a ceiling, and honestly, I don't know many men who would welcome my career."

"What about Jake? He wouldn't place a ceiling on your music. He doesn't even try to hide that he likes you—correction, in his mind, he's trying. It's cute to see him so caught up." She giggled as she gulped down the rest of her drink.

"Oh, he's anxious to see how far I can go. But is he a man who can settle down? Is he the marrying kind? He told me he's not into relationships. The other night, he left the showcase with Rene Starr, his last girlfriend."

Sophie wrinkled her nose. "I thought he was done with her."

"Well, she was at my showcase, and they left in his car. How long were they together?"

"A minute. I started working for Jake toward the end of their thing. It was toxic. She's probably the reason he doesn't want another woman. They cheated on each other. She was heavily using, and he was drinking even more than he does now. They were high rollers, dropping crazy money everywhere, and this power couple. Then, one day, it was over around the same time as her third album tanked because of her affair. Jake refused to say anything about her, and we didn't see her around the studio anymore. We knew he still saw her, because he would disappear whenever she called. He hasn't disappeared in so long. I assumed he'd finally gotten her out of his system. Men love crazy."

"They do," I agreed. Rene exuded a wildness in her sexuality and beauty. She had an edge and talent. I understood his attraction to her.

"My advice is to decide for yourself what's more important. If it's your music, then you need to have an honest discussion with Phillip and be prepared for it to end. If it's him, then you need to sit down with Jake and figure out how to navigate your career so that you and Phillip can live happily ever after. Also, be prepared for the sacrifices you'll have to make."

"I know." I flopped my head down on the table and covered it with my arms. "One is ignoring how damn fine Jake is."

She whooped. "And that kiss? Tavion and I couldn't get over how hot you two looked. So nothing is ever going to come of that?"

"Nope. We're like those characters on a TV show who ultimately end up with someone else."

"Which show is that? All the ones I know, the characters eventually hook up, and some even marry."

I waved my hand. "I'm sure there's a show out there. Just can't think of one, or maybe we'll be the first." I lifted my head. "By the way, want to spend a couple of nights at Hartland? Jake is moving me somewhere nearer to the studio later this week, and I thought I might want to actually enjoy Hartland before I leave. I need a buffer between me and Jake. Phillip may still be coming this weekend. Getting some and inserting reality in this fantasy will keep me from drooling over a man who isn't for me."

"Then we better ask Tavion too. Maybe even get Domino to hang out. You need all the buffers you can get until you see your man."

We tapped glasses again.

"Excuse me, ladies." The same man who'd loaned me his guitar walked up to our table. "Can I interest you in performing here again? The two of you make a good team."

I smiled. "I have to ask my manager, but we can probably make that happen. Can I have your card?"

"Yes, ma'am." He passed me his card. "I'm the talent coordinator for the club. Tell him or her to call me."

This time, we squealed in excitement as we tapped glasses. I had my first serious gig.

TWENTY-NINE

Jake

My decision to stay at Hartland served dual purposes. One—to show Amara the beauty of the land without the pressures of a looming show. We'd done a lot in prepping for the show, and we'd had time to create more music. Time to decide which demos to drop to generate buzz and anticipation for Amara's debut. Time to do more promotional shows and appearances to introduce her to the music world and to record label executives. She needed to be on everyone's radar and be a crossover star. I wanted her to surpass those countless Black women and men who'd tried before her.

I'd already instructed Sophie to start Mari Johnson Instagram and TikTok accounts, posting photos from rehearsals and her showcase, including the original video from the Peabody. Sophie would begin to post daily by capturing Amara while she remained in Nashville. I also told her not to post any photos that clearly depicted Hartland. Within hours, Mari Johnson had gained forty-five thousand followers on IG and almost double that on TikTok. We were well on our way.

On Wednesday, I walked into the kitchen of the main house and heard splashing and music in the pool area. From where I stood, I could see Amara, Tavion, and Sophie in the pool. Domino sat on the edge on his phone. The crew was all here.

"Love the sound of people having fun in my home. Hartland was built for laughter, fun, music, family, and love," Evelyn said from behind me.

She was the other purpose for my being here at Hartland. I steeled myself against reacting in anger and disappointment before turning around. She stood in the doorway in a vibrant turquoise kimono with her red hair piled in her customary bun. Evelyn spread her arms wide to embrace me, and I sighed deeply, remembering that she was the woman I'd always known. I didn't want to see her any different.

Her familiar flowery scent wafted underneath my nose as I hugged her. She'd been a surrogate grandmother, imparting wisdom, kindness, love, and even discipline over the years. I loved her deeply, and that wouldn't change no matter her and my father's actions.

She eased onto a stool, watching me as I grabbed a water out of the fridge. "I'm so glad you're here. I didn't like how yesterday went down."

I opened the bottle and almost gulped down the entire bottle before I answered, "We're here for a couple of days. I plan to show her around, as you suggested. Thank you for allowing her to stay as long as you have. I'll secure another place for Amara over the weekend. Maybe a hotel, or I'll lease a space."

Evelyn clasped her hands together and rested them on the marble counter. "She can stay as long as you need. I spent time talking to her and her mother. Amara isn't and won't be Rene."

"You and my father meant what you said yesterday. Amara needs to be in the city anyway. She just landed a gig for Friday night, and she'll get more before the summer is out." I tapped the counter of the island.

"I saw a video of her performance." A soft, proud smile crossed her features. "She has that elusive 'it' factor. She has a bright future, Jake."

"It's why I pursued her and wanted to sign her." I inhaled and blew out my anger before I asked calmly, "Is that why you or my father decided to go behind my back and send Amara a contract from Barnes? She was offered more than what I suggested, and my father doesn't offer advances to anyone. Her NDA wording was even updated to include that she couldn't give out any information about Barnes Management, including me or you."

Only the slight widening in Evelyn's eyes told the tale. She didn't know, but she would defend my dad. "We didn't go behind your back. We sent her a standard contract with an incentive that we give any talent who stays at Hartland and performs songs created in the studio."

"That contract wasn't standard, and we're not about to fight over these songs. Those songs are Amara's. She wrote the lyrics and the music, and just because the magic happened in your studio, doesn't make it yours." My blood began to boil with what I already suspected, making my decision to not fully confront her that much harder.

She held her hand up. "Those songs will remain Amara's. I'm only explaining why the email went out. Your father doesn't send his own emails anyway."

I didn't respond. My father didn't send his own emails, but he didn't order his assistant to send contracts on a Sunday either.

Evelyn rose from the stool and reached out to touch my wrist. "We don't need bad blood between us. Just found out Ellie is in town and refuses to visit me. I couldn't stand it if you did the same."

"Then make sure my father backs down."

She removed her hand. "William makes his own decisions with Barnes Management and always has."

"No, he doesn't. You started the company together. He listens to you and relies on you more than anyone. One of the reasons my mother didn't like living here."

With fire in her eyes and a flushed face, she pointed her finger at me. "Your mother was and still is jealous, and she's never had a reason to be. She made you distrust me."

I calmly replied, "Mama has never spoken a word against you in my presence, and she isn't jealous. She hates the hold you have on my father, and I never questioned that until now."

Evelyn's forehead furrowed. "Why would you ever question anything about me and your father? We've been working together for years. He's family."

"Like two peas in a pod. He'll do anything for you, even if it means hurting people you love." Before I said anything else without receipts, I jammed my right hand in my pocket and walked out the glass door to join my friends. Evelyn wouldn't follow. She had too much pride and ego to ever run after anyone. And I needed more information before I confronted her and my father. Information that I needed now. Information that I could possibly glean from Evelyn's only child—Ellie Hart.

The crew listened to "Wreck Me," and Sophie and Tavion harmonized while lounging in the pool. Amara glided through the deep blue water.

Domino noticed me first and reached out to dap me. "Was wondering when you were going to get here. Your idea and you're not even around."

I glanced around at the charcuterie boards and wine. "Looks like y'all figured it out."

Tavion and Sophie stopped singing long enough to wave.

"You're off today. Relax." I smiled.

"We happen to rock this song in our spare time. This better be her first single." Sophie propped her arms on the side of the pool and looked up at me.

"We can test a few songs with the gigs you're about to get," I added as Amara swam to me and pushed up to sit on the edge of the pool. "A couple of other clubs want you to perform, and I could secure more. You have about a month left here with us. Let's make it count."

She assessed me quickly. "You good?"

I smiled faintly. "Yeah. Never better."

"No, you're not." Amara frowned and rose to her feet. She wore a one-piece fuchsia-pink bathing suit, and I dragged my eyes away from her ass and thick thighs that she covered up with a matching sarong.

I spoke in a low voice meant for her ears only. "If this is your way to get back at me for opening my door shirtless, baby, you won."

She rolled her eyes impatiently before she grabbed my wrist and pulled me away from listening ears and seeing eyes. "Stop flirting to throw me off."

"That's not what I'm doing. You look damn good in this bathing suit. Trying hard to keep my eyes trained on your face."

This time she blushed while she insisted, "I can tell something's wrong. Your energy is off."

"Just some family shit. Nothing for you to worry about," I reassured her, hating that I had to lie when I'd promised myself I wouldn't do that to her.

"You can talk to me." She touched my forearm, and concern etched wrinkles in her forehead.

"I appreciate you. I really do. But I don't need you to hear my problems. I..."

"You have Rene Starr for that. Got it." She stepped back and studied her bare feet. "Um…so…what's the plans for today?"

"Don't be like that." I reached for her, and she evaded my hand.

She lifted her head with a weak smile. "No…no, I'm not being like anything. You keep drawing the line, and I keep crossing it. We're good. You're my manager and producer. That's it. I'm excited about performing again and being in the studio. After Phillip gets here and we talk, then you and I need to discuss how to handle my career from Atlanta and if it makes sense for me to still teach. I really want this to work, Jake. When I'm on stage, I come alive." She blinked back tears. I wanted to hold her and tell her we would figure everything out, but that was her fiancé's role.

"It will work," I managed to quietly reassure her. I wanted to correct her erroneous assumption about Rene, but if that was what Amara needed to keep her distance, then I would let her believe that I had another woman. "Listen, I need to go back to the city. Something just came up. I'll be back later, and we can jam in the studio—or on the porch—since the crew is here. Maybe Jess and Evelyn will join in. Tomorrow, we'll have our own trail ride. Then we can check out a couple of places for you to stay."

"You're leaving? You just got here." She looked so crestfallen, I kissed her forehead impulsively.

"Promise, I'll be back, and I'm spending the night so we can sit on the porch and talk more. Want to check in and see how you feel about everything. We haven't had time to really do that since the show."

"All right, I'm holding you to that. I do need your advice and to figure out how often you need me here in Nashville once the summer ends. If teaching interferes with your plans for me."

"I know we have a lot to discuss." I squeezed her shoulders. "The sooner you let me go, the sooner I'll be back."

She eased out of my hands. "So arrogant. I'm not holding you here. Go." She abruptly turned around and headed back to the pool. "You better not be looking at my ass."

I admired the sway of her hips and butt. "Too late."

Ellie Hart, a younger version of her beautiful mother, from her figure and porcelain skin to her red hair, sat at a table on the rooftop of the Four Seasons on her cell, drinking a Bloody Mary, probably her second or third, and eating shrimp cocktail and ceviche when I walked up. She smiled and quickly ended her call once I settled in the chair across from her. "Jake Barnes, if I live and breathe. I wouldn't expect you to be Mama's errand boy."

"Man," I corrected her. Ellie still saw me as that teen who'd lived in her family home. Unlike her mother, who broke through barriers to include people of color in her band and on her team, Ellie still considered me and my mother the hired help. I never knew if it was how she perceived Black people or if it was specifically for me and my mother because she resented that we were more of a family than she and Evelyn had been.

She smiled harder. "Of course, Jake. You know I don't mean harm. I knew you when you were actually a boy. Sometimes I forget you've been growing for years. A handsome rake, from what I see and hear on these Nashville streets. Glad you've seemed to calm down, because your rep for stealing already-owned hearts was starting to precede you. Wouldn't want two degenerates from the great and powerful Hartland running around the city." She pushed her plate of ceviche and French bread toward me. "Eat. You look hungry."

She as usually known for her witty and biting sarcasm, but Ellie's factual words didn't dig under my skin as she'd probably intended. I barely glanced at the food. "I'm good. I don't plan to stay long."

She shrugged, pulled out a glittery gold vape pen, and inhaled. The fruity scent covered up whether it was nicotine or weed. I would wage the latter, given her drooping eyelids. "How did you find me?" Ellie asked.

"You still use Barnes Management credit cards for your travel, and I tracked you."

Her hazel eyes narrowed. "Mama gave me permission to use that card."

"Somehow, I doubt it, since your mother no longer owns any part of Barnes Management."

"You can't prove Mama didn't give me permission." She sipped on her Bloody Mary before returning to her pen.

"I really don't care that you use the company card, especially because I'm no longer a part of Barnes Management."

For the first time in probably a long time, her Botox-injected lips curved into a genuine, bright smile. "Good for you. Always thought you were smarter than William, brought in more business than he ever did, and needed to be out from under his thumb. I wish you much more success than I ever wished for William or my mother."

"I'm not sure if that's a good thing, knowing how you feel about the two of them," I remarked in a droll tone.

Ellie lightly squeezed my forearm. "It's a fucking wonderful thing, since I actually give a fuck about you, Jake. I used to be so jealous of you and your mother that you found William, and he whisked you away to this grand life. But I always cared about you and adored your mother."

Before I could protest that William had never been that white savior to our Black family, her eyes drifted away, and she puffed on her pen. "Jealous because I wanted Evelyn and me to be a team like you and your mother. A team of two. And I wanted a good man to fall in love with my mother once my bastard of a father left us, and that man would love me like his very own. Except that never happened. My mother seemed only to attract losers, and the occasional winner she lost because she only wanted him to kiss her ass," she spat out bitterly.

"Why? Why do you hate your mother so?" I plainly asked. Like her mother, Ellie appreciated brutal honesty and would hate it if I kept this conversation going without getting to the point.

Her forehead wrinkled briefly, and she looked out at the city. "Did she send you to ask me that?"

"No. I came here of my own accord. I never understood why you mistreated your mother when she'd given and still gives you so much. I'm an only child like you and can't imagine not seeing my mother if I lived out of town and only came home on rare occasions. What did she do to you? At one point, you loved her. I can tell from your old pictures."

She looked back at me, assessing me. "For once in my life, someone considers that maybe, just maybe, the great Evelyn Hart…did something to me. Ever since I was a teenager, I've been called the bad seed and the troubled child of Evelyn, as if a child's blossoming exists without the watering nurture of parents."

"I can imagine that having such a force of nature for a mother couldn't have been easy," I replied.

"It wasn't. Lonely days and nights with a nanny who didn't like me, while my mother loved the world and my father just didn't care." She gulped down her drink and winced when she placed the empty glass back on the table, before signaling the nearby waiter for another. "You still haven't answered why you're here."

"Why do you hate her? She spends most days since she's slowed down at Hartland with Jess and Craig. She's lonely and hurt that you don't visit her. I want to understand why you don't want to deal with your mother when all she really wants is a relationship with her only child."

"Guilt trip doesn't work with me, darling." She puffed on her pen.

I held my hands up. "No guilt trip here. Trying to understand because me and William are having conflict, and I don't want to end up like you and Ms. Evelyn."

She scoffed, "I may not like him, but he loves you and your mama. Whatever you're going through will pass. It works like that in functional families. Families disagree, argue, and may even physically fight. That strong bond brings them back."

"Maybe if my biological father bonded with me, I would believe that me and my adoptive father can survive all wounds, self-inflicted or otherwise," I said, admitting openly and to myself for the first time that maybe I'd chosen my career path and followed William blindly out of fear of losing him like I'd lost my father. Maybe that was why his potential betrayal was like a stab to my soul.

Ellie waved her vape pen. "At least you know that William wanted you. He adopted you and wanted you to have his name when it wasn't necessary or a requirement." She met my eyes and confessed softly, "How can I love a mother who doesn't love her own child? My mother didn't want me."

I leaned closer. "How can you say that? All Ms. Evelyn talks about is you. I was just at Hartland before I came here, and she told me she didn't want her and me to end up like you and her. I believe your mother loves you as much as you believe William loves me."

She chortled. "Really? Maybe she does now, since she didn't end up with the man she wanted to leave me and my father for. I found this letter."

My breath caught in my lungs, and I felt faint as I whispered, "How old were you when you found out your mother had an affair?"

"I was fifteen when I found a from a man apologizing for standing her up and not choosing her. That he didn't feel right running away together when they both already had children and that she would eventually agree with him. My whole world shook. My own mother was willing to give me up for a man. After that, my heart hardened toward Evelyn."

"And you never confronted her about the letter? Do you even know when the affair happened?" Although it was possible Evelyn's lover wasn't Stoney, the letter Ellie talked about sounded similar to the ones from Stoney's love affair.

She shook her head. "Why? So she could either lie to me about the affair or, worse, tell me to my face that she never wanted me? At least I can pretend she wanted me until she fell in love with a man who wasn't my father."

"Ellie, we've both done and said things we regret. We definitely know that love makes you do crazy things. Even if your mom thought she would leave you at one time, it didn't happen. Or maybe she planned to bring you once she and the man settled somewhere. You won't know how she truly feels or felt if you don't talk to her."

We grew quiet when the waiter brought another Bloody Mary for her and a Perrier for me. She took a long sip, and her eyes became even glossier. "I think I saw him once."

"Who?"

"The other man." She snickered. "We always say 'the other woman' because, typically, the husband cheats and not the wife. I'm sure my father cheated on my mother, which may be why she went looking for love outside of her marriage. As much as I hate my mother, my deadbeat father is ten times worse."

"When did you see the other man?"

"This was years ago. I was home from college at Hartland, and Mama was married to her second husband. Another son of a bitch country singer who only used her for her fame and fortune. Her husband was away, allegedly on business, and I happened to look out of my bedroom window. My mother was locked in a passionate embrace with another man." She inhaled a long time before slowly blowing out fragrant wisps of vapor that dissipated in the air. "They weren't kissing, but the way they held each other, you knew at one point they were lovers. I'd never seen my mother look at any other man how she looked at him. Hopeful and happy. I almost felt sorry for her, because it looked as though the man probably loved her at one point, but the visit wasn't about getting back together. They soon had words, and the tearful, loving reunion turned ugly fast. The man jumped back in his car and skidded away. My mother covered her face and rushed back inside."

"Do you remember what the man looked like?"

"I couldn't see him clearly because he wore a fedora. He seemed handsome from his build and profile. Knowing my mother, if she were to date outside her race, he would have to be drop-dead gorgeous."

I slowly exhaled. "The other man was Black?"

"Yes. My mother is an equal opportunist in every way." She settled back in her chair. "Do you know this man? Is that the reason you're really here?"

I nodded.

"Who is he? Is he, like, your kin or something?" Her sculpted brows dipped. "Is that how your parents met? Through Mama's lover?"

"I don't think that's how they met. But that man is like family, and I wanted to know if Evelyn knew him." I rose from my chair with lead weighing heavy in my heart. "I think it's time you stop running from your mother and discover the truth, from her mouth to your ears. You don't seem very happy, and neither is she. Maybe together you can find some peace. Who knows? You may actually find some happiness, too. No matter the past, she is your only mother, and you're her only daughter. Work that shit out."

I left a hundred on the table and a reflective Ellie Hart staring at the Nashville skyline.

The minute I drove away from the Four Seasons, I called Nathan. When he answered seconds later, I said, "Like Easy discovered in *Devil in a Blue Dress*, solving the mystery isn't neat and tidy and involves a problematic interplay of race and power."

"What? Stop sounding like a book report and speak plain."

"I don't know how I will fucking tell Amara that Evelyn Hart was a scorned lover who stole her grandfather's songs. Is that plain enough?"

THIRTY

Jake

After my conversation with Ellie, I drove straight to Barnes Management, a block off Broadway. My father wanted to be close enough to new talent to have the option to leave the office and walk to any of the restaurant bars and sign someone immediately. I barely greeted his assistant, Cheyenne, as I barged into his office.

My father was on the phone in his expansive chrome and steel office. He frowned at me as I entered, then held his finger up, and I shook my head. "We need to talk now."

He sighed loudly. "Listen, Barry, my son is here, and we must deal with something. Call you back, or we'll talk more over drinks later."

The minute he clicked off the phone, I started. "It was never about me. You were afraid that people would start digging if Amara and Evelyn were connected in any way. Even sent her a contract with an ironclad agreement that she wouldn't mention anything about me."

William leaned back in his chair, and his shrewd blue eyes challenged me. "Tell me what you know."

"Naw, tell me what you did and why you implicated me in your dirty dealings." I rested my hands on the arms of the chair and sat with my legs apart. "If you ever loved me, tell me the truth."

His forehead wrinkled. "Don't make this a test of my love for you. Your life is a testament to my love for you."

"How so? When you stopped trusting me after Rene? Or when you used me to do your guilty work and pay off Stoney? Please tell me how."

"Stop." He slammed his fist on the desk then cleared his expression, taking a deep breath. "I fell in love with your mother first, and she made it clear that you and her were a package deal. If I couldn't love you, then we had no future. Admittedly, I had no idea how to connect with a Black teenage boy with daddy issues. But I fell in love with the parts of you that were your mother, and then I began to see all of you over time. I didn't adopt you to make a point to your mother. I did it because I wanted you to know I chose you. Even if your mother and I didn't make it, I would always be your father. So whether I tell you the truth you think you want to hear has nothing to do with my love for you."

"If you ever loved me, then tell me the whole truth," I repeated resisting the urge to rub my burning chest. "It's not about whether I want to hear the truth, it's about you standing on what you taught me. Honor. Respect. Truth. Isn't that what you lectured me about endlessly? And when I didn't demonstrate those values, you expressed disappointment. Your opinion of me mattered as much as my mother's. I *never* wanted to disappoint you. Never questioned any of your decisions in business or why you had me travel to Memphis twice a year to visit an old musician." I hit the desk. "I was so fucking afraid of losing another father, I didn't question the hush money you gave me to deliver to that man." I scoffed at myself. "Still didn't question your motives or involvement with Stoney even when Amara wanted answers about her grandfather. I might be your son, but I'm also a Black man in an industry where my people have had so much stolen from them. You made me culpable in whatever you and Evelyn did to him. I'm a fucking sellout to my race. You owe me the truth."

My father ran his hands through his still-thick, graying hair. "Evelyn didn't know that I sent money to him. You were why I wanted to show him remorse for something I didn't decide. Watching you grow from a youth to a man, navigate your life, seeing evidence of how you were treated differently. The same conversation that flowed easily with me didn't always flow so easily with you. Yet you excelled in college, had your choice of any industry, and wanted to follow in my footsteps. Watching you hustle hard and spend your summers in my office instead of enjoying them filled me with pride. I'd done a good job with my son. I don't even know if you remember, but you stumbled upon one of Stoney's songs and wondered why he didn't go further."

I nodded.

"Your interest in him reawakened old guilt that filled my spirit, and I wanted to do something. Stoney didn't believe in handouts, and I couldn't say it was for payment for records he'd written and produced. I sent you instead. Figured with your charm and energy, he would accept the money and not ask any questions."

I bitterly corrected him, "You mean because I was also Black, Stoney would somehow receive the money he should've received years ago from me better."

"It wasn't about your race. I couldn't be seen giving him money as Evelyn's manager."

"Bullshit, William. You could've used anybody in the company to give him cash. You chose me."

The ends of his mouth curved down when I called him by his name. "I was trying to rectify a situation the best I could."

"That man didn't care about the money. I don't know what he did with it, because he lived in a dump and drove a car on its last legs. The best way would've been to credit the man for his accomplishments. Now tell me the truth, or I'll tell Nathan to blow this secret wide open."

He studied his hands. "It was my fault. I was this young man, barely seventeen, already an outsider from New York, trying to break into the country business. Nashville is friendly to its visitors until you want to make her home. Then she becomes protective, ensuring your motives are pure and that your reason for staying is out of love for her. Evelyn was a young singer making waves with beauty, talent, and brashness. She struggled to juggle marriage and motherhood while trying to reach that elusive national and crossover appeal. I promised her, as a manager, I would deliver that star. She laughed at my youth but recognized the spunk in me, the desperate need to prove myself as she once had.

"I'd just witnessed the talent of Stoney Johnson at a blues festival. His talent, charisma, and stage presence had everyone on their feet as he performed." He mused, "Amara is so like him on stage it's so uncanny. What I saw in Stoney was the same way you knew Amara would be big. I approached him about being his manager. He laughed and asked what a young white boy could do for him. He had three more shows, and I was in the front row for every one of them. Impressed that I stayed, he agreed to meet with me.

"The more we talked, the more I realized he had no interest in being managed by anyone. When I told him, I wanted him to write for Evelyn and to write country. He became excited. He'd seen her perform around Tennessee and loved the challenge of writing outside of his genre. He'd already written blues and R&B songs for other artists with some success. As a native of Memphis, country music would be a new experience yet dear to his heart.

"How was I supposed to know that two married people of different races in that time would fall so deeply for one another? I pretended I didn't see the longing looks and secretive smiles. All I cared about was the music. Together, they created beautiful hits. Songs that would place her on the trajectory she wanted."

"Evelyn co-wrote the songs?"

"It would make all this so much simpler if she did. She could at least argue the songs were hers, too." William shook his head sadly. "He wrote and produced him, and her voice brought them to life."

"How many songs?" I asked. My emotions were numb as I listened to my father.

"Nine. Four eventually went number one. Three won Grammys. All hit the charts at some point. The world would've never known Evelyn Hart without Stoney Johnson's songs."

I slumped in my seat and closed my eyes.

"She loved Stoney, and they made plans to leave their respective families and ride off in the sunset as this dynamic force. Except Stoney changed his mind and stood Evelyn up at the Memphis airport where she waited for him. He couldn't leave his wife and son, who'd always loved and supported him. Evelyn loved Ellie but hated her emotionally and physically abusive husband. She saw Stoney as her escape and didn't understand why he would discard her as he did."

"Hell hath no fury," I murmured.

"Evelyn lashed out and hurt him the only way she knew how. Taking credit for his songs."

Jabbing the desk, I shouted, "Stole his songs. She *stole* his songs. She stole his legacy. She stole his rights to a life of riches and fame. That man died alone and broken. Let's call it what it was. He probably didn't sign any papers, and even if he did, you made it null and void. She knew he couldn't demand the rights back. Who would believe a struggling Black man over a white woman, especially America's sweetheart?" I wiped angry and disappointed tears from my face. "Why did you let this happen?"

Remorse filled his flushed face. "I confronted Evelyn when she insisted on including the songs on her third album, and demanded she put his name on the records. She told me how she'd been hurt by men her whole life, and now it was time for payback. No man would ever hurt her again. I was the only man she trusted. She promised that we would be a team and that my career would soar with hers. Besides, Evelyn had spent months with Stoney, and the record label wouldn't give her more time to produce more songs. The label would drop her if she couldn't deliver music, and what other company would sign a married woman with a child who'd only had a modicum of success in country music? She promised me that if the songs were hits, she would pay him for them.

"I shut my mouth as Evelyn's career surpassed our expectations. Stoney had been paid by the music company while he and Evelyn worked together for the two songs under the original agreement. On his own, he produced the remaining seven. I told myself that any time I felt any guilt."

"Does Mama know?"

He shook his head. "Please don't tell her. I will."

"And what will I tell Amara? Huh? Do you think she will trust me? Believe that I had no clue why I gave her grandfather money for years? Shit, I'm the shady record producer and manager that convinced her to sign with me after bilking millions from her family."

"I'll fix it. Give me some time to talk to Evelyn and work it out."

I rose, straightening my slacks. "You had fifty years to come clean."

He stood too, facing me. "If you ever loved *me*, give me a chance to make this right. Don't say anything to your mother, Evelyn, or Amara."

Refusing to agree to anything, I stalked out of his office and drove back to Hartland, trying to figure out how to tell Amara the truth. A truth that could change the trust she had in me.

THIRTY-ONE

Amara

My feet were submerged in the water, and I leaned back on my elbows, allowing the sun to naturally dry my skin. Something troubled Jake, and it hurt that as close as I thought we were becoming, I could only get *so* close. I understood why it had to be. Still, I wished for an alternate universe where we could be the type of best friends that truly shared everything with one another. Underneath the chemistry and not-so-secret glances, we genuinely had similar interests and could talk tirelessly for hours. I'd never met someone who truly got me as he did. Never had that friendship with anyone where we had to see each other or talk to one another every day.

Being here at Hartland during the summer was like the adolescence I wished I'd had, lounging by the pool, snacking, listening to music with beautiful, talented people without a care in the world. The longer the sun warmed me, the more it evoked the urge to write. Without saying anything to anyone, I pushed myself up, slid on my flip-flops, grabbed my robe, and headed inside the main house.

"Where are you going?" Tavion asked.

"Need a moment. I'll be back," I responded without turning around. I slipped into the cool kitchen and shivered from the suddenly cold air.

"You hungry? I can make something quick."

I startled as my eyes quickly adjusted from the sunlight.

Evelyn sipped from a glass cup of tea. "Jess is gone to the store to make a big meal for later. She's going to try to convince Jake to grill for us."

I smiled. "Then we're in for a treat. He grilled me a steak the other night at his place." At Evelyn's knowing smile, I quickly amended, "He prepared a meal for me and his friend, Nathan."

"You like him," she stated.

Instead of denying an obvious truth, I compromised. "It's complicated."

"That good love you can't turn away from is always complicated." She quirked a brow. "Do you want something to eat?"

"No, ma'am. Is it okay if I go to the studio?" I asked, suddenly feeling like I needed to ask permission.

She chuckled. "You weren't going to ask my permission if you didn't see me."

"Um…I'm sorry…Jake said I had…" My words faltered.

"Stop stammering, darling. It's not a good look. Do I intimidate you?" she asked as she peeked at me over the rim of her cup.

"Yes. I mean…I've only seen you on TV, and you're larger than life even in person. I don't want to do or say anything stupid in front of you."

"Do you have that worry around Jake?"

"No."

"I'm no different than Jake."

"With all due respect, there are layers to who you are in this world, and my perception of you probably won't change."

She tilted her head. "And there's no way you'll ever see me differently?"

"Honestly, my stomach has been queasy since you asked if I was hungry."

Evelyn twisted her lips and rose from her chair. "Then we need to spend more time together." She walked briskly out of the kitchen. "Come on. Let's go make some music."

Anxiety and anticipation warred inside me as I followed her, and she beckoned me to walk closer.

"We walk together. How you position yourself in relation to others dictates how people treat you. Make sure if it's a meeting about your career, you sit at the head of the table. If someone is already sitting at the head, make sure you choose the other end. Never on the side. At a round table, keep your hands clasped on the table, head and shoulders up. Show the men you won't take their shit or pity, because powerful men still control the industry."

I added, "White men."

Evelyn slanted her gaze at me. "Men are men."

"Come on, Ms. Evelyn, you know that's not true. I'm a woman like you and have experienced sexism. But I'm still a Black woman, and you broke down walls to join the good ol' boys' club. Men who look like your father. Men you see every day. Very seldom was there a Black man in these meetings. 'Good ol' boys' might mean to you a man who embodies traditional Southern values—friendly, unassuming, and down to earth. 'Good ol' boys' for most Black people translates to racist men. Sitting at these tables as a proud Black woman can be easily translated to 'angry Black woman,' or a bitch who dares to want a seat at a table never meant for her."

"The table wasn't meant for me either. You don't think I've been called a bitch or worse? Treated horribly simply because I wanted a chance to soar?"

"My story doesn't negate yours, Ms. Evelyn. I can't imagine all that you endured to rise to the top in a genre dominated by men." We started walking down the stairs. "I don't know all that I'll encounter yet. Everything has been so smooth thus far, I'm almost afraid to push it. Acceptance here in Nashville doesn't necessarily mean acceptance in the world."

Evelyn opened the door to the gold studio. "Acceptance in Nashville is all that matters if you want to remain in country music." She picked up a guitar in the corner and sat in the producer's chair. "Jake tells me you never considered a music career until now. You have the voice to do any genre. Why country?"

I pulled the strap of my acoustic guitar over my head, deciding to stand near her. "I asked Jake the same question."

She scoffed, "Darling, if you lead with 'Jake told me to do country,' your career is dead before it's barely had a chance to breathe. This music is honest and not a trend."

Nodding, I started strumming. "I wasn't finished, Ms. Evelyn. He showed me how country music, especially for us true Southerners—which I am—is as a part of our history as blues, R&B, and rap. Elvis sang the blues and we have blue-eyed soul singers like Justin, Sam Smith, Teena Marie, and George Michael, who sang the hell out of anything they touched. They didn't just choose songs expected of them because of how they looked. They chose songs that moved them." I looked at Evelyn, who'd been watching me with a soft smile as I played. "You know what song moved me more than any song? My grandfather's lost song. He was a bluesman out of Memphis who inspired me to do country. Jake might have led me here." Tears burned my eyelids. "Stoney Johnson will keep me here. Anything I do is my way of honoring him…my acknowledgement of the path he began that I have every intention of finishing."

Evelyn blinked back her own tears. "Can you play his song?"

"I've been playing it with a capo." I looked around the room. "Probably back at the cottage with my other guitar."

"Stop stalling and play." Evelyn tapped her guitar. "I know some of his work. Never heard his country music."

"I…" I started to defend myself and then figured she would believe what she believed. From the moment I plucked the first string, I disappeared into the song. Any nervousness about performing in front of Evelyn faded as I performed "A Man's Luck."

Like any musician worth her salt, she picked up the rhythm and joined in with her guitar, making the song that much grander. We smiled at each other as she continued to play while I sang.

She shook her head slowly, her eyes still glassy. "Can we produce that song together as a tribute to your grandfather?"

I stared at her. "Wait…you want to do a song with me?"

Evelyn rested her arms on the top of her guitar. "The question is, do *you* want to do a song with *me*? I'm on my way out, and you're just beginning."

I placed my hands on my hips. "Now, Ms. Evelyn, don't start acting white on me. Who do I look like, turning down an opportunity of a lifetime because our skin color differs? I've seen you perform duets with plenty of blondes, brunettes, even redheads like yourself much younger than you. I can go blonde if that'll make it easier, though I'm sure Jake will have a whole fit."

Her head fell back in laughter. "All right, Ms. Mari Johnson. Point made."

"We can get Jake to produce it."

Evelyn's smile slowly faded. "I know enough to produce it. We'll keep it simple, just like we did now. I want to keep the original sound of him as much as possible."

"I have to talk to him about it. He's my manager. I signed the other night."

"Congratulations, darling." She smiled, though the warmth didn't travel to her eyes. "Jake is a good manager. He'll take care of you. Your grandfather would probably have approved."

I smiled. "That's how I met Jake in the first place. He knew my grandfather. He visited him over the years and got a chance to know him. I don't remember Stoney Johnson…didn't even know that people knew him by that name. I didn't know he'd made enough of an impact in the blues world to be in the museum in Memphis until Jake." I pushed through the ache in my chest. "We don't even have a picture together. My father and grandfather didn't speak, so I never had a chance to know him. Music is my chance of knowing him, if that makes sense."

Evelyn replied softly, "Makes all the sense in the world. I also know why Jake means so much to you, too." She reached for my hand and squeezed it. "Did Jake ever tell you how I got started?"

"No." She released my hand, and I removed my guitar and placed it next to me on the sofa across from her. "I've *read* about how you got started."

"What you read is probably a mixture of truth and fabrication. My story is like so many musicians. Humble beginnings, born and raised in Chattanooga, and music the only way out of poverty. My parents were horrible people. I mean that in the truest sense. They fought each other any chance they got. Most fights my father won, and those were better days for me. The times my mother won, I bore the brunt of his emasculation.

"Never really dug school or wanted a man to take care of me and wind up like my mother, so I left home at fifteen. I had a job washing dishes at a restaurant to pay for my room at a boarding house. The restaurant would have local and nationally known singers perform. Sometimes the owner would allow me to sit at a table and listen." Evelyn chuckled. "I swear those were the best days of my life. I wore this big, cheesy grin, happy to be free of my abusive father and fighting parents. My job paid for my freedom and inspired my love of music. I'd just turned sixteen when a singer canceled at the last minute. I took it as my moment and boldly walked on the small stage and started singing Patsy Cline's 'Crazy.' I sang that song like it was my last day on Earth. The best singer has the craziest backstory, and I had a hell of a beginning. My troubled past guided my soul and my voice. All I ever knew was to be honest and raw. The audience that day believed in me and demanded that I be hired.

"I finally started making decent money and bought a guitar, taught myself how to play, and began my journey. For a lonely girl who believed she was unlovable, those people made me feel loved. Perfect strangers stood up for me because of my voice. How could I do anything else but sing? Oh, there are stories I can tell you about how men treated me during this winding road. I refused to let anyone stop me. Not even the devil himself kept me from my destiny once music hit my soul. Music saved me from repeating my family cycle of poverty and violence. It just didn't bring me the love I've always wanted."

Her story, told lyrically, had me mesmerized. She closed her eyes and began to hum a melody so melancholy yet beautiful, it reminded me of my grandfather's life. Or at least the life I'd pieced together.

In my peripheral vision, I spotted Jake standing right outside the studio. His hands were fists by his side as he stared at Evelyn with wounded eyes. The studios were soundproof, so he couldn't hear her words, and she was so caught in the past that she didn't notice him. If she did, she would have yet another line to add to her story. She'd clearly hurt someone she loved deeply during her journey to get here.

Jake slid his gaze from Evelyn's to mine as he opened the door with a smile. "Hey, been looking for you."

"We've been getting to know each other more," Evelyn said.

I clapped my hands once, hoping that my news would change the tension that seemed to emanate from him. "Yes. What do you think of a remake of 'A Man's Luck' sung by me and Ms. Evelyn? We could alter the words slightly. Maybe change it to 'A Woman's Luck.'"

Jake finally acknowledged Evelyn with barely veiled contempt. "I thought you wanted to distance yourself from Amara since she's signed under me?"

Her eyes narrowed. "That was your father's wish. Not mine. You asked me to openly endorse her. This is the best way to do this. 'A Man's Luck' can be my swan song."

Jake assessed Evelyn before asking, "Am I producing the song?"

"It's probably best that I do it myself. We'll keep it simple and do it right here." Evelyn waved her hand dismissively. "Leave me out of the pissing contest between you and your daddy. I told him the same thing."

Instead of addressing her, Jake reached for my hand. "We'll discuss and get back to you."

Confused about the energy flowing between Jake and Evelyn and needing to talk to him alone, I allowed him to pull me up.

"Amara, a man has a way of stunting a woman's growth," Evelyn said. "His ego is fragile, and when threatened, he'll do whatever he can to regain control of his power. It doesn't matter who he hurts, right, Jake? Care to share what's got you threatened?"

He retorted, "Trust me—you don't want me to share."

Her green eyes flashed. "Try me."

Jake glared at her and then turned to me. "Let's go."

Evelyn sighed with annoyance. "You and I know that my name attached to Mari Johnson will legitimize a woman who has no ties to this world beyond a grandfather who's an old blues singer from Memphis. Don't be a fool."

"We'll be gone before the night's over." Jake's chest heaved up and down as he firmly gripped my hand and pulled me away from Evelyn. I wanted to jerk from him at her reminder of how the core of me had thus far been stunted by my father and Phillip. But the little voice inside of me whispered to follow Jake and give him a chance to explain.

His mouth formed a stern line, discouraging any questions from me as we hurried up the stairs. When we reached the top, Jess and Craig walked in with bags of food. Jake bit out, "No time, Jess. The crew can stay if they like, but Amara and I are out of here."

I looked apologetically over my shoulder at Jess and Craig as Jake stormed out of the main house. I released his hand once he pulled me down the steps and we headed to the cottage. "Can you tell me what's going on?

Why are you so angry, and why are we leaving here when we made plans to be here for the next couple of days? Our friends are in the pool waiting for us. We can't just leave them hanging."

He stopped but didn't turn around. "We can explain everything later. Right now, we just need to get your stuff and go."

I hurried around to face him. "Explain to me now."

Jake narrowed his eyes, assessing me before he dragged his hand down his face. "I don't want to lie to you."

I grabbed his hand off his face. "Then don't. What's wrong?"

He stared at me a long time and then dropped his gaze to study his shoes. "Because I'm splitting away from Barnes Management, my father believes it's best you leave Hartland. We had words, and I just want to get you away from here. Please, can you just pack and let's go, before the others know? I don't feel like talking to anyone."

I'd never seen Jake this upset. Underneath his anger was hurt, and all that mattered was comforting him. I tapped his foot with mine. "All right. Let's just go, and I'll get Sophie to pack up my stuff and bring it to me later."

He raised his head, wearing a frown. "You sure you want to leave like this?"

I looped my arm through his and turned him back around to his car. "If you think I should leave, then I'll leave. I don't want to be anywhere I'm not wanted."

Jake looked down at me. "Sorry. You're caught between me and my family."

"No apologies. I'm proud to be your first client." As we approached the car, the butterfly doors of his car lifted high. "We'll just have to stop and get me something to eat. And I want a penthouse suite with room service, since I'm missing out on Jess's good food for you."

THIRTY-TWO

Jake

"Jake, what do you think about that arrangement?" Amara asked while she sat on a stool with her guitar, interrupting my rumination about the confrontation with my father. It'd been three days since we left Hartland. She had a performance tomorrow, and we were repeating the songs used in the showcase and trying to determine if any order should be changed.

"Play it again," I instructed her.

"Only if you pay attention this time." She raised a brow.

I folded my arms and paced in front of her as she performed at the closed bar that would open at four, determined to focus on her. She was less nervous than she'd been for the showcase last week. My nerves, on the other hand, were shattered. Phillip would be in town tomorrow. I felt even less deserving of her than I already had.

"Jake, you're still not paying attention."

I waved my hand impatiently. "That's because you got it." I looked at Sophie. "Tell her she got it."

"You called rehearsal, boss," she reminded me. "You say she got it, she got it."

"Bet he'll pay attention to this." Amara smiled, shifted her guitar behind her, and started playing the keyboard. Domino picked up the rhythm. "Been thinking about this song, especially since tomorrow's crowd will be a little more brown."

I inhaled deeply when she began to sing that she wanted to be free, a song by Deniece Williams that I'd heard my grandmother play back in Houston. A song my mother also loved and played loudly on Saturday mornings. A beautiful song about being allowed to be yourself while in a relationship. A classic song that many may not remember before tonight, but how Amara sang it, it would be remembered.

When she finished, before I could approve of her choice, hands behind me clapped. Amara glanced at me before her lips spread into a smile. She hurried past me, and the crew smiled politely. Sophie threw a sympathetic glance my way, and I ignored her. I already knew who was standing behind me, and I slowly turned around as my stomach dropped to my slightly shaky knees. Locked in a passionate embrace, the engaged couple kissed.

Hot fire burned like acid in my stomach, and I had to resist the urge to bolt. Leaving before she introduced me to him would wave dangerous yellow flags. Instead, I jammed my fists in my pockets and studied my shoes, waiting like the rest of the crew for them to finish their—very public— private reunion.

Amara, with a smiling face, dragged him to me. "Hey…umm… I know y'all met on the phone the other day."

Phillip regarded me for a second and offered his hand. "Thank you for taking care of her while she's been here. She speaks well of you."

I accepted his hand. Strong handshake. "No problem. She's easy to take care of."

His eyes crinkled at the corners as he patted my shoulder before walking past me to meet the rest of the crew. Amara's eyes were soft. "He surprised me. Didn't think he was coming until tomorrow."

"It's cool. You can leave if you need to. I know it's been a while since you've seen each other. You're ready for tomorrow night."

"If you don't mind, can we do a run-through of the show again? I want him to hear me without the crowd. Just hear me and the crew, pure and raw."

"He'll see you pure and raw tomorrow night," I said as I reached into my pocket for my cell, prepared to find someone to help me forget about Amara.

Then Evelyn's taunt about the fragility of a man's ego struck my conscience. "You know what? Go for it." I drummed up enthusiasm from somewhere deep, though I wanted to get the hell out of Dodge.

I strode back to the stage and picked up the fiddle. Phillip looked surprised when I walked on the stage as she introduced him to the crew. He soon exited to sit at a table and watch. If anyone could make me escape from my life for a little while, it was Mari Johnson.

Domino counted off, and soon, I forgot my troubles.

THIRTY-THREE

Amara

I slid my arm under Phillip's as we strolled down Broadway to the hotel. "So?"

"So what?" His tone held a hint of irritation.

"Did you enjoy my show?" I asked, wanting to really hear how he felt. He'd clapped and whistled when I finished, even praised my voice and the crew. Yet I still sensed he had more to say. Maybe he wasn't as impressed as he'd projected earlier.

"I told you I did. I didn't expect anything less. I have a hotel two blocks from you. Why don't you pack a bag and join me there?"

"Okay. But why didn't you tell me you did not intend to stay at my hotel?"

"What kind of man stays at a hotel with his woman paid for by another man?"

"The same man who expected me to stay in hotels sponsored by his company?"

"My company isn't taking care of me like I'm his woman."

A seemingly happy couple holding hands walked around us on the bustling sidewalk. The man smiled as he accidentally bumped my shoulder. "Excuse us."

Phillip and I watched the couple move ahead of us and kiss each other.

I glanced at him. "That should be us."

His jaw tightened though he didn't look at me.

I softened my tone. "Jake isn't taking care of me like I'm his woman. I'm a new client, and I can potentially make him a lot of money. Of course he's going to treat me well, because I have options."

"You mean pimp you out?" he scoffed.

I stopped in my tracks, and with a shaky voice, I demanded, "Take back what you fucking said, or I swear I'll never speak to you again."

"Sorry. I shouldn't have said that. You have unbelievable talent. But I can tell he struts around like he owns you." He shoved his hands in his pockets. "Still trying to get used to all of this. Your hair, the way you dress, and the late nights. I don't fit in with any of these people."

"That's just Jake. He's like that with the crew or any talent he works with, but he listens to me and respects my wishes. Whether you get along with those people back there shouldn't stop you from wanting to support me. Would it be nice if you fit in? Of course, but it doesn't change my feelings about you." At his continued frown, I jumped in front of him. "All right, let's reset before we start another argument. You came down here to enjoy it. I can pack a bag and go to your hotel, and then we can order room service and catch up. Or I can get my clothes tomorrow and just go to your hotel now."

He slung his arm around my neck and kissed me on the cheek. "Let's just go to my suite. Been missing you."

I breathed a sigh of relief. My emotions were so ragged. I'd been unprepared for both men in the same space.

I pointed out different bars and which celebrities owned what before we finally arrived at his hotel. I leaned on his shoulder as we rode in the elevator together. I sniffed his arm. The familiar scent of his soap comforted me. He never gave me the butterflies Jake gave me just by being in his presence. Still, butterflies weren't enough to build a life, especially with a man who preferred dating over relationships.

When we settled in the luxury suite, completely clothed on top of the bed, Phillip found the menu on the TV. "Whatever you want, let's go for it. We're celebrating."

I snuggled against his side. "Your deal and my signing a contract with an agency who'll potentially help me make millions."

Phillip snorted. "He'll get a huge cut after whatever record label gets theirs. I wouldn't bank on clearing that much from it."

Pushing myself up to rest on my elbows, I snapped, "I guess I can say the same for you with your deal. You just brought your company millions for years to come, and what was that bonus again? Seventy-five thousand? Sounds like you didn't get much of a cut either."

"This tit-for-tat shit has to end," he replied. "We won't make it if that's your go-to every time we argue."

"We won't make it if you keep shitting on my dream."

He shifted on his side to face me. "This dream that started five minutes ago because you're so strung out on him? Don't think you can fool me. It's not about the music. It's about being around him. I know his type. He'll say and do anything to get what he wants from you and then drop you once he does. You're too naïve and trusting to see what I see. He couldn't stand that I was there today. Jealous, not because he really wants you. He was jealous because you dare love someone other than him."

"No, you're jealous because I'm not that wallflower, that doormat you're accustomed to, and he sees me. Do you know how many times in two years you changed our plans because your career was always more important? I went along with it because at least it wasn't another woman. That's my bad for making it acceptable to change our plans on a whim simply because you know how to be faithful, which should be an expectation of any relationship." I pushed up on my knees and faced him. "I need to be heard. I need to be me in this relationship. And the woman you saw earlier tonight is the woman I should've been all along. I let my father's issues with *his* father keep me from my destiny. I've never felt so free as I have this summer. I've never felt more like myself, and I refuse to put myself in a little box for you, my father, or any other person again."

He rapidly nodded. "Yeah. I'm hearing you loud and clear, and this person isn't the woman I asked to be my wife."

I pressed my palm on his chest. "And you're still the man I accepted to be my husband, flaws and all. Can you accept me now that you see I'm changing…that I'm happier?"

"Is a part of that happiness Jake?"

I shook my head slowly. "If it's about Jake, we no longer have to work closely together. He'll understand."

"You didn't answer my question."

"He was the first person to believe in me. The only person who could give me information about my grandfather, because he spent time with him. Jake opened me to this world, and he'll always have a special place in my heart," I answered honestly, treading lightly around the chemistry that raged between me and Jake.

He snarled, "Did you fuck him?"

"No. No." I touched his arm, and he jerked away from me. "I swear I didn't."

"You wanted to, and if he was down, you would've." He squinted. "That's it. You haven't fucked him because he doesn't want you like that. See? It's what I said. He teases you and pretends he wants more to string you along. Not enough for the deed to actually happen, because then that would make it hard for you to work together."

His words hit too close to what I often thought about Jake's interaction with me. He was too aggressive and determined to let the fact that I had a ring on my finger stop him from pursuing me if that was what he truly wanted. I jumped out of bed. "All right. Fine, you figured it out. I do like him. Have a gigantic crush on him. I'm giving up everything I know and love, hoping that Jake will give me a piece of his heart. I'm so stupid over him that I can't see that I'm losing a good man. The fact that music is in my blood has nothing to do with why I'm here. Nothing at all. The joy I feel performing is because Jake is right there with me. Yep, you're right. Thanks for showing me the light."

Phillip slowly lifted his legs over the bed and sat up. "Take him out of the equation, and you'll soon realize that this life isn't what you want. Better yet, I'll give you a pass. Fuck him and see what happens after that. You'll see I'm right. This isn't you, Mari. People know they want to sing their whole lives, not when they're thirty years old. Get a fucking clue. You're a has-been before you even start, just like your grandfather."

His voice held such contempt that I grew nauseated. He'd spoken his truth, and moving forward had become an impossibility.

Refusing to utter another word, I pulled off my ring and threw it at him. As he called my name, I grabbed my sandals and purse and walked barefoot out of his room, slamming the door behind me.

Distraught, I caught a Lyft to Jake's music studio instead of my hotel. I needed peace; outside of Hartland, his studio had become my sanctuary. He'd given me free access once I signed the contract, and I needed to be there to erase the ugly words that Phillip had just spoken.

When I opened the door, my heart dropped to my stomach. The song we were still working on, "Wreck Me," played as background music. A shirtless Jake was stretched out on the sofa, his pants half undone and his arm flung across his face, asleep. I spotted a turned-over empty glass next to a bottle of whiskey. I backed out the door quietly, not wanting to disturb him or for him to look at me with pity. He'd warned me about Phillip, yet because I wanted Phillip in my life, Jake did what he could to honor that and pushed his own feelings about my fiancé and his attraction aside for my career. Why couldn't Phillip see that love meant sacrificing for the other person's good? Jake, who'd only known me for a couple of months, understood that and was truly there for me. He wouldn't have invested in me if he didn't see my potential.

Before I started crying again at the impossibility of being with either of the men, I hurried out the door. As the door closed, he softly called my name. "Mari, are you okay?"

I couldn't lie to him, so I stepped back into the studio. "No. I'm not."

Jake jumped up and peered down at me in the faint light from the monitors and the mixing desk. "Hey. Why are you crying? What happened between you and Phillip? Why are you here?"

The concern in his eyes started a new round of tears. I gripped his arms and pressed my face into his naked chest, unable to look at him. I had too many confusing and conflicting emotions. I couldn't deny my attraction to him. Phillip had the right to be jealous or not trust me around Jake. Yet my crush on Jake didn't stop my sense of loss that the man I'd been building a future with didn't see himself with the me I was becoming. Phillip's taunt about my being too old cut to my core because maybe I was foolish to chase a dream I'd never known I had. My heart ached that I no longer had Phillip and that I could never have the man holding me.

My engagement wasn't the only reason Jake and I couldn't be together. He had a woman, and more importantly, we had a professional relationship that neither of us wanted to fuck up. Those thoughts made the tears come faster and harder.

Jake rubbed my back with one hand and locked the door with the other. He walked backward, still holding me, and lay back down on the sofa, curving his body to mine, and didn't say another word as I sobbed.

His soft lips pressed against my forehead as my tears subsided, and I opened my eyes. My gaze zeroed in on his slightly gaped mouth. He shook his head gently, and I ignored him and kissed him. Jake didn't respond as I brushed my lips on his again. The third time, his breath hitched, and the fourth time, I used my tongue. He returned my kiss and shifted his taut body over mine and moved between my legs. I moaned at the evidence of his virility against my center as I indulged in his whiskey-flavored tongue and soft lips.

Jake's mustache and growing beard brushed my cheeks as he deepened the kiss while his hand found my breast. He whispered in between kisses, "You're too vulnerable. I don't want you to wake up with regrets."

"Stop trying to control this, Jake. I am vulnerable, but I've also wanted you since I met you. This is the life I want, and eventually, I'll meet a man who accepts all of me and is willing to grow with me. I'm not expecting you to leave other women alone because I'm not with Phillip anymore. Let me have you tonight, okay? I need you so desperately. Tomorrow, we can pretend we never happened."

He caressed my cheek. "What if I can't pretend? What if I know I can't ever let you go if we do this?"

I studied his face. "What are you saying?"

"What if you already met the man who accepted all of you and wants to grow with you? What if that man is me?" he earnestly replied.

My heart pounded viciously at the words I didn't think he would ever say to me. "You can't mean that. You told me you weren't good for me. You have other women. You have Rene."

"I still think you're too good for me. No, I don't have a woman, or women. Rene's my ex, and I'll always care about her and help her in any way I can. I no longer love her and haven't for a long time." His thumb traced my trembling lips. "I didn't correct your perception once I realized you thought she was still my woman. I needed to have a barrier between us because I fucking want you so much and figured you would keep your distance because of her." He chuckled. "Guess I was wrong. Turns out you don't care if I have a woman when you want me bad enough."

I buried my head in his neck, relishing his scent. "I didn't come here tonight thinking I would see you. I came here because it's become my sanctuary. My peace. I'm not usually that woman who doesn't care if a man is already in a relationship, or kiss another man when I'm taken."

He kissed me, cutting off my words. "I know who you are. You don't have to explain. Makes me feel good that I make you forget what your mama taught you."

I dropped my head again. "Mama isn't going to like you for a very long time. She warned me that you had feelings for me and that I needed to watch myself that day we met at the repast."

He lifted my chin to see my face. "Why didn't you listen to your mama?"

"Because every time I tried to picture my life without a Jake Barnes in it, I couldn't. Fate brought us together. It's up to us to decide whatever that means."

"Then I want us to decide. I've tried to ignore my feelings for you. Put me more into the music, exercising more, drinking less, drinking more, being mean to you. Anything to stop this maddening express train to falling in love. I was so fucking jealous of Phillip I couldn't see straight. Took it out on the crew again after you left. They could see my hurt, so I know they'll forgive me."

"I'm sorry. I know that had to hurt." I kissed his nose.

"When you left with him tonight, my heart broke, and I came here to remind myself that what we have is bigger than our feelings. To force myself to let you go and to get over my love for you." He held my face between his smooth palms. "Tell me that I'm not just a consolation prize, or you're settling for me because the man you really want can't accept you?"

I kissed his palm and confessed, "The night you picked me up at the airport, I knew I was in trouble. I'd just promised a man that my love for him wouldn't change, that no matter what, we would find a way to be together, even if my life changed in ways we had never imagined. I promised him that two hours before you waited for me by your car, happy to see me. My heart and soul swelled at the sight of you. And I hated myself for already betraying Phillip. So I stuffed down my feelings, though I anticipated every moment I would see you again and missed you whenever we parted. You are my reason for waking up in the morning.

"I do hurt because I know the end of my engagement hurts beyond me and him. We were building a life together. Until music captured my soul, and you stole my heart. So, no. You will never be my consolation, but you are my prize." I opened my legs as far as the sofa would allow. "And if you still have any doubt about how I feel…" I started singing the song that he had on repeat in the background.

> *"In the twilight's soft embrace,*
> *Your eyes hold a storm I can't replace.*
> *Touch me soft, whisper low,*
> *In your arms, I let go."*

His breath hitched as we locked eyes, and I shifted to straddle him, wanting him to truly feel me.

> *"Wreck me, in the shadows we find,*
> *A love so fierce, it's one of a kind.*
> *In your kiss, I find my defeat,*
> *In your arms, my heart skips a beat."*

My hands roamed and caressed his chest, and the intricate tattoo of a treble cleft was surrounded by small musical notes on his right pec. I trailed over the soft hair on his lower abs, leading to his half-opened pants.

"Under stars, our silent confessions,
In each touch, those whispered questions.
Love's a ghost in our embrace,
But with you, my heart finds its pace."

I undulated on his thick erection while continuing to feel every dip, rip, and angle of his chest and abs. His intense gaze never wavered from mine, though his hands gripped my waist.

"Wreck me, in the shadows we find,
A love so fierce, it's one of a kind.
In your kiss, I find my defeat,
In your arms, my heart skips a beat."

I bent over him to kiss his lips, feeling my body begin to spiral at the sensuality of this moment that I never dared to imagine. I moaned in his mouth as I continued singing.

"Love, like fire, wild and free,
In your eyes, is where I want to be.
Hold me close, don't let go,
In this dance, love's all we know.
Wreck me, in the shadows we find,
A love so fierce, it's one of a kind.
In your kiss, I find my defeat,
In your arms, my heart skips a beat."

Once I finished singing, Jake roughly gripped the ends of my t-shirt while he dipped his tongue into my mouth, insistent, sure, and strong. The way his lips touched mine, soft yet sensually demanding as he kissed me, reminded me of his words when he kneeled before me. He'd known that if he pressured me, he could have me. His kiss alone had me wanton and wide open for his every carnal wish. He quickly slipped the fabric over my head and stopped it at my arms, effectively trapping me. I was at his mercy as he massaged my breasts through my lace bra before freeing them for his pleasure. Hot desire like molten lava pooled in my panties, already slick by just the sight of his muscular chest and arms.

I moaned when he captured my rigid nipple in between his teeth. He gently nipped and sucked while his fingers rolled and pulled on my other nipple, all while our lower bodies danced to an erotic rhythm old as time. Jake maneuvered us until he was back on top of me. He licked down my body and tongued my belly button on his way to my honey pot. I gripped his strong shoulders, anticipating his touch, his lick, or his kiss as he lifted my hips higher. I writhed and relished the feel of his scratchy beard and mustache in between my legs. His mouth and tongue took turns teasing, sucking, and pulling until my body started to buck uncontrollably to release the building pressure. He pressed against my clit. I keened, and he eagerly relished my explosion as he sucked and sucked until I shuddered.

"No…no… Mari, we're not done yet." He chuckled before he slipped a finger inside me, readying my body for him. My breasts rose and fell rapidly as he removed his pants. I inhaled at his well-endowed maleness while he slid on a condom taken from the back pocket of his pants. Jake knew the charming effect he had on women before they ever encountered his sexual prowess. I understood more than ever why he might have fifty problems, but a woman wasn't one. I closed my eyes, spreading my legs wider, my impossibly wet center starved for his attention. "Please."

He pressed his chest against my breasts, and his dick teased my entrance as he whispered, "Please what? Tell me what you want me to do to you." When I didn't immediately answer, he fisted my hair and tugged. "What do you want me to do to this body that I've been dreaming of fucking since you slid next to me at the Peabody?"

I moaned, "Fuck me."

With one hand, he trapped my wrists and pushed my arms above my head. His other hand curved to my hip as he thrust so deep that I lost my breath for a second. "Your pussy is better than I ever imagined."

He slowly pulled back and slammed into me over and over, driving my body insane with his rhythm. Although he fucked at a steady pace, my body still spiraled as if he'd increased his rhythm. Once my breathing quickened and I bit his shoulder, he began more rapid and forceful thrusts, urging me to come hard for him when he tightened his grip on my waist and pounded me fiercely. Every ram, every plunge, I cursed him more and moaned loudly, wanting to be freed of this torturous yet rapturous building explosion. And when I thought my body couldn't take much more, Jake pumped incessantly at breakneck speed until we both loudly started our ascent into ecstatic bliss. He kissed my lips, promptly shifted, and I collapsed on his chest.

Right or wrong, I fell in love with Jake Barnes the same night I ended my engagement.

THIRTY-FOUR

Jake

Although the skies were dull and gray, all I could imagine was the sun as Amara snuggled closer to me. She would awaken soon and wonder why I hadn't slept. We were in my bed at my home, where we'd been for the last two days after we left the studio. I didn't want the rest of the world into our private haven. Not yet. The world meant sadness, hurt, and the pain of betrayal.

I squeezed her tighter to me, wishing our love wasn't marred by a past that had happened long before either of us existed. How would she feel when I told her that the woman she admired and respected was the other woman who'd stolen Stoney's music?

I brushed back the curls that tumbled over Amara's forehead. I loved this woman, recognized it as love the day we first jogged, and she recited "A Born Legacy" while we were in the midst of Mother Nature. My heart had thudded against my chest as she calmly and proudly relayed the start of her new journey, lying beside me on the grass. Amara had been an unattainable love, or so I believed at that time.

Yet we were here together and loving each other. I needed to tell her, and every time I gathered my strength to, she would smile, tease me, or kiss me, and I punked out. Now that she was mine, I was too afraid to lose her. I was afraid to see the other side of her. The side of her where she no longer looked at me with admiration, desire, and love. The side of her that would somehow blame me for being culpable in what my father and Evelyn had done to Stoney because I gave him money for years.

My stomach burned with acid every time I thought about how I'd been used, and that Stoney had known why he received the money and still treated me with respect. I wanted Evelyn to own her shit and tell Amara herself. Then maybe she would forgive me for not telling her once I knew the truth.

"Mmm." She kissed my chest. "I think I want you to cook for me."

I twirled strands of her hair around my finger. "Can I get a 'good morning' before you start making demands?"

Amara grinned. "Good morning, and I want steak and eggs. Please and thank you."

I smacked her bare ass. "After we jog."

She groaned. "Here we go."

"I thought you told me you like running."

"I do. But you make me feel like you're trying to change my body or something."

I shifted on my side to face her. "I love jogging, and I love swimming. It's cool if you don't. You keep making it about your weight, and I keep telling you it's about the stamina you need to perform because you're always front and center." I dragged my index finger down the middle of her full, luscious breasts. "Your body, with its dips and curves, is so fucking sexy that I can look at you all day long. These breasts—damn, these breasts—make a man want to do right, just to have a taste." I licked her nipple and moved lower to the diamond stud in my belly button, and her stomach quivered. "This might be the hottest part of your body."

She giggled. "And not my tramp stamp of a sun?"

I smiled against her stomach. "Oh, I plan to hold on to that as I hit it just right from the back. Matter of fact…" I turned her over on her stomach so fast she gasped as I placed a slow kiss on the small of her back. She writhed on the sheets, anticipating more, and I exceeded her expectations. My worries about the future vanished into the pleasurable present.

The rest of July and August sped by in a blur. Amara and I were caught up and so in love that we made the crew blush, though we'd both initially tried to hide that we were exploring being together. Tavion had been absolutely right—we couldn't seem to get work done. The minute Amara started singing to me when we were alone in the studio, I would drag her from the booth and fuck her on the sofa. On the floor. In the chair or against the mixing board. Anywhere we could, we fucked. When the crew were around, I became impatient and short when they wanted to linger, and I wanted Amara to myself.

Her eyes would light up with amusement, and she would purposely keep the conversation going when she sensed my impatience to be alone with her. And she felt every inch of my frustration the minute we were by ourselves. She loved her effect on me and that I didn't mind open displays of affection. I was madly in love with the woman who was perfect for me. We had no more barriers. She still had to deal with the fallout from her family about the end of her engagement with Phillip, and I had to deal with an angry Rene, who'd discovered through social media that Amara and I were a thing. None of that really mattered, though, because we had each other.

She was also in demand in Nashville and performed almost nightly. Mari Johnson had a gift, through her voice, that transcended race and gender or any arbitrary, socially defined construct that divided us, and she crowded every bar she performed. She decided not to return to Atlanta to teach and had been spending every night at my place, though she insisted that she needed her own home. I kept her so busy with rehearsals, performing, and recording demos that she didn't have time to seriously look for her own apartment. I wanted her to fall so deeply for me that when the truth about Stoney and Evelyn came to light, she would believe I'd been kept in the dark. My father and I hadn't spoken since I left his office, and we wouldn't talk until he addressed the theft of Stoney's songs. I'd messaged him a few times, demanding that he and Evelyn take responsibility for what happened to Stoney's songs and make amends with Amara and the Johnson family, to no avail. I kept receiving the same response, that he needed more time. Because he was my father, I owed him. But he had to get it done soon, or I'd tell her myself. Withholding the truth from Amara prevented me from fully loving her the way I'd envisioned: a love where secrets never lived.

She wrapped her arm around my waist as we strolled through the Gaylord Opryland Resort. "Why have I been here since June, and you're just bringing me here? I could've stayed here instead of that hotel downtown and truly been inspired."

From the outside, the resort deceived passersby as an ordinary Marriott hotel. Once you walked inside, guests were in an oasis of trees, plants, and waterfalls amid restaurants and pathways. Hotel rooms and windows looked out onto the lush gardens. We were slated later tonight to enjoy the water park, an adults-only adventure inside the resort.

She pinched my nose. A habit she'd started before we became a thing.

Playfully, I knocked her hand away. "Quit it. You can touch me anytime and anywhere now. You'll leave an imprint on the bridge of my nose like I wear glasses."

She ignored my hand and pinched it again. "You mean the glasses you need but are too vain to wear?"

"I can see."

Amara squeezed my waist. "Baby, you're always squinting. It's okay. You'll be even sexier with glasses."

I slung my arm around her neck and kissed her cheek. "I still have perfect vision."

She glanced around the atrium of the resort and pointed to the left. "Okay, what does that sign say over there?"

"*You* can't even read that," I argued, since I couldn't decipher anything about that circular object in the distance. I've needed glasses most of my life, and I even had them as a child. I would never admit that to Amara, or that I only drove to familiar places without any trouble at night. I wasn't ashamed to admit that on this subject, I was indeed vain.

"If you can read it, you can do anything you want to my body while we're in the pool later."

"Even with other people around?" My dick jumped at the possibilities.

She impishly grinned. "Mm-hmm."

"Bet," I said, then jogged a few yards to the sign and shouted, "It says that the Cascades and the gift shop are in that direction."

She rolled her eyes and marched in the opposite way. I rushed to her and hugged her from the back, kissing her neck and the side of her face. "Don't be mad because I think quicker than you."

I kept kissing her until she turned around in my embrace and wrapped her arms around my neck. "You make me happy."

I nodded. "I've never been happier."

Amara looked at me expectantly, perhaps waiting for me to declare my love. She knew I loved her, as I knew she loved me. We just hadn't spoken those three words out loud. I wanted everything out in the open before I told her. I didn't want her to think more than she probably would that I'd manipulated or coerced her into forgiving me.

Instead of the words I knew she wanted to hear, I smiled. "We need to hurry up if we're going to make that tour at the Opry House."

I ignored her look of disappointment as I held her hand, and we headed to the place where dreams came true for those in the country music world. She retorted, "I told you I already had the tour with Tavion and Sophie."

"Not with me. And please tell me you didn't stand in the circle for a photo like a tourist?" I asked, half in jest but also in earnest. At the Grand Ole Opry, the six-foot circle of wood centered at the front of the stage, cut from the Ryman stage and carefully installed without as much as a fresh coat of paint, is considered hollowed ground. Only those who perform there as part of the Opry family stand in it, akin to an artist's rite of passage. It's not just any piece of wood, it's a symbol of the Opry's enduring legacy and the essence of those who stood there.

"I swear to you I didn't," I replied solemnly. "For the last time, I didn't jinx myself. Tavion and Sophie skirted around the group and took pictures of us from the wings. When it was my turn in line to move up for a photo in it, I respectfully declined. My spirit spoke and told me not to step into that circle."

I squeezed her hand. "Stoney told you not to."

She smiled. "He did. I treated the circle as sacred."

This time, I pinched her nose. "Good job."

Amara dragged her nails down my back as she yelled her release and immediately went limp against my shoulder. I held her against the wall by the balcony door, still pumping in and out until I finally reached my pinnacle a few seconds later. I eased her back to her feet and panted, "You're good?"

"Next time, warn a sistah that I can't walk around with your t-shirt on." She patted her curly hair as I pulled up my shorts on my way to the bathroom to discard my condom. "I need to keep my hair braided around you. Straightening it so you could sweat it back out is a waste of money and time."

I kissed her neck. "What can I say? I lusted after you since that very first day back in April. We have to make up for lost time."

"You can say we have all the time now that I plan to live here." She adjusted her flowy skirt, which she'd paired with one of my t-shirts, and tied it to show off her belly button and tramp stamp.

"That's right. You're not going anywhere, and I get to have you to myself." I grinned as I returned from the bathroom. "How long will you be gone?"

"I don't know. Want to walk around the hotel and catch a vibe. I have my notebook and my phone to capture whatever inspires me."

"I'll call you when I'm ready to eat. Need to do some work myself."

"Sounds good." She caressed my nape while she kissed me.

I grabbed her ass. "Don't get me started again."

She removed my hand. "Nope. We both have work to do."

"We do." My cell rang. "And duty calls."

She left, and I picked up my cell. I cursed when I saw the text from my mother.

Call me immediately. I'm not playing with you. 10:54 a.m.

I plopped down on the sofa and did her bidding. "Hey."

"What's going on with you and William? You gave up the business? I thought you were starting your own and still working with him."

"Mama, you know I've wanted to do my own thing. That's what I'm doing now. I still have some clients with Barnes, and I have no intention of poaching any of his roster, if that's what he's worried about."

"It's not him. I'm worried about the two of you. When was the last time you spoke to your father? He keeps telling me everything is crazy because he's planning Evelyn's last tour, but he's not sleeping or eating. You don't call him like you used to."

"If he didn't tell you, it's not my place. He's your husband." I ran my hand over my bearded face, frustrated that William had done nothing.

"You were my son first. Tell me what's going on…" A muffled sound came on the line, and Mama replied, "It's Jake. I'm asking him if you don't tell me what's happening. And you know he'll tell me." The phone went silent. Probably muted. I pulled my cell from my ear and started to press the red button and let them hash it out.

Then my father started speaking. "Listen, I know…I know… Jake, give me more time."

"I stalled Mari enough. She's been itching to go to Memphis. If we do that, I'm going to tell her. I can't pretend I don't know shit when I know it all. You need to tell Mama and then make Evelyn do right."

He seemed exasperated. "You can't make Evelyn do something she doesn't want to do, especially now, with so much at stake."

I scooted to the edge of the sofa and hissed, "Stop with the excuses. I can't keep lying to her about Stoney. I love her, Dad. Can't you see I can't keep this from her any longer?"

"Keep what from me?" The door slammed.

Startled, I looked at Amara, who'd slipped in so quietly I didn't hear her.

"Is that Amara?"

"Yes, and I'm telling her." I hung up against his protest.

Amara slowly approached me, her eyes already nervous and her hands at her sides trembling. "What do you have to tell me about my grandfather?"

THIRTY-FIVE

Amara

I'd forgotten my pen when I settled down to create, and I wandered into a nearby gift shop, searching in vain for something to write with. I sighed. I needed to return to the suite and hope I didn't get caught up in Jake. I couldn't stop the crazy grin that crossed my face whenever I thought about him. I'd known we had chemistry. I just hadn't realized that sparks ran amok almost every time we touched. I'd never been this deliriously happy, never dared to believe I would be this insanely in love with another human being. Knowing the feelings were reciprocated only made my rainy days bright, too.

When I approached the door to the suite, his voice was raised; from what I could tell, he was on the phone with his father. I opened the door when I heard Stoney's name.

"What can't you keep from me?"

His drawn-out sigh exacerbated the dread that crawled across my body when I'd heard some of his conversation on the other side of the door. Jake patted the sofa next to him, and I shook my head.

"Tell me now," I demanded.

He straightened his shoulders and leaned forward. "Evelyn is the mystery woman in Stoney's letters. When he broke things off with her to remain with your grandmother and father, devastated because he was the love of her life, she didn't give him credit for the songs he wrote." He reached for my hand, and I moved it behind my back. "He wrote nine songs. All hits. Four went number one, and three won Grammys. His songwriting catapulted her into superstardom. My father tried to make Evelyn give him credit, but she refused. She made a deal with him that as she rose in the world, so would his career. Years later, my father tried to make amends by sending Stoney money through me."

Suddenly, my head itched, and I started scratching my temples, digging my nails into the skin. My lungs were being squeezed, or was it my heart? I'd *trusted* him. "How could you know and not tell me? How long did you know? Or were you just humoring me this whole time? I mean, hey, you've known my grandfather for years, giving him hush money. Or did you give him anything? He sure didn't seem like he was a millionaire. You and your father probably made fun of me behind my back. The naïve school teacher who has a decent enough voice who wants to do more digging. Let's offer her a deal so she can't ever say a word when she discovers that the people she just started to trust have been lying to her the whole time. Let's offer her a life she could only imagine to erase that we took away her grandfather's life. *His life,*" I screeched.

He grabbed me and pulled me into his arms. "Please...please stop hurting yourself. I just found out myself. You know how we both kept hearing that familiar chord progression in 'A Man's Luck'? That's because it's the same one used in Evelyn's song 'A Red-Headed Woman.' When I made the connection and gathered more information, I confronted my father, who told me the truth. He asked for more time to figure out how to best handle everything. I told him I would tell you myself if he didn't make things right with Stoney, and with you. I hadn't spoken to him since that day in his office until my mother called just now, trying to figure out what the hell was wrong. She didn't know either. Still don't know if he told her, because everything was happening as you walked through the door."

I held myself stiffly in his arms and stared at him. "How long have you known?"

"The day we left Hartland when I came into the studio while you were with Evelyn."

"Why didn't you tell me then? You were angry enough to do so. I saw it all over your face. Why did you keep your mouth shut?" I pushed against him so hard that he almost slipped off the couch. "No, you already knew. Probably have known since you first brought money to my grandfather. You were mad about something else."

He eased to his knees, grabbed my waist, and implored me with those mesmerizing brown eyes of his. "Please, please. You heard me on the phone. I love you. I didn't plan to fall in love, but I fought it as hard as possible, and it happened."

"Of course you didn't. You didn't plan to fall for the woman who could ruin Evelyn Hart and Barnes Management. Keep your enemies closer, right?" Blinding pain struck my heart. How could I be such a fool to believe he would love me when he'd made it clear he didn't believe in relationships? I tried to remove his arms, and he held them firm. I yelled, "Let me go, Jake."

"I can't. I know once you walk out that door, we're over." He tucked his head against my stomach, and my resolve slipped. *Fuck.*

"Move." I tried unsuccessfully to shoo him away, and he only gripped me tighter.

"I can't lose you when I've just found you. Tell me how to make it right, and I'll do it." He pressed his lips against the diamond in my stomach. I grabbed his head, torn between giving in to the heady, intoxicating allure of this powerful man on his knees begging me to stay and making him suffer for his involvement with my grandfather. Jake didn't get to have me when he'd lied to him all this time. He didn't…

Oh, God, why is he so hard to resist?

With his slow lick of my belly button, I pressed his head into me and allowed him to push up my skirt and slide off my panties.

Jake lifted his head to kiss me thoroughly, savoring every inch of my mouth before he eased down between my legs. With every lick and tug on my clit, he apologized for not telling me the moment he'd discovered the truth. I didn't allow his declarations of love and apologies to penetrate my heart, and as he asked with his eyes if he needed a condom, I opened my legs wider. I wanted to feel him without any barriers. I wanted to feel him, raw and skin against skin. I didn't care about consequences as he stroked me, replacing the dread with pleasure. I held on to him as he began to buck, spurring my own climax. I needed to experience Jake sexually the way we were meant to experience each other—because this would be our last time.

THIRTY-SIX

Amara

Two days later, I stood at the threshold of my grandfather's home. I glanced over my shoulder at the cemetery, debating whether to speak to him before going inside. I decided against it until I knew what to say.

Today was a bright end-of-August day. Much different to the day I'd entered his home four months ago. Now, the face of his house didn't seem sad. Just indifferent. So much had happened so quickly since I'd last been here. I had to be sure everything had really occurred and that I hadn't awakened from a nightmare. I checked my phone for the selfie I'd taken the first day in front of Hartland with Jake in the background. Melancholy assailed me as it did every second Jake crossed my mind.

After we had sex, he'd carried me to bed and held me as he dozed. Once he was in a deep sleep, I eased out of bed and grabbed my guitar, notebook, purse, and cell. He could have my clothes at the resort and his home. I just wanted to leave before I got sucked into him again. I caught an Uber to the airport. I longed to fly home, climb in bed with my parents, and pretend I was their child again, when they'd take away my hurts with a simple hug.

Standing at the counter debating which flight would take me home the fastest, I'd heard a whisper. "Think that's her."

Then I felt a tap and turned around to two smiling young women, one of whom was wearing a t-shirt from Fisk University, a historically Black college in Nashville. "You're Mari Johnson, right?"

I nodded, trying to place their expectant faces. "I'm sorry. Do I know you?"

"No." The shorter one grinned. "We just saw your show last week and couldn't stop smiling. We love country music and don't like saying it too loud, even in Nashville. Watching you perform inspired me."

"Are you a musician or a singer?"

She shook her head. "Naw, my singing would hurt your ears." Both women giggled. "I heard your story, and you inspired me not to be afraid to go after what I want. I can't explain it except to say you looked really happy on that stage, and if I could have a little bit of that happiness, I think my life would be just fine."

The quieter one shyly asked, "Can we take a selfie with you?"

I smiled. "Of course."

The three of us had taken selfies with their phones and mine. I needed to remember this moment whenever I had doubts about my career. About my talent. About my destiny. About my born legacy. Jake may have broken my heart, but without him I wouldn't have ever taken such a leap of faith into who I really was.

When the airline rep asked about my destination, I'd told her the next flight to Memphis. Now I stood at my grandfather's door, using the code for the new system my father had bought, and walked inside.

The house looked the same, except I'd used some of my advance to hire a cleaning service to keep the house tidy and dust-free. We kept the temperature at seventy-five. The front room still held the two pictures of me and my parents. I walked up the stairs and stopped when I reached the step where I'd hidden from the guests until Jake Barnes walked in and immediately spotted me.

I pushed through my sadness and went back to my father's old room. I had to admit to myself, it was eerie to be alone in this house. Yet, at the same time, it was comforting to know that this home was my grandfather's last connection to me. He'd given me this place. The granddaughter he only met twice. I went into the closet where I'd found the guitar, searching for any more clues.

After searching for thirty minutes, I wandered back downstairs and stared at the photos. I moved closer and lifted the one of me and my parents when I was a baby. It seemed heavier than the typical frame. I turned it over and pulled down the back of the frame to reveal a folded letter with my father's name written on it taped to the back of the picture. With a racing heart, I then looked at the back of my graduation photo and found another letter with *Amara* written across it. I held the letters to my chest before I placed both frames on the coffee table and rushed across the street.

I went to the marble headstone that Jake had ordered and paid for a couple of months ago. I ran my fingers along the engraving that I'd chosen, a quote from *Montage of a Dream Deferred*. I'd ended it with my own dedication:

Marcus "Stoney" Johnson, Sr., a musician who knew the blues too well and who loved his family most of all.

I wiped tears as I glanced up at the window that I'd stared out of four months ago. Then, I didn't quite understand the gravity of what it meant to be Stoney Johnson's granddaughter. Had no idea that this journey would make me feel so close…so attuned to a man with whom I'd never ever taken a photo.

"Whew. Um…this is really hard. Like, crazy hard to be here with you like this when I barely remember you. It's like I have an idea, and then it fades. I can speak to you anywhere now, and you'll hear me. Still, this is where you rest, right across the street from where our family lived.

"I wanted to say thank you for my talent. Your love of music and gift for words courses through my veins. You inspire me. Even finding out about your affair with Evelyn makes me closer to you because I know personally how someone suddenly shifts your heart in ways you never imagined. I fell in love with one man after promising to marry another. Sounds familiar, doesn't it? And like your affair, it ended in betrayal." I touched the top of his headstone. "I wanted to read this letter I just found before you. Figured it only fitting." When I unfolded the letter, a snapshot of me as a little girl holding a guitar while he stood behind me with a beaming smile drifted to the ground. I couldn't have been more than four or five. My grandmother probably took the picture. I jumped up and down at the unexpected find before retrieving the picture. I believed that a photo of the two of us had never been taken. Then there was a photo of him showing me the guitar.

I wiped away more happy tears.

Dear Amara,

I always hoped to see you again before taking my last breath. I asked your father about you when he came to help me put my affairs in order. He didn't really want to talk about you. Barely wanted to talk to me, though he honored me enough to help me plan my burial. Not that I blamed him. I hurt him deeply, as I've hurt others who couldn't seem to let go of the pain. If you found this letter, I hope you also found the others. I left them because I wanted you to know the truth about Natalie Hartwell, who you may know as Evelyn Hart, and me. I did love her. Thought for a minute that I could give up my wife and be with her. But I couldn't leave your grandmother or my son, who I've loved with every breath I took. I wrote him a letter and hope he'll believe how much I regret that we couldn't be the father and son I envisioned for him when I first held him. But this letter isn't about him—it's about my beautiful granddaughter with an ear for music.

I cherish the day your father decided to bring you to see me when I visited your grandmother. She'd finally forgiven me, and we'd developed a friendship. If she'd lived, I would've asked her to marry me again. She did her best to get your father to forgive me. He couldn't seem to let go of the past. So when he agreed to let me see you, he didn't tell your mother. I guess he didn't want her pressuring him too.

Your father dropped you off and didn't even stay to see me. Although his leaving hurt, seeing you so bright, talented, and talkative warmed my heart. I had my guitar out, playing one of your grandmother's favorite songs, "Ain't No Sunshine" by Bill Withers, when you walked to the guitar, cute as a button, and bopped your head and sang along. You didn't know the words, but your tone and melody were clear. We knew you could saaang! Then I showed you how to pluck the guitar, and you clapped in joy. Oh, how I wanted to be the one to teach you. I could see you already had natural gifts.

I was ecstatic when your father told me you were a music teacher engaged to a good man. I hope you love him with all of who you are. It's the only way to love. I hope he deserves your love and sees you for who you are.

Speaking of good young men, a man named Jake Barnes visited me for years and gave me money each time. I looked forward to his visits. I liked to think of him as family, because he would never seem in a rush and wanted to spend time with me. We would share a meal and talk about music, love, and life for hours. I could tell he didn't know the real reason he brought me money on behalf of his stepfather. He was too starry-eyed about working with Evelyn Hart. He had no idea that the people he loved were trying to quietly pay me off for making millions off my records because of a love affair with Evelyn that ended the only way that it could. Something about his energy charmed me, and instead of turning him away or rejecting the money, I welcomed him into my home and kept the cash, though I never used it. All I ever wanted was credit so that my wife and son could see that their sacrifices for me weren't in vain.

I could go on and on talking about how proud I am of you, and how I probably should've written you before now. I didn't because pride kept me from doing it—I was too afraid you'd reject me like your father did. I hope that the picture of us and my letters are enough for you to forgive my sins, for you to be proud of me, and for you to know you were deeply loved by me.

Your loving granddaddy.

P.S. The money I didn't spend is in my living room. Underneath my recliner, there's a floorboard that blends in with the rest. Step until you hear a creak. Open it and there should be over two million dollars in cash. Keep it for yourself, or share it with your father. It's yours to live your dreams.

In disbelief, I hurried across the street, back up the stairs, and through the door, hoping some thief hadn't discovered his money. I moved the recliner and stepped across it several times before I heard hollowness. I then ran to the kitchen and scrounged through one of the drawers to find a hammer to help me lift the boards. When I finally managed to lift the board, I sat back on my haunches, beaming. Stacks and stacks of hundred-dollar bills.

This money would never erase what was stolen from him, but it was a start.

THIRTY-SEVEN

Jake

I drove up to Hartland a week after Amara had left me while I slept. I understood why she'd left like she had. We had an undeniable magnetic attraction, and we were powerless to ignore the pull whenever we inhabited each other's orbits. I only sent one text.

I love you.

I didn't expect an answer, and sadly, she met my expectations. I missed her terribly after talking and being with her every day for almost three months. The crew missed her, too. I couldn't explain what happened between us except to say that I'd fucked it up and hoped that she would forgive me one day. I was sure they probably thought it was about another woman, and in some respects, it was.

Evelyn Hart had dictated so much of our lives that my father had partnered with me so I could handle the roster while he focused on her career. How could I ever expect my father, who'd been beholden to Evelyn since he was a teen, to demand anything from her? He couldn't.

I parked in the circular driveway, grateful that Evelyn rocked in one of her chairs on the front porch. I didn't want to enter the house and run into Jess. This wasn't a social call. I exited my car and stopped at the bottom of the steps. "I think you know why I'm here."

Evelyn chuckled and tilted her head. "Yes, you fell in love, and now you want to destroy my legacy when I'm at the end of my career to prove your love."

Taking off my shades, I drawled, "William actually had the balls to at least tell you what I know."

"He's still your father." She pointed at me.

"Maybe I'm not ready to claim him again after his duplicity."

"He didn't deceive you, Jake."

I retorted, "Using me to give Stoney money for years without telling me wasn't deception? The same man who criticized me whenever I lied or made bad choices and made sure to tell me in no uncertain terms his disappointment."

"Yet he always claimed you. Always been proud of you, even when you messed up. He's torn up about what this is doing to your relationship."

I laughed. "Stop deflecting. Do what's right, Ms. Evelyn."

"Right, for who? Stoney? The man who left me at the airport like a damn fool waiting for hours when he knew he'd changed his mind? He promised to love and treat me better than any man. I believed him. For once, I believed in a man. I'd been beaten by my father, raped three times by men in this industry who threatened to ruin my career before I began. I foolishly married a man who was just like the father I ran away from when I was fifteen. All this happened before I met Stoney when I was twenty-four and he was twenty-seven. He made me fall for him, and I thought maybe… just maybe, God gave me real love." She tightened her fists. "How dare he hurt me like he did, and there's no consequences for his behavior. So when the record label asked for the two songs they paid for, I added the remaining seven he wrote because he'd been inspired by me and our love. I told them they were mine and that he had released his rights to the first two songs.

"Years later, he drove all the way out here, and once again, I thought he wanted to finally be with me, and all he wanted was his name on my songs. He would call me when the mood hit, asking for his music. Never wanted me again. I can admit I started to feel sorry for him when I heard his wife and son had left him anyway and that he struggled. When I offered money, he refused."

"You already punished him. Why not give him the credit he deserved?"

"Because it was too late. I became an icon and a role model for women everywhere. My legacy is not my own, Jake," she reasoned.

"And because Stoney made the honorable and right decision for him and chose his family, you stripped him of everything." I walked up the stairs until we were at eye level. "You might as well have accused him of rape."

She gripped the handles of the rocking chair and rose proud and with indignation. "How dare you, Jake Barnes, fix your mouth to say that I would ever tell such a lie on Stoney or any man. Any time a woman lies about rape makes the next woman's story less believable."

I nodded slowly. "Oh…I dare. I dare." I spread my arms wide. "Like all the many Black musicians who had their legacy, their rights, stripped from them because of someone's lies. Then, when the next person steps forward and complains, no one believes him. For centuries my people have been literally and figuratively raped, left to feel powerless and helpless by people who believed they had the right to do that to us. I thought you were different. Thought that race and skin color didn't matter to you. Felt proud that I knew and loved you."

Evelyn's shoulders wilted, and she clasped her hands in front of her. "What happened fifty years ago shouldn't change how you feel about me." Her voice trembled as she continued, "I'm still the same Evelyn you've known for over half your life. I'll never stop loving you. What I did to Stoney was spiteful and mean. I'd had a rough beginning. I was young, angry, and hungry for stardom. Would I do the same things again? Never. Let sleeping dogs lie, Jake. He's gone now. What does saying anything now really do except destroy our family?"

I yelled, "Stoney Johnson was like family to me. For fourteen years, I visited him twice a year. He was a broken man who drove a bus during the day and played his music alone in his home or at some hole in the wall at night. He kept two pictures in front of him where he sat every night watching TV—his son and his granddaughter. His life meant something. His music meant something. He wasn't just a man who broke your heart. Stoney was brilliant, funny, loyal, and loving. No matter how embarrassed I am that I never questioned why my father sent me to his home with an envelope of cash twice a year, I am forever grateful that he sent me." I tapped my heart with my fist. "I am a better man because I got to know a man like Stoney. I helped the woman I love to feel closer to him. To know him a little more. To be proud of him." I stepped closer to Evelyn. "And I swear to God, I will bring Stoney Johnson's legacy to light, not just through his granddaughter's music."

Evelyn's green eyes sparkled like emeralds as she reached for me before dropping her arms to her sides. With heaving chests, we stared at each other.

Jess came to the door and opened it. "Everything okay?"

"Yes." Evelyn's gaze didn't waver from mine as she held her head up higher. "Bringing Stoney's legacy to light could bring mine and yours into darkness."

I stepped back on the stairs. "That's the difference between me and you. Excuse my language, ladies, but I don't give a fuck."

Jess shook her head and went back inside. She probably knew the truth about Stoney, since she and Evelyn shared most things. Evelyn snapped her mouth shut and remained speechless, standing on the porch as I jumped in my car and sped away.

Once I made it to my office, I called Nathan. He answered on the third ring. "I want you to publish the story on Stoney Johnson with concrete evidence. The whole truth."

He drew in a ragged breath. "This could ruin your relationship with Evelyn and your father. May ruin any future you have in this city and this country for besmirching Evelyn Hart's name, even if it's the truth. Amara may still not come back."

I replied, "I'm fully aware of the consequences. I promised Amara that we would find out everything we could about him, and I'm keeping my word to her."

"Aww… That's some real love."

"It is, and I hope she'll believe in me again." I drummed my fingers on the desk. "And please stop using your SAT words on me. 'Besmirching,' really?"

"Wait, are you still jealous I scored much higher than you?"

"Man, I ain't jealous of shit." We chuckled together before I grew quiet. After losing Amara and being at odds with my father, I needed my friendship with Nathan more than ever. "Seriously, thank you for always being there."

He paused a beat and then replied, "Always got you. Now, let me get back to work." He clicked off.

I leaned back in my chair and picked up my iPad with the electronic copy of Amara's contract saved on it. I took a brief video showing me deleting the contract. I sent her the video along with a message.

Nathan will release the truth about Evelyn and Stoney as soon as he finishes gathering evidence. There may be fallout from die-hard Hart fans, but your grandfather's talent will be recognized. I sent the video to prove I've deleted your contract. You owe no one. Whatever money you earn and will earn is all yours. You're free to sign with someone else. I'm relinquishing any rights to your songs and demos we produced in the studios. If you want the crew to be your band, I can also release them from their contracts or do an addendum where they can work with you and me. The crew loves and misses you, but not as much as I do.

After I sent it, I opened the drawer on my desk and searched for a number I'd written on a notepad. I stared at the phone for almost thirty minutes before I gathered the strength to call. I allowed the phone to ring, though I wanted to hang up before he picked up. He answered, his voice still the same. "Hello."

"Is this Jakobi?"

"Jake?" he asked, and I could hear the smile in his voice. I looked up toward the heavens, thankful for this sign.

"Yeah, it's me. Wanted to see you. Maybe talk."

"I would like that. I really would. I have time now if you want to talk."

"I have time." I propped my feet on my desk and began a much-needed conversation with the man who'd given me life.

THIRTY-EIGHT

Amara

My father had been my rock ever since I could remember. I had been a daddy's girl and always wanted his approval. I'd earned good grades to see his smile and hear his praise. Hid my passion for music because I knew he disapproved. Everything I did or didn't do was for his love. Until now, and because he'd been unused to me not bowing down to his demands, we hadn't spoken in months.

Stepping into the home I grew up in inevitably invoked nostalgia and the little girl inside of me. Mama had conveniently gone shopping to leave us alone to really talk. He was in his favorite recliner after playing a round of golf. A professor in criminal justice at Morehouse, he had his summers free. Usually, he spent them working on his research, playing golf, or taking mini trips with Mama.

When I walked into the den, he looked up and just as quickly returned his attention to the TV. I eased down on the sofa and called out answers for categories that I knew while we watched *Jeopardy!*. After a few, he joined in like we used to when I was young. By the end, we'd answered many clues and high-fived each other. The tension between us was replaced by our strong connection.

"Are you finally back?" he asked.

"No, just came to talk to you. I don't think I'm coming back to Atlanta to live. I'll live between Memphis and Nashville, figuring out my music career. I want to fix up Granddaddy's place too. Not sure if I'll live in it, but I'll rent it out or something."

He tsked. "You could've kept that information to yourself."

I scooted to the edge of the sofa. "Why can't you forgive him? He's gone now, and you're still holding on to anger. He messed up, and he lost his family as a result. Before Grandma died, she forgave him. She was the one he hurt. Not you. So why can't you forgive him?"

He pushed up from his chair. "I'm not talking about this."

I jumped to my feet. "Yes, you are. He loved you. He never stopped loving you. I found over two million dollars and letters in his home that he left for you and me a week ago."

Daddy snapped, "I don't want his money, nor do I want to read any more of his letters. The last one I read was when he made plans to meet up with his woman. I tried to tear the picture of them together I found with the letter, but only managed to rip her head before I heard my parents come home. I loved that man with every breath inside of me and would've done anything for him, but my father chose another woman over Mama and me. Do you know how devastating it was to know that he contemplated leaving us and going off with this white woman? He was not only risking his family but his life. We were still getting lynched, and he was willing to risk everything for her. I was eight years old, and the day I thought he was going to leave, I physically ached. My stomach and head hurt. I couldn't even focus at school, wondering if I would ever see him again." His pain-filled eyes glistened and his hands clenched into fists as he unshackled his hurt.

The show of raw emotion and anguish from my taciturn father held me immobile. I was scared to move or even breathe, worried that any action would break this truth spell and my father would return to that familiar, reserved man.

He blinked rapidly. "When I got home that day, he wasn't home. I remember running upstairs to see if his clothes were in his closet. I started crying when I saw his clothes were there. Then he walked through the door with roses for Mama and candy for me. I couldn't enjoy the candy because I didn't know if he planned to leave on another day. I couldn't sleep, worrying if he would leave while I was asleep. I would cry whenever he left. This went on for about two weeks, and my mother had enough. She demanded to know what was wrong with me, and I showed her the letter I'd kept."

A lone tear fell down my father's cheek. "They had a horrible fight. Mama destroyed most of the house, including my father's favorite art that she'd painted. She beat on him, and he took her licks, cried, and promised that he wouldn't ever cheat on her again. That he did choose her. Mama was hurt by his betrayal, especially after struggling by his side while he'd pursued his dream. She and I left in the middle of the night, and every time he tried to call, she ignored him, or my aunt cursed him.

"I missed him terribly at first and hated that I was the one who broke up the family. I messed up our lives showing her that damn letter. I heard my father beg for another chance. Listened to the agony in his voice. Knew he loved us. I felt sorry for him until those words I read popped into my mind. He was going to leave us, and in the end, he did." He glared at me. "And you're just like him. Breaking off your engagement to be with another man. A man who you haven't known that long just because he shares your foolish dream."

I wiped my eyes using the back of my hand and stood proudly before my father. "I didn't break up with Phillip to be with Jake. I broke up with Phillip because he doesn't believe in my 'foolish' dream, as you call it. I broke up with him because he refused to see the real me. I wanted to make it work, but I can't live in the shadows anymore. Like my grandfather, I'm meant to be center stage and proud. I'm meant to be a performer and plan to do it for as long as possible."

Daddy punched his palm with his own fist. "We were too poor to live anywhere other than beside a graveyard because my father just had to be this *musician*." He stepped closer to me. "Why would someone so smart want that life, huh? You saw how he ended up—alone and broke."

Refusing to allow his contemptuous words to alter my dreams, I lifted my chin higher. "If you can't accept my life, you can't accept me, and I'm prepared to live without you." He shut his eyes tightly, and I had to push through the hurt I'd just caused to speak my piece. "I love you as you loved your father—with every breath inside of me—but I won't punish myself as my grandfather did for his actions. He punished himself because he was about to give up everything he loved for Evelyn Hart."

Daddy's eyes flew open, and I nodded.

"Your father changed his mind because he loved you more, and, as a woman scorned, Evelyn took credit for his music, won awards, and became a star because of his songs. She betrayed him, and he felt foolish because he still lost you and Grandma. He was told no one would believe him when he demanded his credit."

I touched my father's forearm. "Can you imagine what that must have been like for him? To be that close to his dream and what he thought was his destiny and not achieve it? Disillusionment and losing his family killed something inside of him. When Evelyn's people started giving him money out of guilt, he didn't want it. He saved that money and left it for us." I passed him the letter. "Forgive him, Daddy. Read it."

His eyes widened at his name on the envelope, and he shook his head. "What does it say?"

"I don't know. I didn't read it."

He tried to hand the envelope back to me. "Read it for me."

"No. I've read enough letters that weren't meant for me. Please remember that you once loved him so much you couldn't function without him. I'll see you later, Daddy."

When I moved past him, my father caught my wrist. "Stay while I read his letter. I'm not prepared to live without you."

I sobbed in relief and hugged him tightly. "I promise I'm going to make you proud of me."

He pulled back wearing a frown. "Mari, I've always been proud of you. You don't have to do anything else on this Earth to make me prouder." My father patted the arm of the sofa. "Now, stay and tell me about Nashville so your mama knows we made up and she'll let me back in our bedroom."

Knowing how much that had to hurt my father, who lived and breathed for my mother, I winked. "I'll make sure she knows you begged for my forgiveness. She'll love that."

"She will." He chuckled as he returned to his recliner, holding the envelope. "I have my girls back."

"Yep, you do." I clasped my hands together, empathizing with his nervousness as he stared at the letter in his hand. "And you can have Granddaddy back, too."

My father took a deep breath before he slowly opened the letter from *his* father.

A month later, on a cool late-September evening, I sat on the deck of my new home in Nashville with my guitar, strumming and humming with Sophie. Using some of my inheritance, I'd bought a modest three-bedroom home a short drive from Music Row and Broadway. I wanted the freedom to play and sing without disturbing neighbors, and I had the money to afford more than an apartment.

"I like how that sounds… So mellow." Sophie took a swig of beer from her bottle.

She and I had grown even closer after I returned to Nashville in time for a set I had at a bar. It'd been weird to perform without Jake. Although he wasn't always on stage with us, he was always in the audience. When I received his video canceling the contract the same evening my father and I reconciled, I'd just finished dinner with my parents at their home. My heart skipped a beat and I had to excuse myself to the bathroom.

I'd leaned my butt against the sink and listened to his message. His deep voice soothed me as he released me from any obligation to him, and I'd wanted desperately to call him. To hear him tease me or to at least arrange to pick up my grandfather's guitar, which I'd left at his house. Then the familiar ache of betrayal the day I found out about Evelyn and my granddad squeezed my heart. No, I needed more time. More time to heal from my broken engagement and the lies from people I'd begun to trust. More time to see if I could do this new life without Jake Barnes.

"I like it, too. Getting nervous about meeting with Lunar Records." I picked up my beer bottle.

"Jake will still help you negotiate without a contract," Sophie reminded me.

"I know. I guess I want to see if I can do this on my own." I swallowed the apple-flavored ale and looked out onto my manicured lawn. "Don't get me wrong, I appreciate all that Jake did to put me in this position. Without him I wouldn't have taken a chance. Without him I wouldn't have these gigs in the city. Without him I wouldn't have met you and the rest of the crew. You've become more than a band. You're my friends now."

Sophie held her bottle up. "Naw, we're family."

I grinned and tapped it with mine. "Yeah…we are."

She gulped down her beer and rose from her wooden chair. "Good, because families forgive families, right?"

"What did you do?"

"It's not what I did." She scurried into the house.

I shook my head and continued strumming my guitar, thinking of Jake and if he'd already started seeing someone else.

She walked back out holding a purple guitar case with a bow.

I frowned. "I told you no birthday gifts." Today was my thirty-first birthday, and I wanted it to be a low-key, relaxing day, which it had been.

Sophie placed the case on my deck table. "Open it, please."

"Okay." I smiled as I unclicked the latches and lifted the lid. "Oh my God."

Sophie peeked over my shoulder and nudged me when the tears started. "It's from Jake. He didn't know if you would take it from him, so he called me to pick it up earlier today."

I pulled out my grandfather's newly restored acoustic guitar. The gloss of the paint twinkled even in the approaching darkness. I checked the tuning pegs, and the broken one had been replaced.

Sophie pointed toward the case. "He told me he left a card."

I looked back down, and just like the first time I found this guitar, the instrument wasn't the only thing in the velvet-lined case. An envelope bearing my name written in horrible scribble teased me with its contents when I picked it up and heard a rattle.

Sophie squealed. "So freaking romantic. I had no idea Jake had it in him."

I'd never considered myself the romantic type either, until Jake.

I opened the envelope and pulled out the purple card, along with a thin gold necklace with the broken peg of my grandfather's guitar.

Wreck me, in the shadows we find,
A love so fierce, it's one of a kind.
In your kiss, I find my defeat,
In your arms, my heart skips a beat.

I hugged myself at the lyrics he'd written on the card. Words I'd sung to him the night we first made love. I laughed. "This man knows how to get what he wants."

"Then I suggest you give it to him." She arched a brow. "He might just be at the studio if you want to see him."

"Of course I want to see him." I admired the necklace and the thoughtfulness to keep the peg so I could still have what made Granddad's guitar uniquely his. "But we said that if we crossed the line, it could ruin everything, and it did. Maybe we shouldn't go back."

"Evelyn and her bullshit ruined it, not you or him." She grabbed my shoulders. "You obviously still love each other, and you'll get through this." Sophie then pushed me toward the entrance to my house. "It's your birthday. Go and fuck his brains out while I sit here and enjoy this beautiful night. I'll lock up behind me."

Unadulterated anticipation and excitement of being with him again seeped through me as I grabbed my keys and my purse and headed to the front of my house. When I swung open the door, Evelyn Hart stood there in a denim dress and a cowboy hat, poised to ring the bell.

"Hey, darling. Think it's about time we really talk."

The thrill of seeing Jake quickly turned to dread. I stepped back and allowed the woman who'd haunted my grandfather into my home.

THIRTY-NINE

Amara

The room was quiet, save for the soft whisper of an evening breeze through an open window. Sitting at the old wooden desk that had once belonged to my granddad, I opened his weathered journal to a rare blank page.

I reached for one of my pens, feeling the weight of history in my grasp, and began to write. The black ink bled onto the page as I wrote carefully within and outside of the page's ever so faint, yet well-defined lines. What flowed from me would not be just a song—it was a declaration, a sacred vow to him and to myself. My words poured out, a mix of resolve and reverence, a song to weave our spirits together on the stage he never truly left:

A Song for Stoney

With every chord that I strum,
With every beat of the drum,
I step onto the stage with you,
Echoing truths only we knew.
Broken chords and stolen rhymes,
Now restored, credited in time.
But this spotlight I seek today,
Is claimed by right, not just to repay.
I'll carry your legacy, proud and strong,
With every note, I right the wrong.
Not out of spite, nor to reclaim,

But to honor our name on fame's vast plain.
Stoney, through your music, through my fight,
Your soul and mine unite in light.
Bound by blood and chords that blend,
I play your legacy to the end.

Love Mari Johnson, your granddaughter.

I closed the journal slowly, sealing our pact with the ink that still glistened on the page. Walking over to his old guitar case, I placed the journal carefully inside, right next to the Yamaha guitar—his legacy, now intertwined with mine.

As I prepared to leave the room, I reached to turn off the lamp, and my eyes caught the edge of an envelope peeking from the drawer. It was the one Evelyn had given me, her hands slightly trembling as she did.

"I'm trying to make things right, Amara," she had said, her voice thick with a regret that seemed to carry the weight of years. "This is all I can undo," she confessed, acknowledging the limits of her atonement.

I pulled the envelope out again, sliding my fingers under the flap I had already opened once before. Inside, the letter from Evelyn's lawyer was formal yet resolute, a testament to a promise kept: *Pursuant to Ms. Hart's instructions and in recognition of past oversights, the masters of all songs credited to Evelyn Hart but created by Mr. Marcus "Stoney" Johnson are hereby reverted to the estate of Marcus Johnson, Sr., effective immediately.*

The words were a stark reminder of how much had been taken and how much was trying to be returned. Evelyn's attempt at restitution, while significant, was just a step, not a conclusion.

Rereading the letter, I felt a deep, solemn connection to the past and a clear path forward. It wasn't just a legal correction, it was a moral one, handing back what was never rightfully hers to claim. And with it, a baton was passed—not in triumph but in quiet acknowledgment of errors and efforts to amend them.

I folded the letter delicately, placing it back into the envelope. This document was more than paper—it was a symbol of justice, however delayed.

I slid it into the top drawer of the desk, a secure and fitting place among Granddad's other important papers.

As I closed the drawer, the weight of responsibility settled on my shoulders. Evelyn was no hero in this narrative, and her actions spoke more of necessity than of valor. But they also didn't paint her as a villain beyond redemption. She'd reopened a door, and now it was my turn to step through it, to elevate Stoney's legacy to the heights it deserved, on terms that honored him and were once again rightfully his.

FORTY

Jake

I fingered the lettering on the gold-plated invite as I sat in the back seat of a chauffeured SUV, wondering if I should even be here tonight. My stomach churned with emotions. I'd been surprised that Evelyn hadn't crossed me off the guest list. She and I hadn't spoken since the day I confronted her. Yet she knew the article with damning evidence was finished and would be released in the coming weeks. Could I walk in this auditorium with a room full of fans and industry people who knew me and my family and pretend that the shit wasn't about to hit the fans? Was I even ready to deal with the consequences of that article? Would I still be standing after everything was out in the open and chaos ensued among my family, friends, and the people I loved? Barnes Management and my new company might take an unrecoverable hit once the world realized I was behind exposing one of country music's treasures.

I tapped my Stetson against my chest. I'd done the right thing, regardless of the fallout. I owed it to Stoney Johnson and the countless others who looked like me who'd been fucked over in the music industry.

"Are you ready, Mr. Barnes?" the driver asked me.

I stared out of the tinted windows at the people dressed in their finest, excited to see Evelyn Hart's last performance at the Ryman, the theater that kicked off her career. With her big voice, sass, and sex appeal, she'd become a music legend in this country and beyond.

"Yes." I stepped out of the car, donned my hat, and ignored the flashing lights of cameras as I walked behind starlets and music legends all headed inside to laud Evelyn.

I blinked, adjusting my eyes to the theater's darkness after all the bright lights outside. Jess stood near the entrance to the auditorium, wearing a long, formfitting red dress with a red cowboy hat. "Don't you look jazzy," I said.

She held her arms out, and I hugged her. "Jake, where have you been?"

"I needed a break from everyone. I've been working since I was eighteen and rarely take vacations, so I did some traveling." I'd had to leave Nashville for a while to avoid falling back into old behaviors because I missed Amara so damn much. I'd thought the restored guitar I gifted her on her birthday would've brought us back together. Instead, she sent a text thanking me for an amazing gift and that she wanted us to talk soon. That was two weeks ago.

"Are you back?" Jess smiled as people walked around us on the way to their seats.

I nodded.

"Good." She grabbed my hand and pulled me with her. "Evelyn wants to see you."

"Of course she does."

We weaved through the crowd, and I waved at the familiar faces I always saw at these events. Some I liked, some I'd slept with, and some didn't like me. Yet this was my world. My parents were in the VIP section, near the front of the auditorium, and happily waved when we passed them on the way to the backstage area. I smiled at both and pointed toward the stage.

After reconciling with my biological father, I'd reached out to William. We spent a weekend together, hashing out our issues and dividing the business. By the end of the weekend, William reassured me that his love for me had never been conditional. We determined that we had an unshakeable bond and could get past any differences, and that he would support any decision I made in regards to exposing Evelyn. Through my conversations with both, I'd finally seen them as men first, capable of making errors like any human being. Then I saw them as fathers whose actions made me doubt their love for me. Spending time with both, I'd learned it was far from the truth. Having the tough, hard discussions with both had allowed old wounds that festered to heal.

I owed my decision to forgive my fathers to Stoney, the man and the talented musician whose biggest regret was not mending his relationship with his family. He would've given anything to hear from his son and granddaughter before he died. I'd spent years with a person who had so much regret as a man, as a husband, and, most of all, as a father. I prayed that somehow, in his last days on Earth, he'd made peace with his actions and the consequences.

I checked my watch as we wandered through the staff and guests behind the stage. "Jess, it's almost showtime. I promise to stay and speak to her afterward."

She looped her arm through mine. "She's not going on without seeing your face. We miss you, Jake. Besides, her dressing room is right there."

Evelyn's familiar Tennessee twang sounded clear even through the thick door. "I told you I needed my lashes added before you added the foundation. Why can't you just do what I said? Then this one over here trying to fuck up my nerves with this last-minute run-through of the show." I smiled as Jess knocked on the door, and Evelyn yelled, "Come on, darlings, I can't seem to get shit done anyway. Might as well as have another interruption."

Jess opened the door wide to show me standing at the entryway. Evelyn's eyes immediately teared up. "Now, why did you bring him back here now? I didn't expect him to show up. He's messing up my look." The makeup artist immediately started dabbing at Evelyn's eyes. She shooed her away and stood, still wearing a satin robe. "Come on in and give an old woman a hug."

I walked in, but hugging her was something I wasn't ready for.

She looked around the room. "I need everyone to leave but Jake. I might be late getting on stage. They'll be all right. This won't be the first time my fans had to wait on me." The three people and Jess scurried out of the room. The minute we were alone, Evelyn stepped back. "The older you get, you just get better looking. When are you going to settle down and make me a great-grandmother?"

"Ms. Evelyn, did you really want to see me to ask about my marital status? Truth be told, I've been taking a sabbatical from women. I've been focusing on myself. Traveling. Getting my business together and slowly developing talent."

"I heard through the grapevine you're already making a name for yourself with all this cross-genre music." She gripped my biceps. "You can't give up on love yet. Trust me, it's lonely out here."

"Sometimes love don't love us." I ducked my head, not wanting to talk about this, when my heart still ached for Amara—especially not with the woman who was a part of our origin story just as much as our breakup. It'd been two months since Amara walked out of my life. I knew she did shows in the area and Memphis, because she'd hired the crew as her band. As I'd predicted, I also heard labels were vying to sign her. I couldn't be prouder, though we no longer spoke.

"Sometimes and sometimes, we have to take a chance again."

I kissed her forehead. "Ms. Evelyn, tonight is about you. Not me. I need to go find my seat. You go on in ten."

She gripped my arms. "I can't go on the stage until you forgive me for what I did. Please say you forgive me."

Shaking my head, I looked down at the woman who'd been the matriarch of my adopted family. "You'll never change. You won't guilt me into saying anything. I love you and will always love you. Forgiveness, when you don't seem to have remorse, is another matter."

"I forgive you."

I jerked back. "What do you have to forgive me for?"

She waved her hand. "For having your friend write a story on me without my permission."

"What? I warned you and my father. The story won't drop for another week or so, the way you wanted it. You'll have your moment tonight before all hell breaks loose." I turned away, feeling my temper rise.

"Say you forgive me."

I looked over my shoulder at her. "Ms. Evelyn, now's not the time. You need to focus on your last show." Someone knocked on the door. "See? They need you."

Impatiently, I opened the door, and my breath caught in my throat. Amara stood before me, beautiful and fierce, wearing a strapless purple sparkly dress hugging all the parts of her I'd claimed as mine for the short time we were together. The necklace I'd had crafted with Stoney's damaged tuning peg adorned her neck. She wore thin braids that hung low on her back with a purple Stetson.

She cocked her head to the side and placed her hand on one hip, with eyes that danced with flirtatious energy. "I was wondering if you were going to show up."

I balled my fists instead of pulling her into my arms like I longed to do. "How have you been?"

"Real good. Amazing, actually."

Her smile widened, and my stomach painfully clenched. I hoped the pure joy she embodied wasn't because of a man. Maybe Phillip had realized he was a fucking idiot and begged for another chance. Or maybe she'd met someone new. "Glad to hear that. You look good. Then again, you've always been beautiful to me. I've missed you so damn much."

"That's all I needed to hear." She waved at Evelyn. "Kill it tonight. I can take him now."

Evelyn smiled. "Please take him. I still need to get dressed. He was about to curse me out when all I wanted to do was bring you two back together. I know you wanted to surprise him. I wish you had told him before tonight that you still want him. Had me all nervous he wouldn't show."

I looked back at Evelyn. "So you don't need my forgiveness?"

"If I lived my life hoping people forgave me, I'd be dead. Go on and kiss her already. It's my fault you broke up. You're too good together. So go on and work it out. I'm ready for them, babies." She pushed me out of the door as Amara took both of my hands in hers.

"I don't understand…" She pulled my head down before I could finish my thought and captured my lips in a soul-wrenching kiss. Her tongue sought and found my so-eager tongue. I dropped my hat, wrapped my arms around her, and lifted her to deepen the kiss.

Only the whistles and catcalls around us brought me back down to earth. She lifted her head, wiping the lipstick off my mouth. "God, I love you."

"I love you too." I gazed into her eyes. My heart threatened to burst from her declaration that I'd started to believe I would never hear.

"I was hoping you'd waited for me," she teased. "I know how you love the women."

I held her tighter. "I love you and only you. I don't care if you don't want me to be involved in your career. I just want to be with you again."

"I want to be with you too, and I want you all up in my career. Like, I need help figuring out which label is best. I can't do this without you anymore. Just needed to prove to myself that my love of performing wasn't entwined with how crazy I am about you."

I finally put her feet back on the floor and picked up my hat.

"I am so happy on that stage, but I would be much happier if you were there with me," she said.

Evelyn opened the door and strolled past us. "Y'all still making up? Come on, darlings, we have a show to do."

"What the hell?" I whispered to Amara as we trailed Evelyn.

"She came to my house to formally apologize for her actions against my grandfather and asked me to be a guest and be on stage the whole time." She entwined her fingers in mine. "And I want *you* to be on stage with *me*. You know all the songs we're doing. Just let Domino count out."

"I had no idea I would be performing tonight. I would've worn a purple suit," I joked before nudging her shoulder as we walked briskly through the corridors. "Evelyn never shares her stage the entire show."

"This is her way of apologizing for Stoney."

I brought her hand to my lips and kissed it. "Is it enough for you?"

She shrugged. "It's a step. And it's a boss business move for my music. A show with Evelyn Hart at the Ryman? Come on, can't get better than this."

Admittedly impressed by her confidence and the command of her career, which was a far cry from the woman I'd met six months ago, I grabbed her chin and kissed her soundly. "Can I tell the world how much I fucking love you?"

Amara pinched my nose. "Well, I already told you in a song, so technically it *is* your turn to profess it."

As we neared the stage, she looked at me. "Sorry I didn't reach out, especially when I received the guitar. I needed to heal in so many ways. Needed to trust you again. I have so much to tell you."

"Shh. We have time to talk…" I bent my head to whisper, "Well, after we fuck all night."

Amara leaned against my shoulder. "Mm…hmmm. I missed that part of us the most."

We grinned at each other, and suddenly, I knew all would be well again.

FORTY-ONE

Amara

Having Jake by my side again as we walked on the stage behind the curtain made my night complete. I clasped my hands together behind my mic as he greeted the crew and hugged an enthusiastic Tavion, Sophie, and Domino. He introduced himself to the young bass player I'd hired a few weeks ago. The uber-talented Alcee seamlessly fit with the crew. They were officially my band, and we'd decided to keep The Crew as their name. I gestured at the piano, and Jake donned his Stetson again, since we were all wearing hats. He sat down and tickled the ivories, ready to play.

The last two months had been a time of healing, revelations, and mending rifts. My parents were together in the audience, anxiously awaiting my debut at the Ryman. My father and I had spent time cleaning Stoney's home from top to bottom. Being in his childhood home opened up my father, and he'd relayed good memories of Granddad. We'd bonded in ways he and I never had. We'd also counted all the money. The amount was closer to three million dollars than two. My father insisted I take all of it. I'd simply deposited a million in my parents' account to avoid further arguments.

The emcee started talking about the night and getting the audience hyped as she ran through Evelyn's long list of accomplishments and hit records. The butterflies that suddenly sprang to life in my stomach warred with the stones holding my limbs down. This would be my biggest audience yet. I strapped on my acoustic guitar, kissed the peg around my neck, and looked back at Jake. He mouthed, *I love you.*

His reassurance calmed me, as it always did. I pictured his voice and dimpled smile whenever I grew nervous about a performance. He hadn't allowed his ego and hurt to stunt my growth. Jake had shown me love.

The lights dimmed, and I closed my eyes as the curtain rose, prepared to give the performance of my life.

Evelyn strode across the stage with a fitted red dress and a tail that dramatically billowed behind her. The audience applauded and stood up as she stood center stage with her arms outstretched. People clapped and howled for at least five minutes before she smiled and picked up the mic.

"Listen, you know I love all this attention. It's better than drinking the finest Tennessee whiskey." More howls sounded through the theater. I smiled along with everyone else, though I was confused about what was happening. We were supposed to play "Shady, Low-Down Men," one of her biggest hits, to start the show. "I wanted to use tonight, the very place where I sang 'A Red-Headed Woman' for the first time, to confess my sins. Is it okay if I confess my sins tonight?"

A resounding "yes" echoed through the auditorium.

She inhaled. "Years ago, I claimed songs that weren't mine. Songs, including 'A Red-Headed Woman,' written and composed by my guest Mari Johnson's grandfather, Stoney Johnson." The adoring audience grew silent as she, indeed, confessed. "He's no longer here with us, and I'll always regret not honoring him when he was alive for the contribution he made to my career. Without him, I would still be Natalie Hartwell and not the Evelyn Hart you all know and love." She laughed. "This is the first time I've said my real name aloud in years. I almost forgot it." Some fans chuckled along, and the tight smile she wore relaxed.

"Without the bravery and courage of a man who's been like a grandson to me, who called me on my shit, I wouldn't stand before you ready to deal with whatever consequences of my misdeeds." She blew a kiss at Jake, who had tears in his eyes. "I already told the Hall of Fame what I did and will no longer be inducted next month. The announcement will be released tomorrow." Some of the audience booed, but most listened. "No booing.

They made the right decision. There's honor in being a part of greatness. My actions weren't honorable." She smiled brightly at the audience. "But I tell you…there's nothing like telling the truth and freeing the cages of secrets and lies from within. Fifty years of stones weighed me down, and I can suddenly breathe again. It's my farewell tour, and y'all have done more than right by me. I think it's time I did right by a man I loved for a long time. Let's all stand and yell as loudly as possible for one of the greatest musicians I'd had the pleasure to know, Marcus 'Stoney' Johnson." The whole Ryman gave a standing ovation as five photos of my grandfather were projected behind me on screens that dropped down, including the picture of him teaching me the guitar. Tears flowed down my face at the thought that she'd chosen one of the most significant moments of her career to honor my grandfather.

In the VIP section in the front row, my ordinarily stoic father's face was flushed with tears as he held my mother. I looked back at Jake, and our wet eyes locked. Evelyn was making up for her past wrongs, in her fashion.

"My time in the spotlight has been long, but it's time for new voices to sing the songs of our hearts," she continued, settling her gaze on me with a mix of regret and resolve. "Tonight, I pass the torch to an extraordinary talent, Amara 'Mari' Johnson, whose roots and wings are equally strong."

The crowd, moved by her words, erupted as Evelyn gestured toward me. Stepping forward, I felt a surge of empowerment. This was more than a debut—it was a reclaiming of Stoney's legacy, a celebration of his life through the music we both loved.

Evelyn put her mic back on a stand and glanced at Jake. "I need a guitar." People started stamping their feet and clapping as if they wanted an encore before the show had even started.

Jake picked up the guitar on a stand by the piano, brought it to her, and kissed her cheek. "Jake Barnes, everyone. He probably won't ever admit it, but I believe he brought my baby back to me. Ellie Hart is in the audience. Wave and show people how damn beautiful you are. A chip off my block— the better side of me, of course, if I do say so myself."

The spotlight shone on a younger version of Evelyn, graceful, beautiful, with a hint of devilment in her smile as she rose from her front-row seat next to Jake's parents and waved at everyone.

Evelyn strapped the guitar around her neck. "Take it, Mari."

"How y'all doing?" I laughed as the crowd responded. "Whew…like, how am I supposed to follow her? Thank you." I wiped my eyes and gestured to Evelyn. "One more time for Ms. Evelyn Hart!"

Evelyn gestured for quiet, then looked at me with a nod that felt like a benediction. "Let's show them what the future sounds like," she said, her voice tinged with pride.

Domino counted off with the drums, and Sophie started playing the electric guitar while Alcee plucked the bass. While Tavion played the tambourine, I held my purple glitter guitar pick up in the air.

With a deep breath, I launched into the song born from one of Granddad's unfinished pieces, now a symbol of our intertwined legacies. As the band joined in, the music swelled, filling the Ryman with the sound of redemption and new beginnings.

Evelyn walked over to me, smiling, strumming her guitar like a woman at least thirty years younger. The minute I started singing, my voice strong and clear, the crowd howled their approval. Evelyn joined in, adding harmony, but it was clear this was my moment, my song, with the audience responding not just to the music but to the rightful return of Stoney's legacy through me.

Under my lead, we captivated the Ryman Auditorium all night. Her final bow. My inheritance reborn.

BONUS EPILOGUE

Jake

Six months later.

With my headphones attached to the piano and covering my ears, I tickled the keys in my music room, trying to capture the right note to describe my feelings over the last year. Love had changed me. Undeniably and irrefutably, Amara Johnson had changed me. No other woman appealed. She'd cured me of my affinity to drown my sorrows in a bottle. I wanted to be…I *had* to be a better man for her and myself. My career was no longer my everything because she and I were part of something bigger. We were love personified. We were the legacy of our ancestors who dared to dream of the life we were presently living.

My mother and I had become closer again. She approved and had grown to love Amara like a daughter. Mom didn't allow a week to pass without asking about potential wedding plans and grandbabies, no matter how often I reminded her that Amara was beginning her musical career and we had time.

My mother's faith and belief in her husband's heart—and that he'd tried to make amends by giving Stoney money over the years—made it possible for her to forgive him for his past transgressions against a Black man and move forward, while my relationship with William was slowly being rebuilt. We still didn't have the easy connection and flow we once had. He wanted us to go back to how we used to be, but I knew the impossibility of that. We would and could forge ahead as father and son—but with the full knowledge that as much as William loved me, he didn't quite understand how his dishonest actions toward Stoney involving me had impacted my soul as a man.

I would always love my stepfather for adopting me and being there when my father wasn't, but I was glad about my decision to call Jakobi. This was my way of honoring Stoney. Confronting the past had helped me fill the void and deal with my inadequacies about being a man and truly loving a woman.

I was happy with Amara. We'd rarely been apart once we reunited months ago. We lived between our two homes, and we implicitly trusted each other. She didn't know the man who drank and partied hard. Or the man who slept around and played with love. She knew the man who worked hard and willingly came home to her. When we were apart, we would talk on the phone like teenagers until the wee hours of the morning. If we attended parties, it was on behalf of my artists to promote their music. We spent most days in the studio thinking, envisioning, and creating. In addition to producing the songs for Amara's album—set to release in four days—we'd worked on records for other artists on my label.

I still demanded and expected perfection in her performances and the records we produced. Although we clashed during those moments, I ultimately deferred to Amara in any decision that involved her professionally and personally. We were a great team in and out of the bedroom. Our passion remained hot, and she'd become my best friend, who continued to get me more than any other person. We inspired each other to grow in ways neither of us had even imagined.

While I was lost in the refrain of my newly composed song, the soft touch of her lips on my neck and her rose-honeyed scent captured my attention. Joyful surprise erased the flash of irritation at the interruption of my flow. I pushed my headphones off my ears.

She grinned. "Love the song already."

"What are you doing here? Thought we were meeting up in Memphis on Monday."

We'd decided to host a press conference to celebrate the release of her first album in Memphis at the Rock and Soul Museum, where Amara first heard Stoney's songs. She was set to arrive tomorrow, and I was headed there Monday night after meeting with another artist in L.A.

"I didn't want to wait another day to see you." She rested her cheek on my shoulder and dragged her hand down over my bare chest and abs, stopping at the waistband of my basketball shorts, arousing my lower half.

"I missed you more," I said, and twisted to cup her face, noticing the wariness beneath her happiness to see me. "How did you get home?"

Amara was now recognized as a rising Black country star, or the woman who brought Evelyn Hart down. I wanted her to travel with security to avoid any fans who wanted to take selfies, or enemies seizing an opportunity to attack her for her perceived role in their queen's downfall. Whenever she didn't, we argued.

Her face flushed, and she lowered her gaze from mine. "Sophie."

"No security? I worry enough when I'm not with you. If something happens to you, I won't forgive myself."

"Shh… It's okay. Short notice, baby. I couldn't get security. This is why I look like this." She pulled off her Spelman baseball cap and placed it on the piano. Her hair was in a ponytail, and she wore a sweatshirt and leggings, appearing more like a college student than a woman who had performed before thousands. "No one recognized me."

Before I could protest, she playfully nipped my lower lip and rubbed my pecs, successfully distracting me from my worry and concern. "Mm…this was so worth the risk of coming to Nashville without security. Come on, Jake, don't be mad. I'm safe, and I'm home with you where I belong."

I gazed into her beautiful face, impishly grinning, and brushed my lips over hers. "I believe I created a monster. I spoil you way too much. I planned to surprise you and cook your favorite meal once we returned home."

"You still can. I didn't eat dinner." She hugged my neck.

"I've been in here for hours. What time is it?" I glanced out the window into the sparkling night sky. It'd been daylight when I came in here.

"After midnight." She shrugged without looking at her watch or cell.

I quirked a brow. "You want me to grill you steaks in the middle of the night when you need to be in Memphis tomorrow?"

"I already arranged for a driver and security for the four-hour drive before you go off about keeping schedules. Don't feel like the drama of the airport." Amara kissed me and tapped my nose. "We can talk while you grill, then eat, have sex, and sleep until I have to leave."

My hand drifted to her breast, and her nipple puckered through her t-shirt at my touch. "Or we can fuck now and then do everything else tomorrow."

Her eyes closed, and her forehead wrinkled as I rolled her stiff bud between my fingers, needing her right now. She pressed her hand on top of mine and released a sigh. "Technically, it's already tomorrow. It's so late, and you're not going to want to talk if we have sex."

I growled. "Then don't come in here teasing me, touching me everywhere, if you don't want to get fucked. It's been a week, and then you'll leave again tomorrow, baby. I need you."

"I missed you and need you too. I just need to talk more, Jake."

"What's wrong?" The wariness in her eyes returned, and I picked up her hand.

"Everything and nothing." She rubbed the back of my hand against her cheek. "Can we talk while you cook, please?"

The need to comfort her pushed down my desire. She'd been away from me for a week, and we'd spoken every night. She seemed happy to be home with her parents, and last night had been dinner with them. Something had happened to make her forget her plans and hurry home to me.

I entwined our hands and led her out of the music room and into the kitchen.

We gathered ingredients and prepped for the steaks and spinach salad, making light conversation about the song I was working on. I patiently waited for her to talk. I'd learned that Amara needed time to process before discussing her feelings. She preferred to flow and not be rushed or forced, whereas I would dive headfirst into a conversation.

Holding a glass of red wine, she settled on the island across from me as I placed the Wagyu steaks on the grill. She took a sip before she said, "Last night, I ran into Phillip and his new woman while out with my parents."

My stomach churned, though I nodded and picked up the package of feta crumbles. We hadn't really discussed him since they'd broken up. I hated that the mention of his name still affected me after so long.

She stared at her glass. "I don't know. I've been more uneasy and restless the closer we get to this album release. Then going back to Atlanta and running into Phillip last night made me feel out of sorts. I couldn't sleep."

"Why didn't you tell me you saw him when I called you?" I kept my tone neutral and sprinkled the salad bowl with the cheese and dried cranberries.

She placed her glass down. "I wanted to see you when I told you because I didn't want you to think that whatever I felt meant anything regarding us."

I gripped the side of the island. "You came here instead of Memphis, and you barely talked to me last night. Are you sure it's nothing?"

Amara rubbed her stomach. "Sometimes I replay what would've happened if I never approached you at the Peabody. Or what my life would be if I had woken up in an alternate universe where I was still this teacher engaged to an everyday man living in Atlanta because my music didn't take off. Being around my parents felt so good. Familiar. Normal—until we went to eat. Probably wasn't a good idea to hit a downtown restaurant on a Thursday night."

Her lips curved into a wry smile.

"It took a minute for my parents and me to adjust to people trying to get my attention as security whisked us from my father's car to the private room in the restaurant. Until then, I was the daughter they'd always known, not Mari Johnson, the country singer. Once we finally relaxed, we could laugh and joke about my new fame, and dinner went well." She tapped her nails against the marble. "Then we bumped into Phillip, his new girlfriend, and his parents on our way out. We all hugged each other politely. I even embraced Phillip and the new woman as if we were just the children of old friends and nothing more. Neither of us could look at each other. Talk about an awkward situation." Amara chuckled as she met my gaze. I could only manage a slight smile.

"Did it bother you seeing him with someone else?" I asked quietly. She'd loved him and planned to marry him. It couldn't have been easy, despite how they broke up and that she was with me.

"Not the way you think. Seeing him made me miss the normalcy of my old life." She hugged herself and leaned closer. "Baby, I'm only telling you because I want transparency in this relationship. No matter what it is, I want to be able to tell you."

"Just because I want that too, it doesn't mean it's easy to hear that you might regret being with me. I know I can be difficult and demanding, that sometimes I push you too hard when I should let you be."

She rushed around the island and grabbed my chin. "I don't regret being with you. I love you so much that it physically hurts when we're apart for too long. But sometimes, the magnitude of this path I'm on is downright scary. As much as I know I'm meant for this, I wonder if it will all fall apart one day. I fear this insane happiness is fleeting and that the bottom will fall out when I least expect it. I'm scared that this ride will end, and I'll wake up wondering if I'll end up like my grandfather. He risked it all for his music and ended up a cautionary tale. What if I'm no different?"

"Why do you feel it will end?" I searched her face as if her expression gave me the answer.

"Baby, you are of this world and have been since you were a teen, and even if exposing Evelyn ruins *my* career, you'll be fine in the long run. You have too many connections and established artists who are accepted no matter the genre." She blinked back tears.

I gripped her waist. "Your career won't be ruined. You have the hottest album dropping next month. Period."

She shook her head. "Maybe I'm a fool to believe I can rise high in country music."

I narrowed my eyes. "Did he say something to you?"

"No, but seeing Phillip with another woman and his parents like we used to do made me question my journey."

Her words stung. Did she still prefer the life she'd had before me?

Releasing her, I picked up the tongs and flipped the steaks over. "Then you regret being with me, because if you for a second think you would be better off with him, then what are we doing, Amara?"

"Shh." She turned off the grill and took the tongs out of my hand. "It's not about him. I don't *long* for him. I could never choose to be away from you for months like I'd planned to do with him last summer. You are etched in my soul forevermore. It's what he represents—my regular life where no one knows me but my family and friends."

We faced each other. "I get that. I also remember how you had your feet in two different places when you were with him. You can't go backward now. We've come too far. Before you left, you weren't talking like this. I know it wasn't your parents making you second-guess yourself and everything we've built. What did he say to you, Mari?"

She lowered her gaze to my chest. "It was what he said to me when we broke up. He said I was a has-been before I even started, like my grandfather… He thought I was too old to start all of this. What if he's right?"

"You never told me he said that to you." My temples throbbed. "With all your success in the last year, seeing him again made you doubt yourself?"

"Maybe it wouldn't bother me if I didn't sing country or wasn't associated with Evelyn."

Her words gave me pause. I touched my forehead to hers and asked, "Why do I feel like you still blame me somehow?"

"Oh, I do blame you for everything." She squeezed my nose. "I blame you for making it impossible to walk away from my destiny. I blame you for opening me to a new world of friends and the love of a lifetime. I'm trying to explain my feelings, and you're taking them as a slight to you, when all I'm trying to say is that I'm scared out of my damn mind that my album drops in three days. Singing at venues in and around Nashville and a couple of late-night shows is nothing compared to what the rest of the country will say once that album drops and if I can handle it."

I reminded her, "'Wreck Me' was number one for four weeks straight on the pop charts. Your other song was in the top one hundred for months. You're already a success. Of course I take everything you're saying as a slight, because I don't operate with doubt and second guessing. I don't make mistakes when I see talent. I didn't step to you because I was attracted to you. I stepped to you because I saw that spark that would set the music world on fire."

She took a step back. "Why do you sound angry with me? This isn't *about* you."

I slapped the back of my hand into my other one. "You didn't speak to me for two months because you didn't trust me and believed I'd lied to you and your grandfather. So, yes, when you've been in Atlanta for a week away from me, back in your old world, and come back talking small again, I do take it as a slight."

Amara's face softened before she buried her head in my chest and held me tight. "I'm not trying to hurt you."

Inhaling her familiar, sweet scent removed the temporary blinders that she had any doubt about me. I wrapped my arms around her and kissed the top of her head. "I'm sorry. I know all of this scandal has made everything harder than it already is. It still bothers me that if he accepted who you really are, that you wanted to sing, you wouldn't be with me. That he might have been the better man for you. I replay *that* in my mind. I've never loved any woman like I love you."

She rubbed my arms and chuckled while tears slowly trailed down her cheeks. "I really would've been my grandfather and had a torrid affair, because even if Phillip accepted my desire to sing, he never saw me the way you do."

I gazed deep into her eyes. "I do see you. I've been a part of the music world most of my life and forget how overwhelming it can be for new artists when success happens as fast as it did for you. But my experience also tells me that you won't be your grandfather. Stoney paved the way for you to have the career he dreamed about. Please…please, trust and believe me when I say that no one can destroy or deny what and who you are destined to be. And I will always rock hard for you even when you doubt yourself."

Amara released a sigh. "And this is why I wanted to talk to you in person. I needed to hear this."

I lowered my head to whisper against her lips, "I love you."

"I love you too." She breathed before slipping her tongue into my mouth.

"What about the steaks?" I asked in between kisses, my passion growing again as her hand roamed over my back and ass.

"Right now, I'm only hungry for you." Amara slipped off her leggings and curved her arms around my neck, pressing her body to mine.

I lifted her to the clean side of the counter, pushed down my shorts, and thrust inside her as I once again possessed her heart, body, and soul.

Amara stood at the open door of the back seat of the car. "I wish you were riding with me. Would love more time with you before the album drops."

I kissed her. "Me too. If I didn't have to be at Helm Records, I wouldn't be."

She nodded.

"I'm going to do my best to fly into Memphis Monday morning instead of night. I hope to finalize the negotiations as soon as possible so we can spend the day together."

She pouted prettily before easing into the car. I closed the door and waved at the driver, then watched the car until it turned the corner.

Amara invaded my heart and soul. When she hurt, I ached. When she smiled, I glowed. Watching her grow into her own woman over the past year, making decisions about her career without my constant guidance, had swelled my heart with pride.

After months of hard work, a week in Atlanta had shifted something inside Amara. Last night and this morning, she'd almost seemed like the unsure woman with the bold and soulful voice I first met. Maybe I should've gone with her for at least a few days, like she'd asked me. I'd thought she needed to be with her parents without me, and used her absence to refocus on my building roster of acts instead of being there for her. It was enough she was traveling alone to Memphis to visit Stoney before her release on Tuesday because of my obligations to another artist when she should've been my priority. She needed me with her, and I wouldn't let her down again.

Amara

A rush of melancholy assailed me as we pulled in front of my grandfather's house in Memphis on Sunday afternoon. Realizing Stoney's gift and learning about him, though beautiful, also reminded me that I would never be able to touch or hug him or play my guitar with him. I held back tears that threatened to fall. I didn't want to cry unless the tears meant joy. My grandfather had left me the means to do whatever made me happy and free. He didn't want me to stay stuck and lonely in the past, as he had. It was still surreal how the trajectory of my life had shifted so dramatically because of Stoney Johnson. I'd hired a driver to transport me from Nashville to Memphis simply because I could—a far cry from the woman who'd driven a used compact car.

The driver opened the door, and I stepped out with my guitar to admire my grandfather's home. The windows used to look sad and gloomy. Now, with the renovations and my family's determination to make this home a designated historical place in Memphis, the windows seemed content. No— the windows appeared happy. More important, his home appeared *alive*.

His gravesite had also been transformed from a barren headstone to one overflowing with flowers and guitar picks from fans and curious tourists. We'd hired around-the-clock private security to ensure his home and burial site remained undisturbed. After Nate's exposé was finally released, people from far and wide visited the home and final resting place of the bluesman who once crafted hit music.

Before I entered the cemetery, I asked my driver, "Mike, can you give me a few minutes alone at the graveyard and make sure no one disturbs me?"

Mike nodded at the hulk of a man standing guard at the front of the house before leaning against the driver's side of the car with arms folded.

"Hey, Granddad, it's me." I rubbed the headstone. "I can't believe it's been a year since I sang for you when we said goodbye. Because of you, my life has changed in so many ways. Because of you, I'm living out loud and am no longer afraid to be me. Because of you, Daddy and I are closer than ever. Because of you, I'm breaking down barriers in the country music world. Got an album debuting in two days and everything." I gripped the neck of my guitar. "Because of you, I met the love of my life. You were right about him. Jake is a good man who's good to me, and he loved you too."

I smiled. "I know Jake and Daddy have been out to see you. We decided to each take turns coming to see you so that you're never alone for too long. God, how I wish you were on this side again so I could give you the biggest hug, or we could play the guitar together." I wiped my eyes and whistled. "I said I wouldn't cry unless my tears were happy. And I'm so happy now. Well…most days. Still scared of what's going to happen on the other side of my album release. I worry if Jake can accept that though I love the world he's brought me into, I still love the world I left behind. He's had this huge life for so long that it's hard for him to accept that I don't need it to feel like I've made it. All I need is him and my music. Sometimes I wonder if that's enough for him." I hummed, plucked a melody on my guitar without thought, and chuckled. "Guess that's my answer."

Unchecked tears trickled down my cheeks as I played to the beat of my heart and mind. My chest swelled with inspiration and belief in my abilities as much as when I first found his guitar and notebook. The doubt about my path that had clouded my vision dissipated more the longer I remained before my grandfather's final resting place, strumming my guitar with renewed faith and vigor, ready for the release of my album. I kissed my palm and touched the top of his headstone. "Love you. Until next time."

I gladly waved at a few clapping fans who'd watched my private performance from the front of my grandfather's house and adjusted my dress as my driver held the limo door open. I eased into the back seat, feeling more joy than when I'd arrived. I'd *needed* to see him alone and not with Jake or my parents, as I'd originally planned.

Peace settled over me as we drove through the old neighborhood back to downtown. I picked up my cell to write down lyrics inspired by my impromptu song at the gravesite. Maybe this could be a prelude during one of my performances or go on the second album.

I pressed my cell against my chest. I'd been too afraid to focus on anything past this first album, but after seeing my grandfather, a second album had become inevitable.

My cell rang, and I answered, expecting Jake. "Hey, baby."

"Nope." Sophie giggled.

"Oops…I should've checked my caller ID. Jake said he would call around this time." I covered my face with one hand as if she could see me.

"It's all good. Are you still with your grandfather?"

I smiled, loving that Sophie understood my connection to him without explanation. "I'm in the car, headed back toward downtown."

"I knew today wouldn't be easy, especially without Jake."

I released a deep breath. "In some ways, it wasn't. Of course I wish my grandfather was here beside me. Yet when I'm at the house or the graveyard, I feel so close to him—and inspired. I'm finally ready for this album to drop. I also have songs tumbling around in my head as I'm talking to you. All in all, today was a good day."

"Okay, Ice Cube." Sophie squealed in delight. "Well, I'm at the Peabody waiting for you. Let's have drinks, hang out, and forget about the release for a little while."

"You're in Memphis already?" I asked.

"You came with the crew?"

"Nope. They'll be here tomorrow. Nate wrangled me into this new project in Memphis. Hired me to be his social media manager, since I've done a good job with Jake's company and promoting you."

"Nate's already here too?" I asked, the lingering sadness replaced by anticipation of seeing my friends. "We are definitely hanging out. Jake won't be back from L.A. until tomorrow anyway."

"Then let's do this. We can hit Beale Street as tourists and not entertainers after we leave the Peabody."

"I want to go, but I'm not up for fans. Just want to bounce from place to place." I looked out the window as we headed toward downtown Memphis. "Still weird that I have to think about how I move."

"Then we do our best to hide your identity, and even if someone recognizes you, this is Memphis and not Nashville. We're in the city of blues and Stoney Johnson. Relish your legacy. Come on, Mari, please say you're down."

I grinned. "This *is* my dad and granddad's city. I'm down. Just need to tell Jake where I'll be, since he expects me to be at the hotel."

"We'll be in the lobby at the Corner Bar, where you and Jake went viral." She paused. "What are you wearing?"

"Aww…that bar was fun." My heart fluttered when I remembered that evening and how Jake looked at me with what I now knew was the beginning of love. "And stop sounding like Jake, who has a stylist for every occasion."

"Well, did you listen to his stylist?" Sophie teased.

Rolling my eyes, I retorted, "Jake had an outfit waiting for me in my suite when I arrived yesterday. I'm wearing a Prada mini-dress and heels. Is that good enough?"

"Jake would be proud that you actually decided to wear it." She laughed.

"Yeah, well, I have nothing else to wear except cowboy boots, a crop top, and sweats until tomorrow. See you in a few minutes." I clicked off my cell and then called Jake.

He answered on the first ring. "I was just about to call you. Are you okay?"

"Yeah. I am." I shifted in my seat. "This was such a good idea to come here early. I needed to see my grandfather to remind me of who I am and my legacy. I even started working on a song for my second album while I was at his grave. Think it's going to be a hit."

Jake chuckled. "That's my Mari."

The warmth in his voice tickled my soul. "I am so grateful for you. You've never stop believing in me and supporting me throughout this whole journey."

"And I never will."

I gripped the phone. "I know. One of the many reasons I love you."

"Mari…" He paused.

"Yes?" I tucked a leg underneath me on the soft leather in the back seat, twirling strands of my ponytail around my finger. I could listen to his deep voice all day.

"Please believe me when I say if you ever decide you don't want to perform or you no longer want this life we've been building, it won't change the depth of my love for you. I'm here to support whatever you want to do or whoever you want to be, do you hear me?"

Tears flooded my eyes. "Baby, I wish I could see you."

"I'll cut my trip short and fly to you right now if you want. Say the word."

I smiled wide, knowing he would do whatever I asked. "As much as I want that…you have a business to run and others to manage. Besides, I'm almost at the Peabody to meet Nate and Sophie at the Corner Bar. They're here in town early for some project."

"Ain't that a bitch. You're bringing them to our spot when I'm not there?" he asked half seriously.

I laughed. "It was Sophie's idea."

"Sounds like Nate trying to fuck with me because I told him earlier how I was missing you… Hey, let me finish this call with Amara, then we can talk." Jake must be addressing someone else.

"Go ahead. I'll call you later tonight once I get settled."

"Okay. Have fun. Love you."

"Love you." We were pulling up to the Peabody as I clicked off. I donned my shades and patted my sleek ponytail, and the driver assisted me as I stepped out of the car. A few guests stared or snapped pictures while I walked into the lobby, making a beeline to the Corner Bar.

"Surprise," yelled the small crowd in the bar.

I stopped moving, too startled to process what was happening and why everyone I knew and loved was beaming before me. I scanned the space behind me, and people gathered, trying to get a peek into the bar. I then looked back at the familiar faces in the unexpected space and time.

"Oh my God, what's happening?" My heart beat rapidly as Sophie approached me at the entrance, reaching for my hand.

"We wanted to celebrate Stoney today, and your first album, without all the media."

Stunned, I allowed her to pull me into the dark, elegant bar that had been transformed into a vision of white. Pearl-colored balloons and candles and walls of white roses enveloped the small space in a romantic dream.

"I can't believe everyone is here." My friends and family surrounded me in a circle. The members of my crew grinned widely. Nathan stood next to Sophie and waved. My parents and Jake's parents smiled at me from the other side. Even Jess proudly stood near the entrance. I clasped my hands together, shaking my head in disbelief at Sophie. "It is noted that you're good at keeping secrets."

She flipped her blonde braids off her shoulder. "It definitely wasn't easy."

Nathan nudged Sophie's shoulder. "Um…don't let her take all the credit. I helped."

Sophie punched him in his side playfully.

He winced while grabbing me in a brotherly embrace. "How are you holding up with everything?"

"I'm better now," I reassured him. No matter how hard it'd been since the truth was revealed about Evelyn and my grandfather, I appreciated everything he and Jake had done for my family.

Jess walked up to me hesitantly. "I hope it's okay that I'm here."

I hugged the first person besides Jake to welcome me to Nashville. "Of course."

She smiled. "Evelyn asked me to tell you that whenever you're ready, she'll be waiting."

"Tell her thank you." I kissed her cheek. Forgiveness was a winding road. Maybe that road would lead to Evelyn.

Jake's mother and stepfather greeted me with huge smiles. William held my hand warmly. "We're so glad to be here."

"I wouldn't want it any other way." I reached for Mrs. Barnes's hand with my free one. "Thank you both for being here."

She squeezed it and kissed my cheek. "You're family now."

Last but not least, I hurried into my parents' welcoming embrace. They hugged me tightly, tears raining down on my face. "You must have already been here when I called you this morning."

My father nodded. "It was hard not to tell you, especially when we knew you would visit Dad. Jake had asked us to be here at the hotel for you instead of waiting for the release party."

Wiping my eyes, I sniffed. "Why does he always seem to know what I need?"

My father glanced past my shoulders and answered, "Because he loves you."

"And because I see you even when I'm temporarily blinded by ambition."

The deep, melodic voice from behind me brought another round of tears from my mother, who clasped her hands over her mouth in surprise.

I closed my eyes and breathed through the clamoring of my heart. He was here. Jake was here.

I slowly turned around, and his copper eyes glistened when our gazes collided. He'd never been more handsome or sexy in a gray tailored suit that coordinated with my pale lilac dress. Behind him, the people trying to peek into our private party were a blur of faces.

"Hey," Jake whispered as he took the last few steps to me.

My stomach clenched painfully. "That's what you said when I sat next to you at the bar. I remember thinking that that simple greeting felt like so much more."

"Because it was." He wiped my tears with his thumbs. "I was so surprised to see you—and taken with you. It's all I could say that day."

"And all I wanted was to see you today to touch you and hold you." I slid my arms around his waist. "I can't believe you did all this."

"Don't you know that I would do anything for you?" He glanced up as if holding back tears. "A year ago, we met on the steps inside your grandfather's house, and I had no clue you would have such an impact on me. You forever changed me when you sat beside me and ordered that old fashioned. You shook my world, Mari Johnson, and I don't want another day to pass without showing you, our family, and our friends how much you mean to me."

I whistled. "You're doing a damn good job."

Our guests' laughter startled me off the island of two, and I buried my heated face in his chest, which shook from his amusement.

Jake rubbed my back soothingly as he said, "We both forgot where we were."

My mother replied, "And we are so here for it. She's been waiting for this."

"Mama," I warned.

"I've been waiting for this too." Mrs. Barnes chimed in.

"Pay them no mind." I looked up at Jake apologetically. I never wanted to pressure him into marriage. During pillow talk, we'd discussed being married and having children one day, but in the unforeseeable future. We were too focused on our careers. "I'm just happy that everyone I care about is here to celebrate my grandfather and my album with me. How can I ever repay all that you've done and been to me?"

"Marry me." Jake's eyes twinkled, and his lips curved into a dimpled smile.

"What?" The rest of my thoughts tumbled in a ball of emotions. I scanned the familiar faces with expectant expressions, trying to process what was happening, then pressed my hands to his broad chest. "Wait? Are you *proposing* to me?"

"I wanted to ask you to marry me on the anniversary of the day you arrived in Nashville. The moment I picked you up from the airport, I was lost to you forever, and I've been planning this big speech on bended knee..." His heart raced under my hand, and he stopped speaking, his eyes filled with tears. "But, um..."

His nervousness calmed me, and I smiled. "It's okay, baby. Take your time. I'm not going anywhere."

He inhaled and exhaled before gazing into my eyes again, gracing me with his dimples. "My legs are too unsteady to get down. I might not get back up." As we all laughed together, Jake sobered first. "I realized that you needed reassurance that I also wanted marriage and family and to share both worlds with you. And no speech can truly describe how I feel about you and how much I want to make you my wife." He slipped his hand into his pocket and pulled out a diamond solitaire ring.

I lifted my trembling left hand from his chest.

He asked softly, "May I?"

Nodding emphatically, I replied, "Yes."

While everyone cheered, Nathan teased, "Thank you for agreeing to marry this man, because I need my sleep. He's been driving me crazy since yesterday morning, scared you'd reject him."

"Excuse me," Jake said to our parents as he raised his middle finger at his best friend.

While our guests joined in the laughter, I only had eyes for Jake Barnes, my future husband, as he slid the ring on my finger and declared, "This ring is my promise always to love you, to always support you, to always be whoever you need me to be…your manager, your friend, your man, and hopefully one day the father of your children."

When the ring fit perfectly, he breathed a sigh of relief. I spread my fingers, staring at the big rock on my hand before almost knocking him off his feet by raining kisses on his face and neck. The claps and sounds of approval of our family and friends were muted as he captured my lips in the sweetest kiss. Together, he and I would climb impossible mountains and swim treacherous seas. No one and nothing would stop us from whatever life sent our way.

He was forevermore my refrain.

RIFTS AND REFRAINS

In the quiet where all worlds fade,
You and I remain, steadfast and unswayed.
Around us, the chaos of life falls away,
In our sanctuary, where only whispers stay.
Your eyes hold a universe, calm and serene,
In your gaze, I find peace, previously unseen.
Every moment with you, the rifts repair,
In our song's refrain, I breathe my truest air.
Nothing else matters, nothing competes,
When our fingers entwine, my world feels complete.
Your voice, a melody that sets me free,
In your presence, I am who I wish to be.
Through the storms, our love stands firm,
Against the tide, together we affirm.
In our echo, no rift too deep,
No night too dark, no hill too steep.
In the harmony of what we share,
Every worry dissolves in the air.
For nothing even matters, when I'm with you,
Our love, the refrain that forever rings true.

AUTHOR'S NOTE

Writing "Rifts and Refrains" has been an incredible journey, and I am deeply grateful to everyone who contributed to bringing this story to life. First and foremost, I want to express my sincere appreciation to Keisha Mennefee of Honey Magnolia for her belief, creativity, and collaborative spirit, which infused every step of the journey.

I am indebted to Leland Taylor for his invaluable brainstorming sessions and for lending a listening ear during the creative process. To my beta readers and editors, your insights and feedback have been instrumental in shaping "Rifts and Refrains" into its best possible form.

I want to express my heartfelt thanks to Beau Braswell for giving me a glimpse into Nashville's vibrant culture, treating me to a memorable tour, and introducing me to some truly exceptional cuisine (that brisket lingers in my mind!).

Keio Stroud deserves a special mention for being a guiding force in exploring Amara's musical roots, enriching the narrative with depth and authenticity.

Lastly, I want to express my deepest gratitude to my family, especially my daughter, for their unwavering support and patience throughout this endeavor. Your understanding and encouragement sustained me through the long hours and late nights poured into this project.

To all who have journeyed alongside me in the creation of "Rifts and Refrains," thank you for being a part of this story.

- Tiye

ACKNOWLEDGMENTS

This project was created to celebrate the profound contributions of Black artists to the country music genre, acknowledging both celebrated luminaries and lesser-known pioneers whose talents have significantly shaped this American art form. This story also honors the rich tradition of Black love, intertwining it with a collective passion for music, illustrating how deeply music and love are connected in our experiences.

Special thanks are given to the well-known and unsung heroes of country music, whose enduring spirit and creative genius continue to inspire and influence generations. Recognition is also extended to the silent legacies of individuals like Amara's grandfather, whose stories and sacrifices, though seldom spotlighted in history books, resonate powerfully through the music and lives they have touched.

This acknowledgment serves as a tribute to all who have used their voices in this rich genre, regardless of whether these voices have received mainstream recognition. Their impact on music and on our hearts is deeply felt and forever cherished. Here's to the music, to the love, and to every voice that sings the unsung hymn of Black excellence in country music